CODE

THE OTHER END OF THE STETHOSCOPE

BLUE

DEBRA E. BLAINE, MD

This book is a work of fiction. Names, characters, places, and incidents either are products of the author's imagination or are used fictitiously. Any resemblance to actual events, locales, or persons, living or dead, is entirely coincidental.

Under no circumstance should any portion of the content of this book be construed as medical advice.

ISBN: 978-1-7337955-7-9

Blaine. Debra

Edited by: Monika Dziamka and Amy Ashby

Published by WARREN Publishing
Charlotte, NC
www.warrenpublishing.net
Printed in the United States

For my brother
Robert Kenneth Blaine
March 17, 1957 – October 28, 2000
I miss you every day.

"When I was young, I admired clever people. Now that I am old, I admire kind people."

–Abraham Joshua Heschel

PROLOGUE

September 22, 2000

"**W**hat the hell!"

The techie smacked his hand on the table, careful to avoid hitting his custom-crafted personal computer. It had never let him down like this. He had rebuilt his Compaq, installing a brand new 933 MHz Intel Pentium III Xeon Processor and added an additional four GB memory board. For his current project, the little machine was perfect. He even preferred it to the Cray supercomputers he used to work on, until he had been hired as a consultant by Financier, Inc. about a year ago. They were paying him ridiculous money—almost three times what he had gotten from Cray—to develop a specific software to create databases of medical records. They wanted theirs to be the first really viable electronic health record in the world and dominate the market.

He was in his early forties and had some serious health problems of his own, which had added to his decision to leave Cray Research. Creating an electronic health record, or EHR as it was being called, seemed more relevant than the work Cray was now doing in graphics and business, and he was sure computerizing health records would be the wave of the future.

Except for this sudden glitch, he had basically completed the project. He had no idea if they'd want him to stay on after the software was written, but he was not worried about income. He had been working on computers since high school, and he knew he was one of the very best in his field. He knew it as a fact, and not as something to boast about. Having started with the monstrosities that each took up an entire room in the early seventies, he intuited computers as if by instinct. If he weren't such a rationalist, he would have said they had a "relationship" of sorts. In college, he had studied computer science in its infancy, had written a few languages himself, and had soon surpassed his professors' knowledge. If there was no program that did what he wanted, he'd always just written one, so employment had never been a concern for him.

He hit search again, setting the criteria for all medical history recorded, and again the result set came up with data anomalies. The program had only pulled specific diagnoses, like organ failure needing transplant, with subsets for heart, liver, and kidney. There was a separate queue for dementia, divided into Alzheimer's and Parkinson's, and then STDs, or sexually transmitted diseases, were also highlighted. The search logic had obviously been linked elsewhere.

Why these disorders in particular? They seemed to have nothing in common. There was no mention of hypertension, diabetes, or any surgical history, which he knew he had inputted. The software was supposed to disclose *all* of the medical conditions of any patient entered into the system. As requested, he had set up the program to also collate by diagnosis, so it would have maximum usefulness for epidemiological research, but that was designed to function only in the background, so it would not be intrusive in the running of the software. Somehow, this selectivity had become a primary operation, and the application was defaulting to *these* diagnoses only. He had to debug the program immediately, he'd already told them it was complete. Where had this issue come from?

Everything had an electronic footprint, so he backtracked to find the source and how it had ended up on his software. It might connect to the previous guy that Financier had assigned to the project. Rumor was, that guy hadn't worked out so well, and was gone now; maybe he had left behind a few stray lines of programming that still needed to be deleted.

As the techie traced the issue backward, the screen blinked at him: *ACCESS DENIED*. Now, why were they trying to keep him out? He was being paid a lot of money to write this program, and something was malfunctioning. He needed to fix it before Financier noticed the flaw. He inhaled sharply and hacked in, decompiling the dynamic link library, and was even more puzzled than before.

All the comments were in Russian. What had happened to Financier?

"Okay," he said out loud. He often talked to himself when he was stressed. "What if I run this forward. Why are you looking for transplants, organ failure, STDs, and dementia? Let's see ..." He started typing rapidly.

Suddenly, he broke into a cold sweat and snatched his fingers from the keyboard as if it were a bed of burning coals.

"Holy shit!"

October 31, 2000

The piercing beeps slowly penetrated the deep fog in Tobi's head. Again and again, they sounded off. She groaned as she reached for the alarm. It can't be morning already, she thought, it's pitch black. The noise stopped, and then it started again. Geez, that's the phone! She sat up on her elbow and felt around for the little lamp next to her bed, and looked at the caller ID. It was her mother. *Now what?* She flipped the light off and answered the phone.

"Tobi! Reuben's dead! He died!"

Tobi sat bolt upright and turned the light back on. Her heart sprouted wings and tried to fly out of her chest.

"What?"

"The police are here."

Tobi waited. She waited to hear more, she waited to wake up—she wasn't sure which, but she couldn't speak. Her heart's new "wings" smacked the inside of her rib cage.

"Are you there? I haven't been able to reach him for three days, so I called his friend Ken and he went to Reuben's apartment, but there was no answer, so Ken called the police. They broke the door down and found him … they said he'd been dead for at least a couple of days. I *knew* something was terribly wrong, I just *knew* it. My mother's intuition again. Darn it!

"Say something, Tobi! Are you there?"

"Yeah, yeah, I'm here," she whispered, but she couldn't seem to fill her lungs with air. "I just spoke to him a few days ago, or … what's today?" She looked at the dutifully quiet alarm clock. It was 3:54 a.m.

"I did too, on Saturday. You know, *he* calls me every day. Or, he did. Tobi, what am I going to *do* without him?" Mom sobbed. "Thank God your father isn't alive to see this. It would kill him!"

The room started tilting, and for a moment, Tobi thought it might turn upside down. She gripped the bed and clenched her eyes shut and willed her mother to stop screaming just this one time. She felt like she had just entered some eerie corridor, that space between the worlds of the living and the dead.

"What happened?" Tobi asked.

"Nobody knows. They think he had a heart attack, but they have to do forensics to rule out foul play. Can you imagine? That means an autopsy, right? I've had *such* a bad feeling the last three days! But an autopsy? Everyone loved Reuben. Who could possibly want to hurt him?"

The wind suddenly kicked up outside and a branch brushed against the window. Tobi shuddered in the dim light of the bedside lamp.

"Tobi, talk to me! Are you coming down? You can't leave me alone now. I'm all alone. And I can't pay for a funeral, you know, it will have to be you."

"Yeah, of course I'm coming down. Just … give me a few minutes, okay? I'll call you later."

"Later when?"

"Later today."

"Tobi!"

"I'll call you when I have reservations." Tobi hung up.

Her heart was racing a million beats a minute and her chest hurt. She forcibly resisted the impulse to check her pulse rate, because knowing that number could only make her feel worse. Sometimes being a doctor was not an advantage.

She got up unsteadily and tried to slow her breathing. As she walked into the hall, she glanced into Benny's room. Eight-year-olds can sleep through anything, she thought. But then, it wasn't as if she had made much noise. She dismissed the urge to wake him up and hug him. They had that extra closeness that single mothers have with their only children, but that would be completely selfish, especially since he'd barely seen his uncle in the last few years. Not that Reuben had made much effort to be part of his nephew's life, but Tobi hadn't pressed it, either. The word "dysfunction" had been invented to describe Tobi's family, and then she had married into more of the same. She'd read that people tended to unconsciously reproduce their childhoods in their choices of spouse. Now she tried mightily to keep

Benny as shielded from drama as much as possible. She let him sleep. She would tell him in the morning. Gently.

She walked into the playroom where the computer was and tried to process what she had just heard: Reuben was dead. Just like that. She repeated it to herself, but she couldn't hold the thought. And Mom had felt something was wrong for days but hadn't called her. Right. She only called about inane things, like the price of shrimp being such a bargain, and acted like that was monumental. Whatever. Tobi needed to book flights.

She went to the American Airlines website. Last minute flights were a fortune, and she was exhausted as soon as she printed the boarding passes. She tried to lie down on the couch, but it was useless. She got up and paced the house for a while, and then went back to the computer and sent out an email blast to her friends.

> I'll be in Texas for a few days. My brother was found dead in his apartment. If you need to reach me, call me at my mother's, 210-555-7734. I'll try to check email occasionally.

She marveled at the technology of email. Who would've thought you could connect with so many people at once, and so quickly, without even waking them up?

A memory from eight years ago suddenly flooded her: Reuben showing her his first laptop and describing this thing he called the *internet*. He thought it was going to be the rage of the future. She had humored him at the time but hadn't believed it would ever amount to much. Reuben was always at the cutting edge of his field.

She almost called Troy. She *needed* to call Troy. But his last words just two days ago burned in her brain. *I'm sorry, my love, I cannot see you anymore. I cannot even tell you why, so please do not ask me. This is good-bye.*

She had no clue what had prompted their sudden break up after three years together. He had just asked for her ring size. He wasn't the type to get cold feet, he was always poised and self-aware. But there was something about his tone that told her it was for real. He and Reuben had been friends too, so she had included Troy in the email she'd sent, but the truth was, she desperately hoped it would prompt him to call her.

Reuben couldn't be dead! Her big-little brother. He was almost four years older, but his soul was childlike and naive while Tobi's felt ancient. There was too much unfinished business between them, but she had always figured there'd be time to make up and set things right.

The dog had been following her from room to room. She sat down in the dark and stroked him absently while the wind hammered eerily at the windows. Chewbacca's tail thumped nonstop and comforted her, and at 6:15 a.m., she called her friend Pam, who worked in the same practice. Tobi obviously wasn't making it in to the office today, and she needed someone to cover her shift. Unfortunately, she woke up her husband.

"I'm sorry to wake you, Pete. It's Tobi. Is Pam there?"

"Do you realize it's six o'clock in the morning?"

"I know, I'm … I'm really sorry. My brother just died. I was—"

"Oh! Oh, sure, let me get her. I'm very sorry."

Suddenly, Tobi was drowning in a deluge of tears. She had wondered why she felt nothing, but as soon as she heard herself say those words out loud, she couldn't stop crying. Chewy brought her a rope toy and pawed at her nervously when she wouldn't play. She tried to keep quiet, because she didn't want to wake Benny yet, but there was a knife stuck in her chest. Forever came and went, and finally, Pam got on the phone.

"Oh my God, Tobi! What happened?"

"I don't really know, Pam. My mother called me a couple of hours ago. I'm supposed to work today, but I have to leave…." Her voice cracked.

"Of course! Which office? I can cover you until two. That should give them time to get someone else. He was young, wasn't he? Was he sick?"

"Forty-three. Yeah, I mean, he had a-fib, diabetes, and congestive heart failure. But he was doing really well. My old med school buddy was taking care of him, and he never mentioned him being *that* sick. He'd lost weight—he even got off insulin. Pam, I had *no idea* he was sick enough to just—die!"

"Mommy?" Benny padded out into the living room. "What's wrong? Why are you crying?"

Chewbacca bounded over to Benny, his tail whipping at everything in its path.

"Pam, I gotta go. Benny just woke up. I can't thank you enough."

"Don't even think about it. Stay in touch, okay?"

Tobi hung up and turned to Benny. He was rubbing his eyes with his fists, incredibly keeping his balance even with the golden retriever bumping against him. Chewy actually weighed more than Benny did. She knelt down and put her hands on his little shoulders. "Benny," she said softly, "I have some very bad news. Do you remember your Uncle Reuben? He used to carry you on his shoulders, remember?" Benny nodded sleepily. "He died last night."

Benny touched her wet face. "I'm sorry, Mommy," he said. "Is that why you're sad?" His upper lip quivered.

"Yes, Benny, I'm very sad." She took a deep breath and faked a smile. "So, guess what? No school today. We're going to Texas to help Grandma."

"No, Mommy, it's Halloween!" Benny shrieked. "I don't want to go to Texas! I want to stay home!" He twisted away and ran back to his bedroom.

Tobi fell back on the floor, stunned for a minute, and then realized she should have been prepared for this behavior. By the time he was four, Benny could name all the planets in the solar system and their order from the sun, *including* how many moons orbited each. Frequently, his intellectual precocity had made him seem older than he was, but he was still only eight. He'd been through hell with the divorce, and although she hadn't told him yet that Troy was gone, she knew he sensed something was very wrong. He was becoming too adept at shielding himself from emotional pain, often with denial, and it broke Tobi's heart. Somewhere in his brilliant little head, he must have already asked The Question: if Mommy's brother can die, can Mommy die too? Way too scary for a little boy, and much easier to run away from than to face. She started to follow him when the phone rang. It was her best friend, Sally.

"Tobi, you poor dear! I got your email, I'm so sorry! What can I do? Who's taking Chewbacca? I'll take you to the airport, and then I can take Chewy home with me. What time is the flight and which airport?"

"Oh, Sally, I love you. I hadn't even thought about that yet." She looked guiltily at the dog, now pawing frantically at the closed door to Benny's room. "It's JFK, 3:00 p.m. I don't know what to do about Benny. He's … reacting. Not well. He needs time, I guess, and I feel so muddled."

"Of course, you do, baby. Oy, and now you'll be spending a week with your mother too. Benny will come around. Just breathe. I'll head over as soon as the kids are off to school."

Chewbacca had managed to open Benny's door and was lying panting on the bed. Benny was hiding under the covers, and she heard his muffled voice as she walked into the room. "I'm not going!"

Chewy thought it was a game of hide-and-seek and pawed at the blanket. There wasn't a lot of room for the three of them, so Tobi sat on the edge of the bed and rubbed Benny's back through the covers. "I know this is very upsetting, Benny-Ben. Sometimes things happen that are very sad and very difficult, and we just have to help each other get through them."

"But it's Halloween!" Chewy sniffed at where Benny's voice had come from and sneezed. He tried to pull the blanket off with his teeth, but Benny held fast. "We have a party in school and everything, and I want to go trick-or-treating!"

"There will be other Halloweens, Benny. We have to be there for Uncle Reuben's funeral." She didn't mention they'd have to wait until the coroner was done with him. What had her mother said? They had to check for "foul play"? Tobi couldn't fathom the idea that his death might have been intentional. That kind of horror only happened in movies, not in her life.

"I *need* you to be there with me, Benny. I'm very, very sad that I lost my brother, and I need to be with the person I love most in the whole wide world, and that's you." Tears were streaming down her face again.

Benny's head peaked out from under the covers, and Chewy found him right away. He barked and licked Benny in the face, but Benny pushed the dog aside and stared at Tobi. His eyes were wide and frightened. "But if he's dead, Mommy, he won't even *know* if we go to his funeral."

Tobi hugged him tight. "Hush, Benny-baby, it'll be okay. Funerals aren't for the dead. Funerals are for the living."

Chapter 1

Present Day, 2019

The pelting rain brought an early evening, and the flashing blue and red lights reflected off the droplets, brightening the misty twilight in the parking lot, as the EMTs hurriedly pulled the stretcher out of the back of the ambulance. It bounced once on the wet pavement before they steered it into the urgent care office, where the receptionist was holding the door for them.

Inside, Dr. Tobi Lister had just finished putting an IV into her patient. She used the back of her elbow to push aside her dark brown hair, and for a second, hints of gray reflected the fluorescent light. Her face was tense, but she smiled kindly at Barry as she reached up to adjust the oxygen cannula at his nose. His damp hair was stuck to his forehead, and his breathing was rapid and shallow. Tobi's medical assistant, Esther, glanced at her anxiously and started cleaning up the IV tray.

"You're going to be fine, try not to worry," Tobi told him.

"Have you ever seen this before?" Barry's voice was weak and tremulous. "I thought I just had the flu."

"You do have the flu, and yes, I have seen this before. Your heart is an organ that can get an infection just like any other." She had actually only seen it once before outside of the hospital. It was a long, hard road back, but that patient had made it.

"Yes, but it's my *heart*. I have two kids at home, and a wife."

Tobi could not get over how much Barry looked like Reuben. He had the same forehead, and the same beard thing going on. Reuben had been a scuba instructor and underwater photographer as well as a genius with computers, so he had ditched the mustache to be able to make an airtight seal with his face mask, but he had kept the beard, trimmed away from his cheeks. Barry had the same unusual facial hair. She felt the familiar guilt again too. Her own brother, and she hadn't kept close enough tabs on him. How easy it had been back then to believe they were invincible.

"You're going to be back home with them soon," she said.

The paramedic's wet jacket dripped on the tile floor as he brought the stretcher alongside the "cardiac" room where Barry was lying. That room was designed with a curtain instead of a door and was just behind the providers' work station, so patients could be observed more carefully. The crash bag, defibrillator, and IV supplies were all stored in there too. "Talk to me," Jack said.

Tobi pulled him aside and spoke quietly. Since telling Barry he needed to go to the hospital, he had become frightened and short of breath.

"This is Barry, he's thirty-nine years old, and he came in with classic flu. Three days of fever, cough, and sweats, and his test is positive for Influenza A. He has no cardiac history, but his heart was too rapid and very irregular, so I did an EKG." She showed the paramedic the tracing.

Jack raised an eyebrow. "Heart rate 217, really? What were his initial vitals?"

"The pulse oximeter read him at 95, which was consistent with his 102-degree fever, but, look—he's in atrial fibrillation," Tobi replied. "So far his BP is stable, 126/82."

Reuben had had a-fib too, she thought, diagnosed when he infarcted his spleen and part of his left kidney. But this is new onset, she told herself, and Barry isn't going to die. She still wasn't sure why Reuben *had* died, since he'd been undergoing treatment for his cardiac disease.

"He came in today because he felt a little lightheaded when he got out of the shower this morning," Tobi added.

Jack nodded. "Good thing he did. Good pick-up." He clapped her on the arm. "We'll get him right over. If they can't convert his heart rhythm in the Emergency Department with medication—or synchronized cardioversion if he deteriorates—he'll go straight to the cardiac cath lab and electrophysiology. We'll take good care of him."

While they had been speaking, the EMTs had loaded Barry onto their stretcher and transferred his cannula to their own oxygen tank. They hooked him up to leads, and the loud "*beep, b-b-beep, b-beep, beep-beep-b-b-b-beep*" echoed in the waiting room. As Barry was wheeled toward the door with his jacket tossed over him, he looked back at Tobi in a panic.

"Doctor, I don't want to die," he said in a whisper.

She walked over to him. "You're going to be fine. I'm going to call your wife and tell her to meet you at the hospital." She squeezed his hand as they wheeled him away. It was soaked in sweat.

Tobi turned her attention back to the busy waiting room, where six or seven people were watching the activity. The energy level was high with a mix of impatience and curiosity, and most were either looking at the wait time or staring at the ambulance personnel. A little girl in a pink ballerina outfit under a pink hooded jacket was wearing Disney boots and twirling between the patients' chairs, sometimes stepping on their feet, while her mother was too engrossed in her phone to notice. Two more people had just arrived and were waiting to check in.

Two more exam rooms were still full, and Tobi's mouth was dry. She washed her hands and turned toward the breakroom to grab a soda, when she heard a commotion at the front desk. A middle-aged woman in a black workout outfit and large clanging bracelets with matching earrings was shaking rain off her umbrella and onto Patty at the front desk.

"I just need to get my throat swabbed. It'll only take a minute, I'm not even feeling sick," she said. "My son's friend was over yesterday and the mother just called to tell me he has strep. Can you have someone just do it real quick so I can leave right away?"

The ambulance was lingering at the curbside, and the lights were now blinding in the rainy darkness. They created a strobe effect inside the office, and thunder crackled overhead.

Patty braced her posture, as if she knew what was about to come. "I'm afraid that won't be possible. We just had an emergency. We still have two patients in rooms, and there are four more waiting to go in who are ahead of you. The wait time is at least an hour."

"But this is supposed to be *urgent care.*" The woman spoke very slowly as she pulled off her wet gloves, as if Patty were daft. "That means I should be able to be seen *right away*." She took off her rain-soaked jacket and regarded it at arm's length. "Why did that person even come here?" she nodded at the ambulance. "He should have gone straight to the hospital." She turned to Patty. "All I need is for you to swab my throat." She presented Patty with her insurance card and smiled, as if it were a done deal, flashing long pink and gold acrylic nails as she did so.

Patty frowned but took her card. "That's not how it works, ma'am, I'm sorry. We don't operate like a lab. We have to get your medical history and do an exam too."

Patty was in her late forties, mouse-brown hair pulled back in a short pony tail. She was forthright and old-style Italian, not the type to debase herself for entitled people who could not conceive that the needs of others might be greater than their own. In short, she wasn't really cut out for customer service medicine, but she did the best she could. "They're not 'customers,'" she'd say, "they're patients, and they should behave like patients."

"Well, that's ridiculous!" said the woman, but she let Patty sign her in, and then sat on the edge of her seat, tapping her foot restlessly. Then she looked around, pulled up Yelp on her phone, and started writing a nasty review.

Tobi had never liked the layout of her office. The exam rooms were arranged in two half circles on either side of her work station, which allowed for visualization of all of them at once, and each had stylish wood doors, except for the oversized cardiac room, which closed with only a curtain. From this circle, there was a straight path back to x-ray, the stock room, and the break room, and a short, wide hallway leading up front to the reception desk. From her work station, Tobi could pretty much see the entire office. This meant the entire office could also see her.

She turned back toward the break room, trying to shut the woman out of her mind for now. She was still trying to stem her adrenaline rush. If Barry had coded … well, it could have been bad. The last time she had seen such severe myocarditis, or a viral infection of the heart, in the outpatient setting was over twenty years ago, and she had been working with RNs. Together, they had started intravenous cardiac meds when the patient developed heart block, but the patient's pulse had still dropped to 32 and her blood pressure had plummeted. Miraculously, the patient never actually lost consciousness, and they didn't have to use the defibrillator paddles or the intubation set, but they had taken them out in preparation. That patient had grabbed Tobi by the arm and commanded her: "Don't let me die! I have two small children—you can't let me die!" Tobi had prayed for her every day of the two weeks she spent in the ICU in total organ collapse at New York University Medical Center. The woman had come back with flowers twice over the years to cry on Tobi's shoulder.

Nurses were too expensive for most medical offices these days, so Tobi had no idea how a full code would have gone here at B. Healthy, LLC—or even what life support training her medical assistant had. Although Esther was exceptionally competent in their day-to-day routine, the angry woman at the front desk had been right about one thing: this was no place for super critical emergencies.

And now I have another "unsatisfied customer," even before she is seen, Tobi thought. I'm sure I'll get a zero for her visit, and that will drive down my "scores." Her review will be counted instead of having saved Barry's life—since he is unlikely to take a customer satisfaction survey while he is in the cardiac care unit. She quailed. Welcome to 2019, where modern medicine has degenerated into a high school popularity contest.

Jorge met her halfway to the breakroom. He was always upbeat and full of energy, and although he was actually an x-ray technician, he'd do anything to help with patient care except draw blood. Tobi had known him for years and had personally recruited him to work at B. Healthy. She hoped he didn't regret it now.

"Don't worry about that crazy lady, Dr. L., we saved a life today. Who cares what she thinks?"

"Umm, corporate?" Tobi grinned. "I just can't wrap my mind around the things they consider important sometimes."

Jorge fished a Sprite Zero out of the fridge for her. "They have no clue," he said. "They don't work the front lines, they don't deal with sick people, and their only concern is dollars. But I've never known you to care what anybody else thinks, not even in the old days when we both worked for those creeps on the south shore. You always just do what's right. I respect that, and we all love you for it."

"Thanks, Jorge. I love you too." She flashed him a smile. "How's your new little bambino? How old is he now?"

"He's a handful, but he's amazing! He was two months yesterday. I want to be home with him more, but I need to pick up more shifts too. We need the money now; kids are so expensive! And—I'm not getting any sleep at night!" Jorge was grinning from ear to ear as he thought about his newborn.

Tobi chuckled. "It doesn't get easier anytime soon, I'm afraid, but it's definitely worth it."

"Oh, yeah, don't I know it. The whole world feels different now. I never knew I could love anyone so much."

As they turned to head back up front, Dr. Ismar Rufini walked in. Tobi's stomach lurched and tightened as he came straight toward them. He was a swarthy, saturnine, and unscrupulous man in his late thirties, with a stocky build, getting larger as the months wore on. He had been educated in his native Turkey before coming to the States, and he seemed to find capitalism very favorable. He was their regional lead physician, and by far the slimiest person Tobi had ever met. He was barely a mediocre doctor, and for some reason she could not quite put her finger on, he always made her skin crawl. The other regional leads were intelligent, caring, and valued high-quality medicine. She wasn't sure why her zone had drawn such a short straw.

"Hello, Dr. Rufini," Jorge said. He gave Tobi a knowing look and quietly slinked back up front.

"Hey, Tobiii," Ismar drawled in his thick accent. "You look busy."

"Hey, Ismar, what brings you out on this rainy night?" Tobi tried to sound casual but was feeling self-conscious about the overcrowded waiting room, as if it were her fault.

"Yes, I just stopped by to pick up some flu tests for the south shore," he said in his sing-song voice. "I see your wait time is, like, over an hour." Ismar squinted his eyes and peered at her as if she had just committed a crime.

"Hopefully you left us some," Tobi said. "We've been going through them pretty fast." She ignored his comment about the wait time and took another quick gulp of her Sprite Zero as she started to walk past him to get back to her patients. He had to have seen the ambulance and she didn't have time to discuss the case with someone who wouldn't even care. Tobi noticed the strobe lights were no longer illuminating the waiting room, but they were clearly visible through the front windows as the ambulance exited the parking lot to head up the block toward the hospital.

He surprised her by taking an interest. "That patient was cardiac, yes? And young. The young heart patients are expensive ones." He gave a self-amused laugh, and there was an odd sort of hunger in his eyes. "You know, you are not the primary care doctor here, you don't have to spend so much time. Just give patients, like, some helpful medicine and discharge them. That is what they want. The patient in room four says he has been waiting a long time."

Did he really think she should have just given Barry a cough medicine and sent him to his primary care doctor? She did not have the time to discuss standard of care with a half-wit who was supposed to be her boss, so Tobi just stared at him and chose to say nothing rather than something she would regret.

"Okay," he continued, "so, I'll let you get back to work. I will be coming with Molly Baker, like, one day next week. Just routine, we go over all the providers' productivity and, like, their customer satisfaction scores."

"Sure, Ismar, see you later then."

Tobi headed back up front, thinking he had lost his mind, and definitely should not be practicing medicine, let alone be a supervisor. How *did* he ever end up as lead? He must've come cheap, since he had very limited experience. Money was always the deciding factor in a place like B. Healthy. Ismar went into the stock room.

Patty looked back at Tobi as she walked up to check on the next patient in the queue, and rolled her eyes, as if to say, "You need this now?" None of them had eaten in at least five hours, and they still had several hours to go, so their endurance was wearing thin. The two patients before Barry had needed nebulizers and one of those, a chest x-ray. This flu was causing a lot of respiratory compromise, even in the immunized, and there were few simple in and out problems today.

Tobi walked into room three to see an elderly couple who had been in a few times in the past. Mrs. Lenman was eighty-two years old, and a few hours ago, had tripped over her rambunctious miniature Chihuahua, while making her famous potato leek soup to bring to Thanksgiving dinner tomorrow. She had caught herself on the counter, and by some miracle, did not fall to the floor, but her right hand was swollen and bruised and some of the thin fragile skin had been scraped off. She had been holding an old beige dish towel against it, which was now sitting on a chuck on the table, soaked with blood. Esther was in the room, cleaning the wound.

"This is terrible," Mrs. Lenman was saying. "I didn't finish cooking. It started bleeding, and we came straight here. How can we go to Thanksgiving dinner without the soup? We get invited for the soup, they wouldn't ask us otherwise, because I always get in the way, just like little Daphne." She looked up at Tobi as she came in. "She's my rescue puppy. But she's so cute, you have to forgive *her*. Me, I'm just old."

Esther shook her head and smiled at Tobi. "I told her that was crazy."

"Oh my gosh, of course they want you there! Soup or no soup," Tobi said as she grabbed a pair of gloves. "Let's look at your hand. I saw you're on Aspirin; that's why it bled so much. We're going to x-ray your hand to make sure you didn't break anything, and we'll put a special sponge bandage on it called PolyMem, to help it heal. There's nothing here to stitch, the skin is too fragile. I'm afraid you won't be able to get it wet for a while."

"Oh, Harry," she sobbed, turning to her husband. "What will I do about the soup? We can't go without the soup!" She looked at Tobi. "It's my daughter-in-law, she doesn't like me much, but she lets me come because our grandchildren insist they want my soup. They say her soup isn't as good as mine. I think they just say that, though, so she'll ask me. She makes good soup too."

Tobi completed her debridement of the woman's hand and gave her a tetanus shot. Why were people so hurtful to each other?

Tobi saw a patient with a urinary tract infection while Jorge took Mrs. Lenman's x-ray, then she went back in as Esther was finishing dressing the wound.

"Great news," she told Mrs. Lenman. "Nothing is broken, but I do want to see you back in three days to make sure there is no infection. I'll bet you'll have a wonderful Thanksgiving. Remember, you're not allowed in the kitchen, so you'll have to sit in the living room and hang out with your grandchildren."

That put a twinkle in her eye. "I have a new great grandchild on the way, you know! I hope she likes my potato leek soup."

The Lenmans left, and Tobi unlocked the EMR. It tended to time out frequently, often even while she was using it. If she clicked on a new window, even within the same chart, suddenly, she'd have to sign back in to the whole program all over again. It was a waste of precious time.

She put in the details of the procedure, indicating the wound had been cleaned, debrided, and dressed with a PolyMem bandage, and she added the charge to the billing page. Then she opened the box that said, "right hand x-ray" and recorded her reading, specifying in the redundant but necessary manner "three views of R hand," and typed "no fracture or dislocation, moderate degenerative joint disease." She documented the neurosensory exam she had performed and then described the injury precisely. Then she grabbed the empty tetanus syringe to record the lot number, expiration date, and where she had given the injection. Next, as instructed by the billing auditor, she chose the most specific diagnosis she could find in the long list of ICD-10 codes, so the maximum bill could be sent.

Each part was on a different screen, and each screen had to refresh, so notation took several minutes to complete—and that was with the EMR running at its usual painstaking speed. When it was sluggish, it could easily take twice the time. But if she did not do it correctly, she'd get persistent emails from billing telling her she needed to unlock the chart at a later date and adjust the documentation, and she hated to do that. If a chart ever went to court, the lawyers would be able to see that she had modified it after the original visit, and that could potentially discredit her. She'd been taught over the years to treat every chart as a potential court document. You never knew.

Jorge had just turned over another exam room, and Esther had finished cleaning and spraying down the cardiac room. She was already triaging the next patients.

Tobi saw two quick sore throats, and a shingles patient named Antonio. He was there with his daughter Amelia, who was a regular patient of hers. Despite the bothersome shingles, they were very excited about their good news. Antonio's kidneys had shut down about five years ago, but he had just gotten onto the kidney donor list. Tobi allowed herself an extra sixty seconds to warmly congratulate him and wish him luck. He was a relatively young guy and a sweetheart and he deserved a chance to escape dialysis for the rest of his life.

For a bit, it looked like she might actually catch up, although the longer times still showed in red on her spread sheet. There was nothing she could do about that. She completed Antonio's chart, noting his renal failure and new kidney donor status. It helped her to remember her patients' stories so she could ask about them the next time she saw them, and it made her job feel more personal and satisfying. Corporate might have frowned about the extra time it took to write those additional notes, as they preferred the turnover be as fast as possible, but they also expected her to be friendly and appear unrushed so the patients would want to come back. It was a no-win scenario. As she glanced through the next chart, she overheard Jorge down the hall, standing at the scale next to a mother and her little girl.

"Just step up here, little lady, we need to see how much you've grown."

"No!" The little girl stamped her foot and grabbed her mother's leg. "You can't make me!"

Jorge looked at the mother. "We need her weight in case the doctor wants to prescribe any medicine," he said.

Mom looked down. "Please, Jilly? Do what the nice man says."

"No! I don't want to!" She clutched tighter at her mother's leg and glared at Jorge.

Mom shrugged her shoulders and looked at Jorge. "She doesn't want to."

Jorge looked exasperated. "It doesn't hurt, Jillian, see? Look, I'll step on it first. All you have to do is stand here for a few seconds." Jorge demonstrated, and looked again to the mother for support.

At that point, Jillian, who looked to be about five years old, started screaming and stamping her feet, and buried her head in her mother's leg. Tobi shuddered and went in to see the next patient, a simple ear infection after a diving vacation in the Caribbean.

The visit took less than five minutes, but when she came out, the waiting room looked even more crowded than before, and Ismar's visage hung in the air. Tobi did her best to record everything in the EMR quickly, but it kept stalling on her, especially when she tried to send prescriptions. She would get the little spinning circle, which she called the "blue circle of death." If she became impatient and clicked again, the whole screen would fade, and the program threatened to shut itself down, so she just had to wait it out. She didn't have time for this today. She had already spent a half hour with just Barry in an office where she was expected to see forty-five patients a day by herself. At least Ismar was nowhere to be seen.

She walked into Jillian's room next. The little girl was sitting on the exam table, plastered against her mother who stood beside her. Tobi noted that vital signs were miraculously in the chart, including a normal temperature, and the weight read forty-seven pounds, or twenty-one kilos. She didn't even want to know if that was today's weight.

"Hi, Jillian, I'm Dr. Lister. Those are cool boots. Is *Frozen* your favorite movie?"

Jillian pouted but nodded slightly.

Tobi looked at the mother. "Are you Jillian's mom?"

"Yes, I am. Jilly felt a little warm today, so I brought her in. She's also had a stuffy nose for a couple of days."

"Did you happen to take her temperature?"

Mom shook her head and smiled. "She doesn't like thermometers."

"Okay, any other symptoms? Has she been coughing or complaining of a sore throat? Is her appetite normal? Or has she been cranky or clingy recently? Sometimes kids get like that when they're sick."

"Nope, just her usual adorable self," the mother smiled again. Jillian was quiet, but she kept her eyes riveted on Tobi as they spoke, and Tobi felt their daggers. She would hate to see this child when she was cranky.

Tobi picked up her stethoscope and addressed Jillian in her most reassuring voice. "I'm just going to listen to your lungs, sweetie, like this." She placed the end of the stethoscope on her own arm, then on Jillian's arm. "I'm going to put it on your back now and I want you to take deep breaths."

Jillian held her breath and jerked about, but Tobi held her gently but firmly by the shoulder. "See? That's all. It doesn't hurt. Can you take a big breath for me?"

Eventually, Jillian had to breathe, but she sure wasn't making it easy. Tobi managed to auscultate her lungs and then her heart. She pressed gently on her tummy while Jillian squirmed, but she displayed no additional discomfort and did not push Tobi's hand away. Looking in her ears was equally tricky, but the real trouble was looking at her throat.

"Would you open your mouth for me? I have nothing but a light, see? No sticks. I'm not going to put anything inside your mouth."

"No!" Jillian pressed her lips together tightly and covered her mouth with both hands.

Tobi wondered if this child ever said yes to anything.

Tobi looked at the mother, who made no move to help or take the child's hands away. "I need your help with this," she told her.

"Jilly, we can go for ice-cream if you open your mouth," her mom said.

"No! You always promise, but we never do!" she said from behind her hands.

Tobi hated to reward bad behavior with treats, but she was feeling desperate. "We have lollipops and potato chips. You can have either one if you help us take care of you today—if mom is okay with that.

I just want to look." She glanced at the mother, who had squatted down on the floor to plead with her daughter.

Suddenly, Jillian turned her back to her mother, looked straight at Tobi and opened her mouth wide. No tears, no fuss. Her throat was irritated, but not swollen and no exudate.

"You did great!" Tobi told her. "You get to choose which snack you want." She turned to the mother. "She has some minor irritation, but no swelling or pus. It looks viral to me."

"So, you'll give her an antibiotic?"

"I wouldn't treat her with antibiotics, I don't think they will do anything for her. Not unless she had a positive strep," Tobi said. "But her throat doesn't look excessively red, I think it would be negative."

The mother frowned. "Jilly, do you think you could let them take a throat culture?" She looked so doubtful, it would have been a miracle if the child had agreed.

"Nooooo!"

At that point, Tobi was done. The child was not seriously ill, was afebrile in the office, and she felt like her job was over.

"I think she will do well with fluids and Tylenol and you can take her to her pediatrician if she is not improving," she told the mother.

"Can't we just try?" She turned to Jillian. *"Please* baby?"

After another resounding "No!" they headed up to the front. Tobi wrote up the rest of the chart and was printing instructions when they came back with Jillian trailing her mother by the hand and whimpering.

"Doctor, she says she'll let you do it. I'd rather know."

Tobi turned to Jillian, trying to erase the picture of *The Exorcist* from her mind. "Okay, sweetie, but we will only try once, okay?"

Jillian hiccupped and nodded. Esther went into the room with them while Tobi went to collect the lollipop she had promised and Jillian's printed discharge instructions. Esther was back after a short minute. "It's not happening, Dr. L., not unless you want me to hold her down. But her mother won't touch her, so …."

"No, Esther, you're right. Mom has to participate, otherwise we'll be in trouble."

She walked back to her work station and found that her tablet had restarted itself. In fact, it didn't seem like the same tablet, but she hadn't looked carefully beforehand to see which one she was using, and they all looked the same except for the numbers on the back. Now *she* was losing her mind. It was true that any of the tablets could restart themselves at any time, even while she was using them. Tobi often blamed it on "office gremlins," since there seemed to be no rhyme or reason to it, but something felt weirder about it this time. She looked at the bookmark bar—no, it was definitely a different tablet. Now what was that about?

Tobi was exhausted. She felt like she should care about this but was just too tired. Twelve hour shifts seemed to get harder and harder, even though she should have been used to them by now. Maybe I'm just getting older, she thought. She downed the rest of her Sprite Zero and dreamed for a split second of the untouched turkey sandwich she had in the fridge before heading into the next room.

By 7:30 p.m., Esther had the last three patients in rooms, all stuffy noses without fever for less than two days. Those visits were such a waste of resources, both time and money. When she was a kid, no one had gone to the doctor for a stuffy nose, but these days, people piled in, complaining about the wait time and their $30 copays, while the insurance companies forked over the same reimbursement for each visit, regardless of whether it was a concussion or a sniffle—if it was billed properly—and B. Healthy made sure of that. These spurious visits were the only context in which she understood the rising costs of insurance premiums and decreasing benefits.

It was even more frustrating when the very sick patients needed imaging or expensive procedures and were not able to get authorization for them or had huge out-of-pocket expenses. It was as if they got stuck paying the price for all these unnecessary office visits.

Mrs. Perrin was the last patient. She was wearing a sleek charcoal-gray dress and three-inch heels and had just applied fresh bright red lipstick. Despite the rain, her hair was perfectly coiffed to show off heavy sapphire earrings and a matching sapphire pendant. She said she'd had a runny nose and a post nasal drip that had woken her up last night, and it hadn't gone away all day. She had no fever or muscle aches, no fatigue, except for not getting a good night's sleep, and no cough, wheezing or trouble breathing, but she did have a slightly scratchy throat. "I suffer from sinuses," she said. "I need a Z-Pak, it's the only thing that works for me."

It was always such a challenge to practice responsible medicine with patients like Mrs. Perrin, especially when providers were being encouraged by corporate to be people pleasers. Tobi told her that without fever or other systemic symptoms, this was a cold, which was a viral infection, and colds can make a person feel uncomfortable for up to a week. It happened to be in her sinuses, so yes, technically, it was a sinus infection, but not a bacterial one that would respond to an antibiotic like azithromycin. Viruses were not affected by antibiotics at all, because they were too small, and they lived inside the cells where the antibiotics couldn't get to them.

Mrs. Perrin looked at the doctor as if she were an ignorant child, and told her she knew her own body, and she needed her Z-Pak.

Tobi sighed, thinking it would be so much easier to give her whatever she wanted so they could all just go home. She wondered if she should try to explain that the inappropriate use of antibiotics for viral infections was causing massive resistance across the globe, and that in some areas, people were dying from simple infections that were once easily treated. Antibiotic research was barely able to stay ahead of the mutating bugs, which led to "super bugs," like "flesh-eating bacteria" and MRSA (she saw several cases a month), and it was even getting harder to treat something as basic as gonorrhea.

Then there was the risk of getting overgrowth of another gut bacteria, called *Clostridium difficile*, which could happen when taking any antibiotic, and the more frequently taken, the greater the risk. That kind of intestinal infection sometimes caused so much damage, it would require the patient to have part of their colon resected. Then they had to live with a bag tied to their abdomen, instead of using their rectum to poop the normal way. It wasn't a pretty sight, but even then, many people still didn't get it.

She felt Ismar in her head like a specter, telling her to just give the patient the Z-Pak and keep her happy. Instead, Tobi said, "We have learned we need to use antibiotics more responsibly than we have in the past. There are too many resistant organisms now, and we know for sure that colds are caused by viruses, and that an antibiotic has no effect on them. I'd like to give you some medicine to help you feel better, which is really what you want, right?"

"You don't understand. I don't have time to be sick right now, I have too much to do."

In her nearly thirty years practicing medicine, Tobi had never heard anyone tell her "now" was a "good" time to be sick. She plodded on.

"I'm going to prescribe a nasal spray to dry up your nose. You can also take a decongestant, like Allegra D, and you should drink a lot of fluids to support your immune system. These will make you feel better until the cold passes."

Mrs. Perrin stormed out of the office. So much for doing the right thing, Tobi thought, and now I have another bad review for the day. More ammunition for Rufini to yell at me, and Mrs. Perrin will probably find another doctor tomorrow to give her a Z-Pak anyway, just to shut her up. The ISIS extremists may not prevail after all, but the bacteria will get us all in the end. And the insurance premiums will continue to rise.

Chapter 2

Ismar Rufini sat in his study in his mansion on Centre Island, a room his wife was forbidden to enter. Downstairs he smelled the after aroma of dinner and what was supposed to be zaatar spiced lamb with couscous. Jennie had tried to read up on his native recipes, but she just didn't have the right flare. You had to be born into it, he supposed. She made up for her cooking shortfalls with her seductive, exotic silver-blonde hair that flowed back over her shoulders, but he cringed to see her go out in public like that and was glad no daughter of his was growing up in this country. He had even told Jennie they were not having any children unless they could be sure to have only boys.

He thought his wife was being quite unreasonable. Now that they were married, she should be appropriately modest. It wasn't like he would have insisted she wear a burka, which would cover her entire face, so what was her problem? He considered himself to be fairly liberal. He frowned and opened the little locked box in the bottom of his drawer and took out the faded photo. The woman in it was wearing a hijab, so her face was quite visible. High cheekbones and dark eyes under pronounced brows looked straight at the camera, so wherever he moved, the eyes looked right at him. Like an accusation. He tried to ignore the fleeting feeling of guilt as he gazed at her and the two small children by her side and then he put the picture away. Why did he torture himself like this? At least he knew they were safe.

His life here in America was far more lucrative than it had been in Turkey, and he turned his attention to the present. He smacked his lips and looked at his harvest for the day. Out of the three offices he visited, he had four potential clients for the Project. Lister's cardiac patient with the new onset a-fib might not be viable, unless there was so much viral damage to the heart muscle that he needed a transplant. It was more likely he would make a full recovery, unless he died, of course, but he was worth watching at any rate. He made a note of the hospital Barry had been transferred to and would check on him in a week. Perhaps Barry could be convinced he was at grave risk of a relapse and could be signed up anyway. Now that was a novel idea Ismar could suggest. The others he'd found would definitely bring him a pretty little lira. Lister was very good at writing notes; the program might not have otherwise flagged the shingles patient just accepted onto the kidney donor list. Perfect.

The software made it so easy. All he had to do was attach the flash drive to the tablet and tell it to run the RKS program, and—*voila*! It recorded all the pertinent findings right onto the drive, leaving the EMR program untouched. He could detach the flash drive from the USB port and be gone without even leaving a footprint—unless someone with real computer savvy checked the history of the hard drive. If he were ever found out, though, he'd be screwed for sure.

He compressed the files, encrypted them, and sent them off on the secure server he'd been given before he stuffed another piece of baklava into his mouth. He smiled and licked the honey off his fingers.

Chapter 3

They were restocking rooms and tallying money, and Tobi was checking her charts before locking the EMR. They were all exhausted, as the offices were chronically understaffed and overstressed, even if they were due for a bonus. All the B. Healthy employees' bonuses were based on their visit volume, door-to-door times, and patient satisfaction scores, but the staff were paid less up front since they were promised a bonus every three months. A few unsatisfied "customers" could really ruin a quarterly incentive check.

Jorge told Patty about the Lenmans. "She really thought she wasn't wanted at her son's house for the holiday," Jorge said. "It made me so sad."

"I'd like to just smack that daughter-in-law," Patty said. "That sweet old lady does not deserve that! People just don't appreciate each other. I mean, she's eighty-two years old, how much longer does she even have? Imagine, making her feel she's only wanted for her soup! My grandmother passed when I was ten, and I *wish* she were coming for the holidays!"

"Hey, what ever happened to the woman who came in for the 'quick strep test' when EMS was here?" Tobi asked. "I expected a score of zero from her."

"She left without being seen," Patty said. "After she wrote whatever she wrote on Yelp, she said she was going to another, more 'convenient' urgent care, and she'd never be back. I wanted to tell her that was just fine by me, but I behaved, and said only 'that might work out better for you tonight.' Grrr! I hate people sometimes!"

"It's just as well. We saw forty-eight patients as it was. We barely even got to eat," Esther said, her stomach rumbling loudly. "What did Dr. Rufini want?"

Esther was the sweetest of them all, a soft-spoken young woman from Ecuador in her mid-twenties, who quietly managed to take care of things before Tobi even realized they needed doing. She had the work ethic of an older generation and was never found sitting down if there was work to be done.

"What does Rufini ever want?" Tobi asked. "He likes to throw his weight around and watch his bank account get padded."

"Has he ever offered any helpful advice?" Jorge asked. "Seems like he just tells everyone what they are doing wrong. 'Not fast enough, scores too low.' If he were so concerned, he could have stayed a few minutes and seen a couple of patients for you. In fact, I thought he was going to do that, I saw him looking at a tablet for a while before he left. For a minute, I actually thought it was yours."

Tobi frowned. "Why was he messing with my tablet? I knew my tablet was switched! I wasn't sure at first, but when I reopened it, UpToDate wasn't on the bookmarks bar. I thought he left ages before that, anyway."

"He did, but he came back in, like he forgot something, and went to your work station, and then he was in the back checking numbers or something," Jorge said.

Tobi furrowed her brows. "Rufini was definitely acting weird today. Whatever he was doing, he would have had to use his own login, so why didn't he just use the tablet he left me if he wanted to look at charts, instead of switching them? The thing times out fast enough, and he doesn't have my password, so how far could he have gotten, anyway?"

"I think you can change the tablet security to keep them from timing out so soon, if you have the authorization code," Jorge said.

Tobi stared at him.

"Just saying."

Tobi let it go and her shoulders slumped. "I don't know. I'm just as happy Rufini didn't stay, he just adds to the stress. Dr. Milton speaks up well enough for both of us about needing more help, and all it's gotten us is more criticism. It's not worth it."

They all grabbed their things. "Drive carefully everyone, it's slippery out," Tobi said.

Chapter 4

Mannfort Tzenkov liked his life. Private jet, women when he wanted them, fine wine, and travel anywhere around the globe. Today, for example, he sat overlooking the Coral Sea on the east coast of Australia, in a little town called Port Douglas. He liked Port Douglas because it was relatively quiet, unlike the big party city of nearby Cairns, where the majority of tourists headed. Mannfort liked to keep most of the hoopla and decadence at a distance.

His IT guy had been tracking some circumspect activity that appeared to be monitoring the Project and needed to be handled. The activity had originated in this part of Queensland and was probably from a hacker. Whoever it was, they were smart, leaving few breadcrumbs and spending only seconds at a time, making them hard to trace. Mannfort's people were just starting to close in, but a few weeks ago, the trail suddenly went cold, so Mannfort had decided to make the trip himself. He was due for a vacation, and it would set him up to be close by if anything else emerged. If the offender were less principled, Mannfort might recruit them. If not, they'd have to pay the price for their vigilante activities.

The sky was cerulean blue, crystal clear, and it mingled at the horizon with the peacock blue water. The lush green brush covered mountainous slopes less than a mile away and extended nearly to the white sand beach. The place was as picturesque as anywhere he'd been. He sat at a table on a deck a hundred yards from the water, with a gentle breeze caressing his face. His laptop pinged with the notification that the next payment had arrived in his account.

He smiled. The Project was brilliant. He and his partner Alexei Bereznikov had started it nearly twenty years ago, and it had progressed from targeting the powerful and desperate to the general populace, which had proved even more lucrative. Back then, it had been easier to be invisible, but writing the program was more involved. The current software was a cinch to tweak to maximize revenue. Though it should have been more discoverable with modern technology, it didn't seem to matter. With everything already in place, no one knew any differently, mostly because they hadn't bothered to look. Best place to hide was always in plain sight. Alexei had recently met with an untimely death, which left the management of the Project to Mannfort, along with a hundred percent of the profits.

The genius guy who created the original software even had the good graces to die all on his own, so Mannfort didn't have to get his hands dirty on that one. Good thing, because for a little bit there, it looked like he was starting to catch on. Nerds. They never saw the big picture. He stretched his legs in the sunshine, content to enjoy the surf until IT contacted him again. He glanced over at the pub just a few yards away, and decided he wanted to try that Australian Pirate Life beer. It seemed wickedly apropos.

He locked his laptop and left it on the table. In its protective sheath, it was safe from sand and moisture, and he would be close enough not to have to worry about theft. Besides, the height of travel season was still a couple of weeks away, and this beach was close to deserted, which was exactly what he liked about it, and the locals were known for watching out for each other. With a couple of bucks in the right places, he had ensured they would look after him and his property too. Rolly, the bartender at the Ocean Breeze Bar, was one of those "places."

The outdoor pub gave a flawless view of the water some two hundred feet away and the laptop was clearly visible on the isolated table to Mannfort's left. Instead of taking his beer back to the hard wooden bench, he found a lounge chair at the bar to face both the water and his computer and settled into his beer and a Cuban cigar. He watched a blonde babe walking the beach, while stroking the bottle absently. The wind shifted a tad, then grew stronger, and he noticed how she stopped and lifted her head as if sniffing the air. She glanced in his direction as if she felt him staring, and then turned and started briskly back, away from the shore. Rolly motioned Mannfort to come back under the canopy, but he brushed him off. After a few minutes, the wind kicked up and started gusting, and the sky darkened ominously. He tossed the cigar and started toward his laptop. He wasn't worried about the rain, but the laptop was lightweight, and the wind could toss it off the table. The bartender ran around the counter and nearly threw himself in front of him.

"What are ye doing, mate? It's about to lightning!" he said.

"My laptop is out there, I have to get it," and he shoved Rolly aside.

"Suit yourself," the bartender muttered under his breath and took shelter within the enclosed section of the pub.

Mannfort hurried along the walk, and onto the sand toward his table. He was in reasonable shape for a man in his early sixties who partook of simple pleasures, but he had an arthritic left knee, which tended to give out on him at the worst possible moments, and it slowed him down on the uneven seashore. Thunder cracked, and the sky opened up like a faucet. Mannfort was soaked in an instant, and buffeted backward by the fierce wind, but he pressed on. It took him less than a minute to get to his laptop, but it was already lying on the wet sand. It wouldn't close properly, and he grabbed it up and ran back for shelter. The storm seemed to have come out of nowhere, but within ten minutes, the rain settled into a gentle sprinkle. Mannfort stayed at the bar under an awning, inspecting his laptop, and twenty minutes later, the clouds began to dissipate, and the whole thing was over.

"What the hell was that?" Mannfort demanded of Rolly when the bartender finally emerged again.

"That there was a thunder shower," he answered. "This is rainy season, mate. It happens. Only don't want to be on the beach and get struck by lightning, if ye know what I mean. Don't worry 'bout it, it's over."

"My laptop!"

The bartender looked at him more closely. Mannfort was cradling the device like a baby. "Oh, that's bad. Water *and* sand. Hope you got that little Joey backed up."

"Mostly, but not for what I did today," he said. "The cover is resistant to sand and water, but it looks like it cracked. Is there anyone around here who can fix it? I know time is essential for these machines. I can pay for it—handsomely!" Mannfort had pulled the protector off, which had revealed a three centimeter fissure in the heavy plastic and he was wiping down the keyboard vigorously with several napkins.

"Yep—a-a-actually, nope. There *was* a guy who could fix anything on a computer. Hardware, software, recover your whole drive if ye needed, debug anything … but he just passed a few weeks ago. Tragic diving accident. He used to own that dive shop down the road. You might go on down there, Marcus runs it now. He might know somethin'. Walk straight down this main drag and take the fourth right. You can't miss it."

Mannfort walked straight over, but he was seething. He'd paid the bartender enough to guard against theft, he'd have thought he should've been warned about the weather too. He saw the dive shop as he came over a shallow ridge, adjacent to a dock where a twenty-foot dive boat was tethered.

A man in his early forties was inside, hitting on the blonde babe from the shore, and she was flirting timidly back at him. Her royal blue bikini fit just right over a perfect ass, crumpled on one side, and there was no tan line where there should have been. Her breasts were full and seemed to speak their own language back to the store owner, but Mannfort had little time for that now. He positioned himself boorishly between the two of them, facing the divemaster.

"Are you Marcus?"

"Depends who wants to know," Marcus answered slowly, annoyed by the rudeness. His skin was a deep tan and his biceps flexed as he placed his elbows on the counter and turned to Mannfort. Each muscle in his forearms was clearly defined as he locked his fingers together slowly and stared at him.

"My laptop was caught in the storm. Do you know someone who can fix it? I can pay well. Very well."

Marcus eyed Mannfort and his laptop up and down for several seconds. He rubbed is hands together and glanced at the blonde. She gave him a subtle nod. "I'll catch you later, Marco," she said softly, and she left the shop.

"So, you're in a spot with your computer, are ye? I'm not the man you want. Wish I was. Robain taught me a thing or two, but no one has the brain he had. I can't do nothing with that."

"Where is this Robain? I'll pay him a couple of grand, US, if he can fix this thing for me this afternoon. Cash."

"Ah, Robain woulda done it for free. He was that kind of guy. Never did understand why he didn't put his talent to better use, he could have been a millionaire."

"Where can I find this guy?"

"Horrible mistake. He saved that little darling you just saw. Couple weeks ago, her brother Patrick come up from the reef screaming that Missy was caught in the coral. Robain had just finished his second dive, didn't even get all his gear off. Hell, he had no business going back down, I think he was in dive group U? He needed to stay out at least an hour, but he was only up about ten minutes, so let's see, he woulda been in group R. He grabbed a full tank and went right back down again. Patrick said Missy was at thirty-five feet but turned out she was at fifty and caught in some rock. Man, she must've been sucking air like crazy, she was on empty. Panic does that to you."

"So, where is this Robain now?" Mannfort was losing patience. He couldn't care less about "dive groups." Why did Australians *talk* so much!

"Well, that's what I'm tellin' you, mate. He's dead. He shoulda made a decompression stop, but he come up way too soon, like three, four minutes after Missy and Patrick. He was having trouble breathing and clutching his chest. Everyone thought he threw an embolus. Bends, you ever hear of the bends, mate?" Marcus was looking at Mannfort like he was an ignorant tourist. Mannfort gazed back at him with open hostility.

"They packed him up and went straight to the hyperbaric chamber in Townsville. Passed right by Cairns Hospital. Fuckin' A! He was having a heart attack. Not the bends, no embolus, just an old fashioned, freak heart attack! He died in the hyperbaric chamber. I hear he had some heart problems back in America, but he didn't talk much about that. I only knew he was on meds and he saw a doc down in Cairns from time to time. I think he got worse, 'cause he stopped teaching, but he still liked to do a few dives now and then for himself."

"Damn," Mannfort said under his breath. He didn't care a wit about this guy Robain, he needed his laptop fixed.

"Yah, damn shame. No purer soul on this Earth. He never wanted no money, except just enough to get by. Always helping people. Like he was paying off some terrible debt only he knew about. And brilliant! I mean, easily the smartest man you ever knew. And we don't even know who to notify. He did all this beautiful underwater photography … he was incredibly talented. I'm sure his family would want some of it, but he never talked 'bout no family if he had one. He had one friend used to come 'round now and then, also American, but we haven't been able to reach him.

"It was like Robain just appeared here one day and spent his time doing good and enjoying the sea. I'd have said he was a monk, but he wasn't religious or nothing. Don't think he was Christian by birth, he used to say he didn't think there was a God. Kinda lonely, you know? Missy feels terrible ever since. No matter what we tell her, she blames herself."

Something was itching in the back of Mannfort's head, and he credited his intuition to much of his success. American, genius, computer master … diver? He *had* come here looking for a hacker. "What was his last name?" he asked.

"Sack or Sacks, something like that. He just went by Robain. His doc would know."

"And when did you say he showed up?"

"Geez, I dunno. 2003, 2001? Maybe 2000. It's been a bit of time," said Marcus.

Mannfort set his chin. "So, where can I get my laptop fixed?"

"Beats me. Maybe in Cairns, you could find someplace. Might have to go to Brisbane." Marcus half turned and started stocking his shelf.

"Tell you what, *mate*. You help me fix my laptop, and I'll help you find this Robain's family."

CHAPTER 5

The now-freezing rain battered the windshield and Tobi could hardly see ten feet in front of her. The wipers were on maximum speed, which she hated, because it always made her feel like her heart was racing, and now the roads were icing up. She flipped on her fog lights and reduced her speed to fifteen miles per hour. She passed a fender bender pulled over to the side of the road, police already on the scene. The frozen rain reflected her headlights in the darkness and gave a surreal feeling to the ride. She left the radio off to concentrate better on the road, and the pinging of the ice on the car added to the sense of being completely cut off from the world. It felt like an episode of *The Twilight Zone*.

Imagine if you will … She played it out, hearing Rod Serling in her head:

It is the year 2019. Medical offices are so overcrowded that it can take weeks to get an appointment, even for a serious matter, causing a large percentage of illness, both critical and insignificant, to be funneled into America's urgent care centers. These centers are exploding around the country, multiplying faster than an unchecked mouse population hiding in your walls in the springtime, and medical practices of all specialties are swiftly being gobbled up by venture capitalists. Many entrepreneurs view these urgicenters, and medicine as a whole, as a new best way to make it onto the Fortune 500. And so, what was once an essential human service is reborn as a revenue-generating commodity ....

Tobi chuckled to herself. She would go crazy without her sense of humor, but it really wasn't funny. At her last medical school reunion, she and her former classmates had bitterly bemoaned that their profession had come to this. "Productivity" measured by volume and speed, not quality? Customer satisfaction surveys? Patients weren't customers. If it were realistic to assume that patients knew how they should best be treated, there would be no need for doctors. Just come into the Emergency Department and dial up an appendectomy or a cardiac stent, or some antibiotic—oh, and don't forget to check if the medicine you want is chemically related to your allergies or if it interferes with your other medications or has consequences for your current medical conditions. You heard about it on a TV commercial? Well, then, it must be your perfect cure. And then there's the insistence: "I have bronchitis, I need an antibiotic," when in fact, you have no cough, fever, or congestion at all, you just have chest pressure, and you need to be evaluated for a possible heart attack.

Enter the unrestricted media, teaching patients that they should never have to be physically uncomfortable and then terrifying them with the horrible possible consequences of not getting this medication or that treatment—all to raise the pharmaceutical company's stock value. And then put all that in the hands of an increasingly rapacious and privileged population, like the community Tobi worked in, and what do you get? A culture of anxiety-ridden, entitled people who have no coping skills and feel justified in demanding whatever treatment they saw on television or read about on the internet. It was a great recipe to feed corporate greed that focuses on profit margins rather than on improving health in the population. The tycoons must be laughing all the way to the bank.

There were many communities where people respected and appreciated medical care, but it seemed the more affluent the neigborhood was, the more importunate and entitled its people behaved.

Long Island had plenty of sick and injured people who *should* be coming to urgent care for treatment, and Tobi wanted to focus her energy on *them*. But corporate was much more interested in rapid turnover, meaning people who were not particularly ill. Corporate giants, like Big Pharma, pandered to a culture of impatience, and fostered general anxiety about health onto unwitting Americans, who already had few coping skills. It was simple math; increased volume meant increased charges, but a wheezing patient should get a nebulizer, which tied up a room for another fifteen minutes. So, the real money was in the people who came to urgent care like a stop at the grocery store, not for a genuine illness. And like any business model designed to sell product, the corporate giants tossed their net wide to ensnare the market, even if it meant creating a need where there was none, just in order to increase revenue.

Like a "must have" at your favorite specialty store, urgent care offices made more money if they had more sick people to prey upon, so advertising campaigns encouraged people to come in with the most minor concerns, like a post nasal drip, and then promised that all patients would be in and out in less than an hour. But no matter how you slice it, Tobi thought, without fever, a stuffy nose for less than a week is still a cold, and there is no magical formula to make it go away any faster.

But of course, when those patients did not get what they wanted, and without delay, they sent scathing Press Ganey scores that stuck to dog-tired, diligent health care workers like cat fur on a flannel shirt—as if B. Healthy were selling Apple TVs instead of treating human beings.

The model was clearly unsustainable, and when the profits peaked, Tobi was sure B. Healthy would just cash out and sell their business as they would dump a stock that was about to tank. They had no vested interest in helping human beings and cared nothing for the destruction they might leave in their wake. She felt the niggling in her head again, telling her this place was going to fall hard on its face, and she should get out now, while she could.

Chapter 6

Mannfort Tzenkov grabbed his laptop and his wallet and secured his trusty silencer in place, then fastened his piece to his hip beneath his shirt and hopped in his rented Maserati Granturismo. He had left the top down, but fortunately, the Sheraton on the Sea had covered parking, or it would have been soaked from the storm. In a couple of minutes, he was cruising south on Captain Cook Highway toward Cairns and the contact Marcus had given him. His GPS said an hour and ten, but he planned to push that up and he hit the accelerator.

Smartass guy, that Marcus, he fumed. Thought he could just dismiss me out of turn, did he? Didn't want to give up his connection? What, money wasn't enough? Just so happened, they were both interested in finding out about this Robain guy, or Mannfort would have popped him as he drove away.

Mannfort hadn't been involved in any first-hand bloodletting in a while, and he sorely missed the rush. That was, after all, why he had chosen to come do this job himself. Now he was savoring the idea of knocking that smirk off Marcus's face for good.

He found the little back street shop in Cairns easily enough. It didn't show on his GPS, but Marcus had given him an address nearby and precise directions from there.

The a-hole behind the counter didn't want to help him even for five Gs until Mannfort mentioned Marcus by name. Then he was pretty friendly. He suggested Mannfort get a drink and a bite to eat. It would take a couple of hours to retrieve the files, so he took a walk amidst the bustle and music of Cairns. He stopped in to Bon Aliment par la Mer, a pricey little French restaurant for a juicy steak and a glass of Ringbolt cabernet sauvignon.

Mannfort savored the decadent cuisine at a side table with a view of the Coral Sea. Where else could you get a crocodile appetizer, grilled to perfection? He called his contact in Kiev.

"Kazimir, talk to me. What do you remember about the American who wrote our first software?"

"He had a terrible car accident, Mannya, you grow forgetful."

"No, not the first guy. The really smart one who developed the blueprint completely, so we could start using it. He started snooping at the end and then died in his home of a heart attack, but he finished the program before he died. We're still using it, with a few tweaks."

"We had nothing to do with that. He had a bad heart, they said."

"*Nyet*, Kazimir, I know all that. But who was he, really? What else did he do besides write software?"

"What, Mannya, you going soft on me? You want to know what he was like? After all this time?"

"Yes, Kazi, I want to know everything we knew about him. His hobbies, his interests, his family ties, and where they are right now."

"You want me to dig in his old file?"

"*Dah!* That's what I'm saying! Dig, and get back to me."

Mannfort hung up the phone. He hated being called "Mannya," and Kazi knew it. He had gone to great lengths to remove the stain of poverty that had riddled him before Yeltsin came to power. When the Russian economy had privatized, it finally opened up new opportunities for the courageous and fortuitous like himself, and he had jumped on them. He didn't even mind being called a *kleptocrat*. Swiss banks were always safest, and he had plenty of cash he needed to stash these days. The more the world digitized, the easier it was for the Project to bring him profit. But he hated the name *Mannya*. It reminded him of the days of hunger.

His laptop was not salvageable, but the a-hole had retrieved all his data and put it on an external hard drive. Then he transferred it to a new PC and told him he didn't owe him anything more, the five grand covered it.

Mannfort opened the new laptop and checked to make sure everything was there and not corrupted. He asked for the hard drive he'd used for the information transfer and took his old laptop back. Then he told the a-hole he wanted to give him a little something extra for his trouble. Mannfort reached under his shirt and pulled out his Makarov pistol, its silencer still attached, and shot him in the chest. The a-hole fell with a look of disbelief on his face. Mannfort shot him once more in the head, just to be sure.

He smiled and holstered his pistol and got back in the Maserati, feeling the rush of adrenaline, like endorphins in his blood. This time he closed the top. It was dark and chilly, and he preferred the tinted windows now. He was back at the Sheraton on the Sea by 10:00 p.m.

Chapter 7

The Bluetooth sounded above the noise of freezing rain on the windshield.

"Hi, Tobi, it's Chloe. I know you're probably up to your elbows cooking—"

"Actually, I'm in the car on my way home. What's up?"

"I thought I heard rain ... I'm just feeling stressed," Chloe groaned.

"How's Larry doing? He's not due for chemo again for a couple of weeks, right?"

"Yes, and he's such a trooper," Chloe said with a sigh. "He gets really tired a few days after, but so far that's it. By the next week, he seems to be mostly back to normal. For now, anyway. He's still got a long way to go. The week of, he says he feels like he's being poisoned. His body gets very heavy."

"Well, he *is* being poisoned."

Chloe was one of Tobi's closest synagogue friends. She didn't go every Friday night like Tobi did, but they made it a point to get together for lunch at least once a month and on some holidays too. At a glance, Chloe looked like a privileged soccer mom, always dressed to the nines, but she was actually one of the strongest, most compassionate, and most introspective people she'd ever met. Tobi felt blessed to have her as a friend.

"Tobi, have you ever come across this supplemental insurance called Kordec? These people approached Larry with it, said that with his type of leukemia, he'll likely need a bone marrow transplant at some point. Kordec is for seriously sick patients who may encounter a lot of bills that could break them. After his regular insurance maxes out, it covers hospital bills, rehab, and it gives a stipend if he's disabled and can't work anymore. But it's super expensive—like crazy—and so far, Larry's doing pretty okay and he's able to work. He doesn't want to spend all our resources paying for this supplement when we're getting by with the Blue Cross, but it would be so hard to get insurance on him now."

"Is it life insurance too?"

"No, that's the only thing they *don't* cover, I guess because they figure he's not a good risk." Chloe's voice caught.

Tobi pulled into her driveway. "Never heard of them. But don't worry, Chloe, I think he's going to beat this. He's doing amazingly well."

"I hope so. We have Sebastian's wedding coming up next summer too, so money is an issue. My baby boy! I should be so happy for him, what's wrong with me?"

"How is that going?"

"We're trying to get them to keep costs down. At first, they were talking about this hundred-thousand-dollar-wedding, but we just can't swing it, and I don't think her family can either. And we'd rather they use the money we have for them to start their life, not pay for a party."

"It sounds so unnecessary," Tobi said. "I mean, unless you're a millionaire, and a hundred K isn't a big deal, but you could still feed a thousand homeless people for a week with that. I went through this for Ben's bar mitzvah. I gave him the option to have the expensive four-hour party or a modest party with games and a DJ, and we could go on a trip somewhere. So, we went to Australia for two weeks. It was incredible. We hiked in the Blue Mountains, fed wallabies and kangaroos, and Ben got to dive the Great Barrier Reef on his first real scuba trip."

"That sounds amazing. What made you think of the Great Barrier Reef?"

"I don't know. Reuben always wanted to go there, but he never made it, and Ben was saving his first Israel trip for his father. Plus, it was summer in Australia, and they speak English. Driving on the left side of the road was a challenge, though." Tobi chuckled.

"I bet! I hope Sebastian does something like that, make it a destination that would also make for a magnificent honeymoon, all for the same price. But he doesn't listen to me anymore …."

"Give him time, Chloe, and trust him. He's a smart kid. I mean, we really can't make decisions for our kids after a certain point. We just have to hope we taught them everything we could and then have faith in them to live their own lives, wisely."

"I know. It's so hard to let go."

"That's a big add-on to your stress right there, girlfriend. Between your oldest leaving the nest and worrying about Larry, it's amazing you're not completely strung out," Tobi said. "Give yourself some credit!"

"Maybe you're right. Are you home yet?"

"Just pulled up."

"Okay, I'll let you go. Thanks for the chat. Have a great holiday!"

Chapter 8

Mannfort paced in his penthouse suite for an hour until Kazi called him. It was only 11 p.m., but he hated to be kept waiting.

"Did you find what I need?" Mannfort asked.

"*Dah*. Reuben Sokowsky, American. Born in New York City. Excellent with computers, he wrote our first successful program, and it was even better than expected. He started snooping though, and we thought we'd have to treat his, ah, curiosity, but he did it himself. Found dead in his apartment in Austin, Texas, on October 31, 2000."

"Interesting ... anything else about him?"

"He had a pilot license, was a PADI certified Divemaster and scuba instructor, and did freelance underwater photography ... sold some of it. Employed by Cray Research and Superior Oil before us and worked at NASA on the American space shuttle project. Graduated University of Texas, Austin, 1979. That's it."

"Positive ID on his death?"

"Looks like it; it was a closed case. Identified by friend, then cremated."

"No DNA confirmation?"

"Mannya, no one did DNA testing back in 2000, not unless the vic was some Big Shot. But there is something strange ...."

"What, Kazi, what?"

"Well, we lost one of our insureds about that time. Guy named James Arlan. He was scheduled for a heart transplant. Diagnosis was cardio … carmayo … oh, hell, I can't pronounce it. Some heart condition. Was going to cost a fortune. We were about to take care of it, but he just disappeared. The weird thing is, he never got the transplant, either, so we let it go."

"People don't 'disappear' unless we make them, Kazi."

"I know, Mannya, but I don't see any follow-up on him, or any charges to Kordec Insurance for the surgery. I guess nobody noticed."

"Hell of a thing to not notice. Nobody looked for him? What about his family?"

"Arlan didn't have much family, and not in America anyway. He was presumed dead by his Canadian cousins after his wallet turned up in the Colorado River. That case was closed too."

"Body was found in the river?" Mannfort asked.

"*Nyet*, nothing found but the wallet. Maybe was assumed he went downstream."

"Kazi, you're sure we didn't do it?"

"Positive, Mannya. Maybe he committed suicide."

"Why would a man about to get his heart transplant commit suicide?"

"No idea."

"What about Sokowsky? Did *he* have family? Kazi, some hacker has been poking around in the Project's files, as recently as a few weeks ago, and I'm wondering … scuba instructor, huh? I want to know about every job Sokowsky had, every hobby traceable back to his last known server, and every email he ever sent to anyone. There's always some kind of trail. Start with the information we had on him back then and work forward. Understand?"

"*Dah,* Mannya, *dah.* Give me more time on that, it was a long time ago. I'll call you back."

Chapter 9

Tobi walked in the house and was greeted by her dwarf cat, Pantelaymin, who was a muted tortie on her back, with vivid calico colors on her tummy. Her deep gray and beige markings made a flawless line down the center of her face, giving her a certain harlequin appearance. There was also a perfect line down the length of her belly, so she was a great genetics lesson. It was like seeing the fusion of the neural tube. And, like a mirror, she always seemed to embody Tobi's own emotions and reflect them back to her.

Tobi barely got through the door, with little PanniKat rubbing against her legs. The cat purred loudly and gazed up at her with those wide green-gold eyes, looking very concerned by her human's lateness. Tobi took off her wet coat and sneakers and picked her up. The fatigue of the day began to dissolve with the soft, rhythmic vibrations against her chest. They nuzzled each other, face to face, and then little Panni rubbed the top of her head under Tobi's chin.

She changed clothes and was ready to tackle the kitchen to prepare for Thanksgiving when Ellie Milton called. She was the doctor who worked opposite Tobi in their office. In her usual style, Ellie started the conversation without preliminaries.

"So, Rufini wants to meet with both of us this time. Like, really? I already met with him last month and he was a jackass. Why do I have to do it again? He already told me I was the slowest provider in the whole company, so what else is there to say? Oh, happy Thanksgiving, by the way."

"Hey, you too," Tobi said. "Are you doing dinner? And you can't be the slowest, he said I was."

"Going to my mom. Thanks for the kugel recipe, it looks yummy."

"Hope you like it. Ismar came in today, right after an ED transfer. Patient was really sick too, flu and new onset a-fib; he looked a mess. Of course, Ismar made a comment about the backup wait time that caused, and he mentioned the meeting next week. And somehow my tablet was switched, and Jorge thinks it was Ismar who took it and was using it in the back."

"He's not supposed to do that!" Ellie said. "Did he change anything?"

"I have no idea, Jorge told me when we were closing up. I just wanted to get out of there, and I didn't think to go through all forty-eight charts and see if anything had been changed. Kind of ticks me off."

"It would me!"

"He said Molly is also coming next week," Tobi added, with disgust. "She's some high up muckety-muck now, right? She comes off so sweet, like she's supportive and understanding, but she'll cut your throat if you close your eyes for a second. And she doesn't understand medicine at all, which is the most frustrating. What was she in her former life, a bookkeeper for some small business, I think? How is she running the corporate operations of a medical giant?"

"Something like that," Ellie said. "How she landed so high up in the B. Healthy food chain is beyond me. I think she just 'stepped in shit,' as the Italians say. That's crazy, we should talk to Dr. Chagall again. *He's* the medical director for all of B. Healthy, Rufini is just one of their little lackeys with a god complex. I talked to him last time about all the negative criticism without offering solutions— just telling us we're losers? Dr. Chagall was like—'that shouldn't happen.' And you should definitely ask about him about Rufini using your login."

"I didn't actually see him do that … I don't know. I do love Steve Chagall, though, he's a doctor and a mensch. He cares about patients first and revenue second. It should be like that, right? If you just do the right thing, the money will take care of itself? All this focus on profit makes me feel like I need a shower. I'm glad he got the position when Daniel Comet left."

"I miss Dr. Comet!" Ellie moaned.

"Me too," Tobi said.

"I can't blame him for leaving, though. This place has become so pecuniary," Ellie said.

"He hasn't come out and said that's why he left, but I'm guessing it was a big factor."

"So, what did slimy *Isssmar* say to you today?" Ellie hissed his name when she hit the "s." "Why did he even come?"

"Ostensibly to pick up flu tests. I guess they were running low on the south shore, but he made a point of telling me he and Molly are coming by next week to go over the customer satisfaction scores and door-to-door times, and he was acting really weird. He said 'young cardiac patients are expensive,' like, what the hell does he care? He's not paying the hospital bill. It's all about the money for these people, Ellie. And then they say they will bonus us based on our 'productivity.' What does that even *mean*? What are we producing? For sure they aren't measuring health. Ismar doesn't get any of that, but I suppose he'll go far in the corporate world. Why did he become a doctor, anyway? There are easier ways to get rich."

"Much easier ways. Do you know he told the staff in the east site that they shouldn't pretend they cared about patients, because they only care about their paychecks? They were pissed! That's probably just how *he* feels. He seriously should be working for a hedge fund instead."

"We're *owned* by hedge funds, Ellie. Ugh."

"I think our times are longer because we document after we see each patient," Ellie said. "I can't leave the charting for the end of the day or the next, like some do. But, yeah, that makes me slower."

"I know, I always finish my charts as I go—I can barely remember all the details about a patient who left two hours ago—which could be ten patients ago. And I'm not staying after hours or taking charts home with me, either," Tobi said. "And I know for *sure* you aren't. Not with three little kids who already don't get enough of your time."

"Absolutely not," Ellie said.

"But even though they don't care about human beings," Tobi said, "there's always the law suit to consider. Don't they get *that* part? This is Long Island, one of the most litigious places in the country. That patient I sent to the ED had his heart rate recorded at 95 in his vitals, but his EKG said 217! Can you imagine if I hadn't done it, just sent him home with a cough syrup and chalked his tachycardia up to the flu? It would have been 'quicker.'"

"Wow. Yeah, and he might have died. What do you think, myocarditis?" Ellie asked.

"That's my guess. But can't you just hear the lawyers if I'd sent him home? 'Dr. Lister, you saw Barry just three hours before he died. Did you even listen to his heart?'"

"Yeah," Ellie said, "then when they had to pay a huge settlement, maybe B. Healthy would be concerned. It's the only language they understand. Hey, maybe we should rename them 'B. Wealthy, LLC.'"

"Very appropriate," Tobi laughed.

"Well, I think I'm not going to be available for this meeting," Ellie said. "I don't need to hear Rufini tell me again that I should be more motivated. You're on that day, so I'm going to be spending time with my family. I'll talk to you later. Happy Thanksgiving!"

"You too. I don't know how you do it with three kids, this job, plus your moonlighting, *and* go to the gym every morning!"

"I guess I'm just selectively motivated," Ellie cackled.

They hung up, but Tobi couldn't shake her feeling of unease. She did not want to meet with Ismar and Molly at all, much less by herself, but she couldn't blame Ellie for bowing out. Still, she'd been living with the corporate nightmare for a several years now, so why was she suddenly feeling paranoid?

Chapter 10

"**M**annya, I got it."

"Spill, Kazimir."

"Reuben Sokowsky had no wife or children. Mother and father are both dead, but he had a sister living in New York. Doctor. Name is Tobi Lister."

"Doctor, huh? Where does she work? Do we have eyes in her institution?"

"That I don't know. But, wouldn't she have talked years ago?"

"Well, find out! Maybe he just told her."

"But, Mannya, Sokowsky died in 2000."

"*Nyet*, Kazi, I'm thinking Sokowsky was the hacker who was active up until a few weeks ago when this 'Robain' guy died. It makes sense, him checking up on us. Who knows what he found out and who he told. Leave nothing to chance."

Mannfort hung up and paced his hotel room, figuring his next move. He hated waiting, but Kazi was much more suited to research, and his loyalty to Mannfort was unquestionable. Their history together went way back. Kazi's father had been a soldier, like so many Soviets, and was killed just when the long nine-year Soviet-Afghan war was finally over. Kazi was only fourteen at the time, but Mannya had been "taking care of" his mother Anya for years while his father was away. Once Kazi's father was not coming home, Anya expected to make it a permanent arrangement. Mannfort wanted nothing to do with marriage, so he split, but Kazimir wouldn't go away. He barely remembered his father and had grown used to Mannfort filling that role. Like a bad ruble, he kept turning up. And then he'd just hang around all day. Mannfort wasn't generally the sentimental sort, but after a while, he'd felt bad for the poor kid and ultimately, he'd taken him under his wing. By the time Kazi was eighteen and had gone off to fight in the Georgian Civil War, Mannfort had become rather attached to him, and they developed a business partnership of sorts when Kazi returned. Kazimir had always been bright, but the war had matured him into a man and he learned a variety of useful skills in the process, so it even made sense for Mannfort to keep him close. They'd been working together for twenty years, at least.

***

In the morning, Mannfort headed back to Marcus's dive shop to "thank him" for his help, but he stopped just short. There was a well-muscled man standing behind the counter talking to Marcus, with a full head of shoulder-length blondish hair that was turning gray. He looked like he'd been crying, and he kept running his hands over his face and back down the sides of his head. He was shaking his head and looked like his entire world had just collapsed. Marcus hugged him tightly and the man thanked him several times before he walked up the road with his shoulders drooping and his head down, still rubbing his head as if he could erase something in it.

When the road was clear, Mannfort walked up to the counter. "Who was that?" He noticed Marcus' eyes were wet too. Were they all a bunch of sissies, then?

"Just an old friend," he said. "Did you get your laptop fixed? I tried to call Freddie a few times, but he's not picking up. Did you find him?"

"Yeah, I found him."

"Okay, good. Well, I'm getting ready for my next dive class. See you around, then." Marcus picked up a crate full of buoyancy compensators and turned toward the side door, which opened onto the pier. Mannfort pulled out the Makarov.

"Hey, Marcus," he said.

Marcus turned back around, his mouth stretched tight, until he saw the gun. Mannfort shot him full in the face, just as his jaw started to drop.

Marcus fell back and the equipment scattered on the floor. Mannfort shot him again in the heart.

"That is for being such a prick," he said with a sneer. Belatedly, he wondered why Marcus had never asked him about finding Robain's family.

Mannfort turned reflexively in the direction of the "old friend," but he was gone. Was he that one friend from Sokowsky's past who stopped by once in a while?

Mannfort couldn't stick around at any rate. He looked up at the sign over the dive shop. *Tobi's*, it said. He hadn't noticed that before. Yeah, this had been Sokowsky's place all right. He pocketed his pistol and left quickly. Everything was already packed in the Maserati and he'd made it a point to pay up this morning for the next four days to make it look like he hadn't planned to leave. Then he'd given his key to a teenager to use for a few nights with his girlfriend, with the promise the kid would never tell. It was the penthouse suite, and he wanted them to keep messing the room up as if he were still there. Mannfort had already wiped down everything he might have touched.

He stopped into Beachside Eats and lingered for a bite, making himself look conspicuous and leisurely. As he was leaving, he saw several police officers on the beach with a group of divers. The man from Marcus's shop was there and he was no longer crying. He was yelling, pointing, and shaking his hands at the constables. He looked more like he was ranting. Mannfort was not able to hear anything, but he knew it was time to leave. He hopped in the Maserati and drove north on Captain Cook Highway toward Cookstown.

He found an abandoned piece of the beach and unloaded the car. He traveled light for just these eventualities, knowing he could always buy what he needed. Then he put the Maserati in neutral and sent it into Finch Bay. Terrible waste, he thought. He hiked into town and rented himself another car with another set of ID cards, less flashy this time, just a simple Audi sedan. He never used his real name, and he always traveled prepared. He headed back toward the airport and his jet.

Chapter 11

Tobi got up early the next morning. She stuffed the turkey and had just put it in the oven as her iPad pinged.

Troy DeJacob wants to connect on Messenger.
New message from Troy DeJacob.

Tobi stared at the Facebook alert as if it were written in another language. After, what, like nineteen years? The banner disappeared from the screen. Maybe she'd misread that, but she couldn't bring herself to swipe it back down for confirmation.

She waivered for a minute, her heart pounding. Then she put down the iPad and decided not to change her morning plans. She had no intention of ruining her day. She put on a scarf, boots, and gloves for a brisk walk in her neighborhood. It was one of her favorite ways to clear her head. She forced the message out of her mind and focused instead on the nature all around her.

Her little community was lined with trees and shrubbery, and in the spring and summer, flowers bloomed everywhere. There were two little ponds with fountains, and no one got in uninvited or without the guard at the gatehouse checking ID, so she felt perfectly safe strolling around even after dark in the moonlight. She loved to just walk and empty her mind, breathe in the cold crisp air, and gaze at the sky and the trees. It helped her put everything in perspective.

The icy rain had stopped overnight, and there was a silence in the air. The little fountains were shut down for the season, and without the wind, the half-frozen water in the ponds was silky smooth, translucent, and still, as if it were in a deep, trance-like sleep. The tall trees seemed to reach for the heavens in their slumber, their bare branches contrasting starkly with the opaque, almost-winter sky. Their detachment was haunting. On some level, she felt like the oaks understood humanity much better than humanity understood the oaks.

The cold air smelled deliciously clean. She took a deep breath in and felt herself expand into the majesty of the Earth. In moments like this, Tobi felt she could catch a fleeting glimpse of holiness, simply by sensing the world as it was and allowing it to just be. Whether it was the fifty-year-old maple, the neighborhood rabbits, or the soil in the now-dormant flower beds, she felt the essence of life all around her, even in its hibernation.

As she walked, she recited to herself a list of things she felt blessed with, which was a habit she always found to be transformative. The more things she found to be grateful for, the more things she found to be grateful for. She started with the simple things that she usually took for granted, like fresh air to breathe, legs that allowed her to walk despite her arthritis, heat in her home, and the oven working. Then she added her limited ability to experience the immensity of the universe and to feel close to God. And then, of course, her amazing son, her little feline companion, her friends, her home, her synagogue community, and her gainful employment with an opportunity to help others every day.

She tried not to think about the Facebook message still locked away on her iPad.

She walked two miles and came back inside, her cheeks red and her nose running, but she felt at peace. The house was starting to smell delicious too.

Her oldest friend, Sally, called as Tobi walked into the house. Sally had moved to Michigan ten years ago, but they stayed close and always called each other on holidays.

"Hey, you!" Sally greeted her. "How's it going?"

"Hey. I'm trying to muster the courage to walk back in the kitchen. It was such a crazy night last night. I've been out for a walk, which helped a lot, but I've still got so much to do!"

"You poor dear. I forget how late you work. You need a job with better hours."

"Don't I know it," Tobi said. "And better bosses."

"Are you still having trouble with that Ismar guy? He sounds like such a menace."

"He is. He should have gotten an MBA instead of an MD. He's been totally indoctrinated into the corporate flim flam. All he cares about is volume and 'customer satisfaction.' No allusion to quality of care, that's not even in the equation."

"I wouldn't want him treating me or my family then," Sally said.

"No, you wouldn't. He's not even a good doctor. Do you know the *other* problem with these stupid surveys, Sally? I mean outside of the fact that we get downgraded if we don't do what the patient expects, regardless of whether it's appropriate. *Everyone* sends flipping surveys. If you talk to the Microsoft guy on the phone, if you question a bill at Verizon, or if you service your car at the dealership, they *all* send surveys. Pretty soon the gas stations and supermarkets will be jumping on the train. Who has time for them? I called Citibank the other day to activate a new credit card, and the recording asked if I'd be willing to stay on the line to take a brief survey. NO, I would NOT be willing. You know who's *willing*? People with a beef, that's who! Geez, you could spend your entire life doing surveys."

"You're right," Sally said. "I only take those things if I'm ticked off about something, or if someone was extraordinarily great."

"Exactly! And we get so many repeat patients, they're not going to fill out another survey after every visit. They obviously like us or they wouldn't keep coming back." Tobi huffed. "Okay, I'm done ranting."

"But you're right," Sally agreed. "It just adds stress to your already stressful job. Is Ben coming for Thanksgiving?"

"Yup, and as long as he's here, I'll be a happy human. I miss him so much."

"He's not that far away, you know. Do you get into the city much?" Sally asked.

"I would go more often, but I know he's so busy. And I'm sure he prefers to spend his free time with Rachel, not his mother."

"He should make some time for his mother, though."

"He does. He's coming out tomorrow. So ... I think I just got a message from Troy ...."

"What? When? What do you mean 'you think'?"

"About an hour ago. I saw the banner notification, but I haven't opened it. I don't think I want to go there."

"Have you heard from him since he left? That was years and years ago, when your brother died."

"Not a whisper."

"So, are you going to answer him?"

"I don't know. Haven't even decided if I'm going to read his message."

"I don't blame you, he completely broke your heart. But curiosity might get the better of you, so call me if you need anything."

They hung up and Tobi picked up her tablet. The Messenger icon showed one unread message. She had truly hoped she'd imagined it. Screw it, she thought. She took a deep breath and braced herself. Better to just get it over with. She tapped it.

My dearest Tobi,

I hope you are well. For so long I wished to God I could tell you what happened, but I could not. I can now, and I think—I hope—you will understand why I left. My cell is 503-555-9393. Please answer me. Call me, text me, or just send me your number. I have so much to explain. I am so sorry.

Still yours forever, Troy

She stood in a daze, staring at the words. What could he possibly need to explain now, nineteen years later? The world seemed to shift, and she was back in time hearing his voice on the phone, saying, *I'm sorry, my love. I cannot see you anymore. I cannot even tell you why, so please do not ask me. This is good-bye.* She remembered the pain that had vibrated through her entire body so even her hands would hurt, and everything she ate tasted like sand. She'd lost thirteen pounds in three weeks. And for months after, over and over again, she felt the knife stabbing her in the heart, and then twisting, tearing a black hole in the very fabric of her universe and threatening to suck her into the eternal darkness beyond.

She slammed the door shut on the memory, hard. That way lay madness. She closed the tablet and put it aside, shaken, and looked around the kitchen, which now seemed to belong to someone else.

After Troy had disappeared, she tried to be grateful for the evanescent bliss she had found with him but she had failed miserably. So instead, she vowed no one would ever hurt her like that again, and she'd nailed shutters across her heart. She pictured her heart in her mind like an old, wooden shack with a "closed" sign flapping crookedly on the door, banging in the breeze with tumbleweed blowing by, deserted and forgotten. But free of pain.

The last she'd heard, Troy had gone off to the Philippines after touring most of Asia, raising consciousness over the inhumane treatment of animals and the blatant disregard for the planet. He had inherited a great deal of money after college and he put his wealth and his intellect to work by starting an endowment called "Executors for Our Earth." That was only after he'd finally "found" himself when he was in his twenties, studying with the Dalai Lama in India.

Reuben had helped Troy develop some software for his projects, and they had become friends. Troy had begun simply as an animal rescuer, but his endowment quickly flourished to supporting other causes as well, in particular, raising awareness of the malevolent effects civilization had on the planet's ecosystem. In the beginning, he had focused on halting the destruction of the rain forests, whose existence were crucial to the balance of oxygen and carbon dioxide in the atmosphere. In the nineties, Troy had been instrumental in the movement that ultimately blocked the use of chlorofluorocarbons, or CFCs, which had been destroying the ozone layer in the stratosphere, thereby exposing all life to harmful ultraviolet rays.

Tobi imagined he would now be a big advocate for finding even more creative ways to absorb carbon dioxide from the ground level atmosphere—or troposphere—to slow global warming. She chuckled to herself, remembering how he almost never used the generic word atmosphere, but would be specific about which of the five layers he was referring to. Troy saw the unique five layers in his mind, and he would unwittingly refer to each one by its more accurate name. Troy had taught her so much. He had dual-majored in geology and meteorology, and he knew more about the Earth than Tobi ever would. She thought she had seen his name briefly in the credits of a recent NOVA episode describing peridotite, a rock found in Oman that absorbs carbon dioxide directly from the air, but she might have just imagined it. The credits had gone by so fast.

As she reminisced, Tobi suddenly realized she was actually considering answering his message. Oh, no, no, no, she thought. I am not strong enough to talk to him again—definitely not to see him again, sit next to him, smell his cologne, feel his ... "Troy-ness." He had such a powerful presence, even in a crowded room you couldn't *not* notice he was there. Maybe it was from all that meditation in the mountains, but his eyes blazed as if he had seen the Other Side. Maybe he had. Serene and kinetic and passionate all at once, he could see right through a person. It was both captivating and terrifying at the same time. She pictured him in her mind, and thought, Who am I kidding? I cannot go back there again; it would be torment!

She decided to ignore the message.

CHAPTER 12

Troy DeJacob sat in the police inspector's office in Port Douglas, rubbing his hands over his face and down the sides of his head. He knew it was his tell, but he couldn't seem to stop. Archie Bent was going over everything for the third time.

"I know you're grieving, mate, but looks like you are the last person to see Marcus alive, so help me out here. Give it to me again."

So, Troy told him again. He told him how he'd known Robain from years ago and how he hadn't been able to reach him for a few weeks, so he'd come to Port Douglas. He told him how Marcus had given him the news of Robain's death and how shattered he felt over it.

"Were ye mad at him for it?" Bent asked.

"Mad at Marco? No, why would I be?" He put his head back in his hands. "Sounds exactly like what R-Robain would have done, going back down too soon to save someone. And he had some heart problems. I guess they just caught up with him."

"So, why'd ye go back?" Bent asked.

"To the dive shop? Marco and Robain were good friends, and I was going to clean out Robain's apartment and take his things home to his family … I wanted to ask Marco if he wanted any of his stuff—I mean, besides the shop itself. Robain shot beautiful pictures of the reef. They worked together for years, you know? Just something more personal to remember him by."

"And that's when you found him dead."

"Yes, and I freaked. He was just lying there behind the counter. His face was … horrible. I just ran out of there. I didn't know if the killer was still around, you know? I came straight to the beach. I knew Marco had a class setting up and I hoped I'd find your constable, Clyde, with them. I remembered he was a big diver."

"Why was Marcus's blood on your shorts and your right hand?"

"Blood—I checked his pulse at his neck before I ran. I had to make sure. Maybe I wiped my hand on my shorts?"

Bent frowned. "Well, which was it? Did you check his pulse or did you just run?"

"Wait, you think I—?" Nothing was making sense. "Look, this has got to be one of the worst days of my life. I'm not thinking straight. Why would I come running to find you if I did it?"

"Not *the* worst, though, huh?" Bent was still frowning. "We did check you for gunshot residue and didn't find any. Preliminary report is he was dead at least an hour when you came on the beach. Look, I'm inclined to believe you, but I need your full cooperation. Tell me about your last conversation with Marcus. Did he say anything that might give a clue as to who would want to do this to him? Near I can tell, he never hurt nobody."

Troy shook his head back and forth, willing something to come to mind. His thoughts were in a jumble, and the jet lag didn't help. "He told me the story of how Robain died, pulling Missy out of the coral … Robain, he was like a brother to me. Marco asked me if I could contact his family, and I told him I would, although I haven't in years … he said he had no clue who to inform and there were so many things his family might want, especially his photography …." Troy's voice faltered. He didn't want to cry in front of this man and the inspector kept looking at him expectantly.

"Wait," Troy said. "He mentioned some guy had come in, needed help with his computer. He'd dropped it in the sand during yesterday's shower. Marcus sent him to a friend in Cairns when the guy offered to help him find Robain's family. Said he felt like it was a mistake, the guy didn't seem like the sympathetic type, you know? He wondered why this guy would want to help him, but I had never left Marcus any of my personal contact information, and he was desperate. So was the other guy, he said."

Bent was taking studious notes. "Did he tell you his friend's name?"

"I think he said Freddie? Marco told me he hadn't been able to reach him since, and he felt nervous about it for some reason."

"Okay," Bent said. "That corroborates Missy's story. She said some rude mate with a Russian accent was in yesterday, cradling his laptop like a newborn babe. Did you see anyone go in the dive shop after you left?"

"No, I'm sorry. I was so shocked by the news of Robain. I don't think I really looked at anything until I got to his flat."

"Okay, Mr. DeJacob. Look, I can't officially detain you unless I charge you, and I'd rather not do that, so I am asking you to not leave Port Douglas right now. Or do I need to charge you and take your passport?"

"No, I'll stay voluntarily. How long?"

"Not sure yet, but I'll be in touch."

Troy left and wandered back to Reuben's apartment. He'd known something wasn't right when he'd heard nothing from Reuben for almost three weeks, but to find out he had died—and then to find Marco like that, his face disfigured and bloody … it was overwhelming. He needed to center himself, and focus, but he was so tired from the flight. The sixteen-hour jet lag seemed way worse than usual this trip, and to be honest, he had let go of a lot of his old mental self-discipline after he left Tobi, so many years ago. He really needed it now.

The computer system hadn't been shut down in Reuben's flat and it was still humming on his desk. There was an empty pizza box on top of the trash—what passed for pizza here, anyway, a package of cashews, some stale tortilla chips, and a bottle of diet cola in the fridge, along with some batteries. That was it for consumable goods. A high-tech stereo and smart TV took up most of the entertainment center across from the couch.

On the walls were a dozen or so pictures of the Great Barrier Reef, the coral colors brought alive and contrasted exquisitely with damselfish, clownfish, parrotfish and blue tangs. In one photo, Reuben had captured a moray eel tentatively emerging from its hole in the coral. There were many more that were unframed, stacked against the far wall.

The place smelled of old food. Troy emptied the garbage and threw the pizza box out. *Ralph's Pizzeria* was written on the top, and it reminded him of how Reuben had chosen the name Robain. He was too afraid he would forget his new name or not answer to it, hence he chose something so similar yet so unusual that it would naturally make him look up.

Troy took the garbage can to the curb, came back in, and looked around helplessly. For a moment, he considered hiring someone to pack everything up, but a cleaning crew might find something that could give away the charade they had played for so long. He blanched. He wasn't sure he could stand the legacy of Reuben's isolation that was written all over the apartment. Where would he send all this stuff?

He needed to tell Tobi now, that was certain, but would she even talk to him? She probably hated him, if she even remembered him, and this would make her hate him all the more. Hell, she had probably married and moved on. Troy had never been able to. He didn't have a phone number for her, but he had searched for her in the past—not with the intention of contacting her—just to feel her close by, and he'd found her on Facebook. Her profile picture was of her and Benny by the water somewhere. Benny had grown into a handsome young man, and it made Troy even sadder to see what he'd missed. He hadn't seen any pictures of another man, but her privacy settings were pretty tight, and until now, he hadn't been willing to become a stalker, so he'd left it at that.

His mind strayed to that October morning in 2000 like it was yesterday, sitting with Reuben in New York Bagels on Fourth Street in Austin, Texas. He'd met him there after meeting with a large donor to his organization, and had wanted to tell Reuben he was going to ask Tobi to marry him. He had just booked a dive trip to Maui and planned to surprise her on the beach at sunset with the ring.

But Reuben had been too hyped up. He kept looking over his shoulder and told Troy in a hushed voice about some sinister plot one only heard in gangster movies. He seemed genuinely afraid for his life, and he asked Troy to help him vanish.

Troy had connections all over the world. His foundation, Executors for Our Earth, had him traveling from Asia to the Philippines, to the Middle East and South America, evaluating the heartiness of coral, forestry, and animal wildlife, and looking for ways to heal this planet that humans continued to assault. His network had been less developed back in 2000, but he had still gotten around pretty well. He'd told Reuben he could set him up on any of a number of islands in the Philippines and then move him again if it looked like he was being tracked, until Reuben was "lost" for good. Troy could have it all in place within a week.

Reuben had been incredibly grateful. But then he grabbed Troy's hand in both of his and squeezed it until it felt like his fingers would break.

"Promise me—you must promise me! Never tell Tobi where I am. Never. Tell her you don't know. I know things between my sister and me have sucked lately, but I know her, she will be relentless. They will find her and watch her, and if she tries to contact me, her life will be in danger too. Do it for her, Troy, and do it for Benny. You must swear it to me!"

Troy recalled it so vividly. His left hand held in a death grip by Reuben, his right hand in his pocket, holding the ring he had just bought: a 1.9-carat round diamond in a split-shank platinum setting. He had imagined over and over how she'd look when he gave it to her. He'd fingered the ring and then clenched it until he felt the diamond cutting his skin.

Troy didn't know what to say. How could he start a life with Tobi and keep this secret? How could he live such a lie? "But, Reu—"

"Please, Troy! They will torture or kill her to get to me, or hold her ransom. Better that she knows nothing, makes no phone calls, sends no emails or letters. These people are assassins! And no matter where I go, I may not be safe anyway. If you love her, *protect her.* Promise me!"

That was the day the light had gone out in Troy's soul. He remembered feeling his heart contract sharply and his lungs unable to expand. The pain was nearly unbearable. All possibility of love and joy slipped through his fingers, like tiny grains of sand. All the while, Reuben kept staring at him, crushing Troy's fingers, his piercing eyes demanding an answer. Slowly, Troy loosened his grip on the ring in his pocket and whispered a silent good-bye to everything precious in his life.

For a moment it got quiet in the bagel shop, as if everyone were listening to them. Then the buzz resumed, dishes clanged, conversations were animated, and Troy noticed the smell of garlic and lox. The door banged shut as a customer left. It was as if time had stopped for an instant, but Reuben's face had not changed.

"I promise," Troy said finally.

Troy had wrestled with that promise for days, and the battle tore his soul apart. In the end, he was true to his word. Above all, he loved Tobi, and he needed her to be safe. But he could not figure out a way to face her every day and lie to her, so ultimately, he had said goodbye. He'd known in the bagel shop that he would have to do that. He could feel her astonishment, her pain, her sense of betrayal, but she'd seemed to accept it. She wasn't the type to beg or make a scene. He knew how deeply he had hurt her, and he hated himself for it. He had hurt himself just as much.

Two days later, he'd received her email, saying that Reuben was found dead. Troy was stunned. He reached out to contact Reuben and found he was very much alive. Then Reuben explained how it happened that another man had died in his apartment, a last person who Reuben had tried to save before he went ghost, and it had backfired.

But then, Reuben had been "dead," and if he just stayed dead, no one would look for him, and he would be safe. And Tobi would be safe. Troy got him out of the country and gave him ten thousand dollars to get started on a new life; Reuben couldn't exactly access his own accounts after he was "deceased." Crazy to see the impeccably moral Reuben Sokowsky forging new IDs and passports. The fear of death could really change a man.

Any fantasy that one day Tobi might have accepted that Troy had known Reuben was alive and in hiding had dissolved into ashes. She had to believe Reuben was truly dead for this strategy to fool the assassins, and how could Troy have sat with her while she cried over her only brother?

Once, a few years ago, he'd thought enough time had gone by, and perhaps he could call her, but he was afraid. She would be perfectly justified in hating him, and the likelihood that they could salvage anything from their lost love was next to zero. He had vacillated for weeks and finally given it up. He settled for looking at her profile picture on Facebook periodically.

The ring was still sitting in a safety deposit box on Long Island, where it had been for the last nineteen years. Troy had left instructions that upon his death, it be given to Tobi, its rightful owner. Or if she predeceased Troy, to Benny, to do with whatever he wanted. Tobi would never understand, but Troy didn't understand it anymore either.

Troy pulled himself back to the present. It was 2019 and he was in Port Douglas, Australia. Reuben really was dead now. He picked up his cell and opened Facebook Messenger. There was no reason to keep the secret anymore, and he needed to return Reuben's things to her. He had promised Marco, besides. His heart skipped several beats, and he felt himself withdraw, trying to hide deep inside himself. He took a deep breath and told himself: "this needs to happen." He wrote:

My dearest Tobi,

I hope you are well. For so long I wished to God I could tell you what happened, but I could not. I can now, and I think—I hope—you will understand why I left. My cell is 503-555-9393. Please answer me. Call me, text me, or just send me your number. I have so much to explain. I am so sorry.

Still yours forever, Troy

It seemed so insufficient, but he could think of nothing else to write. Nothing that could ever make what had happened to them okay. He drew another deep breath and hit "send."

CHAPTER 13

Mrs. Cappione was waiting at the door of the urgent care at 8:50 on the Saturday morning after Thanksgiving. Jorge let her in early because there was nowhere to sit outside, and she looked like she might need to do so.

But immediately, she came up to the front desk and told Patty, "I was in so much pain all night, I almost went to the hospital, but I hate hospitals—I've seen way too much of them." She was ninety-one years old, and walked unsteadily, but without a cane or a walker, and she was dressed in a dirty, beige fur-lined coat and a yellow and green scarf.

Patty brought her in to the first exam room closest to the reception desk to wait, so she wouldn't have to get up and down so much and took her insurance cards.

"My name is Patty. Here, sit down, and take your coat off. We're going to take care of you, don't you worry. I'll bring your cards right back to you, and Dr. Lister will be with you in just a few minutes."

"Thank you, young lady." She started taking off her coat and scarf.

Tobi walked into Mrs. Cappione's room a few minutes later. "Good morning. How can I help you today?"

Mrs. Cappione explained that three weeks ago, she had been cooking her *pasta fagiole*, and her hand had slipped on the pot handle. It spilled, overturning the pot onto her right thumb. Luckily, the stovetop had barely warmed up, so she didn't have any burns (although, she complained it made an awful mess), but her thumb had been hurting ever since.

"First, I saw my primary care doctor at The Center, and he sent me for x-rays. Then he made me go to an orthopedist, and then I had to go back for an MRI."

She did not have the results of either of these tests, and she was almost in tears.

"They told me I have 'osteoporosis,' and they want me to go for occupational therapy, but I can't get involved with all that. It's too complicated to get car service, and have to keep going out ... who's going to take me? Last night it hurt so bad! Can't you help me? I tried icing it, but it only made it worse. Maybe it's an infection. Can you give me an antibiotic?"

Tobi looked at the electronic chart. Mrs. Cappione had come to their urgent care a week ago, and Ellie had seen her and given her a thumb spica splint to wear, which extended from the tip of her thumb to the mid shaft of her forearm. Then Ellie sent Mrs. Cappione back to the doctors who were already caring for her. Ellie hadn't ordered any imaging because the patient reported it had already been done. It was unlikely she had been given a diagnosis of osteoporosis, since that would only cause pain if it resulted in a fracture, and it didn't appear that she was being treated for one. When old ladies broke their hands, they usually required a cast or solid splint, and moreover, the injury she was describing didn't sound like it was of sufficient force to cause a break. There was, of course, a much more likely diagnosis.

Tobi examined Mrs. Cappione's thumb. It looked like the gnarled branch of an ancient tree. She could almost see right through the skin to the misshapen, arthritic bones. But there was no wound or evidence of infection, not even a healed scratch.

"It looks more like severe arthritis," Tobi told her. "Maybe the splint is making it stiff now, even though it might have been helpful earlier. Would it be okay if I took another x-ray now, since you don't have the results of the last one, just so I can get a look at what's going on in there?"

Mrs. Cappione clasped Tobi's hand in hers and looked up gratefully with rheumy eyes. "Oh, thank you, Doctor, you can do it right here? Please take a picture. They told me it was osteoporosis, but I think it's an infection, it just hurts so much!"

The radiographs were enough to make anyone cringe. The joint spaces were gone; it was all bone on bone, and there were sharp, spicule calcifications jutting out from every joint in her poor hand. Her skeleton was so disfigured, it almost looked like it belonged to an alien. Nothing was broken, though, and the bone density looked pretty much normal for a ninety-one-year-old.

Tobi winced. She was not sure what she could do for Mrs. Cappione's pain, since she certainly couldn't throw narcotics at an unsteady, elderly patient. And since she was on blood thinners for her heart, the patient couldn't even take ibuprofen without risk of bleeding.

Tobi went back into Mrs. Cappione's exam room. She took the patient's hand in hers and raised her voice slightly, but spoke gently. "It's not osteoporosis, Mrs. Cappione, it's osteo*arthritis*, and it's very advanced. That's why it hurts so much."

Mrs. Cappione looked like she might cry. Tobi continued, "I want you to try using heat instead of ice, to loosen up the joints a little. Do you have a heating pad at home?" Mrs. Cappione nodded, her eyes wide.

"And stop using the splint now, I think it's making you sore. You can take Tylenol Extra Strength, or the generic acetaminophen, every six hours, and I'm going to send you a prescription for a lidocaine patch. It's a medicine you put on like a bandage, and it should numb the pain—if you can get it. I see you have Medicare; do you have a secondary insurance for prescriptions?"

"I have that 'harp' thing, so my medicines don't cost as much. They still cost me a bundle, though," Mrs. Cappione looked distraught.

"AARP?"

"Yes, that's it." Mrs. Cappione nodded.

"Okay, good. I'm going to send the prescription straight to your pharmacy. Also, please call your primary care doctor on Monday and schedule that occupational therapy. You might only need a couple of sessions to see what it's about, and then perhaps you can do the exercises at home, all on your own. Many people do. I'm going to write all of this down for you."

Mrs. Cappione scowled. "I don't like my doctor. I tried every doctor at The Center, and none of them ever make me better. I'm ninety-one years old. They can't fix anything that's wrong with me."

Tobi nodded sympathetically. "That's what my Baba used to tell me, she'd say 'don't get old'; but I used to ask her, 'What's the alternative?'"

Mrs. Cappione agreed. "Getting old is the worst—but if you don't get old, you have to die young." She sighed heavily, took the CD that was her x-ray copy, and made her way deliberately out to the waiting room. She thanked everyone for seeing her.

Tobi watched her go, feeling demoralized for having so little to offer. The pharmacy might not fill the Lidoderm for her without a prior authorization, Tobi thought. It was a topical anesthetic and only minimally absorbed, so it was safe in the elderly, but it was expensive, so the insurance companies often wouldn't pay for it unless someone spent forty-five minutes on the phone with them to get it authorized, and they were not even available on Saturdays. She had no idea whether AARP covered it, and even if it had last month, that didn't mean it would be covered today.

Tobi groaned at the futility of it all. Primary care offices had secretaries dedicated to getting approvals from insurance companies for medications, imaging, and procedures, which would not be paid for otherwise. It was an extra expense for the practice just to be able to treat patients, and most urgent care offices did not have such a luxury. Theirs certainly did not, especially since they were cutting her staff. There was no one to spend that kind of time on the phone.

It was going to be a very busy day. There were seven people signed in before they had been open an hour. At a quarter to ten, a family of three had arrived: a mother and her two small children, Amara, age five, and Jonna, age seven. Mom had developed a scratchy throat the night before, and Jonna had completed treatment for strep two weeks ago, so Mom had wanted to make sure he was completely recovered, even though he felt fine. While they were there, she asked if Amara could be checked as well, who, by the way, had no symptoms at all.

Tobi walked into their room at five minutes to ten. Both children felt completely well, but Mom demanded strep tests on both, as well as for herself. All three had completely normal exams, no history of fever, and with the exception of Mom's scratchy throat and slight post nasal drip for less than a day, no one had any symptoms. The encounters and documentation took twenty-five minutes and included triaging three patients, taking three histories, swabbing three throats, and doing three examinations. Everything had to be charted separately in the EMR for each patient.

All three swabs were negative for strep, so three cultures were sent to the lab. The three visits were sent to the insurance company for payment, and the outside lab would bill the same insurance company for the three strep cultures. Mom had to be reassured at length that if the rapid strep tests had missed anything, the cultures would find it, and that they did not require antibiotics in the meantime "just in case." As for their insurance, it was a form of Medicaid, so they had no copays, and they left the office without spending a dime out-of-pocket. Tobi couldn't help thinking that the unnecessary cost could have funded at least a month of Lidoderm patches for Mrs. Cappione.

Esther was rolling her eyes as they left the office. "What, did they not have any plans for the day? What was all that about?"

Jorge said, "That's not even unusual. Last week, we had a couple in here who felt absolutely fine, but the father-in-law had a stomach virus, so they wanted to be 'checked out.' They had no symptoms of anything!"

He turned to Tobi. "What do you think, Dr. L, is it just because they don't have to pay for it? Are they really worried they're sick? Why do people waste their time and our time like that?"

"The couple from last week wasn't Medicaid, they each had to pay a thirty-dollar copay, but it's still costly to the insurance company, and it's a waste of our resources," Tobi said. "Some people definitely do work the system, but what's to gain from this? Except to assuage their *angst*."

"What's 'angst'?" Esther asked.

"It means free-floating anxiety, like an underlying uneasiness that you can't quite put your finger on but that permeates your life."

"Oh, like working at B. Healthy," Esther said.

"Yeah, kind of," Tobi said. "It's not completely unfounded, you know. People worry about losing their jobs if they can't go to work. How many flu patients do we have to argue with to stay home, and they often don't anyway? They'll get better much more quickly if they'd just rest, and they wouldn't infect the rest of their coworkers.

But they say their bosses won't understand, or they don't have sick time. Our culture doesn't support sick people—other than to try to make money off them." She looked pointedly around the office.

"And the media doesn't help, either," Jorge said. "When I'm feeding little Jeremy at night, he falls asleep and I don't want to get up because I'll wake him, so I watch TV. All the commercials are about drugs."

"I know," Esther said. "It's like pills are supposed to cure everything. They play sweet, peaceful music, and you see families at barbeques together or walking on the beach, so you don't pay any attention to the awful side effects they're listing in the background. Some of them are horrible. You can even die!"

"The problem is, people expect life to be easy and for things to just be handed to them," Patty said, chiming in. "I never had nothing handed to me, but I managed and my kids grew up just fine."

"Better than fine, I expect," Tobi said. "Your kids know how to bounce back from hard times. Do you remember Mrs. McCleary from last month? She came in three times in less than one week with the same uncomfortable flu symptoms, even though I explained to her each time that her symptoms would last seven to ten days. We need to teach people how to be strong so they can deal with problems, instead of giving them pills so they feel like they don't have to. There will always be some hurdle that can't be overcome. We have to help people find a way to accept that and move on without falling apart."

Esther nodded. "When I worked for the IRS, I didn't like it at all, but all my friends told me I shouldn't give up all those benefits. I think I was depressed. It was hard to go to work each day, and I felt like there was something wrong with me. But then my *abuelo* sat with me and told me my friends didn't have to live my life, and I have to be happy. He made me feel so much better, and now I am a medical assistant. I help people instead of pestering them." Esther smiled.

"But the extended family is becoming a thing of the past," Patty said. "Remember the Lenmans? They didn't even feel welcome in their kids' home. And children don't get as much time with their grandparents nowadays, they're so busy playing sports and video games or hanging out on social media. And everyone lives so far apart."

"And don't forget, there's no money to be made off our elders' wisdom, so our society doesn't value it," Tobi said. "You have to be able to package something if you want it to be promoted. Biggest mistake in medicine was letting pharmaceutical companies advertise on television. Now all 'cures' come in a bottle—and they have to be profitable. Did you know the United States and New Zealand are the only countries in the world that allow the advertisement of drugs in the media?"

"Aren't we lucky?" Jorge asked, rolling his eyes. "That means we are the only countries whose health values are driven by capitalism."

"Health values and health *care*," Tobi said. "It's a swindle."

Chapter 14

Mannford was seething when he stepped off his jet at Zhuliany Airport in Kiev. That squirrel Sokowsky had evaded him for nineteen years! That punk must have been the hacker gathering info on them, so it was anybody's guess into whose head he'd been funneling all that intel. Strange that there had been no repercussions, unless his "heart attack" three weeks ago had been rigged. Something in his coffee cup? The Project did have some "clients" in Queensland as well as the US and Europe, powerful men who had contracted some nefarious sexually transmitted diseases they'd prefer their family and constituents didn't find out about. Keeping that dirt under wraps cost those men on a regular basis, and padded Mannfort's pockets nicely, but if the Project were to be exposed, it would not bode well for their clientele, and they knew it. If Sokowsky had made the mistake of going to the authorities with incriminating information, he might have been squashed out of hand.

Kazimir was driving toward him as he exited the airport doors, and Mannfort hopped in the car.

"This could be a problem, Kazi. I'm positive Sokowsky was the hacker—this guy had a dive shop named *Tobi's*! We have to trace his communications—check every email that he sent. The nerve! To be out there digging in our stuff. He had to have planned to use what he found, or why else would he bother?"

"You think he was sending information to someone? Maybe he was waiting until there was enough evidence to bury us, so he could come out of hiding, but it took him long enough to try that. Why start now?"

"I have no idea," Mannfort said. "I think we have to go to New York and check on this sister. Maybe question her before we get rid of her. What did you learn about her employment? Can we get to her from there?"

"Oh, *dah!* The sister works at B. Healthy, LLC. We have a toad there, some Turkish guy."

"Good. Tell him we will need additional information on her or we will have to make him a personal acquaintance."

Chapter 15

Ismar was sitting on his lounge chair in front of the fire, listening to a recording of tanbur music with his eyes closed. The minor harmonic scale and peppy rhythm mixed with the lingering smell of zaatar made him feel like he was back home. Except, of course, when his wife Jennie kept pestering him to take out the trash and change the outside light bulb. These were definitely things a woman should be able to handle, and it was cold outside; he had no interest in walking down the long driveway dragging a garbage can. He had provided her with an enormous house and even paid for a servant to come and clean it once a week, something Jennie should have been able to manage on her own, especially since she no longer needed to work. She should not be bothering him with little nuisances.

"Ismar, pretty please …?" Jennie crooned in his ear and stroked him under his chin just where he liked it. Next thing, she had her hand on his chest and was rustling the hair under his shirt.

This woman really knew how to work him! And he never learned, because by the time he finished doing whatever she asked of him, she would be on the phone with one of her girlfriends and would stay there for the rest of the night and then beg fatigue, or she'd pretend to be fast asleep when he came upstairs. He would have to insist and get rough with her, and then she would be angry and distant for the rest of the week. Blasted American women.

Ismar got up and put his shoes and coat on and took out the trash, despising himself for turning into a weak Western man, and wished again that he hadn't had to leave Turkey and his life there. Damn Russians. They had ruined his life. He didn't know who he hated more, the Americans or the Russian oligarchs, who were just slightly better than the neo-Bolsheviks; they all detested Muslims. America was supposed to be the "land of opportunity," but he was sure that giving him the post as lead physician was only B. Healthy's way of satisfying affirmative action, or whatever they called it these days. He didn't believe the company cared about him at all, and yet, he couldn't really complain. They had no idea that the position they had given him helped him gather information for the Project, which, in turn, paid him ten times what he earned in his day job.

Ismar's phone buzzed, telling him to log on to the encrypted server for additional instructions. As he read it, he felt the customary sweaty palms and racing heart that he always got when he was contacted by his benefactors. One day, he promised himself, he would pay off his debt and go back home as a rich man.

And he'd teach Jennie to cover up when she walked outside!

Chapter 16

D
r. Andy Corbet was cleaning out his office. After forty years, retirement felt bittersweet. He'd left much of his active practice behind three years ago, but he had stayed on in the American Medical Association because, as they'd said to him, who else would continue to chair the Council on Constitution and Bylaws? It was a tedious job, with a lot of infighting. He hated playing referee, but he was good at it, so they'd kept electing him year after year, and he'd never been very good at saying no.

Now it was over. He was done. Andy and his wife had bought a little chalet in the Swiss Alps and he wanted to spend his time between there and Big Sky, Montana, where his grandchildren were growing up in what was left of the clean air regions of the United States. He did not think he would miss Chicago, even after all this time, and he was passing his post on to a younger, more enthusiastic—if less conservative—doc, Zack Pryor.

Were his files all complete? He thought he had left everything fairly organized and orderly. He fingered the file containing the anonymous emails; all of them were agitated requests that the AMA look into the patterns and practices of a certain insurance company. He had been getting them for years, and never had decided what to do about them since they seemed to come from multiple addresses, but they never identified the sender. The recent emails had a few names and diagnoses, and one even included a Trojan Horse that could unravel the insurance company in question, or so that email said. There were strict instructions on how to—and how *not* to—use the subversive device, with warnings that once it was initiated, it would of necessity, violate HIPAA laws, but it would also expose the origins of the insurance company and would shut it down. The email cautioned to perform the virus only under the specified, controlled conditions. To Andy, the whole proposition sounded incredulous. Who could possibly write such a complicated program like that? More likely, it was a ploy that would destroy their own software instead.

Well, it wasn't his problem anymore. He'd been receiving the emails for over a decade, never signed, always brief, getting more frantic and frequent as time wore on. Feeling generally suspicious of them, and not wanting to violate HIPAA policies, and because he was just busy with other matters, Andy hadn't explored them in detail. This year their frequency had gone from every couple of months to every week, until suddenly they had just stopped. Funny, the abrupt silence seemed more ominous than the emails themselves.

Happily, they'd be Zack's headache now. Andy was off to enjoy his retirement without the hassles of politics in medicine, and it was well-deserved. He took a last look back, then nodded to himself and closed and locked the door on this chapter of his life.

Chapter 17

The day was going by quickly, and Tobi had a vague sense she had missed something important. She couldn't decide if it was regarding a patient's care or something completely unrelated, and finally chalked it up to Troy's message floating in the back of her mind. Nothing too significant then, she told herself.

At 2:45 p.m., Tobi went into the next exam room, where an older woman was in for a urinary tract infection. Mrs. Brown was sitting on the table, engrossed in her smart phone. She barely looked up when the doctor came in.

"Hi, Mrs. Brown, I'm Dr. Lister. How are you today?"

"Mmm."

"It says here it hurts when you pee. How long has that been going on?"

"Oh, just since yesterday," she said, without looking up.

"Do you have any fever? … Back pain?"

No answer.

"Belly pain?"

More silence.

"Mrs. Brown?"

"What?" She tore her eyes off the phone for a quick second. "No, none of that."

Tobi nodded. "Do you have any allergies to medications?"

"Mm hmm … um, what? No, no allergies."

Tobi shook her head. This happened so frequently, it made her wonder why people came to see her at all, when they obviously had more important things to do. The worst was when the patient was a child, and the parent wouldn't look up from their phone to provide the medical history. She'd have to pull Mom back with a "help me out here," but the attention was never long-lived. The parent would be back on their phone in a hot second. Luckily, Mrs. Brown's urine was chock full of bacteria, which made the diagnosis straight forward.

She must be texting someone, Tobi thought. Good for her, I guess, at seventy-eight years old. Maybe it was a grandchild. She got up and went over to Mrs. Brown to do her exam. As Tobi came alongside her to listen to her lungs, she could not resist a surreptitious glance at her phone, but then had to cough to stifle her laughter. Mrs. Brown realized she'd just been busted and looked up sheepishly.

"You really like that Candy Crush game, don't you?"

"Yes, doctor. My granddaughter got me hooked."

***

Tommy Mitchell was in room two. He was a seventeen-year-old high school senior who had rolled his ankle in soccer practice. He was still wearing his white and blue soccer uniform with grass stains on it. He could not walk on his right foot at all and had to be fetched from his dad's car with the wheelchair. Esther was in the room, gently removing the wrap his coach had applied.

"Hi, my name is Dr. Lister. Did that just happen?" She nodded at his ankle. His right ankle was easily twice the size of his left, and already turning various shades of purple.

"Hi, I'm Mr. Mitchell, Tommy's dad." Mr. Mitchell stepped forward and extended his hand. "Yes, he rolled it during practice today. Tomorrow is the big game. You gotta get him on his feet, doc!"

Tobi looked doubtful as she examined his ankle. "Let's take a picture," she said, and put the x-ray order into the EMR.

The radiographs showed three separate fractures in Tommy's ankle. About as bad as it could get.

Tobi took a deep breath before going back in the room. Tommy and Mr. Mitchell were talking about tomorrow's game, but they both looked up when she walked in.

"So, how do we proceed from here? He'll do whatever it takes," Mr. Mitchell said.

"Mr. Mitchell … Tommy … I'm afraid you won't be able to play tomorrow. You have what we call a trimalleolar fracture. It's broken in three places, here, here, and here." She pointed on his ankle. "It may require surgery. You won't be able to stand on that foot for a few weeks. I'm sorry."

They both stared at her.

"I'm going to put you in a splint and get you on crutches, but mostly your leg needs to stay elevated and iced on and off for the next couple of days to get the swelling down. And definitely no weight bearing for now."

More silent stares.

"Do you have an orthopedist? If not, I can recommend someone for you. I want you to be seen first thing on Monday."

The silence seemed to snap. "No, no, no, you don't understand," Mr. Mitchell said. "We just need to get him through the game tomorrow. He will see the orthopedist on Monday, I promise. Unless—can he see the orthopedist now?"

"Not unless he goes to the hospital. It's Saturday," Tobi said, glancing at her watch, "and it's after three o'clock on Thanksgiving weekend. There's not much else that would be done in the hospital, anyway. He may need surgery, but it's not an emergency, so it's not likely to happen until Monday. Either way, an orthopedist cannot fix this overnight so that he can run on it tomorrow. It's just not possible. I'm sorry."

Tommy was fighting back tears. "But the scouts are coming to tomorrow's game. I'm going to qualify for a scholarship to Duke. Can't you just get me on the field somehow?"

"Tommy," Tobi softened her voice, "you couldn't even walk in here by yourself. How are you going to play well enough to be considered for a scholarship? The scouts will not see a great candidate if you get on the field tomorrow. Better for them to not see you at all than for them to watch you play poorly. And you'd do more damage to your ankle, so it would be an even longer and more complicated healing process."

Mr. Mitchell approached to within an arm's length of Tobi. At six feet three inches, he towered over her. "Listen, *Doctor,* you are going to get my son on that field tomorrow or get an orthopedist over here right now who will."

She backed away reflexively. "I think we're done here, sir. I suggest you call your pediatrician and see what he can do. We'll give you a copy of the x-ray, splint his ankle, and put him on crutches. I'd appreciate it if you would sit back down."

Mr. Mitchell didn't move but continued to stare at her threateningly. Tobi backed out of the room and into Jorge, who was poking his head around in alarm. "I'm not going back into that room alone," she said.

"Don't you dare, I'm coming with you," he said.

Tobi wanted to hug him, but she checked herself. She always tried to appear confident and in control, no matter what. It was an old habit, born of having been the person left to carry the family, beginning at the age of ten. Her mother had been hospitalized for gall bladder surgery and later for a spinal fusion, and both times, even though Tobi was the youngest, her father had expected her to be the one to do the laundry, cook the meals, and clean the house. And, of course, she was not to miss a beat on her schoolwork. Both she and Reuben had recognized early on that they should never argue with Dad; under the best of circumstances, he could fly into a rage at any moment. Tobi had learned to just keep her emotions to herself. She never cried or showed anxiety; there had been no one to listen anyway, even if she had.

She thanked Jorge and they gathered supplies, then went back in to Tommy's room together.

Mr. Mitchell walked out when they walked in and paced the hall, on hold for the pediatrician's answering service, while they wrapped Tommy's ankle in an ortho-glass splint and sized the crutches.

"I know I don't have the grades for Duke, but that's where my dad went, and I can't just go to some stupid state school," Tommy's voice was cracking. "Besides, he'll kill me if I don't get in. I wasn't even supposed to play tomorrow, but Dad talked to Coach to make sure I'm in the line-up, and then Dad's going to talk to the scouts after the game. Even if I don't play that well, he knows them. He makes a lot of money, my dad, he can get me in. He contributes to the school and everything. I can't disappoint us all like this! Where else would I go, anyway?"

"Haven't you looked at other schools?" Jorge asked.

"They all suck next to Duke." Tommy's voice broke completely, and he started sobbing between sentences. "I have to go to Duke, I just have to! And I can't get in just on my grades. I study, it's not my fault the teachers don't give me As! It's those Asian kids, they break the curve. It's not normal to be that smart. But it doesn't matter if I can get in with sports, and I've gotten recognition awards in soccer every year since grade school. But how am I going to do that now? The scouts aren't coming back to Long Island again until May, and that'll be too late." The tears were streaming down his face now.

The pediatrician still had not gotten on the phone by the time Tommy's ankle was splinted. His father looked into the room and glared at Tommy's now swollen face. "We're leaving."

Tommy got up with the crutches and limped after him, struggling to keep up. His father didn't even hold the door for him.

"What did he expect you to do?" Jorge nearly whispered, after they were gone, "perform surgery in the office?" They were both still holding their breath.

"More like he thought I could just wave a magic wand. It boggles my mind how ill-prepared so many kids are to face disappointment— or adults, either, for that matter. I did *not* appreciate the veiled threat from that father—as if I had something to do with his kid's injury!"

"Not so veiled," Esther walked over. Her face was white. "I thought he was going to, I don't know, hurt you or something."

"I was ready to push the panic button!" Patty said.

"You both heard all that?" Tobi asked.

"Well, he wasn't exactly being quiet about it. Sounds like they set their sights too high. I wouldn't want to be at that dinner table tonight," Jorge said.

"It's a travesty. We teach our kids to win," Tobi said, "but we don't teach them how to lose. That's the more important lesson. That's what develops resilience. If they can't lose, they shouldn't play. In my humble opinion, that is."

"That's so true," Patty said. "The tough old birds in my family are the ones who went through the mill and survived. I think there was less mental illness in my grandfather's time, and they went through the war and the Great Depression."

"I've read that too. It's not clear whether there was just less reported or there was, in fact, less. But going through hardships, especially as a community, definitely builds fortitude and purpose and puts the silly things we get upset about back into perspective," Tobi said. "Not that we want our kids to go through war—God forbid—but to encounter a little resistance once in a while is an excellent thing."

"My father-in-law calls them 'first world problems,'" Jorge said. "Like when Giana couldn't find a crib comforter with airplanes on it for little Jeremy. She was driving us crazy! Her dad lived in Africa for a year working for Doctors Without Borders, and the people he treated were a whole different level of sick. He made a real difference over there, not like seeing patients for things that will mostly get better all on their own. He says the things Americans obsess over are completely unreasonable."

"And I bet he didn't have to fill out mounds of paperwork or satisfy insurance companies, either. Must be incredibly fulfilling work," Tobi said, feeling more than a smidge jealous.

"People like Tommy scare me," Patty said. "These are the kinds of kids who could become school shooters, or commit suicide, when they just can't cope with life."

Jorge looked puzzled. "What does it mean that he's always gotten 'recognition awards' in soccer?"

"No clue," Tobi answered. "Seems like everyone gets a prize these days, not just first, second, and third, but right up to the guy who comes in last. It's the same issue. We're so worried about hurting someone's *feelings* that we never ask them to buck up and improve. Look, I'm not saying there aren't children out there who need to be treated with kid gloves, but those are special cases. We do need to teach our children to respect each other and love themselves for who they are inside. But that's quite a different thing from giving them the message that last is as good as first, whatever you do will be commended, and that no one should ever have to be disappointed. It's crippling. You know, parents don't live forever, so the most important thing we can teach our children is how to live without us, as heartbreaking as that is."

"But the parents are afraid to upset their kids," Esther said. "Remember that boy with mono last week? His mother said she lied to the pediatrician and let him play sports anyway because it was so important to him. That's crazy! What is wrong with people? That was her son she was talking about."

"Like a stupid football game in high school, which no one will remember in five years, could possibly be more important than risking a ruptured spleen," Jorge said, rolling his eyes.

Esther looked at Jorge. "We are going to miss you, Jorge."

Tobi looked at him in alarm. "Where are you going?"

Jorge laughed. "I've been meaning to tell you, Dr. L. I put in for a transfer closer to Queens, but then I got recruited for Crystal Clear Radiology. It pays more, and it's all x-ray. Giana's parents live in Forest Hills, so we found an apartment close by. We're moving next week."

"Wow," Tobi said softly. "Yeah, that makes sense. I'm really sorry to lose you."

"Don't worry, I'm staying on per diem, so I'll still fill in here from time to time. Seems like every time we turn around, there's something else we have to buy for little Jeremy!"

Tobi smiled at him sadly. "You deserve it. You'll have help with the baby plus an easier commute and you won't have to do three jobs at once anymore. Stay in touch." She gave him a hug, trying not to think about what the staffing situation was going to look like in their office going forward.

Chapter 18

Troy was restless. The packing was done and he'd shipped all of Reuben's things to a postal code on Long Island. The transit time would be a week or more, but Troy had to get back there to pick it up. He hadn't heard from Tobi, so he'd decided to rent space in a storage unit until he figured out what to do with it all. He went into Inspector Bent's office to ask permission to leave for the States.

"Good afternoon, I'm glad you're here, Mr. DeJacob. I have some more questions for you," Bent started when he saw Troy. "Come into my office. First, what brings you to me?"

"Good afternoon, Inspector. I came to ask if you found out anything about Marcus's murder, and because I've shipped Reuben's effects back to America and I'd like to return there to pick them up and distribute them. I have nothing but pain here right now, and I don't see what further help I can be. I came to ask leave to go."

"Hmm. Take a seat. No good leads yet on Marcus. Where were you last Tuesday night?"

"Tuesday night? I had just landed in Sydney from Los Angeles. I had to stay overnight in a hotel and I took a 7:30 a.m. flight to Cairns. When I got here Wednesday morning, I went straight to Robain's and then to the dive shop and talked to Marcus. You can check it. Why do you ask? Marcus was alive Tuesday night."

"Yes, but his friend Freddie was killed in Cairns Tuesday night. You say you were in Sydney until 7:30 a.m. Wednesday? I'll need your flight information and the hotel you stayed at."

"Freddie was killed, too? Oh my God! Sure, I have it all on my phone." Troy fumbled in his pocket to pull his phone out, but his fingers didn't seem to want to work right this morning. The horror was mounting—now three people were dead! He was exhausted and as shameful as it felt, he just wanted to leave. This beautiful, once paradise was now a nightmare for him. It took a minute to pull up the confirmation emails. He handed his phone to Bent.

Bent took his phone and had Troy wait outside while he made calls. Troy felt himself sink further into depression. He hadn't felt this bereft since he had said good-bye to Tobi. Images flooded his mind. He had urged Reuben to go to the FBI with what he'd found, but Reuben had refused, said "these people" were too powerful, and he even suspected members of the US government might be in on the scheme.

Troy let his thoughts stray. Why *was* Marco killed? He hadn't thought it had anything to do with Reuben, whose death Troy had assumed was random, his heart disease having caught up with him. But now that he thought about it, didn't Bent say it was a Russian who had offered to help find Reuben's family? And now this guy Freddie too? Someone had assassinated them both. Reuben had used that word, "assassination," and that was exactly how Marcus's body had looked. Not that Troy had stayed around long to scrutinize it, but it was a memory etched into his brain: Marcus lying on the floor with half his face blown off, and another pool of blood coming from his chest. Were these murders connected to Reuben after all?

In his thoughts, Troy still heard Marcus telling him about "this guy" who wanted to help him find Robain's family, even though the guy seemed like an unlikely sort to be obliging. And then Marcus had been killed. So, what did that mean? Had the guy found out that Robain was Reuben? Had he found Tobi too?

Troy was beside himself by the time the inspector came back, but Bent just nodded to him. "Your story checks out. But there's one more thing, Mr. DeJacob."

"Yes?"

Bent still had Troy's cell in his hand, and he raised it emphatically. "We haven't been able to find a thing on Robain Sacks prior to seventeen years ago. How long did you know him?"

CHAPTER 19

Tobi called Ellie on the way home. "Did you know we're losing Jorge?" she asked.

"Oh, yeah, I kinda did, but I didn't know it was for sure yet. When is he going? I heard the Queens position is opening up next week. Another rad tech quit."

"Another one? Geez ... well, Jorge's not taking it. Crystal Clear Radiology got him instead." Tobi wondered why she always seemed to be the last to know these things. "You could've told me. Esther apparently knew too. I'm happy for him, but I'm really sad for us."

"I know, he's so good, right? And if Janie quits, we'll have no regular RT. Hey, I heard a rumor we will be merging with Hospitals for Health. That's where Dr. Comet went, isn't it? Do you know anything about that?" Ellie asked.

"Yes, he mentioned it, but nothing is certain yet. B. Healthy would have to relinquish some control, but then they'd get the backing of a huge hospital system." Tobi was gratified that she actually knew something Ellie didn't.

"Yeah, well maybe they'll start considering the patients instead of only their wallets." Ellie suddenly lowered her voice to a whisper. "Hey, did you hear about Dr. Meloncamp, from the Manhattan region? I heard he tried to kill himself! His wife found him with a bullet in his head, and he's at Mount Sinai Hospital. Looks like he's going to survive, but they don't know what the residual effects will be."

"What?" Tobi felt her stomach flip over. Medicine was becoming a profession with one of the highest suicide rates in the country, and it was pretty scary, but this was the closest it had ever come to her own sphere.

"Yeah, I overheard Dr. Richmond, the lead physician for the Manhattan region, talking about it. They're trying to keep it quiet right now."

"Who is he? Did you ever meet him?"

"No, but I heard he's a really nice guy. Super smart, and very sweet. His site was known for patients complaining about stupid things. Rocco, the rad tech, used to work with him, and Dr. Meloncamp would get terrible scores from people because they didn't think they should have to wait for their flu shot no matter how busy the office was, or they'd ask for levofloxacin for colds and he wouldn't give it to them."

"Ugh, Levaquin?"

"Yup, totally inappropriate. He'd say no, because it wasn't the right thing to do, but then he would sulk over the scores. And his office was so busy, he couldn't possibly get people in and out in forty-five minutes, they'd come in six or seven at a time. You know how it gets. And they give us such a skeleton staff. Half the offices don't even have receptionists anymore."

"You think he tried to off himself because of his scores?" Tobi asked. "That's so sad. Nothing like that is worth taking your life over. Does he have kids? Why are they trying to cover it up?"

"I don't know about kids. Dr. Richmond is a good guy; I don't think he's trying to cover it up, but maybe he wants to get all the facts first and I heard him talking about wanting to be able to offer some kind of counseling for the rest of us before making the news public."

Tobi whistled softly. "Yikes. We're such a setup for depression, Ellie. Our population is in the top ten percent in intelligence—because how else could we get into med school? We were all motivated from the outset by compassion and altruism, to sacrifice seven to ten years of our lives *after* college to train to heal others ... often starting our earning careers with a half a million dollars in debt ... and for what? You know, I got screamed at last month for not forcibly repeating a rapid strep test on an eight-year-old kid who'd had a culture *pending from the day before*! The kid almost bit the mother's hand off and broke the tongue depressor in his mouth. He could have choked on it, but the mother wrote it up on Facebook *and* sent an email to the company president, insisting I should have tried a third time—she couldn't wait two days for the culture results that were cooking at the lab."

"Wow, I didn't hear about that. What did Dr. Chagall say?"

"He backed me up," Tobi said, "agreed that someone was bound to have gotten hurt and it was ridiculous, since the results would be back in two days anyway. It still went all the way to our CEO and the legal team got involved. Ultimately, they dropped the case, but it took three weeks.

"You know," Tobi continued, "all our education and arduous training is now just so some vulture capitalist can tell us we have to become sycophants to the demands of entitled people who insist they know exactly what they need and that we must give it to them instantly—or they send nasty reviews and try to ruin us. Then they come back a few weeks later to be seen for something else! But B. Healthy is so afraid the bad press might lose them a 'customer' or two. Geez, those same patients will sue us if their inappropriate but desired treatment causes a bad outcome—like if the mother or kid had been injured."

"Of course, in a heartbeat," Ellie agreed. "Your son is so lucky too, that you're paying his tuition. I feel like I'll be in debt until I'm fifty. And—don't get me wrong—I love and respect most of our PAs, but it's like even the hospitals don't need physicians anymore. Our job can be done by 'mid-levels' who studied for one quarter of the time we did and have a fraction of the debt we have. Why did we even bother?"

"That's exactly why I'm committed to paying Ben's way. So that if he decides when he's forty years old that medicine is no longer worth practicing, he won't be looking at a pile of debt and feel trapped into staying in something that's toxic. There are more and more physicians looking for nonclinical careers now. I wonder if Dr. Meloncamp has looked at other options?"

"If he hasn't, he should," Ellie said. "Monica and I were talking about getting together to do something nice for him and his wife. I don't know what, just something to support them and tell them it's okay, we understand and we love them."

"Please count me in. It could be we're all just a shade away from throwing in the towel at times."

They hung up and Tobi came into the house, shaken and exhausted.

Maybe it was time to rethink her own life. Was *she* close to doing something stupid and just not being honest with herself? She didn't think so; right now, she was on a mission to get Ben through school without loans so he could start his life with a clean slate. But she was so tired when she got home, especially if it were after a few back to back twelve-hour shifts, that with the exception of her frequent chats with Ellie or Chloe, her life had become about going to work and going to sleep, and nothing more, and that first day off after a several-day run was mostly about recovery. She did make sure to always be off on Fridays to get to Shabbat services. It grounded her again and reminded her of what was really important in life, and she got to catch up with her synagogue friends. But otherwise, she often just felt like a hamster on a wheel.

I really have to find time for me, she thought. Time just got away from her, and of late, it felt like she had lost touch with much of herself. The old Tobi would never have put up with this lack of authenticity in her life. She'd have been looking for another place to work long ago, even if that meant leaving medicine entirely. She just seemed to have gotten into a rut at B. Healthy.

Reuben's sudden death should have taught her it was best to enjoy the moments at least, if not the days, because putting life off for later could be a big mistake. It was so challenging to put that into practice, though.

Pantelaymin pushed her knitted green and purple ball over to Tobi and looked up with impish eyes. The cat really was such a gentle soul. Tobi had rescued her from the North Shore Animal League, a large no-kill shelter. So many of their animals had been through hell before they arrived there and were exceedingly grateful to go home to warm and loving families. PanniKat had only been there for twenty-four hours when Tobi found her, and the tiny kitten had been only five weeks old. Panni had no memory of hardship, so she was distinctly *un*grateful, but she was still one of the least destructive or spiteful cats Tobi had ever met.

Tobi had named her Pantelaymin after Lyra's daemon familiar from Philip Pullman's *His Dark Materials*. She loved the idea of a person's inner self reflected externally as an ever-changing animal until puberty set in, and their personality was declared. She was pretty sure that if she had an extrinsic daemon, it would be a cat. And Panni really did seem to understand exactly what Tobi needed, and when.

Tonight, they played ball until Tobi seemed to be the only one chasing it. She made herself a tomato, basil, and mozzarella sandwich on multigrain bread, and hit the bed fairly early, hoping for a better day tomorrow.

Chapter 20

Tobi was standing on a beach. There was a gentle breeze in the summer air and the sand, almost white, was soft and warm between her toes. The water was cool, a pure peacock blue, with white foam where the waves broke, and the air smelled like the sea. She felt motion, like she was being sucked into the sand and then onto the ocean, and for a moment she was sliding on top of the water, surfing without a surfboard.

Waves began to crash behind her and she found herself under the bubbling water, its blue turning into blue-green with a hint of brown, hazel colored, deep and mysterious, alive and transcendent, warm and soft and fathomless. Like Troy's eyes … and then it was Troy, in front of her, and she was drowning. Drowning in those eyes and drowning in love, and then drowning in pain and in loneliness.

Tobi needed to surface to breathe, but everything was a blur and she didn't know which way to swim. She felt the vertigo of being upside down and pain in her ears because she hadn't equalized pressure, and she was being carried away in the flow of the ocean. Suddenly there was a gun in her hand and she found herself trying to buck the current and point it at herself, but she did not know why. Troy grabbed her hand and the gun fell away, sinking into the depths of the water. He leaned over to kiss her, and as his lips touched hers, she inhaled his breath and found a regulator in her mouth, which hissed as she breathed. She extended her head back and it hit the top of a scuba tank, which was strapped on too loosely, as if by afterthought.

She heard Troy whisper in her ear, and it was clear as crystal under the water. "Don't worry, I'm right here. I'll always be here with you."

He showed her the depth gauge from behind her back, and it read forty-three feet. He wasn't wearing any gear, his long, golden hair was undulating in waves above his head, he breathed easily in the water without a mask or a tank, and he hung suspended in front of her without any effort or equipment. Troy's body had not aged in nineteen years, and she was mesmerized by him, recalling every line and angle of his silhouette. Like a magnet, she was drawn to touch him. He was so intensely familiar, so full of confidence, tranquility, and passion all at once. And then, suddenly, he was gone, Tobi's regulator dissolved into sand, and she was gasping for breath and thrashing in her panic, trying to figure out which way was up.

Tobi grasped behind her for the back-up regulator, vaguely wondering why she was not wearing a buoyancy compensator at this depth, and managed to blow the water out first with the last of her strength. She sucked in a long, wheezy breath, and then another. She reached out with both hands for Troy, her teeth clamped too hard on the rubber bite plate so that her jaws hurt, feeling her continued descent by the searing pain in her ears—she must have ruptured her ear drums—and the water darkened around her until all color and light were lost and nothing was discernible.

Too late, she realized she was wearing a weight belt. The belt would not release, and she gave up, stretching her arms out in all directions, twisting her body and searching everywhere for Troy's eyes again, but all she saw was the blackness of the water as she sank further into the murk. "No!" she tried to scream, "come back!" The bubbles traveled sideways toward the surface and she knew abruptly which way to go, but her legs were tangled in reeds and she could not kick.

Tobi woke with a start to Pantelaymin sniffing at her face. She was drenched in sweat and shivering, and her heart was racing. Her eyes burned and were swollen nearly shut from crying. It was easier to keep them closed, but she was afraid the dream would return. Panni put a soft paw on Tobi's cheek and licked the tears from her face.

Chapter 21

smar sat in his study and stared at the encrypted message, sweat beading on his brow. Jennie had sent a couple of gyros upstairs with his favorite tzatziki sauce, but reading the memo had made him too nauseated to eat for once. These people are crazy, he thought. He had agreed to do one simple job, to use their program to sift through charts and give them information on patients with specific diagnoses. It was tricky enough even with the software they'd provided, since he had to hide his tracks while breaking HIPAA policy, but now they wanted him to get dirt on the doctors too? Whatever were they doing with all this, anyway, and why did they care if Lister had a brother? And when would his debt be paid?

Maybe he had focused overmuch on Lister since she wrote comprehensive notes and was fertile ground for his phishing, but now they wanted him to get her personal history as well? Her thoroughness could be costing B. Healthy money in lower volume and turnover, but the Project wouldn't care at all about that. Molly Baker had been riding Ismar because his sector did not produce as much revenue as some of the others, so he was making it a habit to criticize any of the providers who were slow, but it was a constant juggling act. He needed them to be slow and comprehensive for the Project, but he also needed them to be fast and efficient for B. Healthy. There were ten sites in his region, and he was having trouble living up to B. Healthy standards for speed, though he was collecting good fodder for the Russians to use. Why were they so fixated on *Lister*? She happened to have a very high percentage of repeat customers, which was good for business but bad for the Project. The better she knew a patient, the less she wrote in the chart, because it was already in her head.

He supposed he could try to engage her in conversation about both her family and the patients she knew, but he doubted she would give him any specifics. And at the end of the day, Ismar put his trust in the whip over the sugar cube. Whipping Lister to make her faster seemed to be exactly what his American employers found productive, so what would she think if he was suddenly nice to her? But now his Russian "friends" were coming to New York? This could not be good for him.

He groaned and turned his attention to his gyros. He guessed he could eat after all.

CHAPTER 22

I hate Mondays, Tobi thought, as she pulled into the parking lot at ten to eight. The flu was at its height, and their average this month was forty-five patients a day, for both eight- and twelve-hour shifts.

Her phone pinged with a notification from her work email. Her Press Ganey score was being reported. She glanced at it with foreboding and saw the zero from a patient who claimed Tobi "needed more training because she upset her five-year-old daughter and could not get a simple throat culture." That would be the exorcist girl, Jillian. That was the only little girl with issues she'd seen in the last couple of weeks. Perfect. There was also an unhappy patient who was not feeling better after forty-eight hours and angry he was not given an antibiotic "like he knew he needed." Tobi always made it a point to tell her patients that colds last about a week, but it seemed to fall mostly on deaf ears. Was this the kind of thing that got to Meloncamp, she wondered? You work your butt off at an insane pace and then the Press Ganey comes up with a seventy.

Doctors are, by definition, overachievers. Giving them a consistent seventy percent is like someone whispering in their ears on a regular basis, "You are a failure." And B. Healthy insisted on eighty-five and above, or the quarterly incentive checks would shrink. Maybe it was just an excuse not to bonus their employees, but some were bound to break under the incessant criticism. Tobi was starting to think that anyone who was getting a consistent ninety and above on their scores was probably not practicing good evidence-based medicine.

Her crew today was Marta and Connor. Connor was full-time on the south shore and he was filling in for Jorge. Patty had taken off, and apparently, since Connor knew how to register patients himself, someone figured the clinic could do without a receptionist for the day. He also had the unfortunate reputation for being rather lazy, either not wanting to get up from the front desk except to shoot films, or hanging out in the x-ray room for extended periods of time, even after the studies were long completed. The schedule was patchy for a lot of sites now; many of Tobi's shifts this month were not covered with x-ray techs, even though Jorge had given three weeks' notice. She was going to miss him dearly.

Of course, lack of proper coverage impacted their customer satisfaction scores too. She wondered if corporate would stop pressuring the providers for a while since Meloncamp was still in the hospital. There had been an email that went out from Steve Chagall and Joshua Richmond, offering support to anyone who needed to talk, so perhaps they'd have a week or two of respite, but it wouldn't last. How could it? They had to pay the board and their corporate salaries. Neither Tobi nor Ellie could figure out how they were supposed to manage high speed and high Press Ganey scores when they were shorted staff. It felt like the Egyptians telling the Hebrews to make brick without straw.

Suleman was on the schedule to scribe for her, which could cut her documentation time in half. He had made it a point to learn both her and Ellie's styles and preferences, so he could anticipate how they wanted to chart, and as she told the patients what she was going to prescribe, Suleman would order it. He also entered tetanus shots and documented splinting and laceration procedures. He was a foreign medical school graduate, passing time while he applied to American residency programs, and Tobi had written him a superb recommendation. He wouldn't be with them for long, but for now, he was a huge blessing as a scribe and made a fifty-patient day much more palatable. Often, however, he ended up working as a medical assistant, because they had none scheduled. This Monday, he had been sent to another office at the last minute because they had no MA, so now Tobi's office was short-staffed instead.

Around ten o'clock, Tobi walked into a room to see Susan, an overweight thirty-three-year-old with a cough that had been going on for two weeks and was getting worse, with a new low-grade fever that had started two days ago. It was a pretty straight forward visit on the surface and should have been quick, but when Tobi looked at her past history, everything changed.

"Do you have diabetes? The medication record shows you've been on insulin in the past but are not currently taking any meds, is that correct? Did you lose weight, and no longer need it?"

"I wish, doctor. No, I just stopped taking everything a few years ago. I had to change to Obamacare, and my doctor wasn't on that plan. And then, well, I just never got around to getting a new primary. I have no time. I have three children with disabilities who I take care of."

"But this is so important, Susan. Do you know that if you don't treat diabetes, you can go blind? Or have kidney failure, and need dialysis? Or develop heart failure?"

Susan sighed heavily. "I know. And I can lose my legs, and all that. I'm just too involved with taking care of my kids. I don't have time for myself."

"How old are your kids?"

"Twelve, ten, and seven. My youngest is autistic, and the older ones have learning disabilities. Plus, Matthew has juvenile arthritis, he's the middle guy. So, I'm constantly doing what I need to take care of them. They have to come first. That's just how it is with mothers. Do you have children?"

"Yes, I do," Tobi said. "And I know that we women in general tend to put ourselves last on the list when it comes to our families' needs. It's like we're encoded that way. But if you fall apart, who will take care of your children? Taking care of yourself *is* taking care of your kids."

Susan sighed again. She looked completely exhausted, and her respiratory infection wasn't helping.

"I'm going to give you some clarithromycin, an inhaler, and a cough medicine; you're wheezing a tiny bit. Would it be okay if we also check your glucose before you go? And I'd like to look at your feet too. Do you check your feet every night?"

"Okay, you can check my sugar. I know I'm supposed to look for infections in my feet, but I don't take the time," she said, as she started taking off her shoes and socks. "And seriously, it's not easy to find an endocrinologist on Long Island, especially one that takes Obamacare, and the truth is, those medicines they put me on gave me terrible side effects. I couldn't take them. The doctor must've tried four or five. That's why she put me on insulin, but then I got skin reactions to the shots. So … I just stopped going."

Marta went in to check Susan's glucose, while Tobi documented in the chart. "Blood sugar is 211, Dr. Lister, but she says she just had a big breakfast."

Tobi went back in with Susan's discharge papers and told her how high her sugar was. "Don't give up, Susan. There are new medications out there now, maybe they will work out better for you. And try to cut your carbs in half and avoid really sweet things, that'll help some. We know where this road you're on will lead, and I don't want you to have to deal with the complications of untreated diabetes. They're often not reversible and are much worse than the medication side effects."

"Okay. Thanks, doc. And I'll look for an endocrinologist on my plan."

Marta came over after Susan left. "She sounds like she's given up. I feel sorry for her," she said.

"I know," Tobi answered. "She's obviously just trying to get by. I wonder, do humans really have it easier than we did a couple of centuries ago? We don't have to hunt our own food or build our own houses anymore, but we still have to find a way to *pay* for them. We've just substituted one struggle for another, and we live in a culture that only puts a value on helping people if money can be made off them.

"It's true," Marta said. "A lot of the new medications that have fewer side effects are probably not even covered on her insurance. We had a patient in last week who said all his meds had to be changed when he switched insurance because the old ones weren't covered, and he had insurance through his job. He said it had taken his cardiologist a year to get him settled on medicine that controlled his blood pressure and didn't make him feel sick, and now he has to start all over again. His pressure was, like, 160/90."

"Well, some blood pressure medications aren't available right now because of contamination with a carcinogen. If it was an ARB—"

"No, Dr. L, it wasn't one of those. He was so happy that his medicine wasn't in that category, but they still had to change it, because it just wasn't covered anymore."

Tobi shook her head. "What's happened to our country? We don't take care of our own people anymore."

Chapter 23

Troy felt the blood rush to his face. *How long had he known Robain Sacks?* He had lived his life always trying to be honest, but if he answered the inspector truthfully, he'd never get out of there, and Tobi might be in trouble. But if he lied and they caught him, he'd be there even longer.

The hesitation showed on his face, and he knew he'd given himself away. There was no reason *not* to trust the Australian police, except that Reuben's paranoia had been contagious. Troy's first concern was Tobi, and he felt in his gut that she was in trouble now. Perhaps Bent could help him find out who this assassin was. Whether or not she hated Troy, he owed it to her to warn her, at the very least.

Bent was still waiting for an answer.

"I think you haven't been completely honest with me, Mr. DeJacob," the inspector said.

"No, sir, that's not true. Everything I told you is the truth."

"Well then, there is more to the story than you have let on. I think you know who killed Marcus. Let's have it, mate."

"Inspector, I swear to you, I have no idea who killed Marcus. I wish I did, he was a friend of mine too." Troy exhaled deeply. Between grief, shock, packing, and sixteen hours of jet lag, he was worn out. He hadn't been able to sleep the last couple of nights, either.

"Well, then, you know something about Robain Sacks, or whoever he was, that no one else does. He doesn't seem to have a history before he came here in 2002, but I hear he was a real decent type. Good to people, caring, part of our community. It sounded at first like his death was an accident, but now with all this ...." Bent's hands swept the room. "He's a dead man without a past, and that don't fly by me. And now two more people are dead. Good people. Is there a connection between his death and Marcus's?"

"I have no idea. I only heard about his death from Marcus," Troy said.

Bent nodded. "But you know something about who he was before he came here. We can't find a thing on Robain Sacks. It's like he didn't exist until he come to Port Douglas seventeen years ago. How long have you known him?"

Troy suddenly gave in. He felt exhausted and alone, and he needed help to figure out who this Russian guy was before he got to Tobi.

"Inspector ... I will help you all I can, but I would ask a favor from you ...."

Bent scowled at him. "I don't make deals like that, Mr. DeJacob."

"No, no, I don't mean it the way you think. My rush to get out of here ... it's because I believe someone I love is in danger. I need to protect her. I will tell you everything, it doesn't matter anymore. But I would like to know what you find. She is in the United States, and she is Robain's sister. For some reason, this killer offered to help Marcus find Robain's family, so I'm worried that she could be his next target. I need to get to her first, she has no idea—"

"You're talking riddles, mate. Why don't you just start from the beginning. You want some coffee?"

"Sure." Troy hadn't had coffee in years, but he needed something to help him get through this nightmare.

Bent turned around and poured him a cup of Jaques. Then he pulled out a notebook and a pen, old school, and looked at Troy expectantly.

Troy took a deep breath and sighed. "Robain's given name was Reuben Sokowsky …."

Chapter 24

Mrs. Waletski was in room five. She and her family were frequent flyers, and she came to the office several times a month, either with one of her three children, or for herself. The nurse at her son's school had called home at 11:30 a.m. to have nine-year-old Dennis picked up because he had a tummy ache and was feeling dizzy, so she brought him straight over. When she arrived at the front desk, there were two people signing in ahead of her, and she announced that she had to be out of the office in forty-five minutes. Connor told her that was unlikely, since there were other patients already in the back and it could be forty-five minutes before she was even seen. She signed in anyway, complaining loudly about the wait time.

Tobi walked into the Waletski's exam room just about forty minutes later, and had a hard time reconciling the hostile person she'd heard signing in at the front desk with this friendly, familiar patient. Mrs. Waletski looked up and smiled and said, "I'm so glad *you* are on today." Dennis was bouncing up and down on the exam table playing his video game.

After exchanging the usual pleasantries with Mrs. Waletski, Tobi turned to Dennis. He said he wasn't dizzy at all and his tummy didn't hurt anymore. He denied having any nausea, vomiting, or diarrhea, and he had no fever. Tobi checked him from head to toe and found he had a completely normal exam. He even asked Mom what was for lunch.

"He seems to be better," Tobi said. "I don't find anything wrong right now."

"You know," Mrs. Waletski said as she eyed her son, "we went to a friend's house for a party last night. There was a ton of food, and I think he ate way more than I usually let him, including desserts and things. Could that be it? He does look pretty okay now."

"Could be," Tobi answered. "Just have him eat lightly today and watch him. Let me or his primary doctor know if anything changes. Shall we fax these notes to his pediatrician for his records?"

"You know," Mrs. Waletski said, "I called the pediatrician for an appointment today, and—can you believe it? They couldn't get him in until three o'clock!"

Tobi left the exam room shaking her head in disbelief. She went back to her tablet to find the EMR had timed her out again, and as she signed back in, Ismar walked into the office with Molly Baker. They were smiling, as if enjoying a private joke. Ismar stopped to look over Tobi's shoulder as she was charting Dennis's visit. He smelled sour from sweat and garlic.

"Come talk to us in the back when you have a minute," he said.

Tobi gave him a cheerful, "Sure thing," but inside she felt the acid bubbling in her stomach. The EMR continued freezing intermittently, and it took her a while to complete the chart. It was almost like it didn't want her to go back there, either.

"Hi," she said as she entered the break room. "To what do I owe the pleasure?"

Molly gave her a bright smile. "How are you, Dr. Lister? I haven't been out here in a long time. This office has certainly gotten busy!"

Tobi would have preferred to use these few moments to eat something, but although her lunch was three feet away in the fridge, she didn't think she could swallow any of it.

"Yes, it has. We've missed you. Did you guys just come to visit?"

Back in the early days of B. Healthy, the leadership had actually done that. They'd stop in and tell the staff what a great job they were doing, and what their latest gimmick was. All that had stopped about twelve months ago, when the company had tripled the number of sites they opened, and each office picked up volume. Now everything was about maintaining the numbers.

Molly started. "Actually, we came to see how you are doing. Dr. Rufini has noticed your performance has been slipping, and there have been a few complaints."

"Yes, your door-to-door times are up and your Press Ganey scores are down," Ismar said. "And a patient from last week wrote a bad review on Yelp because the wait was too long. She said she didn't even get to be seen. She was told it would be over an hour, just for a simple strep test. You know, those reviews are very bad for business. They can reach thousands of customers and discourage people from coming to our offices. We wanted to check on you and see if maybe you aren't feeling comfortable here."

Tobi hated that she let these people rattle her, but she forced herself to look at Molly. "I think I know the person you are referring to. We were having a very busy day and she walked in just as we were sending a very sick patient out to the hospital with new onset a-fib. I did a call back on him, and the family told me he actually coded in the ED. Thankfully, he was cardioverted and is doing much better now. He did take precedence over several other patients—I'm just glad he didn't code *here*. We're not really equipped to handle that. You were in the office that day, Ismar. You saw him go out by EMS."

"Yes, yes, and I told you the patients were getting restless."

Tobi stared at him. "Are you telling me I should have left a critical patient to see someone who didn't even have a sore throat, but just an *exposure* to strep?"

Molly broke in. "No, Dr. Lister, of course you need to take care of a sick patient like that first, but bad reviews hurt our reputation. We have to keep customers happy so they don't write things like that."

Ismar looked unconvinced. "We also have a complaint from another patient that same day. She said she waited a very long time and did not get her Z-Pak, and her visit was a waste of money."

Tobi took a moment before she answered. She sorely wished Ellie were here with her, but she resolved not to let them bait her. "Have you read up on the CDC recommendations for the use of antibiotics recently?" she asked as evenly as she could muster.

"Your overall times are high, Dr. Lister, and that is why we are here," Molly said, diverting the conversation from something Ismar might lose.

"Well, charting takes a lot longer these days," Tobi said. "There are about six extra fields we're told to fill out and some of our patients resent our asking these additional questions. We're now trying to do a primary care function in the time frame of an urgent care visit."

"Those questions are required by the insurance companies in order to collect the contracted fees we agreed upon," Molly said.

"That's fine," Tobi said, "but it does slow us down. And the office is often not staffed to par, and some visits require a more thorough evaluation. People come in with a wide range of problems, from the sniffles to a heart attack. You know, faster is not always better, not if you want to take proper care of the patient."

"Yes, but what about the other patients, hmm?" Ismar persisted. "They do not have a good experience if they have to wait, and many times they, like, leave and don't get taken care of."

"Well, then perhaps *those* people weren't that sick in the first place," Tobi was getting exasperated, despite wanting desperately to keep her cool. She wondered if Ismar had heard a word she'd just said. "I think it's important to take care of the staff as well and give us backing and not just criticism. We've gotten much busier, but we have not gotten any added support. I don't think we've been consistently staffed in weeks. What it says on the schedule is often not who is actually working in the office, and if you look on the schedule for this month, there are a large number of unfilled slots. Even today, Suleman is scheduled, but he was called away to cover another office."

"Why are you looking at the schedule?" Ismar asked. He had taken out his laptop. "It's not something you should be looking at, anyway. Like, here are the average times patients are spending in the office over the last month. It's getting longer and longer. That's not good for business. So, Tobi, that is what we want to know. Like, to see if you are happy here."

Is he asking me to quit? Tobi wondered. Damn, Ellie would have been much better at arguing their defense. Tobi twisted a little, trying to view what was on his screen and tardily realized she had not been meant to see any of it. "Yes, that's what happens when you have more patients and less staff. It takes longer to see everyone."

Tobi knew Ismar did not have the authority to fire her. She wasn't sure about Molly, but she thought she would have gotten a call from Steve Chagall if she were in that kind of trouble.

"How is Dr. Meloncamp doing? Is he going to make a full recovery?" she asked, pointedly trying to illustrate their complete lack of sensitivity.

"It looks like he will," Molly said. "He will need many months of rehab first. He won't be coming back to B. Healthy, at any rate."

"Look, Tobi, you have, like, one of the highest times in the whole company," Ismar pointed at his computer screen, trying to bring them back to his own agenda. "Maybe this isn't a fulfilling life for you."

Screw it, Tobi thought, and dove in. "So, are you telling me I should be looking for a different job?"

"Oh, no, Dr. Lister!" Molly said. "But it is very important that we keep the numbers up and one of the ways we assure that happens is when patients are satisfied with our services. So, we just want to make sure you're happy working here. Happy doctors means happy patients. And, of course, we don't want any more severely depressed providers." She smiled from ear to ear, lips curled wide, but her eyes were like ice. She suddenly reminded Tobi of the character Dolores Umbridge from the *Harry Potter* series.

Of course, Tobi thought, Meloncamp is very poor publicity. "Thanks for worrying about me, Molly. I will definitely make a point of checking in with myself frequently to make sure I'm doing okay." She laughed it off to make it a joke, and Molly laughed too, but Tobi had no illusions. She skipped lunch and went back up front to see her patients. Molly left, but Ismar continued to hover around.

As Tobi got back to her work station, Ismar sat down next to her.

"Tobiii, are you having any trouble with the EMR lately? Any questions?"

Tobi peered at him. "No, Ismar, I've been using this program longer than you. I seem to remember tutoring you on it when you started."

"Yes, yes, I know, but, like, I wondered if you were trying to do too much, like, maybe that is slowing you down and frustrating you."

"Ismar, I try to do the bare minimum on computers of any sort. There is a lot of documentation that needs to be done for liability reasons and for billing, and I do my best to be compliant with both."

"So ... you haven't had any, like, problems?"

"No, Ismar. Have you?" Tobi tried to be the barest level of polite, but she just wanted him to go away.

He laughed. "No, no, of course not. And you are putting in all the pertinent medical history and diagnoses, right? You know, we have to include all of the patients' other problems, not just what they come in for this day."

More than you do, Tobi thought. "Of course, Ismar, I chart very thoroughly. That's one of things that 'slows me down.'"

"Good. We need to be very complete." Ismar was sweating; he really needed to lose at least a hundred pounds. "Tobi, do you have any siblings?"

"Excuse me?"

"I just wondered, like, we never talk. I know you are not married, maybe you are lonely. Are you an only child?"

Tobi glared at him. "Why do you care about my personal life?"

"Really, I would like to know. Just friendly. And to make sure you are okay. Are you close to your brothers and sisters?"

Tobi's first impulse was to say "we're not friendly," but that would be rude, so she said nothing. Ismar continued to stare at her, waiting for an answer. The sweat was beading on his brow.

"I *had* a brother," she said finally. "He's dead."

Tobi stood and picked up her tablet, closing the conversation. She walked stoically into the next room, completely baffled. In the last two years, Ismar had not asked her a single personal question, why the sudden interest in her private life? Was she happy, was she lonely, did she have siblings … it made no sense. She had a deep sense of foreboding about the last half hour with both of them. She definitely felt like Ismar was trying to get her to leave B. Healthy.

Tobi had been through far worse than Ismar Rufini and Molly Baker, though. She was nothing if not a survivor, which was exactly what had gotten her into urgent care—or what she now called "Fast

Food Medicine." Ben's father had gotten involved with another woman a few months before Ben was born and then had told her when Ben was only a week old, that they ought to split up before their son was one. They fought a nasty custody battle that lasted four-and-a-half-years and rivaled *The War of the Roses* in its ferocity.

In those days, family practice doctors had taken call at the hospital and visited their patients who had been admitted before or after their usual office hours, since "hospitalists" did not exist yet, so the hours were long and variable. Ben's father had told the court that he deserved full custody because Tobi's work required excessively long absences from their baby boy, and she could not provide proper care as a result. It later became clear he'd really just wanted her to pay *him* the child support, but she had been so frightened of losing Ben, she had started doing urgent care when it barely existed. It was a good way to make money and do strictly shift work and it was less stressful than the emergency room, which, in those days, was often staffed by moonlighting psychiatrists.

Those early years had been nightmarish, and she'd had no family support, not emotional or financial. Tobi's father had been manic depressive, occasionally violent, and always unpredictable. She'd remained terrified of him most of her life, and her mother was, well, her mother.

One of the only five or six times her father had ever called her was when she was seven months pregnant. He'd asked Tobi to take out a loan for him for $40,000. In 1991, that was a huge amount of money, at least to Tobi. It was completely unmanageable with baby on the way in, husband on the way out, and a mountain of student loans to repay. She'd said no, and that got her disowned for the second time, or was it the third? There had been about four or five in all, she'd stopped keeping track after a while. Thankfully, a person can only die once. Tobi only felt that vice crushing her heart once. She could only be banished from the home that was supposed to be filled with unconditional love and acceptance once. After that first time, rejection lost its power. How could she be cast out if she no longer belonged? Tobi had learned to make her own way in the world.

Belatedly, Tobi recognized that her mother, Hannah's controlling, narcissistic personality had been, at least in part, compensation for double survivor guilt. As a toddler, Hannah had watched her baby brother die of "consumption," and two years later, the family had fled Poland. That was in 1938, less than a year before the Nazis had occupied, and Hannah had been spared yet again, so anxiety was practically her middle name.

The family had settled in a small town in Connecticut, where all their neighbors spoke Yiddish, so Tobi's grandmother never did learn English. Hannah, of course, had learned in school, and since Tobi's grandfather went to work every day, Hannah was left to translate the world for her mother, a tremendous task to give a six-year-old child. It was no surprise Hannah had grown up feeling she needed to be in control of everything, all the time—while desperate to be taken care of herself. Unfortunately, that extended to Tobi and Reuben. Growing up, Tobi had been told what she should feel, what she should think, and who she should be, and whenever she had strayed from that script, the threat of rejection loomed. It was almost a relief when she'd finally been sent packing.

When he was a teenager, Reuben had run away frequently, but was greeted by a beating from their father each time he was dragged back home. Once he'd even made it as far as Newark airport, but the police had been suspicious of a lone fourteen-year-old with the family dog on a leash, trying to catch a flight to Virginia. Over the years, Reuben had succumbed to pressure and become the dutiful son. Perhaps he had feared being ostracized like Tobi was, and being all alone in the world too. Tobi knew he had given up a big part of himself in the process.

As a child and teenager growing up, Tobi had not understood any of her father's bipolar disease or her mother's neuroses—not that it would have made it any easier if she had. She had watched Reuben's beatings and kept her head low, and focused on learning how to survive. By now, she was a pro. Ismar and Molly were child's play by comparison.

A half hour after Ismar left, Suleman walked in. "Hey, Dr. Lister. They found coverage, so they sent me back over to scribe for you."

"Great!" she said. Privately, she thought management was trying to pretend there was no staffing problem in her office. Whatever the reason, having Suleman around always improved the patient flow, and she enjoyed his company. They often compared their religious practices on various topics, and she learned a lot from him. Judaism and Islam were actually quite similar in language, customs and principles, and they tended to focus on the things they had in common. Once, they had even stepped lightly into the Israeli-Palestinian conversation, and Tobi was pretty sure that, given their good will toward each other, and their both being reasonable human beings, they could have ended the conflict if it were up to them.

Chapter 25

Sipping on his coffee, Troy told Bent everything. He began with the morning in New York Bagels and Reuben's terrified state. How Reuben had discovered the EHR software he had been writing was being used to identify public figures with medical secrets, things that could ruin them if they were known. There was even an FBI director who had been diagnosed with early Parkinson's dementia that he had not yet disclosed, even though it rendered him unable to do his job. He probably didn't want to retire yet. Reuben had traced the findings to a new Russian oligarch named Bereznikov, who was collecting large sums of money from each of them.

"Bereznikov didn't stop with blackmail. Reuben kept digging through the program, and he discovered their front, an expensive insurance carrier whose main niche was high-risk health problems. A significant number of those insured had been meeting with 'accidents' before requiring the costly treatments, mostly organ transplants. Reuben even found the marker indicating who and when was the next target. So this company was taking in high premiums for hospital insurance while guaranteeing they would never have to pay out on claims."

Troy looked up at Bent, whose face was impassive. A little fan in the room created a loud white noise that started grating on Troy's nerves.

"He asked me to get him out of the States," Troy said, "to make him disappear, and I set it up. But the night before he was supposed to leave, he insisted on meeting with a man who had a severe cardiac disease called cardiomyopathy and was a match with a kid who was on full life support and brain dead from a motorcycle accident. The family was expected to pull the plug any day, and this guy, James Arlan, would be getting the kid's heart. Or he should have been.

"Reuben saw his marker. Arlan was scheduled for 'redirection' the next day—that's what they called it. Reuben was sure Arlan was going to be killed. Reuben had wanted to meet the guy at a coffee house in Austin, but Arlan came to Reuben's apartment instead, because he felt too sick to be out in public." Troy paused. The fan bobbed back and forth, its buzz suddenly loud in the silence.

"The guy was severely debilitated, he wasn't breathing well, and he had trouble walking from his car to the front door. His legs were swollen ... he really should've been in the hospital himself, but he didn't want to lie in a bed, waiting to die, and he knew his time was almost up. When Reuben told him about the scam ... he said Arlan didn't believe him at first. But Reuben wouldn't give up. He showed Arlan what he'd found and told him he had to hire protection or at least check into the hospital immediately. When the guy finally did believe him, he couldn't take it. He clutched his chest and fell over. He died in Reuben's apartment that night."

Troy stopped to drink the coffee. His hands were shaking from it, after so many years without caffeine, and he wondered why he was drinking the vile stuff; it was going straight to his head. He struggled to keep his voice even.

"Reuben panicked and ran. He was sure the Russians would realize he had sold them out, with their next target lying in his apartment, so he took Arlan's wallet, hoping no one would identify him and make the connection until he was long gone. He really hadn't planned for anyone to think *he* was dead—if Arlan's body had been found sooner, it would have been obvious it wasn't Reuben. He just wanted time to escape before the Russians knew he'd been talking to one of their clients. He left his own wallet behind so he couldn't be traced by his credit cards or license. And then the body wasn't found for three days, and it was already starting to decompose ..." Troy blanched. "Someone took Arlan for Reuben, and it was a closed case."

"No DNA verification?"

Troy shrugged. "It was the year 2000, who did that back then? They had roughly the same build and coloring, and he was in Reuben's apartment, with no other ID than Reuben's wallet sitting on the table. Reuben had some heart issues too, so it wasn't that much of a stretch."

Bent was writing in his little notebook. "So, where did Reuben go?"

"He spent a couple of years in Guam and did some searching from an internet café, hoping it might have all gone underground, and maybe he could send word to his sister, but instead, he found the operation had actually become more global. He got paranoid and thought the Russians might have detected him snooping online, so he left Guam and came here, and started a new life as Robain Sacks. He was too afraid to surface after that, he thought they'd go after his family too, if they realized he was alive, which is exactly what I'm afraid of now."

Troy rubbed the sides of his face and head again. "There may be more he didn't tell me. I think Reuben was gathering evidence and trying to send it to the States, but he didn't want me involved with anything that could make me a target, so he didn't share that. He said the Russians were ruthless and thought nothing of murdering innocent people to make money off them. He said some in the US government were also in on it as victims of the blackmail scheme and would likely never reveal anything. He was genuinely terrified. That's all of it. That's all I know."

Bent was sitting back in his chair, his mouth slightly open in disbelief. "That's the craziest damn story I ever heard," he said.

"Was for me too, and my life was forever changed by it. I was … I was about to propose to Tobi, his sister, but he made me promise never to tell her where he was. I couldn't lie to her, I just couldn't …." His voice trailed off. *Could I have?* He shook his head. "I left. I haven't been back since. I'm sure she hates me now, if she even thinks about me at all."

"And you mean to go back now?" Bent asked. "The sister is blissfully ignorant, why uproot all that pain for both of you?"

Troy straightened and came back to the present. "If Marco's killer was Russian and suspicious about 'Robain,' then he could be connected to these guys, and if they've sniffed out that Reuben was alive all these years … I don't know. Did he kill Marco because he made the connection? Marco said the guy seemed genuinely interested in locating Robain's family for him, and he didn't know why. If the killer did figure out that Robain was Reuben, then Tobi is in danger—hell, I could be in danger, if Marco told the gunman about me. I have to admit, I've been looking over my shoulder more than a little. No, I have to go home and make sure no one hurts Tobi. I still love her. And I owe her that much, even so."

Troy's muscles were slack, but he felt oddly at peace. He had not told the story to anyone, in all these years. He had not realized how heavy a weight he had been carrying; he had attributed all his misery to losing Tobi.

Bent raised and then lowered his eyebrows and his hand was over his chin. He sat up. "That is such a preposterous story, I'm thinking you couldn't possibly have made it all up. But even if it's true, how many years ago was all that?"

"Reuben went ghost end of October, 2000," Troy answered. "He showed up in Port Douglas in 2002. He loved diving and the Great Barrier Reef. He was afraid to work as a systems analyst and software writer anymore, because he knew his digital signature could be discovered, so he opened the dive shop."

"How'd he get certification to do that?"

"Well," Troy smirked, "he was a PADI Divemaster, so he just certified himself in his new name, using his old name to file the paperwork, and backdated it. I know what you're thinking, but up until then, and forever after, he was straight up."

Bent was scratching his chin. "All I ever heard 'bout the man was good things … but you think the bloke who killed Marcus was from the same people Robain—or, you said his name was Reuben? —was running from?"

"Don't know. It's possible, from how Marco said this guy got curious about Reuben and offered to help find his family. But why would he kill Freddie?"

"Well, that would make perfect sense, seeing as Freddie had access to the killer's files when he retrieved his hard drive. Who knows what Freddie found out. Sergeant Larsen is handling the investigation in Cairns, but this may become a federal matter. If Freddie found something amiss, I'd have liked to think he would have turned it in. If he had a chance to, that is."

"So … you believe me?"

Bent ran his hand through his curly brown hair. It was warm in the office, despite the fan, and there was a dark spot under his arm from sweat. "I don't quite know what to believe, mate. I don't know if I can legally hold you here in Australia, but I'd be obliged if you'd hang around a bit longer so I don't have to get creative. Might could use something you know to catch this mother fucker. As a return favor, I'll share what I can with you as it comes up, and I can see about defraying the cost of your hotel bill."

"No need for that, I can stay at Reuben's place, but I would be grateful for information. I'll stay a few days, if you think it will help."

Now that he had spilled his guts to this man, Troy realized he was reluctant to leave the one person in the world who knew the truth, and he was so exhausted, he thought he might collapse on the floor. He was in no shape to go anywhere right then, anyway.

He straggled back to Reuben's now empty flat. The bed and furniture were still there and the electric was still running, which he had intended to shut off just before he left. But the walls were bare, and the stereo and TV were gone, and his footsteps echoed unnervingly. He collapsed on the bed, with Tobi's face hovering in front of him. The coffee rush was gone and he was crashing. He pulled out his phone again and opened Messenger. No answer. Of course, she wasn't going to make this easy.

Tobi,
Please.
I need to talk to you. It's urgent.

T

He plugged the phone in to charge at the bedside and succumbed to a deep but troubled sleep.

Chapter 26

The long shift was almost over. Rikard was in room four, a pleasant gentleman with a French accent who looked absolutely miserable. His face was drawn, his hair was squashed flat on his head, and his skin was clammy. The flu test was on the counter where Marta had run it, and the small red "positive" line was visible across the room. Both Suleman and Tobi went in with their face masks on, and Tobi introduced them both as they walked in.

"When did you start to feel sick?" she asked the patient.

"Four days ago, but it got much worse on the plane. I just came back from Vancouver. My wife wanted me to get checked when I land, and if I have the flu, she told me not to come home. I can stay in a hotel. She doesn't want me to get her or our kids sick."

"How old are your children?"

"Ten and eight," he answered. "It's okay, I don't mind. How long do you think I'll be contagious? Do I need to burn my clothes, or leave them outside, or anything like that?"

"That's pretty harsh," Tobi chuckled. "Are your children healthy?"

"Oh, yes," Rikard answered, "thank God."

"The teachers have been coming in telling me half their classes are out with flu, so your kids can pick it up at school, even if you don't go near them. At this stage, this could run another five or six days."

Tobi hesitated. "I don't want to get involved in your marriage, but a hotel sounds pretty drastic. It's flu, not plague. Is there a room in your house where you can just sort of quarantine yourself? If your family gets sick, they can come in immediately for the flu antiviral, and you can just throw your clothes in the wash."

"I have an office downstairs, with a couch."

"Perfect. Just wash your hands frequently, clean the surfaces with disinfectant, like Lysol, and cover your mouth when you cough. It's airborne, so take a mask with you, if you want."

Tobi asked Suleman to send a nasal spray and a cough medicine for the patient. As he was getting ready to go, Rikard brought up a question.

"So, I am curious. What is your personal position on who to vaccinate? In France, we say the young, the old, and the sick, but here in America, it seems everyone is supposed to get the flu shot—even though it doesn't seem to be working. Should my children get this vaccine that is not working? Did *you* get the vaccine? Please, tell me honestly, what do you think?"

Tobi shifted uncomfortably on her feet. "Ah, umm … you're right. It hasn't been very effective again this year, so I understand why people are reluctant to get it. And I think that makes the whole practice of immunization confusing to the public. Because people don't understand that the influenza vaccine is unique; they assume other inoculations will have the same potential lack of effectiveness. But the flu vaccine is fundamentally different from most others, and is much harder to produce, because there are so many different strains of flu. It has to be reinvented every year by guessing which strain will be most prevalent by the time it's ready for distribution. We don't have a universal influenza vaccine."

Tobi did not add that the vaccine had seemed to be more effective in the years before it was made mandatory for health care workers and teachers, and the pharmaceutical companies had a guaranteed market. This was one reason she thought the public was becoming increasingly resistant to immunization in general. The flu shot was now obligatory in so many environments, and when people saw it wasn't working, they assumed the MMR, (measles, mumps, rubella), would be ineffective as well.

"You *have* vaccinated your kids for measles, tetanus, and polio, right?" Tobi asked him.

"I think so," Rikard said. "My wife takes care of most of that stuff."

"Good, because not getting *those* vaccines is dangerous and constitutes neglect. Seriously. Those viruses are stable organisms for which we have had excellent vaccines with close to a hundred percent effectiveness for decades, and with virtually no risks. But if you're not vaccinated and you contract them, they'll make you much sicker and are more likely to be fatal or leave permanent defects. We are seeing a huge resurgence of measles now, which is killing people unnecessarily, when we had essentially eliminated it entirely from the United States. I hope we don't start seeing polio and tetanus too, although a couple of years ago, there was a tragic case of tetanus in a little boy who spent months in the hospital; his parents still didn't immunize him after that. I believe in individual autonomy, but I feel like that was a case for social services to step in. It's like we're going back to the Dark Ages."

"I thought you could get autism from vaccines."

"Many, many studies have been done, and there is no link between vaccinations and autism," Tobi said.

"Not even from the flu vaccine? Can my children get autism from that one?" Rikard asked.

"No, not autism—or any other horrible disease," Tobi said. "But as for still getting the flu, I've certainly seen a large number of pretty sick flu patients who were vaccinated. But I'm not going to advise anyone who wants the influenza vaccine *not* to get it." She raised her hands helplessly.

He laughed. "Right, this is America, after all. You have to be careful what you say. In France, we don't sue each other like you people do. I understand." He was smiling for the first time during the visit.

"I'm going to France," Tobi said under her breath.

"You are going to France? When are you going?" Rikard became suddenly animated.

"No, no," she laughed, "I'd *like* to, though." How wonderful it would be to practice medicine without litigation worries, and in a place where pharmaceutical companies were not allowed to advertise and manipulate the public with terror tactics. Rikard's wife, however, was obviously already indoctrinated into the American way.

Randall was the last patient. He complained of having a sinus infection for the last three days and said he got them five or six times a year. He usually went to his primary doctor, who always gave him prednisone and clindamycin, a steroid and a powerful antibiotic, but his doctor hadn't been in today. He had chills and sweats, sinus pressure and a slight cough. His temperature was 101. His nose was dripping and he looked tired. He adamantly refused the flu test.

"I have never had the flu, and I will never get the flu," Randall told Tobi. "I have a sinus infection, like I always get. I came here for my antibiotics and my steroids. That's what I want."

"The flu does cause a miserable infection in your sinuses," Tobi said, "but antibiotics don't treat this kind of sinus infection, they only treat those caused by bacteria. I can give you some medicine to help you feel better," Tobi said.

"I know what I have, I am thirty-six years old and I know my body. I want my clindamycin and prednisone. Now."

Tobi was not in the mood to argue, but giving him those two medications could cause harm. "Randall," she tried again, "all of your symptoms are classic signs of influenza, and we are in the middle of huge epidemic. Antibiotics do nothing against the flu virus, and the steroids can actually weaken your immune system right now and make you worse. I would only use them if you were wheezing or having trouble breathing."

"I realize that is your opinion," Randall said condescendingly. "But I didn't come here for your *opinion*, I came here for my medicine. Now, please send it to the pharmacy for me. I need clindamycin, 300 milligrams four times a day for ten days, and prednisone three times a day for three days."

"I'm sorry?" Tobi was speechless for a minute. "Actually, Randall, my opinion is exactly what you get when you come here. That's kind of assumed when you register. I'm sorry, we aren't a retail store, I have to do what I believe is the right thing. Those are the terms of my medical license."

"Well, I can see you aren't going to help me here." Randall marched out of the office.

"Wow!" Marta said. "What a jerk! Proper medical care is what we 'sell' here, Bozo."

They closed up the office and Tobi went out into the cold night to her car. Another zero. And if Randall complained, she'd be called to task by Ismar for not keeping him "happy," but she was too weary to care. Her breath was frosty in front of her as she walked, and the hairs on the back of her neck stood up. She felt a chill that was distinctly different from the wintery air, almost like she was being watched, and she wondered if the angry Randall were hovering about somewhere. She jumped at the sound of an engine starting across the parking lot and peered into the darkness, glancing behind her constantly until she was locked safely inside in her car. She wasn't usually one to spook easily, but it felt like something was just *wrong*, and she couldn't put her finger on it. Well, she thought, I felt that way for years after Reuben died and it was just me being ridiculous.

Chapter 27

It was only a fifteen minute drive home, which was one reason Tobi had stayed at B. Healthy, but on the way, she called the medical director, Dr. Chagall. She needed to start sticking up for herself.

"Hi, Steve. Do you have a couple of minutes?"

"Actually, I was going to call you. You first."

"Okay. I had a meeting with Rufini and Molly today. Should I be looking for another job?"

"No, why would you ask that?"

"Rufini comes in frequently to tell me I'm the slowest provider in the region, and today the two of them came in and berated me for not seeing patients fast enough and not giving antibiotics for viral infections. And, he asked me if I'm 'happy' here at B. Healthy. You yourself sent out the blurbs citing the CDC recommendations for the use of antibiotics. And I'm not leaving the side of a critical patient to see a case of strep exposure, no symptoms. I'll quit first."

"Tobi, your medical practice is *par excellence*, no one wants you to change that, don't worry. They just want to see faster turnover, but not if it puts someone at risk."

"Steve, you know we never get staffed appropriately, and even if it's on the schedule, Evelyn changes the schedule last minute, not generally for our benefit, and doesn't update it. So, what would you think if someone told you they wanted to make sure you were feeling 'happy' in your life and maybe this place wasn't doing it for you?"

"I think I would feel exactly the same way. I haven't heard anything about this, but I assure you, I want you to continue here for as long as you choose. I'll speak to Rufini about it. Are you doing okay with the news of Tim Meloncamp?"

"And that's the other thing—they avoided that topic completely. Pretty callous of them, I think." Tobi sighed. "I heard about him from Ellie Milton, and it was kind of a shock. I mean, I didn't know him, but it kind of shakes the ground a little. I hope he didn't do it because of the corporate working conditions. I mean, I get it, but—quit, don't kill yourself. Does he have family?"

"He's married, no kids. Lots of loans. He's a sensitive sort. There had to be more going on, but the B. Healthy environment didn't help, I'm sure. He'll be in rehab for months. He has a right-sided hemiparesis and a slight aphasia."

"Poor guy. Guess he's left-handed," Tobi said.

"Yeah, guess so. If you're feeling like you need to talk, you know you can call me. We're working on setting up a buddy chat, maybe five providers to a group, so it's a little more personal. Just so people can vent. We're getting some push back from corporate on it, though."

"Of course, they won't want us bonding over poor working conditions, but it's a great idea. You know, it gets lonely in the office without another colleague to bounce things off of."

"That's the idea," Steve said. "Clinicians need more community. And hopefully, we'll pass out some material on things to look for and what to do if you think someone is heading for a break."

"Thanks, Steve. Is that what you wanted to talk to me about?"

"In part, but there's something else. You know we have alerts that go off when you access someone's chart that you have no direct business in, and lately, you've been snooping in a love of charts of patients who aren't yours."

"Oh, yeah, sorry. I sent some Tamiflu over for Ellie a couple of weeks ago. You know, we can't do it over the phone in New York State anymore, it all has to be electronic."

"I'm not talking about that," Steve said. "You've been peeking in a slew of charts over the last couple of months."

"I don't know what you're talking about. My current patient load is quite enough for me," Tobi laughed.

"Tobi, this is serious, it's a breach of privacy and a huge HIPAA violation. Everything you do on your login traces back to you, you know."

Tobi was floored. "Steve, I haven't been snooping. Really. I have no idea what you're talking about. I mean, sometimes I'll look in a chart if a PA calls with a question about a patient, but other than that, no, I never do that."

"Okay, maybe that's it. But you and a few other docs have been lighting up frequently. I'll check it out with IT."

"But, you know ..." Tobi hedged. "I think Ismar took my tablet last week while I was still signed in."

"Why would he do that?"

"I have no idea. I didn't actually see him do it, but Jorge did. I do know that my tablet was switched."

"That doesn't make any sense, Tobi, why would he use your login? Listen it's nothing official yet, but it looks like we've been given the go ahead to affiliate with Hospitals for Health. We're just cinching up the contract, and this kind of thing will never fly with them. They're very scrupulous."

"Is that why we've been getting so many phishing warnings and the security on the tablets has been upgraded? It times out, like, every three minutes."

"Four minutes, and yes, so we have changed our whole firewall. There were too many holes for H for H's comfort. We actually started that a couple of months ago in anticipation."

"That's fabulous news. Maybe they will be more focused on good medicine and healthy outcomes than on profit and popularity."

"That's the hope. Keep the faith, Tobi."

The guard at the gatehouse smiled and waved her through, and Tobi pulled into her driveway. But as she got out of her car, she instantly felt the foreboding again. She told herself she was crazy, but stared up and down her street, nevertheless, trying to probe through the darkness behind every tree. She suddenly wished Pantelaymin were a German shepherd. She walked into her house and turned the deadbolt as Facebook Messenger pinged again on her phone.

Tobi,
Please.
I need to talk to you. It's urgent.

T

Like hell, Tobi thought. I *needed* to talk to you, you bastard. When Reuben died, when mom died, when Ben cried for weeks over losing you, and then when he graduated high school, and college … I needed to talk to you when the sunset was gorgeous and sparkled perfectly on the surf on Fire Island, and I needed to talk to you when I was at Zion National Park and when I stood on top of the mountain at the Canyons in Park City, and I needed to talk to you when my boss was being a dick … yeah, I needed to talk to you too, Troy. Go fly.

Ellie called as soon as Tobi was inside.

"Hey, so I worked on the south shore today with Monica, and she told me something very interesting. Rufini locked himself in the breakroom for a half an hour the other day, and they could hear him arguing on the phone. When he came out, they said he was sweating like crazy and wouldn't even look at anyone; he just left."

"Ismar always sweats, he's fat. What was the argument about?" Tobi asked.

"Not sure, the first time it was in another language no one could figure out, so probably Turkish." Tobi had an image of the south clinic's staff lined up against a closed door trying to listen, like an old Jackie Gleason episode.

"But then, he was speaking English and it sounded like he was talking to a bank or something," Ellie continued. "Is he being foreclosed on? He's got that huge house up on Centre Island. It's gotta be over a couple mil, how does he pay for that? She heard him saying, like, 'I'll get it to you by next week' and 'please don't do that,' and stuff like that, and she said he sounded desperate. And Monica also heard he was mixed up with some very bad people in Turkey and came here to get away from them. He might even have had a different family that he abandoned when he came here."

"Where do you hear these things, Ellie?" Tobi wasn't in the mood for made-up drama, she had enough of her own right then. And she hated drama.

"Monica knows Rufini's wife's cousin, who's good friends with Monica's brother. Rufini got into it with his wife last week and I guess something slipped out in the argument. Now she's pissed that he was already married in another country and didn't tell her, and she thinks he only married her for citizenship."

"Well, that wouldn't surprise me. But this is a case of 'he said-she said' and mostly in another language that nobody who was listening can speak, so it's hard to take it too seriously."

"Right, but how *does* he pay for that house on Centre Island? I can't believe B. Healthy pays him *that* well. And he didn't come here with any money. He told me once that he was given financial assistance to get through the second residency, which he had to do to get licensed here."

"Well, then, he lives above his means. Residencies do not pay much, but if you're a little bit frugal, you should be able to make it without debt if you have no children, especially if you marry someone who has a job. It's med school that's the killer, tuitions are enormous."

"Yes," Ellie cackled, "we both know—and you know twice!"

"I *do* know twice!" Tobi found herself laughing anyway.

"But you know Ellie? Rufini was pretty weird to me today. He and Molly asked me if I am happy here—"

"That's right, you had your meeting today! How'd it go?"

"Horrible. They want me to quit, I'm sure of it."

"Did you call Dr. Chagall?" Ellie asked.

"I did. He told me not to worry about it, he'd speak with them. But Rufini came over to me after and tried to be chummy. It was odd."

"What did he say?" Ellie asked.

"He asked me if I was having any trouble with the EMR, did I need any help with anything … and he asked me about my family and if I were lonely. It was really strange. He gives me the creepy crawlies, Ellie, I can't explain it."

"That's bizarre," Ellie said. "What did Dr. Chagall say about that?"

"I didn't really mention all that to him. But Steve did accuse me of snooping in charts that were not mine, which was ridiculous, because I don't do that."

"Wait, Tobi! Didn't you tell me that Rufini was using your tablet? Maybe he was doing it under your login."

"Yeah, I mentioned that to Steve, but how would he do that? The thing times out every few minutes and we have to sign back in, and he can access everything with his own login. And he probably has more 'permission' to look at stuff than we do, so why would he bother?"

"Because maybe he's not supposed to be doing it, that's why," Ellie said.

Tobi had a headache and it had been a long day. She groaned. "Maybe. I'm going to hang, Ellie, and chalk all this up to an active imagination fueled by having three small children who live in fantasy worlds. I'll talk to you tomorrow."

Ellie cackled again and they hung up.

Tobi made herself a cup of ginger tea. She had intended to call her friend Sally and talk to her about Troy's messages but found she just didn't have the energy for it. She texted Chloe to confirm they were still on for lunch tomorrow, then cuddled up with Pantelaymin in front of the TV to watch the new episode of *Criminal Minds*.

Tobi barely noticed the commercial showing a woman walking hand in hand with a man and her young daughter among rich green foliage, and then sitting beside a beautiful waterfall. Soft music played while the sweet voice-over said: *this medicine could decrease ability to fight infections, including serious infections like tuberculosis, and these have occurred, as well as lymphoma and other malignancies.* Among the side effects was "death." The medicine was great for arthritis, though. To Tobi, the commercial was just another example of tycoons manipulating the beauty of the Earth to subliminally pray upon the emotional needs of unsuspecting humans so they would pressure their physicians to prescribe something that may or may not be right for them.

She pulled out her iPad and reread both messages from Troy. Why in the freak was he trying to wiggle back into her life now? He wrote that it was "urgent" that they speak. What could be urgent after nearly a generation? The Troy she had known was not given to drama any more than she was, so why would he write something like that?

Chapter 28

Mannfort waited impatiently for Kazi to pick up the phone.

"Dah." Finally.

"Where have you been, Kazi?"

"Mannya! I have good news! We are expanding our catchment criteria and will have many more clients soon."

"Why is it you cannot get one lady doctor out of the way? It should not be so difficult. Do I have to do everything myself?"

"Nyet, Mannya. I have it all under control. I just have to convince the fat doctor we mean business. He was going a little soft. I think he will get the message when I explain it to him again."

"He was always soft, Kazi, he is a fool. That is why we used him. But maybe he outlives his usefulness now, if he is not very careful. We may have to go there and take care of it ourselves. We give him one more chance."

"Dah, dah, but listen, Mannya. We have brilliant idea. We get the patients to sign up before they are so sick. We just scare them by telling them where their condition is expected to go and how much it is likely to cost … it is brilliant. They can pay us for many years, maybe never even get sick at all. No claims to Kordec, just big premiums!"

"You think people are that stupid?"

"They are, Mannya, it is already working!"

Chapter 29

The week went by quickly with no word from Tobi or Inspector Bent, so Troy was not able to leave. He felt antsy just waiting around, but after having spilled his guts to the guy, he tried to be patient. He consoled himself that the Australian police had sizable resources for discovery that he did not have, and he wanted as much information as he could get before heading home. Troy was also not confident he could get through the airport without being detained; Bent could have easily put out an alert for him.

He should have been back at work at least a week ago, and his emails were piling up. He had told his board he was doing some examinations of the Great Barrier Reef, and in fact, he did do several dives. He noted the strikingly increased bleaching of the reef over his last visit four years ago. He had heard how the heat wave of 2016 had done colossal damage, but the sensitive algae that once lived in the coral had been replaced by a heartier species now. The coral was starting to recover, so he was not prepared for the extent of the damage. It still looked like nearly half the reef was gone. He was appalled.

Humans traipse all over the planet without any consideration of what devastation they leave behind, Troy thought. He firmly believed that humans were put on this Earth to be its caretakers, not its conquerors. That was exactly why he had named his foundation "Executors for Our Earth." It was the responsibility of humans to care for the Earth and for life in all its forms, and he did not understand the people who thought accruing wealth was more important, as if they could buy clean air or clean water once it was all gone. There was a reason she was called Mother Earth, the planet that nurtured and sustained them all, without regard to race, conscience, or even species. How she must be crying.

Troy came out of the water and brought his dive gear back to Tobi's Dive Shop. He had decided to keep the business running, sponsored by his foundation, and had interviewed a few locals for the day-to-day upkeep. How could he close a shop named "Tobi's"? Bent had given his approval and offered to assist with transfer of title even after Troy left, since the shop had belonged to Reuben and there was no one else to claim it. It had always been a sort of unofficial not for profit. Reuben had only taken enough income to pay for his rent and utilities. He had bought his inventory wholesale and sold it for little more than cost and was known for giving stuff away. Troy was setting it up so that all revenue generated would be funneled into efforts aimed at restoring the Reef.

Missy and her brother Patrick were running the business end for now. They hadn't found anyone experienced enough to lead dives or teach classes yet, but they rented and sold gear and refilled tanks, so Troy put them on payroll. Missy had gotten down on her hands and knees and scrubbed Marcus's blood off the floor, for which Troy would be eternally grateful. He put his tank down near the compressor to be refilled and placed the rest of his gear onto the counter.

"It's a sad sight, right?" Patrick said.

Troy took off his buoyancy compensator and put his weight belt in the crate on the floor. "You know, you read, you see pictures, you hear reports ... but it's not the same as going down and seeing for yourself. I thought it was recovering better with the more resilient algae transplanted into the coral." He shook his head. "I wanted to cry."

"We all do," Patrick said, "but it is actually looking a bit better than it did two years ago."

Missy walked over to take Troy's fins and mask. "Thank you for keeping the dive shop open. It means a lot to all of us, like a part of Robain is still with us. He was one of the kindest men I ever knew. He saved my life." She swallowed and looked down.

Troy saw her anguish. He was feeling hypersensitive these days. "It's not your fault, you know. That's just how he was. And he had heart disease before he came here that was going to get him sooner or later. No one lives forever."

Missy took his wet gear and walked to the back. Troy looked questioningly at Patrick.

"She hasn't been right since that day. And she's always had some psychological issues. She's been on meds for a year now, but I'm not sure they help; she gets really sad. She took Robain's death hard, and now, with Marco *murdered* … she's scared. We don't see that stuff around here," he whispered. "The worst we get is a robbery, and it usually involves tourists, never *us*."

"You know, she probably saw the killer," Troy whispered back. "I wonder if she remembers anything about him."

"Yes, we know," Patrick said quietly. "Inspector Bent has talked to her three times. I keep telling him she's very fragile and he has to tread lightly. And now she's scared the killer might come back for her, but Bent thinks he left the country already."

"There's something I didn't tell the inspector." Troy and Patrick both jumped at Missy's voice, unaware that she had been listening.

"What's that?" Troy asked gently.

"I saw him that day before he came here to the dive shop with that stupid laptop of his. He was at the table on the beach first and then up at the bar, smoking a cigar and drinking beer, and that's when he started looking at me funny. I felt him before I saw him, he was staring. He wasn't holding a computer then, he was stroking his beer bottle. And it was like ... like he was undressing me with his eyes. I felt like I wanted to get my shirt on bad. And then the storm started blowing in, so I came up quickly, and I went straight to Marco. Who leaves a computer on a beach table if it's so important?"

"Good question," Troy said. "Someone cocky enough to think nature can't hurt him."

"Yup," Patrick said. "Rolly said the guy told him his name was Boris and gave him a couple hundred bucks to make sure no one messed with his stuff, but Rolly didn't feel obliged to tell him about the afternoon rains. It seemed like the guy didn't know our weather patterns. He was an arrogant sort." Patrick snorted in disgust.

"Rolly is the bartender?" Troy asked.

Missy and Patrick both nodded.

"He acted like he should be able to buy anything," Missy said. "A real jerk."

"Did you see him before that day? Maybe in town?" Troy asked Missy.

She squinted her eyes in concentration. "I don't think so, I think I would have remembered. He had that thing about him, like he owned everyone and everything."

Patrick nodded to Troy. "How much longer will you be in town?"

"I don't know. As soon as Bent tells me he doesn't need me here anymore, I guess. Not much longer. I have to bring Robain's things to his sister Tobi."

"Is that who this place is named after? I always wondered, but Robain would just smile mischievously when I asked."

"I will be sorry when you are gone," Missy said quietly.

Troy took her hand between both of his and squeezed gently.

He left them to take his evening run on the beach. He'd been doing three miles both at sunrise and sunset, just to siphon off the nervous energy he could barely contain. It also gave him some respite from his incessant thoughts.

At dinner, he went over his last conversations with Reuben in his mind again, until his head hurt. He felt like he was being sucked slowly into quicksand.

Chapter 30

Blaise Kavandor sat at his desk, going over the paperwork one more time. He had been on the US Senate Committees on Health, Education, Labor, and Pensions for five years, and he had just been asked to chair the next Roundtable Subcommittee on Small Business Health Plans. There were multiple items on the subcommittee agenda, but he kept coming back to one specific insurance company that was up for review. It was ironic because his Russian "friends" had just demanded another large payment from him.

The American Medical Association and several state medical societies had recently voiced questions about Kordec Insurance, and whether it was being fair and reasonable to American patients. They suggested putting a cap on the premiums that could be charged, as many families were suffering undue hardship to pay these premiums for individuals who were not expected to live long enough to benefit from them. Kordec contended that was up to the individuals who optioned to buy the plan, but the AMA argued the insured were being misled.

Kavandor hung in the balance. He could approve discussion of the plan or find a reason to postpone it for another roundtable meeting. He looked again at the text message on his phone.

It is that time of year again.
Remember your wife and your constituents.

A lifetime ago, or so it seemed, he had been less careful with his indiscretions. It took some explaining to his wife Lauren, but luckily syphilis was a disease that could lie dormant for decades before manifesting, and he could have easily contracted it before they had even met. That was probably not the case, but it didn't matter. He might not have even known about the syphilis if he hadn't also gotten the drip. *That* was unmistakable and could have lost him his marriage and the election. He had himself treated before he touched her again, and since, he had learned to cover up or have his partners tested first. The women were fine with that; after all, who wouldn't want to sleep with the senator from Utah? He made sure they received their perks, except that lately his affairs were becoming more treacherous with the whole "#MeToo" movement. And yet, a little danger made it all the more delectable.

Lauren had been tested for everything, but she only needed treatment for syphilis, and he had made sure to double his flower orders and jewelry gifts. She hadn't been much interested in sex even in those days, anyway, so it worked out well. But blast these Russian guys, and however they had found him out. He'd been paying them forty grand a year since to keep his meanderings quiet.

He might never have known that Kordec was connected to his blackmailers, but they had decided having a senator in their pocket was useful and he had been pressured into giving the green light for their insurance agency to operate in the States. He didn't learn the details until he was so far in over his head, there was nothing he could do without incriminating himself. They also made sure he knew how easy it was for them to terminate anyone who did not comply, and all the while, he was supposed to keep paying them. He'd been entangled in this sticky web for nearly twenty long years, unable to break free.

But now, they needed *him*, didn't they? He could bury this investigation for them under mounds of paperwork, or let it play itself out on the roundtable floor. Wasn't that worth forty grand a year?

He sent a text message back.

We should talk. Looks like you need help. I can help you.

He regretted it as soon as he'd sent it. He should have been less assertive and said simply that he'd noticed they might have a problem, and he could try to assist. Damn his impulsiveness. It always seemed to get him in trouble.

CHAPTER 31

Tobi hated Sundays. They always seemed busier than any other day of the week, even though the hours were shorter. She had not seen a rad tech on the schedule, so she was especially dreading it, but when she came in, she found Patty, Esther, and Travis. Maybe it wouldn't be a bad day after all.

"Hi, Dr. L." Travis said. "I heard you needed help today. Apparently, Janie quit."

"Really! Thank you! So she finally stopped threatening and just quit?"

"She got the job down the street from her," Esther said. "She was heading that way for a long time." Esther and Janie used to be good friends, but Janie had gotten weird at the end. She demanded her texts be answered immediately and generally wanted an unreasonable amount of attention at all hours of the day and night. They didn't speak to each other at all anymore.

"Snap-to Urgent Care? Those guys were bought out by the East Coast Hospital Conglomeration last year, so things may change for her there too," Tobi mused. "Right *now,* that hospital system is owned by doctors, but East Coast may be selling to a hedge fund."

Patty cocked her head sideways. "Where do you get this insider information, Dr. Lister?"

"I have connections," she winked. "I've been in this field for decades. So, I guess you aren't going to come over to us full-time?" Tobi asked Travis.

"I can't, doc. I have too much going for me at Cuttles Medical Associates."

"I know you do." Cuttles was a multispecialty group that rivaled B. Healthy, and Travis had just been promoted to Director of Radiological Services. Like so many medical practices, it had begun as a loose association of physicians who prided themselves on their autonomy and banded together for better bargaining power with insurance companies. They were trying to stay independent, but who knew how long it would be before they were forced to sell out to some corporate mogul?

"Did I hear something about us getting bought out by a hospital system too?" Esther asked.

"Maybe," Tobi said. "It should only happen. Not a buy out, but they're talking about a merger with Hospitals for Health. B. Healthy wants to use their name to back our services. Maybe things will improve if that happens. H for H is a monstrosity, but so far, anyway, it's owned and run by physicians, and they still hold quality of care as a priority."

"Hey," Esther said, "have you worked with Dr. Rufini lately? I filled in last week in the south shore office, and everyone is talking about him."

"He hasn't been here much, thankfully, and definitely not to see patients," Tobi said. "What are they saying?"

"That he's been acting peculiar. He hangs out in that office a lot, usually behind a closed door, and sometimes they hear him on the phone, yelling. Friday, he took Monica's tablet and said he'd made a mistake, but he wouldn't give it back. He told her to get another one and he would log her out."

"Was Monica okay with that?"

"She was ticked off, but she said she hadn't opened her email, so she didn't care."

"What about EveryScripts?" Tobi asked.

"Probably already timed her out."

The doors unlocked, and several patients walked in.

Byron was the first patient of the day.

"Good morning, my name is Dr. Lister. I hope you don't mind the mask. I'm wearing it with everyone now."

"No," Byron said, "not at all. You *should* wear it. I'm at death's door!"

"Oh, I'm so sorry. What's wrong?"

"It's this sinus infection. It started yesterday and is just getting steadily worse. I took Nyquil last night, and I'm a little better, but it won't go away. No, no fever. And I'm not achy; I don't think I have the flu."

She ended up treating him with just a nasal spray, and he seemed satisfied with that. I hope he never gets seriously ill, she thought. How would he manage?

There was a steady stream all day. Lunch was discussed, but never actually happened. By one-thirty, they were all getting hungry and a little irritable.

The office manager called. "Hi, Evelyn," Esther said. "I'm fine, how are you?" A long minute passed, and Esther's face darkened. "Well, I don't know. We're pretty busy here. We have three new patients who just arrived, and it's been very steady. We're up to twenty-three and it's not even two o'clock. Can't you find anyone else?" Another silence. "Well, Travis just brought back a fifty-three year old with chest pain, and she doesn't look good. We need to do an EKG, and who knows what else. And then we have two more who need x-rays, so that takes Travis off the floor. It's really not fair to leave us short-staffed, and it's not safe for the patients! And then you want us to get people in and out quickly, right? That can't happen if you're always pulling staff away. How can you expect ...."

Esther stared at the phone, and then slammed it down. Tobi was shocked, Esther was always polite and soft-spoken.

"Evelyn wants me to go to the south shore office to help out. They're even busier than we are, and she doesn't have anyone else to send. Instead of hiring more staff, they just spread us around like peanut butter on toast."

"Haven't they been telling you guys for the last eight months that the shortage of staff problem is getting fixed?" Travis asked. "I'm glad this isn't my main bread and butter."

"Yeah, any week now." Tobi looked at Esther. "It doesn't matter, it's not happening. I can't spare you right now. Let's get our chest pain patient into the cardiac room and taken care of first, and later I will call Evelyn and have a word. Would you get an EKG set up while I'm getting her history and doing an exam? Then Patty can call EMS while we start an IV. She'll need oxygen, aspirin, and nitro spray."

Tobi had lived the evolution of urgent care. When it had started thirty years ago, it was with sincere, caring physicians, who opened stand-alone minor emergency centers as an alternative to a standard private practice. In those days, they were staffed by doctors and nurses, receptionists, x-ray techs, and billers, much as one would expect, and there were very few around. Over time, and as insurance reimbursements across the field of medicine dropped, RNs gave way to LPNs and then finally to medical assistants, because they were cheaper, and the rad techs were given the dual role of either receptionist or medical assistant, because not every patient needed an x-ray so they had a lot of down time. Billing had mostly moved off site.

In many companies now, it was one provider (who could be a doctor, physician assistant, or nurse practitioner), a medical assistant, a rad tech, and a receptionist. Some models had a rad tech and an MA, with either of them doubling as receptionist, and in some ridiculous cases, it was just the provider and one other staff member. Some companies had started employing scribes to help the providers work faster, as it was certainly cheaper than hiring more clinicians. Most other companies added more support staff when their offices got busy, but B. Healthy couldn't even staff the minimum, and would not schedule a regular second provider unless a site was averaging fifty-five or more patients per day.

Having limited support on such busy days was torture for the staff and annoying to the patients—to say nothing of being unsafe when there was an emergency. It was the more ironic, because Urgent Care was finally being recognized as a specialty of sorts, and the insurance companies had actually paid more in the last few years for urgent care visits than they had for primary care visits. Yet they operated with less than half the staff of a primary care office. It was getting harder and harder to find the human connection. Even the patients were left feeling swindled.

The woman with chest pain felt better after the nitro spray, and Tobi sent her out by ambulance on aspirin, oxygen, and an IV. Then she called Evelyn.

"Hi, Dr. Lister. How are you?"

"Hi, Evelyn. Esther has to stay here today. We are much too busy for you to leave me with just Travis and Patty. We just sent out a cardiac patient, and we have a full waiting room. You can't leave us understaffed like that. It's not fair to us and it's not safe for the patients. I told her not to go."

"Oh, isn't Suleman with you today too?"

"No, Evelyn, he isn't. And if he were, it would be more appropriate to utilize him as a scribe, not an MA."

"Oh, I'm sorry. I thought you had him there. That's fine then, she should stay."

Tobi hung up and told Esther.

"But Dr. L., she *makes* the schedule! How does she not know?"

Patty came over. "She knew. She was just hoping no one would challenge her."

Chapter 32

When Troy went back into Bent's office, he was told the inspector was out of town for the next couple of days. He felt like he would burst with frustration. Bent did not seem to need him for any further questioning, so why had he asked him to stay? Although, it had hardly seemed like a request. He felt an enormous pressure to leave, despite his reticence to confront Tobi.

Troy resolved that as soon as Bent returned, he would ask if there was any new information, and state that he was taking his leave of Queensland. If Bent wanted to keep him, he would have to arrest him, and Troy knew there were no grounds for that; it would have happened already if there were. He went for his three-mile run on the beach, and then dipped into the crisp water to cool off and sat down on the sand to meditate. It had been a while, but it was a discipline he would never forget.

Troy had trained years ago on how to silence his thoughts and transcend his physicality, but he had not invoked this mind exercise at all in the last few weeks. It was like he had regressed to the time before he had learned to master himself, but he was ready to recover and prepare to leave.

Troy's family roots were somewhat unusual. He was from an ancient line of Sephardic Jews who had fled to Italy during the Spanish Inquisition, and they were unique in that they had maintained the Ladino language and culture while living alongside their Italian neighbors. Even after escaping to the United States at the onset of the Second World War, his parents had still spoken Ladino at home the way many Ashkenazi Jews spoke Yiddish, and Troy had never quite felt like he fit into American Jewish culture. His family customs differed from common Sephardi, as most Spanish Jews had emigrated further to the Middle East or south to Morocco centuries earlier, and the Ashkenazi from eastern Europe did not know what to do with him at all. Although he felt a deep connection to the God of Israel, he avoided synagogues and the conventional practice of religion.

Both of Troy's parents had died during his junior year in college, in the Chicago Loop derailment in February of 1977. He had been an only child and always a bit of a loner. At the age of twenty, he had felt completely lost. He had one uncle, a successful attorney who had been struggling with lung cancer, and wasn't expected to make it more than another few months. Uncle Franklin had told Troy to stay in school and that he would cover Troy's tuition at Cornell University. While Troy studied geology and meteorology, Franklin sued the Chicago Transit Authority on Troy's behalf, and eleven months later, Troy was awarded $3.1 million dollars. It was the day Franklin died.

Troy had graduated on paper, but skipped the ceremony. There was no one to come anyway. For a couple of years afterward, he traveled the world looking for—whatever he was looking for. He didn't even know what that was. Eventually, he found himself in India and studied for sixteen months with the Dalai Lama, and finally he found peace.

In Tibet, Troy had connected with the Earth and the creatures upon her, and he found solace in his solitude. He was befriended by a stray, deaf, nine-year-old Rajapalayam dog that he named Raj. They were both lonely and aimless, adrift in a world that made no sense to them, but they learned to love and trust each other. Troy began to look at the world through the dog's eyes, through a mind that could see, smell, taste, and feel but could not hear anything at all. He imagined what that must be like and experimented with how different the world seemed without sound. He plugged his ears with beeswax and looked at body language, and found it was often at odds with spoken words. He saw the butcher's menacing movements toward the chicken, which were otherwise clouded by the man's gentle, reassuring voice. Troy reached out with his other senses to connect with the essence of his environment and felt the vibration of the surf with his skin instead of hearing the waves with his ears, translating his surroundings without the audial cues that influenced how he would have otherwise interpreted what he saw.

There were definitely fewer distractions when he could not hear, and it had heightened his other sensibilities. He felt like he was able to grasp a truer nature of things. He began to fathom many lies in life, unpleasant truths that were obscured by clever discourse, and to see things as they really were.

When Raj died a year later, a part of Troy had wanted to die with him, but he felt he owed it to the dog to go on. Raj had had so little but had given him so much, that he wanted to help vulnerable animals everywhere. He was no longer satisfied living in his own head, and he left his inward search and turned outward to find ways to rescue defenseless, tortured creatures, and also to heal the Earth that sustained them all.

He started his foundation, Executors for Our Earth, and it had grown from an organization committed to animal rescue and protesting the deforestation of rain forests to a global agency that sponsored promising initiatives, like using compost such as orange peels to regenerate soil in burned out regions of the Amazon. Recently, they were examining unique rocks that absorbed carbon dioxide directly from the air, and the transplantation of alternative breeds of algae to revitalize coral reefs, like the Great Barrier Reef. The foundation had taken on its own life, and had many affluent contributors, under which it had prospered.

Troy was pleased with the pace of his accomplishments, recognizing the task he had undertaken was monumental, but he had grown restless with the paperwork, however digitized it had become. He was not a man to stay behind a desk, so after a couple of years, he had given over daily management responsibilities of the foundation to his oldest and most trusted friend, Mack Elberg. Mack had studied environmental science and later earned his MBA, so Troy felt free to travel and investigate novel ways to replenish the forests and the atmosphere that was being ravaged by greedy profiteers. It also allowed him to wander and enjoy firsthand the Earth that he loved so much.

It had been on one of those trips in August, 1996, that he met Tobi and Benny. Orcas were common sightings in Puget Sound, and when his travels landed him in the San Juan Islands, instead of taking the private charter he had been offered for free by a benefactor, he decided to join a small boat tour leaving from Washington State's Friday Harbor on the Western Prince II, with no one he knew. He had recently ended yet another relationship and he wanted to be invisible. Just a guy, not the CEO of a huge save the Earth foundation. He could not seem to find anyone who understood him and his need for God and nature. Women seemed mostly interested in his checkbook.

He remembered the boat anchoring in the sound at the location of the last whale sightings, and the smell of brine and motor oil as the engine cut. He felt the cool breeze in the bright sunshine as he walked around the side of the boat, and that's when he saw little Benny. The boy was barely three feet high and bursting with excitement.

"Look, Mommy, another one! And another one! And another one! Look, Mommy! Another BIG ONE! They are spy hopping, Mommy, all of them are coming to look at *us*!" Benny collided with Troy as he jumped up and down pointing at the whales.

"Benjamin! Be careful!" Tobi had said.

"It's fine, no worries." Troy smiled and turned to little Benjamin. "Pretty cool, huh?"

"Yes! The *orca whales* are talking and they tell each other where to find the *humans*. They come to see *us*!"

Tobi had laughed and said "it does indeed appear that way," as more whales seemed to surface every few minutes. "Sorry about your foot," she turned to look at Troy and their eyes met for the first time, and locked.

In retrospect, Troy had fallen in love with them both right then. The woman was kind, solitary, and sublime, and the boy was full of life and joy and newness. He chattered away to Troy ceaselessly for the whole trip.

"That is an orca whale," Benjamin pointed. "They are also called killer whales. Did you know there are two kinds of whales? There are *baleen* whales that have no teeth and there are whales that do have teeth. Now, the orca whale has teeth and so does the sperm whale, but the humpback whale doesn't have any teeth, and neither does the right whale." He shook his head vehemently for emphasis. "And *all* the whales are mammals like us, none of them are fish, and the mommies take care of the babies."

Troy was startled. "How old are you?"

"I am five years old." He pushed his palm straight out in front of him with all five digits hyperextended.

The tour had gone by quickly with his little narrator, and Troy forgot all about his own loneliness. He was very aware of Tobi watching them together with amusement. She kept a distance and allowed her son to enjoy his adventure and his new audience, but was clearly ready to pounce if he were threatened in any way. When they got off the boat, he asked if he could buy them dinner. Tobi had stiffened immediately and started to decline, but she was no match for her son's exuberant acceptance.

They talked for two hours over dinner in a little outdoor café about animals, endangered species, and the forces of nature, and by the time the check came, Troy knew he'd found two kindred spirits and his soulmate. Tobi insisted on paying for herself and Benny, and he let her—that time. He knew instinctively that if he pressed the issue, it would push her away. That in itself, separated her from the other women he had known.

He had almost stopped believing he would ever find another person who respected the vast energy of the universe, connected in some small way to the holy forces of nature as he did, and was open to novel ways of seeing the world. It felt like the three of them had been a family since the beginning of Time.

After dinner, Benny had quieted down and started to fade, looking like he had worn himself out, suddenly the five year old he professed to be. Until the waiter tripped over a napkin on the floor and the hot coffee he was carrying fell from his tray. The cup cracked and the coffee splashed onto Benny's wrist. He wailed and ran into his mother's arms.

Troy felt terrible and immediately offered to take them to the hospital. Tobi looked carefully at the small burn on her son's wrist, and said it was okay, she'd take care of it, and asked the waiter for some ice. Troy protested he might need a doctor, but Tobi firmly declined. "I am a doctor," she'd said.

She ultimately did give him her phone number, but Troy knew it was at least partly because she did not ever expect to hear from him.

Three thousand miles was far away in her world, but for Troy, the distance had been nothing.

Troy settled into the Port Douglas sand, the memory of that day hovering behind his eyes. He let his muscles relax completely, feeling the pull of the Earth below and the surge of the surf beyond, and allowed himself to dissolve into the pulsations of the Coral Sea. He became one with the wind and the tide and let himself—whatever made him Troy—expand. He tapped the energy he felt and fed off it, welcoming in the raw power, emptying his mind and feeling the life force of the planet.

Why was it that he could attain such transcendence best when he was suffering and in pain? It seemed that only when his soul was broken, did life feel truly authentic.

Chapter 33

After EMS left, Tobi went in to see Jenna in room two, a self-pay patient who had been out of work for the last several months after a bicycle accident. She was a single parent and was unable to afford COBRA insurance anymore, so her kids were now covered on Healthy New York, but she had nothing for herself. She was there for bronchitis and was wheezing with every breath.

"I'm going to give you a breathing treatment to open up your lungs and then I'll get you some medications to use at home. I'll see if we have any samples of inhalers in the back," Tobi said.

"No! I can't afford anything more than the fee I already paid, please! That's why I haven't come in sooner," she said. "The kids need boots and gloves, and I can't waste money like that."

Tobi was floored. "I think it's only twenty-five bucks, let me check."

"Twenty-five dollars is grocery money, you don't understand. I already paid $110 to be seen and I have no more. But if you have some samples, I would very much appreciate that."

Tobi stood frozen for a moment. Jenna's oxygen saturation was only ninety-four percent. She was compensating for now based on her general good health, but that wouldn't last.

"You know what? Just take the breathing treatment. I'll ask the manager to waive the fee; if they won't, I'll pay for it myself." She walked out of the office before Jenna could even respond.

Travis looked at her when she asked Esther to set up the nebulizer. "Will you get in trouble for that? She will get billed, you know."

"Then I will pay for it. Geez, it's twenty-five bucks. I spent more than that on dinner last Friday night. I can't let her walk out of here like that. You know, it wasn't that long ago that physicians routinely treated a certain percentage of patients as charity. We expected to. It's only now that we have to answer to some corporate money monger who needs to pad his pockets with every possible dollar that we can't make compassionate decisions on our own anymore."

It took a half hour, but ultimately, Tobi got permission to waive the fee as a "one time courtesy." It felt like a warning not to try this again, but at least she got that. Maybe she had shamed corporate by saying she had already started the treatment and would pay for it herself if need be. Geez, the medication in the nebulizer had to cost all of four or five dollars, maybe less, and the nebulizer itself had been paid for a hundred times over. It was less than $100 brand new.

Not to say that they should treat patients for free. Even before she worked in corporate medicine, Tobi had found that some people tended to think they were entitled to free care even at a private facility. Even when they had just dropped seventy-five bucks on a manicure, they'd come in complaining about their fifteen dollar copay. They did not recognize that there was significant overhead in running a practice. Staff salaries were the biggest payouts, and the reason B. Healthy operated so lean, and there was also the price of rent, utilities, medications, equipment, and supplies, not even mentioning malpractice insurance. All the costs of operating a business of any kind. Still, she should be able to make exceptions for hardship cases without feeling like she had just committed a crime. As Tobi had told the on-call manager she texted for permission, she had to be able to look at herself in the mirror at night. Even the manager did not have the authority to render a decision, although she was in favor, and had to run it by corporate first.

Jenna's lungs were clear when she left, her oxygen saturation was up to one hundred percent, and Tobi had found a sample inhaler in the back closet to give her. Jenna was extremely grateful, and Tobi was sure the positive recommendations and repeat business she had just "produced" for B. Healthy would more than make up for the couple of bucks they'd lost. She congratulated herself for having gone over Evelyn's head from the get-go. Tobi was sure she would have gotten a flat out no; Evelyn was so deep in corporate's pocket, it was ridiculous.

Samantha had signed in at 2:00 p.m. and waited about forty-five minutes before Tobi got in to see her. She was a kind looking woman in her late forties, and she walked into the exam room in a jerky fashion, leaning heavily on her cane and dragging her left leg.

"Hi, I'm Dr. Lister, how are you? I'm sorry about the wait."

"I'm very well, thank you," Samantha said. "No worries, I saw the ambulance. This is nothing, really. I just cut my finger on the cat food can this morning. It bled a lot, so I thought it might need a stitch."

Tobi confirmed her medical history. Samantha was forty-six years old with multiple sclerosis. Her cane was balanced next to her where she sat on the exam table. Samantha saw Tobi looking at it.

"Yes, I haven't been able to walk without my 'buddy' here for years; sometimes I can't walk with it, either, but luckily that's not too often." She smiled. "I've also been hospitalized a few times for asthma, but happily, I'm not allergic to cats, since I've taken up their cause." She fiddled with the cane. "I started feeding a few of the neighborhood strays, and pretty soon, I guess the word got out. They all come to my back door now, and meow like crazy. I feel so bad for them, it's so cold out. But I can't take any more inside. I've already got three. I just took in little Mozart last week, he's only a kitten. This," she raised her bloody finger, "is from his food can."

Tobi came alongside the exam table to remove the bandage. "How many cats do you have?"

"Outside? Must be fifteen or twenty. I had a bunch of them spayed or neutered, and last week, I put a little heated cat house on the porch, now that the temperatures are below freezing. I don't know, I guess I'm a little crazy. I just can't stand to watch poor helpless little creatures suffer."

"The world needs more people like you," Tobi smiled.

"I don't really understand people who abandon them. The kitties are so appreciative too. Especially when I put the heater out there … I find when I do something to help a little creature or a person in need, it makes *me* feel so much better. It gets me out of my pity-pot, you know? I could go crazy, if all I thought about were the things I *can't* do anymore. So maybe, in a way, I'm actually being selfish."

"Not at all," Tobi said. "When you help someone, you always help yourself too. Kindness is its own reward. If you use one candle to light another, you don't diminish the light of the first, but you end up with double the light. So you're just spreading light in the world, and it's lighting up your own life in the process." Tobi thought of how much better she felt because she had gotten Jenna her nebulizer treatment.

"As for your finger," Tobi continued, "I think we can just glue it and spare you the stitches. It will hold just as well."

After she had cleaned, repaired, and dressed the wound, Tobi said again, "Thank you for being so patient with our wait time today, Samantha. I think it's wonderful how you take care of the little ones."

"Thank you for fixing my finger, this was a very pleasant visit." Samantha shook her head. "The wait was no bother, I'm sure your other patients were in much worse shape than me."

Esther gazed after Samantha as she left. "That patient was so sweet. I wish all our patients could be that way. And she doesn't have it easy; did you see her hobble out with that cane?"

"Her 'buddy,' she called it," Tobi said. "Yeah, people who know what it really means to suffer seem to be way more tolerant and caring than people who have it easy. Sometimes we need to get bashed over the head to notice we are all human and all just trying to make our way in the world."

Twenty minutes later, there were again numerous people waiting to be seen. The next man called up to the front desk held his hand over his eyes and spoke slowly and softly. "My name is Bartholomew. Please, help me. I was cleanin' … I think I splashed the bleach in my eyes. They burn something very fierce." He wore an old brown plaid work shirt and had a thick Haitian accent. His hands were dry and cracked.

Esther took him straight to the back, and started irrigating his eyes, while Patty got his information. Tobi did a corneal stain and found chemical burns to both eyes, thirty and fifty percent. She had numbed his eyes with tetracaine, but he needed an ophthalmologist as soon as possible.

Tobi explained to Bartholomew, "Alkaline burns like this are the worst kind. The burn continues to do damage even after the bleach has been washed away. You need to see an ophthalmologist, but none are open on Sunday afternoon, and only a few hospitals out here actually have ophtho departments. How did you get here? Is there someone who can drive you?"

Bartholomew nodded slowly. "The boss drove me here, but my sister is comin'. She's goin' to take me back to the Bronx, where I live."

"Bartholomew, you need to go straight to the hospital emergency room, okay? Even though your eyes feel better right now, that pain killer I put in them will wear off in about an hour." Tobi poked her head out the door, for once appreciative of the circular layout of her office that allowed her to glance up front. "Patty, would you call Montefiore Hospital and make sure they have ophthalmology available?"

"I'm on it, Dr. L."

Bartholomew was on his way with his sister when Tobi walked into Mrs. Jensen's exam room. The patient was pacing back and forth in front of her rapid strep test. "I'm sorry for the delay," Tobi said, "we had an emergency."

Mrs. Jensen snapped at her. "Yes, I know. I saw that guy come in—he took my seat! And then you took him first. Why didn't he just go to the emergency room? If he had an emergency, he should have gone there! Why didn't you just send him *there*? Why did you have to waste time seeing him here, when he had to leave anyway?"

Tobi just stared at her for a second, trying to keep her jaw in it's appropriate position in her face. "You're right," she finally said. "He should have gone straight to the hospital, but once he comes in to my office, I'm responsible. I don't turn away people in need."

"Well, *I* need to know if I have strep or not. Just tell me if my test is positive or negative. It's like a pregnancy test, right? Can you just read it for me? I don't need to be examined, I told them I didn't want my blood pressure taken. Why did she waste time taking my blood pressure? What has that got to do with anything? I need to get out of here; I have things to do!"

Tobi felt her own blood pressure rising. The strep test was negative.

She went back up front, knowing she had just gotten another zero that would paint her as a horrible physician and found a text message from Ellie.

Hey, I'm in the south shore office and Rufini is here. He just took Monica's tablet again. WTF. He went in to the back with it. Monica is pissed!

Tobi wrote back.

Why doesn't she call him out on it?
And she should email Steve.
What are you doing in that office, anyway?

Ellie replied.

They shorted me a shift, so this is make up.

Tobi went back to work. She was too busy to get involved in the drama, but what *was* Ismar's deal with stealing tablets?

Morgan had been pacing in his room and stuck his head out for the fifth time to ask how long it would be. "I checked an hour before I came in, and this office had no wait, but there were five people in front of me when I got here, and now I've been waiting over an hour. You even took someone before me who came after I did. How does this happen? Look, I just need some drops for my eye, I'm sure it's just a sty."

"She'll be with you very soon," Travis told him.

When Tobi got in the room, he looked like he might boil over. "Yes, sir, we did have about a ten-minute period earlier where there was no one in the waiting room, although the exam rooms were still full. We had two very urgent matters that set us back a bit. In this setting, we can never tell how many patients may come in before you get here, and I still have to take care of the emergencies first. I would do the same for you if, God forbid, you needed immediate attention."

He quieted but stayed angry for the remainder of the visit. He did indeed have a sty, and she treated him with an ophthalmic antibiotic ointment and he left.

Later, Patty reported that Dr. Milton had called and told them that Morgan had told his housekeeper—who was also Dr. Milton's babysitter—to tell Dr. Milton, to tell Dr. Lister, that he hadn't realized there was only one doctor on, and he felt bad for having been so difficult.

"That Dr. Milton," Esther said, "she's connected to the whole neighborhood!"

Chapter 34

They were packed up and headed for the door when Rufini showed up. The four of them glanced at each other and Travis let him in.

"Hello, you are all done for the night? See you tomorrow, then." He nodded to Travis, Patty and Esther, then looked pointedly at Tobi. "I can speak to you for a moment?"

Tobi searched desperately for a reason to say no, but she wasn't fast enough. He walked in and put his case down on the counter. Esther looked at her apologetically, but Travis didn't move. Tobi knew he sensed her dread.

"We can wait with you guys, it's no bother," he said.

Rufini shook his head. "No, I don't want to keep you. Don't worry, I will walk Dr. Lister to her car. She will be fine."

Travis looked at her for a long minute. He must be completely psychic, Tobi thought, or else I wear my feelings on my scrubs. When he couldn't come up with a good reason to stay, he nodded at her and glanced toward the parking lot for a brief second before he left.

Locked in an empty office with Ismar was the very last place she wanted to be.

"What's up, Ismar?"

"Yes, so, *Tobiii.*" He paused, and abruptly, Tobi *saw* him. Despite the below freezing weather, there was a thin layer of perspiration on his upper lip, his left brow twitched, and she could smell his sweat. His left hand trembled ever so slightly, holding a package of pastry and his right was resting on something she could not see inside his briefcase.

"I know we have not been, like, social, but I think this is not good. We should be friendly more, don't you think? Here, I brought you some baklava. Peace offering. You like sweets?"

"Now isn't a good time, Ismar. It's been a long day and I need to get home."

Ismar put the baklava nearly under her nose. "Who do you live with, Tobi? Do you live alone?"

Fire alarms went off in her head, and she brushed the pastries away. He always gave her the creeps, but this was ridiculous.

"Ah, I don't think my living situation is really company business, Ismar. Why do you want to know?"

"I told you, Tobiii, I want us to be, like, friends. You started to tell me about your family. You have a brother, right?"

"No."

"I'm sure you said you have a brother."

"I said I *had* a brother. He died nineteen years ago."

"That's terrible. How did he die?"

"Why do you care, Ismar? It's not something I discuss with people. It was many years ago."

"Why not?"

"Because it's painful! And irrelevant. Look, I—I appreciate the overture, but I really need to get home. Have a good night." Tobi spun on her sneaker and nearly ran for the door, leaving Ismar to close up. It was all she could do not to look behind her as she practically sprinted into her car and locked the doors. She looked to her left and saw Travis sitting in his CRV with the motor running. He smiled at her and nodded, and she blew him a kiss. He waited until she pulled out of the parking lot and turned onto the road before leaving, but Tobi still didn't feel safe as she drove down the turnpike, and it was an effort to stay within ten miles-per-hour of the speed limit.

Why was she so freaked out? She tried to analyze her reaction as she put distance between herself and the office. It made no sense to her, she had been compelled purely by some gut instinct, to get the hell out of there. She replayed the scene in her head and kept dwelling on his hand in the briefcase, like he was holding onto something.

This is mad, she thought. I'm losing my mind. He's an ass, but he wouldn't do anything to hurt me physically. And he was just seen with me by Esther, Patty, and Travis, so how stupid would that be? He'd be caught in an instant.

She thought about calling Steve Chagall, but what would she say? It *was* inappropriate for Ismar to have come to the office to see her when everyone was gone. And then to offer her food … ugh. She would never eat anything he gave her. Ever.

She had to stop for gas on the way home, she was almost on empty, but she chose a more expensive station that was full service, so she didn't have to get out of her car. She kept the doors locked and only cracked the passenger window two inches to hand off her credit card.

Christmas decorations lined the strip mall across the street, and it reminded her that Hanukkah was around the corner. Troy used to contend that while every Jewish holiday was a celebration of a major miracle, we often walked sightless every day among unacknowledged miracles that were equally mind blowing, failing to acknowledge the improbable phenomenon that we are mobile, intelligent, breathing human beings who can feel love and appreciate beauty in a universe ruled by entropy. Troy saw God in the blazing colors of a sunset, the first blossoming of a delicate flower, and the chirping of newborn baby birds. It was one of the things she loved most about him ….

Geez, why was she thinking of him now? Still, she knew he was the reason she often listed the gifts of each day, and the strokes of "highly-coincidental good fortune"—otherwise known as miracles. Like the tree that had fallen during the storm last winter and missed her car by eight inches, *and* her homeowners association had it cleared away in less than three hours. Today she counted Travis's just happening to be there to give her a sense of security, making a clean escape from Ismar and the office tonight, and the woman with chest pain who had made it safely to the hospital.

For years, she had prayed every day for the miracle that Reuben was still alive somewhere out there, and that she might find him.

She arrived at her little community and smiled at the guard at the gatehouse who let her in. But when she finally pulled into her driveway, she had another flash of irrational fear when she noticed someone in her rear view mirror who she did not recognize, strolling leisurely down the street. Why would anyone go walking in this frigid weather? Then she saw the dog and understood, but she stayed locked in her car for a full minute, telling herself she was nuts. They couldn't get in if they didn't belong here, she told herself. Finally, she called Chloe, but it went to voicemail.

So, Tobi called Reggie, another friend from her synagogue. He and his wife Lynn were good friends, and Reggie was almost like a surrogate brother, but she usually texted with him or saw him Friday nights at services. She never called.

"Hi, Tobi. Everything okay?"

"I don't know, Reggie, I'm being ridiculous. I'm sitting in my car in the driveway and I'm afraid to get out. I feel like someone might have followed me—which makes no sense, I know, since my community is gated."

"Tobi! Stay in your car. Call the police and I'll be right over."

"No, don't do that … I think I'm just imagining things. I've been really skittish lately, for no good reason, I'm sure. Too many *Criminal Minds* episodes, maybe. Just … would you stay on the phone with me until I get inside?"

"Of course, but that doesn't sound like the safest thing."

"I'm getting out of the car now." Tobi got out with her still full lunch bag and her purse, looking around furtively. The sky was inky black and the street was now deserted under the lamps. "Wow, it's slippery. Winter showed up when I wasn't watching."

"Yes, be careful."

Tobi got inside and locked the deadbolts. "Okay, I'm home and locked up. Thanks, Reggie. I feel pretty foolish right about now."

"Not a problem, kiddo, but I'm not getting off the line until you walk into every room and every closet. Did you check the garage?"

Tobi looked in the garage, behind the patio furniture, bicycle, and gardening tools, and then walked through the entire house with Reggie on the phone. Pantelaymin sat near the stairs, gazing at her curiously.

"Panni doesn't seem to be alarmed. If there were someone here, she'd probably be hiding."

"Unless he brought catnip with him. Did you check everywhere?"

"Everywhere. Thanks, Reg."

"Do you want me and Lynn to come over for a while?"

"No, I'm okay. I have to work again in the morning, and I'm beat. Thank you, though. I'm a little embarrassed …."

"Don't be. Coming Friday night?"

"Of course."

"Okay, I'll see you then. Call if you need *anything*."

Reggie hung up. She knew he was going to text her a few times a day now to make sure she was alright. She did feel embarrassed, but at least now, someone would be checking up on her.

Chapter 35

Ismar Rufini sat in his car down the street from his home with the defroster on. It was 10:05 p.m. He kept looking at the text message he had received, telling him to make himself available at 10:00 p.m. sharp. Finally, his phone rang.

"Dr. Rufini, it is you?"

"Yes." He licked his lips. The voice grated like pebbles on glass and the accent was thick, unmistakably Russian. I'm screwed, he thought. "Who is this?"

"That is not important. I am from the Project, that is all you need to know. Have you been investigating the doctor? What have you learned about her brother?"

Ismar's voice quavered. "She says her brother died many years ago."

"We believe her brother did not die many years ago. Come on, Dr. Rufini, what did you find out?"

"She believes he did, I'm sure of it. And she will not talk to me. She … she doesn't like me."

"That is too bad, Dr. Rufini, because we are not convinced. She has to go, and you are going to have to do it."

"Me? Why me? And why is her brother important?"

"That is not your business. Your business is to do what we tell you. You like your house, *dah*, Doctor? You like your money for your house, and your new beautiful wife?"

"I was thinking of maybe selling … it's … a very big house. You shouldn't have to give me so much money." Ismar's defroster was on full force, but the windows were still fogging up.

"The day we stop giving you money, Dr. Ismar, is the day you are dead. Haha, good joke, *nyet*? Doctor, you just get information to us, we all will be very happy. And the lady doctor. You get rid of her."

Ismar's voice squeaked. "I … I can't. I give you information. Lot of information. Lot of cases. But I can't kill …."

"What did you say, Dr. Ismar?" The voice was icy.

Ismar swallowed hard. "I can't kill. That is where I draw the line." He tried to sound confident but his voice shrilled.

"Mr. Ismar, you kill all the time. Every time you give us the name of someone who is terribly sick, someone we can insure, each time, you kill. You just don't want to get your hands dirty, *nyet*? It is too late for that. Remember, you owe us for solving your 'problem' in Turkey."

Ismar was silent.

"You have one week. If it is not done, bad things will happen."

The phone went dead. The only sound was the white noise from the heater. Ismar turned down the fan and cracked open the window. He put his head back and just tried to breathe.

How would he get himself out of this? His whole life was a saga of going from one disaster to another, but he had always managed to stay afloat before.

About ten years ago, he had made a terrible mistake. Doctors were not paid well in Turkey, so he took a side job—okay, he had known it was underhanded, but that was why it was so lucrative, right? He copied some documents onto a flash drive in Turkey and put it in the hands of Dmitri Medvedev's men, then President of Russia. He couldn't help but think now that had Putin been president, he would have been much more appreciative in the end. The documents were influential in establishing the pact for the Samsun-Ceyhan oil pipeline, from which Russia would have been the larger beneficiary. But the pact fell apart at the end of 2009, and Ismar was discovered and brought up on charges in Turkey. He had been looking at many years in prison—if he were lucky.

Some Russian oligarch had gotten him out, he never learned who, and had told him he was grateful for his service to his country, and set him up in New York. He helped Ismar get into an American medical residency program and start a new life. He gave him money and promised more, as long as Ismar would continue to give information if requested.

It seemed he'd had had no choice, even though he had to leave his family behind, a wife and two girls. Handing over information had seemed innocuous enough in the beginning, and it was something out of which he had made a secondary career, anyway. He was never told anyone's name, except that periodically, men from "the Project" asked for "favors." He was an owned man now, and it seemed his debt would never be paid in full. It was so unfair. He wouldn't have needed to be rescued if he hadn't helped the Russians to begin with.

Ismar knew the information he gave sometimes cost people their lives, but they were already very sick. And wasn't that the way of the world? But ... to kill someone with his own hands? Could he manage *that*?

Chapter 36

smar's words grated on Tobi. Had she said she "has" a brother? She never said that out loud, even though in her heart, she *knew* she had a brother still. Or so she had felt for ages. She realized abruptly that the feeling had finally faded, when she wasn't paying attention. When had that happened? When did she stop believing Reuben was alive out there somewhere? Recently, to be sure, not nineteen years ago. Not even after her mother died.

She remembered that day like it was yesterday. Mom had transformed from the theatrical, narcissistic, and demanding woman of 160 pounds into a tiny, frail, and weak old lady, barely able to speak over a whisper. Suddenly, Tobi was transported back in time to 2013, standing in the doorway of Hannah's room at the Commack Home for the Aged, gazing at her mother until she looked up.

"I brought you your favorite, fried chicken wings from KFC," Tobi had said.

"They said I'm not supposed to eat that anymore." Her mother sighed. "They yelled at me in dialysis after you brought them last week."

"Yeah, well I spoke to your nephrologist," Tobi said as she walked into the room, "and he agreed that I can bring you whatever you want. Better for you to eat what you like then to eat nothing at all. You need calories, Mom, you have no strength."

"I know," she said. "Did you come straight from work?"

"Yeah, it's Thursday, my late night."

"You work so hard, darling. I wish you didn't have to work so hard." Her voice was barely audible.

Tobi sat at the bedside and unwrapped the wings on the hospital table. Tobi never did have anyone to take care of her and no longer expected to, so, of course, she always worked hard. Troy was the one man she thought would always be there, but he had up and left one day with no explanation. "T and T" he used to say. "Dynamite together." But they had quietly blown up for some reason completely unknown to Tobi. To make matters worse, it was the same week Reuben died, just when she needed him most. They were both ghosts in her heart.

Her mother took a greasy bite and put it down, slowly and deliberately wiping her hands on the napkin. She seemed to take an eternity to swallow it. "Mmm, delicious. But that's enough." The one bite had nearly sapped all the strength from her.

After a moment, Hannah managed a weak smile. "Benny came to visit last night."

"He told me."

"He's a good boy. You did a good job with him."

They looked at each other across the chicken. The hospital gown was three sizes too big, and it hung on her mother like a bedsheet on a skeleton. At least she would have closure on this death, Tobi thought. They had never let her see Reuben's body. He had been decomposing for three days when he was found, and the funeral director had been firm. "He doesn't look like your brother anymore. It's not a memory you want," he'd said.

The whole thing had seemed so wrong to Tobi on a gut level. In her heart, she was certain there was a mistake. She had needed to see his body to believe it, but they told her she was having a normal response for anyone grieving. She had even tried to force her way into the morgue, which was no small thing, since she'd been a regular gym rat at the time, but Mom had gotten hysterical and demanded that Tobi follow the funeral director's advice. Of course, because Mom didn't want to see him like that.

Then he was cremated like their father had been, again, because Mom was sure that was what Reuben would have wanted—as if Reuben had thought about it, at forty-three years old. No one had ever asked what Tobi wanted. For years after, Tobi used to fantasize that he had run off to Fiji or someplace, just to get away from all of them. She had always felt it in her bones that he was really still alive somewhere out there. She would have given almost anything to see him one last time. Even after so many years, she hadn't quite accepted that he was dead.

Sitting in Hannah's bleak, aseptic room that day, Tobi had played with her onyx ring. It had been her mother's when she was a teenager, and her mother had given it to Tobi when she was very little, before all their conflict had started. Before she had been disowned so many times, Tobi could barely remember why. She'd started wearing it again in Hannah's last few months. Her mother followed her gaze.

"I'm sorry," her mother said suddenly.

Tobi startled and looked up. "For what?"

Hannah sighed for so long, Tobi thought for a minute she was exhaling her last breath. She felt a sting of fear.

"For everything," Hannah whispered.

Their eyes locked. So much to say. Did any of it even matter anymore? She ached for the loving relationship they'd never had. And never would.

"It's late," Hannah said. "Go get some supper," and she closed her eyes.

Tobi squeezed her mother's hand for a long moment before she got up, and then stopped in the doorway to look back.

"I love you, Mom."

"I know."

Tobi had cried all the way home.

The nurse called her three hours later to say that her mother was gone.

Tobi shook herself out of the past and looked down as Pantelaymin started rubbing her legs. When *had* she stopped believing Reuben was alive somewhere? Not in 2013. Not even last year. Sure, in her head, she "understood" he was dead, but in her heart … he was just … gone. She had stopped trying to think about it any other way, it was of no use. But Rufini's questions made her realize that now, she did *know* he was dead, not just gone. For some reason, it upset her tremendously that she could not pinpoint the exact moment when that knowledge had come to her. As if by doing so, she might have been able to hold onto him a little longer.

Chapter 37

Inspector Bent was finally back, and after his run on the beach, Troy showered and went in to see him.

"Come on in," Bent said. "I'm sorry, I've been away on another matter. I heard you came by while I was gone."

"Yes. I'm not getting anywhere here, it's time for me to leave."

A woman knocked once and came into the office with a message for Bent. While he read it, she glanced at Troy and then looked again closely.

"I know you!" she said. "You're the guy from EE! You were doing studies on the reef for us! You donated the coral transplants two years ago!"

Bent looked up, and Troy tried to hide his first smile in weeks.

"Busted," he said.

Bent looked from one person to the other, puzzled.

"Inspector, don't you recognize him? From Executors for Our Earth. He's the guy. The. Guy." She turned to Troy. "You're, like, the CEO, right?" Troy nodded slightly.

Understanding slowly grew on the inspector's face. "Why didn't you tell me?"

"You didn't ask. Really, I didn't think it was relevant," Troy said.

Bent's entire posture changed. "I'm so sorry I've kept you here so long! I'm sure you have important things you need to be doing.

We really appreciate all your organization has done. You've brought the world awareness of our beautiful, dying reef and the tangible consequences of climate change, and you even funded much of the research that led to our understanding of the algae connection. And the transplants were from you too?"

To the woman, Bent said, "Natalie, thanks for this message. I will handle it later." Natalie left the room smiling and humming to herself.

"No worries," Troy said, "but I do need to be going. I was wondering, did you learn anything about this killer? Anything I might be able to use to track him stateside?"

"Sit." Bent motioned the chair and sat back in his own, now acting collegial. "Some, not much. About three weeks ago, a Maserati was found in Finch Bay that was rented to a Boris Gozinski, as was the penthouse suite here at the Sheraton On the Sea. Once we found the car, we went to the hotel, but there were a couple of kids hitting it off up there, who said some Russian guy gave them his key and told them to have at it, that he wasn't coming back for a few days. Well, you know he never did come back. Suspect he's long gone, and he's our man. Most of the prints and DNA we found were from the kids, except for a half print that belongs to someone else, possibly this guy Gozinski."

Bent looked at Troy sheepishly, and pressed on. "We checked with customs; sure enough, this Gozinski guy came into the country three and a half weeks ago from Hong Kong on a private jet. The jet's gone, but someone with a different name left on it. We have been trying to find him by facial recognition, using the scanned passport photo, to see if he used an alias, but it was a long shot, and nothing materialized."

Troy stared at him. Bent squirmed.

"I'm sorry," said Bent. "I could have shared that earlier, but we don't typically discuss police findings with civilians. If I'd known about the Foundation—"

"Really? *Really?* I've been spinning my wheels here waiting around and you didn't keep your end of the bargain!"

"Well, I'm telling you now, that's all I can say. We looked into this guy Boris Gozinski, and he is known to Interpol as a possible murder suspect from 2012. Became a cold case."

"What was the case?" Troy was trying to keep the steel from his voice.

"Not sure—really, I'm not. Someone fingered him for the murder of a cardiac surgeon in London, but he had an alibi, and they had to let him go. Nothing else on him, except that someone was really convinced he did it, despite the evidence. They didn't give me any other details. It was a long time ago."

Troy remembered Reuben following the London surgeon who was murdered. It was a clear connection. His frustration flared, and abruptly, he'd had enough. He stood up and handed Bent his card. His voice was cryptic.

"I will be leaving in the morning. I would ask you, please, to let me know if you learn anything, particularly if you track this guy to the United States. Another innocent life may be in danger."

Bent stood up too. "I will, and I'm sorry. I wish you luck, my friend. Our reef's friend. Please let me know if there is anything else you need."

Troy nodded stiffly and turned to the door, suddenly energized by his anger. It seemed pretty clear Marco's murder was connected to Reuben, and therefore, to Tobi. He had wasted so much time here and now he needed to cross ten thousand miles to get to her. He felt like time was running out.

Chapter 38

The holiday week was always crazy busy, and the flu was so bad this year, it seemed worse than ever. Today was a steady stream of patients, and since they all seemed to have the flu, the morning flew by in a blur. Tobi smiled to herself, as she answered another text from Reggie, just checking in on her. How blessed she was to have such great friends.

At noon, Tobi walked into room four, another person with flu-like symptoms.

John was sitting on the table, looking slightly agitated. His nose was red and dripping and he had a fever of 101.6.

"Do I have to have that flu test thing? I don't like things stuck up my nose."

"That's okay," Tobi said. "My name is Dr. Lister. We can do without it. They're not always accurate anyway."

"Oh, thank God. I'm sorry, I don't mean to be difficult. I just had a bad experience once."

"It's no problem. Tell me how you're feeling."

"Okay, so I've had fever of 102 for three days now, my sinuses are all stuffed, and I have a headache; I ache everywhere and all I want to do is sleep, but I started coughing last night and couldn't manage to rest at all."

"Certainly sounds like you have the flu. Has it definitely been three days?"

"Yes it started day before Christmas Eve, so … wait, it's been four days. Why?"

Tobi shook her head sympathetically. "The Tamiflu only works in the first forty-eight hours. I can still give you some other medication to help you feel better."

"That's okay," John said. "I've heard bad things about that flu medicine, I don't think I'd want to take it anyway. I just wanted to know if you think I have the flu—without using that swab in my nose."

Tobi nodded. "Yes, you have the flu, like half of Long Island right now."

Tobi looked at his medications. "Let me just get your history verified and see how I can help you. It says you're on levothyroxine and oxycodone. The levothyroxine is for your thyroid, right? What do you take the oxycodone for?"

"I don't take oxycodone. Never have. Why, does it say that? I didn't tell her that."

"Hmm … sometimes the meds come over through the program as something you've had in the past. Maybe you're no longer on it?"

"No, never took it. That's a narcotic, isn't it? Can you take it off?"

"Let me just check something …." Tobi looked John up in the New York State Prescription Monitoring Program and he did not appear. She checked ten other states, as well, and still, no John.

"That is a controlled substance, so I've just cross-checked it, and no, I don't see your name. We're starting a partnering process with Hospitals for Health, and it looks like our program picked it up through them. Have you seen a doctor in that system?"

John started sneezing. "Yeah, my endocrine doctor is in Hospitals for Health."

"That must be where it came from, then," Tobi said. I've taken it out of our records here, but I can't take it out of the system. As far as I know, only the office that entered it can do that. When you're feeling better, you should give their office a call and talk to them about it."

John was upset. "That's not right. What if you hadn't asked me? How long has it been there? I could have been labeled a drug addict."

"We wouldn't label you an addict if it's a legitimate prescription for a legitimate problem, but I do understand your concern. I will bring it up with our IT department, but I think the problem is on the end of the office that misentered your data. That would be human error. Unfortunately with digital everything these days, one mistake has a ripple effect now."

"Yeah. And those records go with me everywhere, right?"

"I think you can opt out of the sharing process. I'm sorry this happened, but I'm glad we discovered it so you can get it fixed."

"Yeah, great," John said. "Just what I need to be doing right now."

Tobi verified the rest of his history and allergies and found no other mistakes. She sent over a nasal spray and a cough medicine and gave him a note for work, and John left. She was sure his resentment would translate to a zero Press Ganey score that would be assigned to her, even though all she did was point out a preexisting problem that needed correcting.

There was, of course, the larger problem. Narcotics could be tracked easily in many states, but what if other medications or allergies were entered incorrectly, or medical history was either omitted or entered improperly? And if that patient arrived in the ED and the attending went by an erroneous account of the patient's medical problems and medications, theoretically, someone could get hurt.

Tobi finished documenting in the chart. She needed to input at least two positive or negative signs in at least five systems for the maximum appropriate bill to be sent for this diagnosis so that B. Healthy would get paid. Under ENT, she wrote "nasal congestion and sore throat" and under respiratory, she entered "cough, no wheezing" and continued on for the other physiological systems. She detailed the medication issue in separate notes at the bottom of the chart as Esther came in to clean the room.

"Esther, were John's meds already in the chart when you triaged him?"

"No, Dr. L., but they tell us to do it like this now ..." she showed her on the tablet. "If you click here, it pulls over all the medication history. A lot of times, the patient's don't remember the names of their medicines, so this helps us out. It's in the new workflow they sent us."

"Yes, I see how that can help a lot. Unfortunately, this last guy had meds in there that didn't belong to him. It's always a good idea to verify everything verbally with the patient."

"I didn't put it there, though, it just popped up."

"I understand that. Someone in another office, probably his endocrinologist, made the mistake, and now it's being carried over. I took it out for us, but it's in the system, so the next time someone uses this workflow, it will pop back in again unless the original office takes it out. Just try to remember to go over everything you see with the patient. The program isn't always right. Pass that along too."

"Sure, Dr. L."

At one o'clock, Tobi went into room five to see forty-seven-year-old Patricia. She was there for a urinary tract infection, but when Tobi asked about her medical history, she revealed that she'd been getting severe, debilitating headaches. They used to be worse with her cycle, but after she went into early menopause, she had expected them to improve. After eight months, she was still waiting. She had been to four neurologists, and had had an MRI, EEG, and a lumbar puncture, but no one could identify why she was in pain. They offered her a myriad of medications and were now suggesting spinal cord injections.

"All they want to do is throw drugs at me," Patricia said, "but I've read the side effects. They cause weight gain and I already have a family history of diabetes. And then blurry vision, dizziness, jerky movements? Like, really? Oh, and headaches. That's crazy, I don't want to chance it. And why would I take them, when no one even knows why this is happening? I've tried changing my diet drastically. I've gone gluten free, lactose free, paleo, then vegetarian, vegan, fat free, carb free—I started magnesium, selenium, chromium, and glucosamine chondroitin. I even completely eliminated artificial sweeteners and stopped drinking alcohol and caffeine. I've sacrificed all my pleasures, and nothing seems to work. It's getting to me!"

Tobi's heart went out to her. "I assume you had your vision checked. Have you ever tried meditation or acupuncture?"

Tobi didn't bring this up very often. One, because time did not usually allow, and two, because most people wanted their quick fix pill and did not want to put much effort into their recovery. Patricia was obviously not that person.

"I've been considering that. I'm glad not all physicians are against such things."

"I think you should try. It won't hurt you, and you never know."

Patricia said, "You know, none of the neurologists ever spend more than fifteen minutes with me anymore. I wait two hours for my appointment, and I feel like they barely even listen. I'm in pain and I'm frightened because I don't understand why, and they barely look at me—they just look at those tablets." She waved at the iPad. "Doesn't anybody care anymore?"

"They do care, or they want to," Tobi sighed. "They're just pressured. Too many patients, not enough time. People complain about the wait, and most just want the quick fix pill they offered you."

"Why do they schedule so many people, then?"

"They try to take care of everyone who needs help, but it's also not entirely up to them these days. It's become almost impossible to have a private practice, so they have to kowtow to whichever corporate they signed on with, and those corporations want to see volume. I'm sure your neurologist would rather be able to spend more time evaluating patients like yourself and less time writing prescription refills."

"Why can't doctors work for themselves anymore, and make their own rules?" Patricia asked.

"Because the insurance companies don't give the same reimbursement to all doctors, even for the exact same service, and individual providers receive a fraction of what corporations get paid. I'm literally talking four to five times less. If you're part of a large pool—and by 'large,' I mean over thirty, and the larger the better—physicians can negotiate a higher rate of compensation. The more patients your doctor's group has on the plan, the more the insurance company will reimburse. That also makes us fertile ground for entrepreneurs to step in and manage these huge composites of physicians. Most of us hate it, but the lone providers get screwed, and the majority have been forced to buy in or retire."

"That's absurd. Feels like us individuals aren't important anymore, are we? Except as numbers."

Tobi raised her eyebrows and nodded. "Our whole culture has become like that, right? Everything is about volume, not quality, form, not content. American medicine is just a microcosm of American values, which are all about how you *look*, and not about who you *are*."

"But you'd think some things would be sacred, no? Like, seeing your doctor when you're sick, and being able to expect them to talk to you? I pay a fortune for my health insurance, but it doesn't get me time with my doctor. You've spent more time with me today than I got at my last neurology appointment."

Tobi flinched. She wasn't supposed to spend this much time with her, either. She raised her hands helplessly. "Medicine has become a profit-driven industry, where the prime objective is to maximize revenue like any other material commerce. We get reviewed the way you'd rate your experience buying a car, or an Apple TV, but those reviews often have nothing at all to do with whether we are making people well. Did you know that Medicare adjusts its payments to hospitals based on the Press Ganey customer satisfaction scores? If the scores are low, the payments are reduced."

"I had no idea!"

"Most people don't," Tobi said. "Some hospitals now put their resources into beautification instead of staffing, so they'll 'look' nicer, since that is a big part of what they're being judged on. But there have also been some studies done showing that higher happiness scores correlate with worse outcomes, because the doctor or the hospital is trying so hard to please the patient. A 'happy' patient can still be dead an hour later. But corporate structures use those scores to reward or penalize physicians with bonuses, or in some cases, even salaries. I'm not surprised that your neurologist can't spend as much time with you as you need. None of us can."

"Ugh. How do you stand it?" Patricia asked.

"It's very disheartening at times. I just try my best to ignore it, so I can live with myself. I'm very sorry no one has found the source of your pain, but perhaps you can try going to someone attached to a teaching hospital. The academics may have more latitude to take time to ferret out difficult diagnoses.

"Meanwhile," Tobi grinned as she continued, "I'm prescribing some nitrofurantoin for your urinary tract infection. For that, you really do just need a pill, and only for a week."

"Thank you, doctor. And thanks for taking the time to talk to me. You've given me back some faith that doctors *do* care. What a mess it all seems!" Patricia glanced down the hall as she was leaving. "I'm afraid you have a crowd out there waiting for *you* now. I hope I get a chance to give you a review, it would be a great one!"

"Oh, I'm sure you will," Tobi laughed. "Thanks!"

Patricia left. As Tobi completed her chart, she berated herself for spending so much time with a simple UTI. This could have been a super quick visit if she'd just redirected the encounter. Why give Rufini ammunition like that? The conversation with Patricia was not relevant to her UTI and must have taken an extra eight or nine minutes, which was eight or nine minutes another patient would be angry about.

She set her jaw and thought: no. If I can't take time to be a person to another human being who is frustrated and scared, what is the point? *I* am not a venture capitalist, and I need to connect with real people about their real concerns. The only thing that makes this job worthwhile is the idea that once in a while, I am able to make a difference in someone's life, even if it isn't about exactly what they came in for. If I'm not allowed to do that, I might as well be flipping burgers.

She tried to send the urine culture and the system froze, the little blue "circle of death" spinning around and around.

"Don't you freeze on me now, Evy-baby," she said under her breath. The screen popped, the culture showed as "sent," and she relaxed. She picked up her tablet and went back to her main work station.

"Dr. L., is EveryScripts working for you? Mine just went down." Esther looked completely flummoxed. "I had to restart, but—wait, it's back up again. Sheesh!"

"Yeah, mine stuttered on me too, but it came back online. Last thing I want to do today is convert to paper and have to document everything again hours from now."

Finally, the last patient was Amelia, whose whole family were frequent flyers. Today she was being seen for a puncture wound of her right great toe. Tobi went in to give her a cheerful greeting, but Amelia was not smiling.

"Hi, Dr. Lister. I just need a tetanus shot, I stepped on a carpet tack this morning. We've all been beside ourselves the whole week." She started to cry.

"What happened?" Tobi brought her a box of tissues. Amelia was not usually the emotional sort.

"Do you remember my father? You treated his shingles a month ago, right before Thanksgiving."

"Sure I do. Antonio, he's a sweetheart."

"*Was* a sweetheart."

"Oh my God, Amelia, what happened? He wasn't that old."

"No, only fifty-three, but he had kidney failure, and he'd been on dialysis," Amelia explained. "And they had *just* found him a kidney! It was a miracle to find one so fast; they said they never expected to, he had a rare blood type. You know he was adopted, and I wasn't a match, so he was in the kidney pool." She started sobbing again. "I'm sorry …." She dabbed at her eyes.

"I remember him well. He was very hopeful he would get a donor. Did he not make it through the transplant surgery?" Tobi asked gently. She stood beside Amelia and put her hand on her shoulder.

"He never *had* the surgery! Last Tuesday, the day before he was supposed to check in … the very day before … his brakes failed …

he had an accident on the Long Island Expressway, and he died. He had a Subaru, they're such good cars, and he had just serviced it in October, getting it ready for the winter."

"I am so sorry!" Tobi felt stricken. Amelia reached up and hugged Tobi, crying on her shoulder.

"He was so close …. Why did that have to happen? We even bought him this super expensive supplemental insurance to cover all the extra costs, but we only ended up making two payments. I just don't understand … none of us understand. And now it's Christmas, and instead of a new lease on life, he's gone! I know, I know I should accept it, I know he's with Jesus now … but he was *so* close!"

Tobi hugged her tight. She had no wise words for an ironic tragedy like this.

"I'm sorry." Amelia straightened up and dried her eyes. "I know you need to get going. I just came for my tetanus shot. And I was glad you were on, you knew him—you just saw him! Life sucks sometimes!"

"I am so sorry, Amelia. May his memory be for a blessing."

Chapter 39

Kavandor had not received an answer to his text message, and he was almost out of time. The subcommittee was supposed to meet right after New Year's. He was sure it was because the Russians considered him a worthless nobody, and it really pissed him off. They had no idea they needed him now. If he did not bury the inquiry into Kordec, their whole gig could go up in smoke. What a relief it would be to not have to come up with hidden money four times a year! But what if there were an inquiry and somehow Kordec passed, and then they found him in the center of it? Wouldn't they strike out at him in vengeance and tell all—or kill him? Right now, they didn't even know he was chairing the subcommittee, as far as he knew, anyway. He would love to have these guys out of his life for good, but if they were scrutinized and *not* discovered for the murderous wretches they were, he could be dead meat. So, if Kordec were investigated, they had best be fried, all while keeping his connection out of the inquiry entirely. It was all or nothing.

Albert Wiseman popped his head into his office. "Hey, Blaise. You're chairing next week?"

"Hi, Al, what are you doing here? Chairing what?"

Wiseman was young, bright, and ambitious. Often a pain in the ass, to be sure.

"Roundtable committee. I was told to sit in on this one, thought I'd pick your brain first. You know the FBI likes to make a show of keeping its nose in the public arena. I'm the new kid on the block, so they stuck me down here where the action isn't. How am I going to display my talents on a round table discussion that has nothing to do with national security? Someone upstairs doesn't like me, that's what I'm thinking. Help me make this interesting, at least."

In that instant, Kavandor decided.

"Well, there is this insurance company the AMA has been complaining about. I don't know anything about them, but they seemed to have pissed off a lot of physicians."

"That's all you got, an insurance company?" Wiseman groaned. "What's the name? I'll look into it, maybe it will cure my insomnia."

Kavandor immediately regretted his decision. Wiseman was not going to take this seriously. "Kodiak, or something like that. Not sure, it's buried under this pile of papers."

"Do they insure people or bears? Email it to me when you find it," Wiseman said, and he moseyed out of the office.

Chapter 40

Troy arrived at LAX the last week in December, exhausted but motivated. He could hardly believe he'd been gone almost a month. Mack Elberg met him as he came through customs.

"Hey, man, I thought they'd never let you out of there. Good to see you!" He gave Troy a bear hug. "That's wild, that your dive buddy was murdered! Did they catch the bastard?"

"Thanks, Mack. Not yet. I am glad to be home, you have no idea. I'm coming in to the office today, but leaving tomorrow for New York."

"You can't do that! We still haven't gotten control of these wildfires. Right now, we need your ingenuity and more funding to get the animals to safety and put these flames out for good. What a horrible season it's been. Haven't you been reading my emails?"

"Yes, I have, but—"

"Come on, let's get you back to the office and up in the chopper. You have to see this to believe it. Really."

Troy frowned. Mack was his closest friend, but even Mack did not know how he had rescued Reuben nineteen years ago. All Troy had told him about this trip and his hang-up overseas was that the owner of the dive shop he used was murdered. He probably could have confided in him, but how could he share the real story with Mack when he had never told Tobi? They went back to the office where Troy always kept a change of clothes. He showered and headed to the roof and their helipad.

The decimation was more than he had imagined. It seemed every year for the last several years, California broke a new record for the largest wildfire in its state's history. It reinforced their research into the North American winter dipole. The dipole phenomenon accounted for the way in which the melting arctic ice was contributing to, if not causing, freezing cold winters from Minneapolis to New York and creating this excessively dry, windy, hot weather in the west. Prime conditions for sustaining fire.

Now that Troy was here, it would be unconscionable to leave California until the wildfires were somewhat under control. EOE had joined the rescue operations on land both for animal rescue and in assisting the National Guard. Troy had long ago given Mack authority to make major decisions in his absence, and he was glad Mack had thrown their resources in for support, but he had not given unlimited access to the treasuries. Mack had reached his budgetary limit.

By December 30, the fires were finally considered to be contained, and with trepidation, Troy turned his attention back to New York and Tobi. She still had not answered his messages and he was getting cold feet about seeing her, while also feeling desperate that her time was up.

He looked her up again through the New York State Department of Education and found she was still actively practicing medicine and took down her work address. He decided not to show up for New Year's Eve, as that seemed presumptuous. He booked a red eye flight leaving the evening of January first, and then looked for ways to distract himself while constantly trying to plan what he would say to her. He still loved her, of that he was sure, but he was so filled with regrets, he didn't know if he could even look at her without falling apart. And what if she wouldn't speak to him at all?

Chapter 41

I t was the morning of New Year's Eve and Tobi had a sinking feeling in her gut. It was going to be a very busy day. Their rad tech was out with the flu, and when she texted Helen, she replied that they weren't getting a replacement until 1:00 p.m. They'd have to make it work. They opened at nine, and by ten, there were already twelve patients signed in.

Around eleven o'clock, Teresa came in, having an allergic reaction. She had eaten a muffin just ten minutes before she arrived, which she mistakenly thought was nut free, and was already bright red everywhere, with swelling in her face and neck. Marta rushed her into the cardiac room, and Tobi left the patient she was just finishing examining to tend to her immediately. Theresa required multiple injections, including epinephrine, and Tobi was starting an IV while Marta put her on oxygen and then went to the front desk to call EMS.

While she was on the phone, Stephanopolis came in with his mother. He was eleven years old, weighed about 125 pounds, and was screaming from an injury to his finger, where the nail was partially hanging off. His mother, Mrs. Tacouris, interrupted Marta on the phone with EMS, and demanded that her son be seen immediately because he was in so much pain.

"Give us just a few minutes, we have a serious emergency. We'll be with you right away," Marta told her. She went back to answering the endless list of questions EMS asked. "Yes, it's anaphylaxis. Yes, she is conscious. The doctor is with her now. She is breathing." Marta glanced backward into the room. "No, she isn't blue, she's red. She's on oxygen. Please, I need to go and help the doctor. Yes, thank you. What is your ETA? Great, thank you." Marta hung up the phone.

"Wait! You have to help my son first," Mrs. Tacouris said, "he is an emergency too! Look how he's screaming!" Stephanopolis howled on cue.

Marta stopped midway back to the cardiac room and looked helplessly at Tobi, who peeked out of the room after taping in the IV. After the first few seconds, Stephanopolis had quieted again, and was standing up, looking around to see who was watching, holding his right index finger out in front of him with his left hand. Tobi quickly noted that he was breathing normally, standing comfortably on his own, and there was no blood dripping anywhere. Screaming kids didn't scare her, anyway, it was the quiet, listless ones who did. She shook her head subtly at Marta and Marta turned back to Mrs. Tacouris. She very politely asked Mom to sign in and take a seat and promised to be with her next.

"If you can't see him right now, call me an ambulance!" Mrs. Tacouris said. Stephanopolis started screaming again, although his hand had not moved, and there was nothing around him that might have jarred his finger.

"Ma'am, you're welcome to take him to the ED, or call an ambulance for him, but we have a more pressing emergency at the moment."

"What could be more pressing than my son?"

When EMS arrived, they had to physically move Mrs. Tacouris aside. Tobi gave them a quick assessment and they rechecked Teresa's vital signs, put her on a stretcher, and transferred the IV and the oxygen to their own equipment. The lobster look was beginning to fade a little from the epi and diphenhydramine Tobi had injected. Once they took over, and she could see her patient was stabilizing, Tobi went back into room four to complete the discharge of the patient who'd been interrupted, while Marta brought Stephanopolis into another room for triage.

Another patient protested immediately. "I'm just here for my flu shot, do I really have to wait? I came in before that woman on the stretcher, and there were already two people in front of me, and now you just took that boy ahead of me too. I thought this would be quick." Visions of zeros danced over Tobi's head.

When Mrs. Tacouris saw Tobi giving discharge paperwork to the patient whose visit had been interrupted, she again demanded they call an ambulance if her son could not be seen instantly. If I'd had time to call an ambulance, Tobi thought, I'd have had time to look at his finger—which was not EMS worthy in the slightest.

Sometimes the hardest part of her job was to quietly make her triage assessments and follow her gut, no matter how many people were screaming at her. Besides, by definition, screaming patients were fully conscious and were never in respiratory distress.

She gave her patient his paper work, grateful that he had been understanding, while Marta tried to assure the flu shot lady that they would be with her as soon as possible. Tobi walked into Stephanopolis's exam room next. He had cut the line of four other patients.

"I'm Dr. Lister. What happened?" she asked without the usual formalities. His vital signs were normal, and he was quiet for the moment. He appeared to have yanked the nail halfway off his right index finger, but there was no active bleeding and the finger looked otherwise intact.

"He caught his finger in the door while he and his sister were fighting. He was trying to shut her out when she was trying to get into his room," Mrs. Tacouris reported. Stephanopolis nodded frantically and whimpered.

Tobi examined his finger, and Stephanopolis held his breath with his mouth open, prepared to scream again at a moment's notice. There was only minimal blood where the nail had partially detached, and he had full movement and normal sensation. "I'm going to remove the nail the rest of the way, which will stop his pain, and we should x-ray it. I don't have a tech here right now, but I can send you to our sister site to make sure nothing is broken."

"What do you mean, you can't x-ray it here? He needs an x-ray! His finger is probably broken. And you're going to hurt him by taking the nail off."

"Whether or not it is broken, the nail has to come off. It's the movement of the nail on his exposed nail bed that is causing his pain; the edge is sharp where it was torn and the nail bed is very sensitive. I'm going to spray his finger with a freezing agent, so he won't feel anything when I cut the nail off. What I want to do will take less than a minute."

At this news, Stephanopolis became hysterical, crying and screaming again so much that Tobi began to wonder if there was an undisclosed psychiatric diagnosis. There was no mention of it in the chart.

"You mustn't hurt him! Don't hurt him! Can't you see he is in pain?" his mother cried.

Tobi stayed firm, revising her assessment: the mother was the problem. "If you want me to fix his nail, it will be uncomfortable for about a minute or less. Stephanopolis is too big for us to hold down, and it is too dangerous for me to attempt using a sharp instrument on a patient who is thrashing around. It will make him feel much better, but you have to decide if you want me to do it, and then he has to stay still."

"Can you sedate him?"

"We don't do that here. If that is what you want, you will have to take him to the hospital."

Mom reluctantly conceded. "Only a minute?"

"Less than a minute."

Marta brought in the ethyl chloride and some betadine and gauze to clean the area, and a suture removal set. Mrs. Tacouris held her son in a great bear hug. "It's all right baby, it's all right, I won't let them hurt you," she cooed at him.

She let him hide his head in her chest and cry while Marta pinned his wrist and hand to the table. Tobi sprayed his finger with ethyl chloride, and eight seconds later, the nail was off. Stephanopolis hiccupped once and then smiled, completely transformed.

"Mommy, can we get ice cream now?"

Tobi left Marta to put a dressing on his finger while she wrote up the chart. Then, Marta called down to their other office, to give them a heads up about who was coming to visit for an x-ray. If there were a fracture, he would need an antibiotic. Mom glared at everyone as she left, and Tobi sent an SOS text to Evelyn.

We are getting killed. Can anyone come sooner?

She went into room three to administer the flu shot.

"I don't understand," the patient said. "Your website advertises in and out in less than an hour, and that's for an illness. This is just a shot, so you should have taken me first! Why do you promise it will be quick if we have to wait around?"

Why, indeed, Tobi thought.

For a split second, Tobi fantasized about putting a "closed" sign on the door, but God must have been watching over her, because Shari walked into the office. She was a rad tech and the staff lead for her own office and theirs. She ordered supplies, changed out their radiation badges, and did some problem solving. She was actually more of a manager than Evelyn, although she needed Evelyn's approval for expenditures.

"Hi, guys, I'm just here for an hour to do inventory. I know, it's New Year's Eve, but they keep begging me to cover other shifts, and I haven't had time to do my administrative stuff." She looked around the overcrowded office. "Geez, you guys giving something away? Where's Jackie?"

"She has the flu," Tobi gave her a hug. "Someone is coming at 1:00 p.m., not sure who it is. If you'd been here five minutes sooner, I'd have asked you to shoot an x-ray on that kid's finger, the one who just walked out."

"Wow. I'll help you guys out. What do you need? I can bring back a few patients. This place looks like a tornado hit it. What happened in the cardiac room?"

"Anaphylactic reaction," Marta said. "And then a crazy mom with a spoiled kid in room five. She thought her son should be seen before a life-threatening emergency."

Shari shook her head. "How typical. Some people think the whole world should revolve around them."

With Shari's help, they got the office put back together, the patients in rooms, and then out with their appropriate treatment. Most of them had simple sore throats or stuffy noses, several for less than a day. By 12:45 p.m., it had slowed down enough to breathe.

Tobi's phone beeped with a text from her wireless service.

Free Message: You're paying per-minute rates on international calls. See how to stay in touch for less with the Unlimited Together plan.

Great, she thought. Why do I always have to find out like this? Numerous times, she had discovered Ben's whereabouts only after getting a text from Verizon, or sometimes from Citibank, informing her that her credit card had been used outside the United States. She copied the text, and below it, she wrote:

Where are you?

... and sent it off.

She went in to the next patient, who was thankfully, a straight forward urinary tract infection. Before she even finished, she heard the "popcorn" sound she had assigned to Ben's texts.

She opened the text, and time slowed to a crawl.

We found a last-minute deal to Nicaragua for the New Year's holiday so decided to jump on it. $300 airfare and hotel! Definitely a little seedy but worth the price and the food is great.

Below that was a picture of him in a blue button-down shirt, jeans, and flip-flops with Rachel in a white summer dress. They were holding hands on a lit-up tile path near some palm trees. There was more.

Apparently, the city government has a deal with the cartel where there's no violence between Christmas Eve and New Year's.

Tobi stared at the phone. Really? Nicaragua? The last time she "accidentally" discovered he'd gone away, it was only to Canada, and before that he'd gone to Mexico. But ... *Nicaragua?* And who would've told her if something had happened? She wouldn't even have known in what country to look for him! She had no words to answer, and she needed to take a breath first and think it out. She went into the next patient's room, an uncomplicated strep throat, but she could barely focus.

Ben *did* these things! He had this attitude about life, that somehow everything would work itself out. She often said that was his middle name: "Benjamin 'I'll-figure-it-out' Lister." The infuriating part was, he usually did. She tried to remember if her text went as an iMessage, as a clue to if he were even in a place with internet access. She couldn't remember if it had sent in green or blue. As if it mattered, it was just to keep her mind off drug cartels in Nicaragua.

Ben had been all over the country and all over the globe, eastern and western Europe, Iceland, Hawaii, Australia, Colombia, and Israel. These days, he usually told her when he was going somewhere. Eighteen months ago, Rachel had taken him to Athens, Greece, for the long Memorial Day weekend, to celebrate his finishing his first year of med school at Columbia University. The two of them often traveled to exotic places that Tobi had barely even dreamed about. Ben was like Troy that way, always ready to hop on a jet.

She discharged the patient with strep on some amoxicillin and set to answering Ben's text. She wanted to shake him—scream at him—*What were you thinking?* But what if something happened down there, and those were the last words he ever heard from her? She wouldn't be able to live with herself. Instead she wrote:

Great. Truce ends tomorrow. Way to give me a heads up. Guess I can't talk to you tonight to wish you a happy New Year. So, happy New Year. You're going to owe me for the Verizon charges.

Popcorn sound.

Are you at work?

Tobi typed back.

Yes. It's crazy
I'll be home tonight
All night

Popcorn.

Ohh Mom, I feel bad then. The Verizon text was because I
called Dad in Israel. I was on the phone less than a minute and
called back to the 516 number. I'm not in Nicaragua, lol, I was
just kidding.

Tobi became aware of her heart pounding and the sweat on the back of her neck. She remembered she was supposed to breathe. Shari was staring at her.

"Are you okay? What just happened? You look ... green."

She swallowed and showed Shari all the texts.

Shari shook her head. "Geez, is this what I have to look forward to when I have kids?"

"I hope not, for your sake. The thing is, it would be completely within character for Ben to have done that. He'll go halfway around the world on an hour's notice, if he gets a good deal and the mood hits him. He's always been like that.

"When he was only eighteen months old, I had him at Long Beach one day. You know the jetties that are spaced every quarter mile or so? He just picked himself up and started walking in the sand, so I got up and followed him. He never once looked back. When he was about to pass the second jetty—had to have been nearly a half mile—I sped up and took his hand and made him turn back around. Fearless, that kid is, always has been!"

Ferdinand showed up at one o'clock as promised, and Shari was done with the inventory by three. She wished them a happy

New Year and left. By four o'clock, there were still a few patients in the office, but it had slowed down significantly, as the community became more focused on their New Year's Eve plans than on seeing a doctor.

Finally, only Mikhail remained, one of her favorite patients. Tobi walked in with her usual sunny introduction, but wearing a mask. She took one look at him, and her heart broke. He was dripping from his nose, which was red and raw, his hair was matted and sticking out in all different directions, and he was coughing intermittently. He looked like hell.

"I hurt everywhere, doc," Mikhail said. "I had a 102.7 fever last night. I was shaking under three blankets. I just couldn't get warm, and neither Tylenol nor Advil helped."

"Looks like you have the flu," she said. "It's most of what I've been seeing for the last few days. When did you first feel ill?"

"Thursday morning, early. It woke me up in the middle of the night, so, three, almost four days ago. It feels like it's getting worse every day."

Tobi examined him. "Your lungs are clear. I can give you a nasal spray to dry up your nose and a cough medicine, which will also help you sleep. Your body needs rest and fluids. Stay away from anyone you like until you're better," she grinned at him.

"Yeah, no kidding. And, if I don't like them? Never mind," he laughed, which turned into a coughing fit.

"Don't worry, Mikhail. You're a young, basically healthy guy, you're going to be fine. The human body is amazing."

As she was charting Mikhail's visit, her phone pinged with a Facebook message. Against her better judgment, she opened it.

Tob,
I know you don't want to hear from me, but I'm coming to
New York. You have every right to flip me the bird, but if
you must, please do it in person. I must talk to you, just
once. After that, I'll go away if you tell me to. Promise.
Love to Benny.

T
It's about Reuben

Tobi's head spun for a second. *Leave me alone!* And that last line, as if he wasn't sure he should write it. What the hell. If she saw him again, if she went *there* again, she could get sucked in again, and she might never be able to come back. It had taken years to get over him the first time. Why would she invite all that pain back into her life?

She shook her head, as if that would remove him from her consciousness, and turned back to her charts.

The rooms were all clean and stocked and it was past time to leave, but a man was banging on the door outside. "I have asthma, I can't breathe. Please let me in!"

Ferdinand opened the door. It was 5:20 p.m., they were supposed to close at five.

"Please, I just need some medicine. I'll be quick."

Marta triaged him quickly and Tobi walked into his exam room. "Hey, doc, remember me? You cured my frostbite over the summer." He smiled mischievously. He didn't look very short of breath.

Damian had a square jaw and ultra-broad shoulders. His upper muscles were hyper-developed, and he was eager to take his shirt completely off for her to examine him. For some reason, he made her think of a gym commercial. Tobi furrowed her brow, wondering why she didn't remember him. She looked at the EMR.

"Oh, right. You banged your arm, and then you put ice packs directly against your skin and wrapped them very tightly with an ace bandage. I remember you, Damian."

Damian seemed proud of this for some reason. "Yup, I wrapped it super tight to make sure it would stay in the right spot. I had it on for about thirty minutes, and when I took it off, my arm was all red and blistered. Man, that hurt like a son of a bitch!"

"Yes, you gave yourself second degrees burns from the ice, like frostbite."

"You do remember me!"

"I do." How could she have forgotten? "So, you ran out of your inhaler?"

"Yeah, a few days ago. I figured I'd come by and see you and get another. Can you give me one of those breathing treatments too? Sorry I came so late, I knew you closed early for the holiday, five o'clock, right? I almost made it. I ran into some traffic, should've been here fifteen minutes ago. Thanks for opening back up or me."

Tobi listened to his lungs, and he was wheezing very slightly. She started an albuterol nebulizer and sent a script for an inhaler to one of the few pharmacies still open on New Year's Eve.

As he was leaving, he asked "Hey, doc, do you think I can still work out tonight? I have equipment at home."

"I'd give it a rest for tonight, Damian. And be careful driving home, people have probably started drinking already."

"Happy New Year!" he called out as he was leaving.

"Is he for real?" Marta asked. She looked like she'd had the day from hell. Tobi wondered if she looked the same.

"Do you have plans for tonight?"

"I did,'" Marta replied. "Right now, all I want to do is crawl into bed."

Chapter 42

Tobi was just pulling into her driveway when her phone sang out Ben's custom ringtone and his picture appeared.

"Mom, I'm really sorry! I shouldn't have done that to you while you were at work," he was fighting back laughter. "It was a good one, though. I never thought you'd take me seriously."

"It's not outside the realm of possibility, you know."

"I know, but I tell you now when I go anywhere. I called Israel to wish Dad a happy New Year."

"I see you called him before you called me." Tobi realized she was trying to guilt him, but she felt stubbornly justified.

"Mom! It's seven hours ahead over there!"

"I know, I know … it's just been a hell of a day. Patients were crazy. I hope you don't regret this decision to do medicine. It isn't what it used to be."

"I can't imagine doing anything else, Mom, I love learning this stuff. Are you going anywhere tonight?"

"I was invited out with Chloe, they're all going to dinner and a show and I have a ticket, and I was also invited to Madelyn's, she's having people over. But I'm so tired, I may just stay home with Pantelaymin."

"You should go out, Mom. Madelyn is just down the block. You don't even have to drive."

"What are you and Rachel doing? I hope you're not going to be anywhere near Times Square. They received threats again, and what a great time for a terrorist to blow it up."

"Ugh, no. I hate Times Square. Too touristy. A bunch of us are making rounds at a couple of clubs and then doing dinner in the Village at Shuka. It's Mediterranean."

"Sounds like fun. I miss you. Hey, so, I keep getting IM messages from … do you remember Troy DeJacob?"

"That dick wad? Yeah. I hope you're ignoring them. You can block him, you know. What does he want?"

"I don't know. He's sent me three, and I have been ignoring them. Today he wrote that it has to do with your Uncle Reuben."

"Mom! Uncle Reuben is dead. For, like, twenty years. He's just trying to find a way in. I hope you're not going to fall for that. He left us, remember? Without a word, just disappeared? Oh, he did tell us he was all right, just could never see us again."

Tobi flinched; Ben had been hurt as much as she had. "But tell me how you *really* feel."

"Seriously, Mom, he's a jackass. Leave that alone. Go—go have fun tonight. You don't hang out with your friends enough. You should go somewhere, I want you to have some fun."

"I wanted to go with you to Iceland last year, and I would have paid for everything. You weren't even going with Rachel." Tobi realized she was whining.

"That was a 'guy' trip. I told you I'd go back with you one day."

"I know." Tobi sighed. "I really am glad you do all these amazing things. Your uncle died so young, but I feel like he did more in his short life than many do in eighty-plus years. You're very like him, you know. You just better live a whole lot longer!"

"I'll be fine, Mom, don't worry. I gotta go, just wanted to wish you a happy New Year. I love you."

"I love you, too Ben. Be careful tonight, wherever you go. Happy New Year and give my love to Rachel."

Tobi shut the engine. She hated that it got so dark so early. She got out of her car and caught her breath at the sound of a dog barking down the block. What was wrong with her? She was literally jumping at shadows, as if she expected someone to leap out at her from behind the trees. Stop it, she told herself. My life is normal. Boring at times to be sure, but there is no reason for me to be so jittery.

Chapter 43

Troy received a call from Inspector Bent.

"Hello, Mr. DeJacob? Happy New Year."

"Thank you, inspector. Same to you. Did you find out anything?"

"Yes, happens we did. Our National Institute of Standards and Technology, or NIST as we call it, got a facial recognition on Boris Gozinski coming into the country. His real name—we think—is Mannfort Tzenkov, known to be one of the wealthiest oligarchs in Russia, with a rather shady portfolio. No idea where he is right now, but I can tell you he holds the reigns of several multibillion dollar companies, and one of them is a health insurance company, called Kordec. I did some digging for you, and they specialize in high-risk patients."

Troy whistled under his breath. "Wow, thank you."

"Yeah, I figured I owed it to you after keeping you rocking on your heels for so long. I wish I'd known who you were from the start …."

Troy kept his voice even. "Why should that have mattered? A human being is a human being. We all deserve the same compassion and respect."

The line was silent.

"But I suppose it is inevitable," Troy said. "I should have used my credentials. Human beings are rarely treated with equality, right?"

Bent stammered. "I learned an important lesson too, Mr. DeJacob. You never know who you're talking to. But please understand that in general, we're not at liberty to share our intel with civilians. I hope this information is helpful."

"It is, and I am grateful that you shared it with me. I wish you health and happiness in the coming year."

"And same to you, my friend, and good fortune in your enterprise."

Troy took out his phone and opened up Facebook Messenger again. He wrote:

Tob,
I know you don't want to hear from me, but I'm coming to New York. You have every right to flip me the bird, but if you must, please do it in person. I must talk to you, just once. After that, I'll go away if you tell me to. Promise.
Love to Benny.

T
It's about Reuben

Chapter 44

Tobi was not looking forward to her shift; the day after the holiday was always a headache. People seemed to come out of the woodwork, as if they'd had no access to medical care in a week, when nearly every urgent care on Long Island was open 365 days a year.

She pulled into the parking lot behind the building and snuck in the back before the doors opened for business. An email popped up from IT about a glitch in the social history section, which should be back up and running in the next couple of hours. She thought about her patient with the oxycodone problem and gave Steve a call.

"Hey, Tobi, happy New Year. What's up?"

"Hey, you too. Quick question. I had a patient a couple of days ago whose chart showed that he was on oxycodone when he never took it. I removed it from our files, but it came from his Hospitals for Health record. Are we able to delete it permanently even if we didn't enter it? Otherwise it will just pop back in again. The guy was pretty upset, and I can't blame him."

"Are you sure he never took it?"

"Yeah, I checked the ISTOP and cross-referenced him in ten other states. He's not in there."

"How did it get in his chart then?"

"I'm thinking it was from his endocrinologist's office, that's the only other place he's been seen that's on the same system. Maybe whoever triaged him there entered it by mistake."

"Not sure; put in an IT ticket and see if they have any suggestions."

"Okay."

Tobi hesitated.

"Is there something else?" Steve asked.

"Yes … I had a disturbing visit from Ismar the other day."

"Disturbing how?"

"He showed up as we were all leaving and asked me to stay, and then he started getting personal with me. He creeped me out."

"Personal how?" Steve asked.

"He was asking about who I live with and about my family, I don't know. It was unsettling. He insisted on keeping me alone with him in the office, after hours."

"Well, that's not appropriate. I'll talk to him."

"Thanks. Also, I was wondering if you found out anything about who was snooping in charts."

"What are you talking about?"

"Last month you told me it seemed like I was looking in patients' charts and violating HIPAA, when I wasn't. I told you I thought Ismar took my tablet, and recently I've heard he has been appropriating other providers' tablets as well. Maybe he's using our logins to do some sort of research or something."

The line was quiet, and when Steve spoke, his voice was stony.

"I don't know what you're talking about. There is no problem with charts. Don't worry about Ismar, Tobi, just worry about yourself."

Tobi stiffened. "What do you mean by that?"

"Just what I said. Anything else?"

"No, nothing else."

"Okay then, happy and healthy."

The line went dead.

Tobi stood frozen for two solid minutes. What the hell just happened? She felt a surge of panic. It was getting harder and harder to convince herself she was imagining things. Something was definitely not right but she couldn't put her finger on anything specific. Why would Steve deny their previous conversation?

Tobi closed her eyes and prayed. Why, God, why did you take Reuben from me? She asked it for the eighty thousandth time. She seemed to miss him more every year, but never greater than at this very moment. She felt abandoned and frightened and confused, and she was desperate for someone to help her sort it all out. And yes, as ashamed as she was to admit it, for someone to protect her.

From her earliest memories and before, Reuben had filled that role. She had been told that as a baby, her mother had lost control of her carriage on the hill in Forest Park, and as it rolled away from her, five-year-old Reuben chased right after it, running in front of the carriage and stopping it before Tobi rolled onto busy Union Turnpike.

She remembered his rescuing her when she was passing the bully's house when she was about nine. She couldn't get home any other way, and she always dreaded it. The boy who lived there was three years older than her and nearly twice her size. He challenged her, as usual. But that day, Reuben was playing street hockey with his friend Kevin down the block. He saw the confrontation and came running to her aid, still holding the hockey stick, and threw the kid on the grass. Then he stood over him waving the stick over his head while he shouted at him never to bother his sister again. Tobi had wanted to cry, half with relief, half with glee. The kid never even glanced in her direction after that.

And then there was the time in college that she'd had an anaphylactic reaction to a penicillin injection she was given at the student health center. By the time she got back to her dorm, she was burning up and started to feel like the walls were closing in. It was a very strange sensation, like her entire body had a toothache. A glance in the mirror revealed she was bright red everywhere, but she was too dazed to do anything except curl up in the fetal position on her bed. Her roommate found her like that and ran to get Reuben, who dragged her back to the health center. When the shuttle bus rolled up, she did not have the strength to climb the high step. The last thing she remembered was saying, "Reuben, you can't carry me," as he lifted her in his arms and onto the bus. She'd woken up the next day in a hospital bed.

Until the early '90s, Reuben had always been her defender, her advocate, her friend. Until her parents started having financial difficulties and demanded assistance, and Tobi found herself pregnant and with a husband who wanted no part of her; until she'd had to put her child's needs ahead of those of her parents.

Tobi had never had a great relationship with either her mother or her father, but even Reuben rejected her for that, having already chosen to submit to their parents' pressure and belong, rather than risk abandonment. Tobi felt utterly alone from then on.

Reuben had given their parents three thousand dollars a month for years before he died, even though they were both working, and they had continued to buy two new cars every three years and live in a three-bedroom house. When their father died, their mother was offered three months bereavement leave at the department store she worked in, but she chose to quit altogether and lean wholly on Reuben. It contrasted darkly with her mother's favorite platitude: *God helps those who help themselves.* How Mom had loved platitudes. Tobi guessed her mother never meant for this one to be applied to herself.

Mom's finances caused a lot of friction between Tobi and Reuben, since Tobi had insisted their mother go back to work and that they should supplement her income, not replace it. But Reuben had promised their father on his death bed that he would take care of Mom, and he interpreted that to mean she should be supported entirely. He resented Tobi for not bleeding money at her like he did. Maybe it was because he did not have children of his own, but he had no clue how hard it was to be a single parent with a mortgage worth of student loans and no family support, even for childcare. It seemed they had always ended up fighting over their parents' financial needs, so that there were fewer and fewer visits and they drifted further and further apart. Ben had barely known his uncle.

How she wished she could talk to the old Reuben now and tell him she was in trouble. That ominous things were happening that she did not understand. There was no question in her mind that he could have figured it all out, and that her safety would have overridden their family disagreements. She needed him so much right then, it hurt.

She spent the entire shift in a fog, terrified by some amorphous phantom she could not quite grasp.

Chapter 45

At 5:45 p.m., Troy drove his rented Jeep Grand Cherokee slowly through the parking lot of the urgent care office. He tried to get a look inside through the front window, but there was traffic behind him, so he moved on. He pulled in behind the office, where there were only three cars parked. No windows back here, but he identified what must be the back door of the clinic. One of the cars was an Outback with MD plates on it. In New York, the specialty plates also had the caduceus, so they were unmistakable. That had to be Tobi's car.

He parked the truck thirty feet from the nearest car and turned off the engine, but he couldn't bring himself to go in. How could he just walk into her office and disrupt her day like this? If she welcomed his communication, she would have answered him. His heart was pounding, and he had to remind himself several times that he was here because she could be in danger and he needed to see this through.

It was dark already, and to his right, he could just see the full moon rising over the buildings in the east. There was patchy ice on the ground and last week's snow still lingered against the perimeter of the lot. From where he sat, he could see the back door and the side of the building, so he decided to just wait for her to get off work.

He sat back and focused on his breathing to calm down. He would have dozed off if not for the cold, but he didn't want to leave the engine running for two hours. His legs were stiff and the windows started to fog, and he was contemplating going somewhere for a hot cup of coffee when a dark red Mercedes Benz GLS 550 drove very slowly into the mostly deserted parking lot. It stopped in front of the car with the MD plates.

A man got out of the SUV and skulked over to the Subaru. That was really the only way to describe it. He moved stealthily, looking all around every couple of seconds. The moon was full and high in the clear sky, and Troy studied him. He was about five foot ten and fat, had to be nearly three hundred pounds. He was carrying some kind of tool in his hand. He got to the Subaru and put his hands just under the front of the hood, looking for the catch.

Instinctively, Troy got out of his car. He slammed the door loudly and started walking toward the Outback, and the guy nearly jumped out of his skin. He quickly put his tool in his pocket and turned around like he was going to sit on the hood, then realized that wasn't such a good idea. He started in two different directions until he ran back to his car, whose engine was still running. The tires screeched as he peeled out of the parking lot.

Troy stared at the car as it left, trying to catch the plate number. He never had understood why anyone would spend nearly a hundred thousand dollars on a car, but anyone who could afford a Mercedes GLS wasn't messing with Tobi's SUV on a whim. Troy pulled his jacket around him. The air was clear and crisp, nineteen degrees and dropping, with wind at five mph, but he barely felt it. He was pumped up on adrenaline. But after fifteen minutes, his nose began to feel numb and he started to feel silly standing in the freezing cold guarding her car. And if someone wanted to get him out of the way, he was making himself an easy target.

He got back in his car and ran the heater for a half hour, then turned off the engine and waited. A few minutes after eight, he saw her. It had to be her. She was walking toward him with a heavy coat and scarf, keys dangling from her gloved hands.

In the shadow, she hadn't changed much. He recognized her by her walk and her profile in the moonlight, and he found himself holding his breath while his heart bounced in his chest. Her dark hair drifted out after her as she turned to look behind her several times. Did she know she was in danger? She had her phone out and was punching on it with her gloves just as she passed his car and did not seem to notice it wasn't empty.

Tobi, Tobi, Troy whispered to himself as she walked past his Jeep. *You have got to be more alert to what is going on around you.*

She stopped a few paces from her own car, as if she had heard him, turned around and looked toward his Jeep and then up and down the street again.

Tobi looked inside her car before unlocking it and getting inside. Then, she started her engine but she did not pull away. After a minute, she got out, looking in all directions again, and came around to the hood, opened it and peered at the engine. She studied it for a moment with a light from her phone then slammed it shut, looking around again carefully, before getting back in the car and locking the door.

"That's a girl," Troy said to himself. Either the man had managed to pop the hood or she just felt something was wrong. She always had been a bit psychic.

Tobi drove carefully out of the icy parking lot, and Troy waited a moment before following her. Before Troy made the left turn onto the street, he noticed the maroon Mercedes GLS had pulled into the lane just behind her. In the light of the street lamps, he could just barely see the face of the swarthy-looking fat man before he turned in behind them both. There was snow and ice on the Mercedes's license plate and he could only make out the first three letters.

Troy could barely keep up with them without drawing attention to himself. Tobi seemed in a rush to get home, maybe spooked by her hood being open, and the Mercedes kept pace. They all exited the LIE and, in another mile, Tobi turned into a gated community. The Mercedes tried to follow, but after speaking to the guard, it was turned away.

Troy hung back and waited, then followed the car as it parked down the road on a side street. The fat man got out and started walking back to Tobi's community.

Troy waited a few minutes after he parked his Jeep. He put his gloves back on and followed the fat man, easily catching up with him but staying back a hundred paces. The fat man hesitated before he got to the guard station, then slunk into the trees on the outgoing side of the gatehouse and slipped past.

Troy considered telling the guard there was an intruder, but then he would certainly be prevented from following—he was an intruder too. He slipped into the same shrubbery on the outgoing side of traffic.

They were thick evergreens covered with ice, and the ground was frozen over, with old snow still lining the curb. The ice from the brush rubbed off and into Troy's jacket, where it melted against the skin on his neck. He made it past the guard and headed up the block until it forked.

Which way had the fat man gone? Standing against a tree in the shadows, he looked up and down and saw nothing. There were soft yellow lights every three or four houses, and with the moon up, he should have been able to see him.

Of course, he's not going to parade leisurely down the street, Troy thought. He himself walked along the road more openly, hoping that anyone he met would assume he'd gotten in legitimately through the gate or that he belonged there. It was too cold for anyone to be going for an evening stroll, anyway. He started looking at cars in the driveways, searching for the Outback with the MD plates, and hoping Tobi had not put it in her garage.

All at once, Troy saw him, at the top of the hill. The fat man was walking around the side of a house about a hundred feet away, looking at the windows and pushing on them tentatively. How he would get himself through one of those windows was beyond comprehension. Troy started to run, slid and skidded on a strip of black ice, wrenching his back, but recovered and followed him around to the rear of the house just as the man was trying to jimmy the sliding glass door on Tobi's deck.

"Hey!" Troy yelled out at him. "Get away from there!"

The man jumped, then turned and peered at him as Troy ran toward him. Did this guy recognize him from the parking lot? The fat man put his hand in his jacket and pulled out what looked like a pair of wire cutters just as Troy got closer, and Troy felt it smack his head just as he twisted the man around, kicked him hard on the side of his left knee, and pushed him toward the ground.

The guy was huge this close up. He made an "oof" sound, tripping over his own feet as he stumbled sideways, but he caught himself on the railing of the deck. Troy's left eye was immediately full of blood, obscuring his vision. He wiped his face, prepared to fight, but the fat man was half running, half hobbling across the lawn and down the street, moving faster than Troy would have thought possible for someone his size.

He was about to pursue him when another man appeared on the road, walking a collie and a springer spaniel. Troy was suddenly aware of how inappropriate it was for him to be there at all, even to call 911. He himself was an intruder, and he didn't even know the address of this house. How would he explain to Tobi or her neighbors that he was in her backyard when the police came?

He pressed his glove against his forehead and waited for the dog walker to pass. The dogs sniffed in his direction and the spaniel barked continuously at someone down the block, probably the fat man, but the neighbor checked the leash and told him to be quiet. Sleepy community, Troy thought, with no suspicions of foul play, feeling protected by the guard at the gatehouse.

He slowly walked around to the front of the house. The blood was starting to freeze on his gray Gore-Tex gloves but was still oozing from his face. As he rang the bell, he considered how this was definitely not the way he had pictured seeing Tobi again.

Chapter 46

Tobi peered through the peephole, expecting to see one of her neighbors. Instead she saw a vaguely familiar face covered in blood. She froze for a second, but she soon realized he wasn't going away. She wavered. She hadn't answered Troy for good reason; she had no interest in communication. But here he was, and obviously injured, and although facial lacerations bled like crazy, she had no idea how bad the trauma was. The jilted woman and the doctor battled inside her for a long minute. Finally, the doctor won. She opened the door.

"What the hell! What are you doing here? How did you get in? What happened to you?"

Troy shook his head and shrugged helplessly. He didn't speak.

Tobi opened the door wider for him to come inside. It was too cold to leave the door open. She closed it behind him.

"I'm sorry," he finally said, "this wasn't the entrance I wanted to make."

"I didn't want you to make any entrance! Oh—geez, sit and let me get you some bandages to stop the bleeding." He sat just inside the door on her brown faux leather ottoman. The contrast of sub-freezing temperatures to heat seemed to make him weak at the knees and he had nearly collapsed. "I hope you have an exceptionally good reason for being here."

She went upstairs and grabbed gauze, alcohol, gloves, and mupirocin cream for starts. She glanced at her old suture set, but she wasn't sure he would need it, and it was years since it had been properly sterilized—no one used autoclaves anymore. Everything at B. Healthy was disposable, but she preferred the higher quality instruments she used to use. She grabbed a disposable stapler and some skin glue instead and went back down. Troy was sitting in the exact same position as when she had left, and he was avoiding touching anything, including the walls, which was a good thing, since he was covered in blood.

"Come in the kitchen. Here, take off your shoes and coat first." Tobi handed him a piece of gauze to press against his head and helped him take off his coat and bloody gloves and put his wet shoes at the door. She hung his coat on the rack. "What, did you get yourself injured so I'd feel bad and open the door for you? What happened?" She ushered him into the kitchen, where his blood wouldn't stain anything.

"Tobi," Troy nearly brushed aside the gauze. "You're in danger. This guy—the guy who just did this to me, I just stopped him from breaking into your house. He was on your deck in the back, trying to force open the door."

Tobi stopped with her hands in midair, one glove on and one off. She looked at the door and then turned back and stared at him.

"That's crazy." A terrible sensation came over her, reigniting the premonition she'd been having all day. "But ... the hood of my car was unlatched tonight when I got out of work. It spooked me. And then I felt like I was being followed all the way home." As she spoke, she raised the blinds on the sliding glass door in the kitchen, looked outside, and checked the lock. She lowered the blinds.

"You were. This guy followed you and I followed him," Troy said. "I'm sorry, but I've been trying to reach you, and I came back because

I felt you were in danger. Now I know I was right. He was messing with the hood of your car, but he drove away when he saw me get out of the Jeep."

"Did you see who it was?"

"He was a big fat guy, darkish skin, beard, drove a maroon Mercedes Benz GLS."

Tobi's jaw dropped. "Ismar? Ismar Rufini?"

"I have no idea what his name is," Troy said, catching a drop of blood on some gauze as it dripped down his face. "I tried to get the license plate number, but it was full of ice. All I got were the first three letters, SLZ. We need to call the police."

"Okay … let me look at your face first. You're bleeding all over the place."

Tobi wet the gauze and gently washed the blood off Troy's face and washed out the wound as he sat at her kitchen table. It felt surreal, having him sitting in front of her, and she grasped for the skills of detachment she used when treating her patients. She needed to keep herself distant, but she couldn't help but smell his skin, like a favorite spice from long ago, evoking memories of love and joy and wonder, mixed with the smell of blood, his shampoo, cologne, and his sweat all at once. She avoided his eyes, those deep blue-green hazel eyes that threatened to wash her away like being drawn out to sea.

The laceration was actually just inside his hairline on his left forehead, so the scar wouldn't show. His blonde hair was graying but still thick, parted in the middle, and nearly shoulder length. As she stood over him, she glimpsed a wisp of gray chest hair poking out from his button down shirt and charcoal gray sweater. It contrasted with his deep tan, so out of place in New York in the winter. How is this actually happening, she wondered. She felt a wave of vertigo and forced herself to focus on the wound.

"So, why *are* you here? Just turned up on cue to save a damsel in distress?"

Troy turned in his chair and put his hands on her forearms and drawing them away from his head. He gaze pierced her eyes and Tobi really did need to sit down.

"Tobi. It's Reuben. He died."

After a twelve-hour shift, fear and paranoia, and seeing him after so long covered in blood, the stress was too much. Tobi burst into hysterical laughter. "That's what—that's what you came to tell me?" The tension definitely got the best of her, and she laughed so hard, she felt she would never stop. She could hardly speak, her chest hurt, and still the laughter came.

"News flash—Reuben died!" she said between guffaws. "Hey, Troy, if you came to offer condolences, you're nineteen years too late! I guess you never got the memo …." Tobi nearly fell on the floor, she was laughing so hard, but the laughter quickly turned to tears and gasps, and she couldn't get control of herself. She managed to put the bloody gauze down on the glass tabletop before she completely lost it. I've got to get a grip, she thought.

Troy looked sheepish. "Yes, I know … I know what you thought. But … Reuben died six weeks ago, not nineteen years ago."

She sobered up abruptly. "What—what are you talking about?"

"I mean …" he stuttered and took a deep breath. "I mean, he was alive until six weeks ago. He was in Port Douglas, Australia."

Tobi stared at him, her breath stuck in her throat. She searched his eyes for the joke and found none. Troy had never been much of a liar. A minute passed, and another, until she started to believe him.

"How …? What hap—I don't understand. Why would he pretend he was dead? Why didn't he tell me? Why didn't *you* tell me?" She felt a fury growing inside her. "Do you mean he just ran away? Do you know how long I've imagined that he just ran away? Do you have any *idea?* I would have been fine with him running away. Hell! I did. I just stayed in the same country, and *I* didn't lie about it!"

Troy put an awkward hand on her arm, and Tobi exploded. She screamed at him and pounded her fists on his chest, as she started to believe what he'd said.

"He was ALIVE? All this time, he was *alive*! And you didn't tell me? How could you have kept that from me? I mourned him. I never got to make peace with him. You stole that from me, how could you? You said you loved me! Do you even know what love means?"

Her fists battered at him as she screamed and he crumpled to the floor, bent over. He didn't raise an arm to protect himself as she hammered at him relentlessly. The bleeding started again from his scalp and puddled on the kitchen floor. She screamed until she had no voice, and then she backed away and started striking herself on both sides of her own head. "NO, NO, NO …. We were *in* Australia! We were in *Cairns*, we could have found him, we could have found him …." Her voice trailed off and she sunk to her knees and leaned back against the kitchen wall.

Troy reacted quickly. He reached over and grabbed both of her hands firmly and made her stop pounding herself, with tears pouring from his eyes. He tried to put his arms around her, but she pushed him away.

She had to be dreaming all this. But here was Troy, in her kitchen, bleeding, and looking completely crushed. Strong, solid, confident Troy; serene, enlightened, mystical Troy; leveled to a lump, with a torrent of tears flowing from those beautiful eyes, and his voice cracking, as he said over and over again, "I'm sorry, I'm so sorry … I'm so, so sorry."

It took at least twenty minutes for Tobi to stop crying, and then she felt empty. She shouldn't have, since nothing had essentially changed. She had thought Reuben was dead and he *was* dead. But all the years she could have spent time with him, talked to him, made up with him … and Ben! He had needed a reliable man in his life to role model. They had both been ripped off. She couldn't decide who she was angrier at, Reuben or Troy.

Once she had calmed down, Pantelaymin came over and climbed into Tobi's lap. Tobi didn't know how long she had been close by watching, but her lap certainly hadn't been approachable until she had composed herself. The cat circled once and settled, facing outward at Troy like a challenge. Troy reached over to pet her and she hissed at him.

"Good girl, Panni," Tobi said.

Troy pulled his hand back. "Please get up off the floor," he pleaded. "I can't stand seeing you on the floor."

"That's funny," Tobi snarled, "you didn't seem to mind it years ago." She regretted it immediately. She watched as Troy's face turned crimson, matching the blood that still oozed from his scalp.

"We need to call the police," he said. "I need to make sure this guy won't try to hurt you again."

Tobi pet Pantelaymin again and kissed her on her nose, then put her aside and got up. She said nothing but changed her gloves and washed the wound again with betadine and then removed the betadine with alcohol. She grabbed the sterile, prefilled staple gun.

"Hold still," she said. "This is going to hurt a bit." She stapled the laceration closed. It was really more of a puncture wound and only took two staples, but she could tell it was tender. He looked cold even in the warm kitchen, but he did not move or say anything more.

"That's going to bruise, just warning you. You'll be purple there for a few days. Did you fall on your head and do you take aspirin or any blood thinners?" The doctor script never slept. He shook his head "no" to both.

She washed her hands and made him a cup of hot tea. "Just so I don't have to learn what you know when you tell the police, how did you know someone was going to try to hurt me, and what, if anything, does it have to do with Reuben?"

Troy sipped at the tea. "Do you remember Reuben's last job?"

Tobi shook her head. "Not really. We weren't actually on great terms. Every conversation came back to Mom. 'We should buy her a new kitchen table,' or 'she needs a new car' ... it was such stupidity. All I remember is he talked about doing an electronic health record for some company that was paying him beaucoups of money, and he left Cray Research for it. It's funny, I thought he was nuts, and now it's the big thing. I never gave him credit for being so savvy, but he anticipated so many advances ... it's too bad he didn't play the market."

Troy nodded. "Yes, well, there was a reason they paid him so much. I don't think they expected Reuben to figure them out, but he told me—"

"Why *you* and not me?"

"Because ... I could get him out of the country and help him disappear. He never intended to 'play dead.' That just sort of happened."

"How does that *just happen*? You're not making any sense!"

"Then stop. Listen. Let me tell you."

Tobi tucked her right leg under her on the seat at the kitchen table. She had changed into navy sweat pants, heavy socks, and a gray Colorado hoodie sweatshirt when she had gotten home, and that should have been downright cozy, but her spine tingled. She considered moving into the living room and onto the much more comfortable Natuzzi sofa, but she didn't want him to get the idea she was welcoming him back into her life. She sat up and looked at him and waited.

"Reuben discovered that the EHR program he was writing for these people under the guise of Financier, Inc., was not to advance patient care but to uncover medical secrets of politicians so they could be blackmailed."

"What kind of secrets?"

Troy cocked his head at her. She used to love it when he did that.

"If you give me a chance, I will tell you. It's not a two-minute read."

"Okay, okay, I'm sorry," she said.

Troy proceeded to spin a barely believable yarn. She was still in shock at seeing him and stressed to her limit by her newfound paranoia, or she might have told him he was full of it. But the Troy she used to know would never have played with her like that, so she listened and tried to digest it all.

Troy's tea was gone but he still held the cup in his hand like he was trying to warm his fingers and Tobi wondered if she should offer him more or something to eat. The Jewish mother instinct to take care of him was strong, but it was battling with her anger and her fatigue, and for once, it was losing.

"Reuben didn't figure out exactly who these guys were, only that they were Russian. Probably the new oligarchs who were privatizing the country at the time, but I actually have a lead from an inspector in Port Douglas. He found a connection to an insurance company whose market is high-risk medical and charges huge premiums, but their patients aren't living long enough to get the benefits."

"What do you mean?"

"The patients continue to pay exorbitant premiums up until the time they need to start using the insurance, and then they have some mishap—a car accident—something, and they die. The insurance company gets to keep the premiums and never has to pay out on the surgery."

Tobi stared at him. He was still the same Troy. His eyes were deep set, with a few more little crinkle lines at the temples and that same little bump on his chin, and his left brow still bunched up near his nose when he was serious. His forehead was starting to swell and turn colors, but there was no further bleeding. She really should get him some ice. She was so focused on Troy, she almost didn't put it together.

"Wait," she said. "What's the name of that insurance company? I have a patient whose father just died in a car accident the day before he got his kidney transplant. Except they only made two payments."

"He said it was called Kordec. Does that ring a bell?"

"I don't know. I don't usually get involved with the carriers. Maybe. I don't think they expected to locate a new kidney so soon, either. Come to think of it, my friend Chloe might have mentioned being approached by them, but they didn't sign up. Why didn't you *tell* me?"

"You never saw him like this, Tobi. I could barely believe it was Reuben. He was completely panic-stricken. He begged me to help him, and then …." he raised his hands helplessly. "Tobi. He made me promise. He made me promise never to tell you where he was or that I even knew. He was afraid you would have looked for him, and then these people would have gone after you and Benny."

"Of course I would have looked for him, he was my brother! But if you'd told me what happened, I would have been discreet. I would have waited. It would have been enough for a while just to know he was okay." Tobi stared at him defiantly. "You had no right to stop me."

"You're right, but I gave him my word."

"And you never told me, even later, when he was safely hidden? So, you didn't *trust* me, is what it comes down to."

"No, Tobi—"

"And that still doesn't explain how he 'turned up dead.' He just happened to find a body lying around that looked like him, to substitute?" Tobi felt her anger rising again. It was too much to swallow after all these years.

"It was the guy scheduled to be terminated before his heart transplant. When he died, Reuben ran, and he tossed the guy's wallet in the river. And of course, he left his own wallet in the apartment—he couldn't use his own name or cards anyway. I think whoever identified the man couldn't tell for sure because he'd been … decomposing for a few days."

"That would have been his friend Ken. They wouldn't let me see him, they wouldn't let me—I would have known!" Tobi put her head in her hands and cried again. "I wanted to see him, I *needed* to see his body." She looked up into Troy's eyes. "I didn't believe it, it didn't feel right, and they wouldn't let me!" She sobbed and Troy inched over to her and put a cautious hand on her elbow. The next thing she knew, she was crying on his shoulder and his arms were wrapped around her.

"Why didn't you tell me? Why wouldn't you spare me that? And … why did you *leave*? I needed you so much back then."

"I couldn't tell you," Troy whispered. "I believed Reuben, I believed it would put you in danger. These people were—are—too powerful. And I left because I couldn't lie to you." He rested his head on top of hers, his tears dripping down his nose and into her hair. At that moment, she felt like they were the only two people alive in the universe.

It was a familiar feeling, her head on his shoulder. She felt warm and protected in a way she hadn't experienced in an eternity, but she recalled her current reality and pushed him away.

"Why did you come back now?"

"Because I think Reuben had been hacking into these guys' program from an independent server before he died six weeks ago in a diving accident. I went to Port Douglas when I couldn't reach him. Someone from this Russian group went looking for the hacker and figured out who he was, and then two other people were killed. One was a friend of ours and Reuben's dive shop partner, and the other was one of *his* friends."

Tobi put her hand over her mouth reflexively.

"And so I come back to make sure you're okay, and I find some guy trying to mess with your car and break into your house. What was he going to do?" Troy started rubbing his hands over the sides of his face and back over his head, flinching as his hand touched his swollen forehead. Tobi remembered he used to do that when he was agitated, which wasn't that often.

"It's 9:45 p.m., we have to call the police," Tobi said. "Why didn't Reuben do that? Or go to the FBI?"

"Reuben found that some US senators and FBI agents had been blackmailed. He didn't know how many were in on it or who could be trusted."

"Geez, and I thought *I* was the suspicious one."

"I did get some help from the inspector in Port Douglas. He found the name of the murder suspect from facial recognition and gave me the name of this insurance company. It's still all speculation, but it makes sense."

"Wow, how'd you get the Australian police to share with you? Just flashed that rapturous smile of yours?"

Troy blushed. "He wouldn't have, not until his secretary outed me as the CEO of the foundation. Let's call the police. Hopefully, that's not a mistake at this point in time, but doing nothing is unacceptable."

Chapter 47

It was nearly midnight by the time the police were done taking statements. Tobi was grateful she wasn't scheduled to work the next day because she wasn't sure she could have managed. The police looked at them both skeptically when Troy told them he'd followed the prowler into the development by dodging the gatehouse, and then Officer Tarman asked Tobi if she wanted to press charges against Troy for intruding. She had glanced at him wickedly and he blanched, but she declined and said she was glad he had come, that he had probably saved her life.

Troy described the fat man with dark skin and beard and his car, license plate letters SLZ, and Tobi told them that Dr. Ismar Rufini and his car fit the exact description, although she didn't know his plate number, and that he had been asking her questions about whether she lived alone or not. Officers Tarman and Weston said they would go to Ismar's house on Centre Island, and they left. No one but Troy could corroborate the story of an intruder and his own presence in the community at that exact moment was spurious.

***

At nine in the morning, Tobi's next-door neighbor knocked on the door, and Tobi invited her in.

"Are you alright? I saw the police were here all night, what happened?" Laila was dressed in black slacks under a forest green winter coat and ankle high boots, her long blonde hair cascading over the hood of her jacket.

"I'm sorry it kept you up," Tobi said. "Someone tried to break in."

"The gatehouse let someone in without checking? You know, sometimes our nighttime staff is not what it should be."

"No, he slipped by on foot. It was … personal, I think. Sounds like it was the regional lead physician where I work."

"Oh my God, did you get in touch with the company? They should know about this."

"I plan to, just wanted to wake up first." Tobi's last conversation with Steve had made her uneasy.

"Is there someone upstairs?" Laila looked up as the sound of running water stopped.

"Yes, that's kind of a long story …."

Laila winked at her. "Good for you, Tobi."

Tobi blushed. "No, it's not what you think. He slept on the couch in my study."

"Okay, no problem." Laila was grinning mischievously. "But if you need anything, let me know. I'm heading out to work."

Troy came downstairs just as Laila left.

His wet hair was combed back away from his face and he was fully dressed. Tobi wasn't sure if she was disappointed or relieved. Maybe both. He had retrieved his Jeep with his suitcase and clothes late last night, and it was now parked on the street in front of her house. The phone rang and she jumped.

"Hello Dr. Lister, this is Officer Tarman. Just wanted to let you know we checked out Ismar Rufini, and he has an alibi. His wife says he was home all night last night from 5:00 p.m. on, so we can't arrest him without more to go on. Are you sure it wasn't one of your neighbors? Looked like the gatehouse keeps a log of everyone who comes onto the premises."

Tobi paled. "I'm sure it wasn't. Troy saw him follow me home from my office, and the description and the car match him perfectly. I even showed him a picture of Rufini that I pulled off Facebook, and he said that was him."

"The partial plate was a match, so we'll keep an eye on him nevertheless, but if you have any other information that can pin him down, or whoever hit your ex-boyfriend, come down to the station and we can talk."

"Okay, thank you, officer." She turned to Troy. "That was the police. Ismar's wife covered for him."

Her phone rang again, this time the president of her homeowners association.

"Hi, Jeff."

"Hi, Tobi. I hear you had some activity at your house last night. The police were asking the guard a lot of questions. First off, is everybody okay? I heard there was an injury."

"Yes, thanks. An old … friend of mine came by and stopped someone from prying my back door open, but he was hit with a wire cutter or something. He's okay, I fixed him up."

"Good, it's nice to have a doctor on the property. Do you know who did it? The guard told me he didn't let in anyone who was going to your house. If he's not doing his job properly, we have to fire him."

"No, no Jeff. This guy snuck in on foot, on the outgoing side of the gate."

"Hmm … he should have had his eyes open. Why would someone do that? Do you know who it was?"

"I think so—well, I thought so, but the police just told me his wife vouched for him."

"Well, I hope they catch whoever it was soon. I've asked security to double their nighttime rounds. You know, we have an unmarked car that drives through the community every shift. If you have any trouble, call 911 of course, but call the gatehouse too, and they'll summon our private security as well."

"Thanks, Jeff, I appreciate it."

"You bet. We've got to keep you safe, doc. And the rest of our residents too. Let me know when they catch him."

"Will do." She hung up. Geez, the last thing she wanted was for all of her neighbors to get wind of this bizarre situation and be frightened.

Troy was in the kitchen and had found the Keurig coffee maker that Tobi kept just for Ben and had prepared a cup of Organics Special Blend. "Since when do you drink coffee?" Tobi asked. "That's not the healthy sustenance you used to endorse. I don't think I can ever remember seeing you drink coffee."

"I started in Port Douglas. I don't know, the world had turned upside down, and me with it," Troy said. Tobi almost felt bad for him.

"Tell me, who else knew about my brother?" She purposely used the possessive adjective rather than calling Reuben by name. He had been Tobi's brother before he ever was Troy's friend.

Troy turned to her, and she was forced to look him in the eyes. "No one," he said.

"Seriously? No one? Not a soul? You expect me to believe you never told a single person?" She realized she was using anger as a shield to keep from losing herself in those eyes.

Thankfully, he looked down as he shook his head. "I didn't even tell Mack. How could I tell Mack when I hadn't told you?" He did look bereft, but Tobi wasn't going to fall for it.

"I wanted to tell you ... so many times," he whispered. "Reuben was dead set against it. You know how stubborn he could be. And then when I thought it was safe, and I was going to do it anyway ... I got scared. I thought you'd hate me and wouldn't hear me out."

"Smart boy," Tobi snapped.

Troy looked up. He resembled a lost puppy. "Look, I didn't come to intrude on your life, but I will not leave Long Island until this is all settled and these people can no longer threaten you. I can check into a hotel, but I am going to spend every night and every day making sure you are safe. It would be easier to protect you if I could use your couch for the time being. But I understand that's a lot to ask."

Tobi vacillated. She hadn't wanted him to come back into her life, but now that he was here, she was torn. Truth was, she was now terrified of Ismar and no longer had confidence in getting help from the police, Steve Chagall, or B. Healthy. Maybe Reuben had been right, and these people were entrenched everywhere. Having Troy nearby did make her feel safe—or at least, safer.

Pantelaymin wandered into the kitchen and regarded Troy with the sassy attitude unparalleled by anyone except a feline. She walked up to him, sniffed at his socks, and after a glance at Tobi, rubbed against him. She circled his legs in a figure eight and started purring loudly. Troy flashed a mischievous smile and looked up at Tobi. He shrugged his shoulders and nodded at the cat, trying to look innocent.

"Change of heart, Panni?" Tobi quipped at the cat. Then she gave up. "Okay, okay," Tobi said. "Only since Pantelaymin approves. But you're staying in the study and using Ben's bathroom. Stay out of my room!"

"Scout's honor!" Troy held up his fingers.

"How is Benny? What's he up to? I missed him too."

"For one thing, no one calls him 'Benny' anymore. He was terribly hurt when you left, as much as I was."

"I never in a million years wanted to hurt him …."

"Well, you did. You hurt us both. But we both survived. He's in medical school now, at Columbia. He has a serious girlfriend, and she's delicious. It's looking like they might get married one of these days."

"Wow, little Benny—or what does he go by now?"

"Ben. Or sometimes Benjamin."

"Ben. A doctor and getting married. I missed it all, didn't I?"

"Yup, you did."

"And what about you, Tob? Would it be out of line to ask if you were with anyone?"

"Nope, Troy, you cured me." He had the good graces to wince, at least.

There was another awkward moment. "What about you?" she asked. "I hear your foundation is a huge success. I even looked you up once on charitynavigator.org; you got four stars."

Troy's face colored. "You know I never did it for money, Tob. It's all for the Earth. And in case you were wondering, no, there's been no one serious in my life since you."

"Guess I cured you too, then." Tobi couldn't seem to keep the acerbic tone from her voice. It was her only defense.

"Well, I need to dive in and talk to my medical director, but the way he sounded on the phone yesterday, I don't think he'll be particularly helpful. There's granola, and yogurt and fresh strawberries are in the fridge, if you want. Don't worry, it's all organic."

Troy's posture changed, and his muscles tightened. "Why do you think he won't be helpful?"

"I don't know. I spoke to him yesterday morning and I told him Ismar was caught using other providers' logins and could access charts and he told me not to worry about Ismar, that I should 'just worry about myself.' It isn't like him to be dismissive like that. And he acted like he'd never said anything to me about my login being used to 'snoop' in charts that aren't mine."

"Wait, so this has been happening in your organization?"

"It's starting to look like it," Tobi said.

"Is there anyone else you can call, besides this medical director?"

"Well, there's Daniel Comet … he was the previous director, but he left. I think he couldn't stand the direction B. Healthy was going in. So much emphasis on profit and no consideration of quality of care. Did you know, Troy, that we don't treat patients anymore, they are now consumers of medical services? And our number one goal is to keep them 'happy customers,' so they'll keep coming back and we'll keep making money, even if what it takes to make them happy is not the appropriate treatment."

Troy raised his hands in the air. "The whole damn world is doing that, why should medicine be any different? They're not selling value anymore, just volume. It's all about greed. The abuses of nature that I've seen, Tobi, it makes me want to cry sometimes. All so some multimillionaire—or multi*billionaire*—can pad his pockets even more. I wonder if he thinks he'll be able to buy clean air and clean water for his grandchildren when it all runs out."

Tobi was quiet. Of course, Troy understood without even being told. He was the same Troy he'd always been.

Troy pushed his hair back on the sides of his head, and flinched when he touched his swollen, purple forehead. "Where is this Daniel Comet now? How well do you know him, and can you trust him? Because I think we have to choose our confidants carefully."

Tobi heard the "we" and relaxed a little. Maybe she wasn't all alone in this snake pit after all.

"Daniel is vice president at Hospitals for Health, which is the system B. Healthy is trying to affiliate with. Yes, I think I can trust him. He used to be my boss, but he's more of a kindred spirit. Like, I feel as if I've known him for centuries."

Troy cocked his head at her.

"No—not like that. He's married, and anyway, I haven't been interested in that with anyone. He's just a friend."

"So, who are you going to call first?"

"I guess I should call Steve first. That would be the appropriate channel. And Daniel if that doesn't go well."

Chapter 48

The first time Tobi called Steve, it went to voicemail, so she sent him an urgent text. When there was no answer after three hours, she called him again.

"Yes, hi, what's up?" Steve's voice was tense and detached.

"Hey. I need your help. Ismar followed me home last night and tried to break into my house. He needs to stay the hell away from me, like in the office too."

"Did you call the police?" Steve's voice was flat.

"Yes, of course, but his wife lied and told them he was with her all night. We're sure it was him, it was his car. How many short, three hundred pound guys with dark brown facial hair drive a Mercedes GLS?"

"Well, if the police say it wasn't him, it's out of my hands. You actually saw him?"

"A friend of mine did, and he picked him out of a Facebook photo."

"I don't know what I can do, Dr. Lister, these are matters best left to the police. My hands are tied. Literally. Okay? I have to run. Be well."

"But—"

The phone went dead.

Tobi felt like she'd been sucker punched. She stood there feeling completely vulnerable. Steve had always been so collegial and friendly. *Dr. Lister?* Really? I'm in deep trouble, she thought. He had said his hands were tied, "literally." He might have been trying to let her know, they'd gotten to him. She called Ellie.

"Hey, Ell, is it busy there?"

"We caught a three-minute break, good timing. What's going on? Wait, let me go in the back and shut the door. Okay, I'm in the x-ray room. I heard you accused Rufini of trying to attack you! What happened?"

"Where did you hear that?" Tobi was astonished. "How did it end up all over B. Healthy already? I just called Steve five minutes ago."

"I don't know, but you know me. I heard from Monica in the south shore office. He's been hanging out there recently, and she overheard a conversation. Also, he seems to have hurt his knee, he could barely walk. He said it just gave out on him yesterday, and he wanted to get an x-ray, and then he didn't want anyone to look at the image. He wouldn't make himself a chart, either. Of course, she looked at it after he left, and he has a fracture of the head of the fibula. You don't get that with your knee just buckling. Hey, don't tell anyone I told you, okay? HIPAA and all that. But he doesn't seem to care about looking in other peoples' charts, or using our logins, so …."

"But how did that get connected to me?" Tobi asked.

"Oh, yeah, he was cursing you under his breath, told Monica you were giving him a hard time, and then Monica overheard him in the kitchen denying he had anything to do with you being assaulted— he mentioned you by name and said his wife had already explained he was home last night. Were you assaulted? What happened? I was going to call you later anyway."

"Ellie, this is all a big mess, and I'm really scared. I tried to talk to Steve, and he was bizarre. He called me 'Dr. Lister.' I think he's wrapped up in it too."

"That's weird. Wrapped up in what? Monica tried to talk to him yesterday about him using her tablets and he was, like, clueless. Didn't he ask you once if you were snooping?"

"Yeah, he did, last month. Now he acts like he doesn't know what I'm talking about. Something bad is happening at work, Ellie. Do you know anything about an insurance called Kordec?"

"Umm, yeah, it's for really sick people. I think they're all like end-stage something or other. A couple of my hospice patients were on that plan where I moonlight. It's super expensive. Why?" Ellie asked.

"I don't know, but Ismar and the tablet issue have something to do with them, I'm pretty sure. Pretty convenient that Monica manages to 'overhear' all these conversations. What does she do, put her stethoscope to the door to listen?"

Ellie cackled. "Yeah, well, she feels like she's getting shafted by this place, so nothing is out of reach to her. I'll call you later, a bunch of patients just came in."

Chapter 49

After three postponements, the subcommittee finally convened. The meeting was dull and cumbersome, and the room was stuffy. Kavandor was sweating. He still had not heard back from his Russian albatross. He kept glancing at Wiseman out of the corner of his eye and praying the newbie really did want to make a career mark.

He drawled, trying to sound bored with the topic. "So, our next matter is this insurance company called Kordec. The AMA has been receiving anonymous emails for years, begging them to look into it. They disregarded the correspondence at first, since no one would take responsibility for sending them. But after about the fiftieth email, they started questioning. The medical association thinks the insurance is costly and provides no realizable gains for the consumer, since the insureds seem to die before they can benefit. They want us to evaluate and possibly shut it down."

There was an outburst from the newbie. "Kordec? The FBI was looking into Kordec a bunch of years ago, and so was Interpol. I was just reading about it!"

Atta boy, Wiseman, Kavandor thought. Come through for me, bro!

"What else did the AMA say?" Senator Hank Hasbrow asked. "Did they find the source of the emails?"

"Apparently not," Kavandor said. "The previous chair, Andrew Corbet, had been receiving them for years but dismissed them. He just retired, and the file was inherited by Zack Pryor. Pryor thought they should be looked at, but he hasn't been able to get past the firewalls that are hiding the source and is looking for help. He also found that several state medical societies have Kordec on their radar, but not with the kind of detail these emails provide. He's asked for an investigation into this company. If what the emails claim is true, then at the very least, these people are making a lot of money preying on disadvantaged patients."

Wiseman spoke up. "I might be able to get some FBI support for that, at least to track the sender. The trail went cold for us years ago. A surgeon in London reported his patients were dying before they got to the OR, but then he died—or was maybe killed—Scotland Yard never did get to the bottom of that. Why is this email person being so underhanded? If there's a problem, why don't they come out and talk to us? We would protect them."

"Maybe they're worried about HIPAA violations," Hasbrow offered. "Or retribution. Who knows why people feel they need to be anonymous. How many patients are we talking about? Is it worth our time?"

"Not sure, but if, as Pryor thinks, it's a multistate action, possibly thousands," Kavandor said.

"Wow. Sure," Hasbrow said. "Let's check into it, then, and see what's going on. If something is fishy and we don't act on it, we could lose votes in next year's elections, especially if the liberals get wind of it and say we ignored it. We can only look good by investigating."

"Okay, Hank, I'm putting you on it. Al, please facilitate with some of your FBI resources." Kavandor felt an odd mix of relief and anxious anticipation.

"Sure thing," Wiseman said. "We can usually break through those firewalls."

Chapter 50

Mannfort sat in first class on Ukraine International, sipping his vodka, lime, and ginger beer. He was sweating under a skin-tight facial mask. He'd had them made up for him and Kazi before boarding. He was sure either of them could set off facial recognition alerts at the airports. He didn't think the Americans were sophisticated enough to spot them unless they were actively looking for them, but Interpol was more thorough, which was why he'd sent Kazi on Air France through Europe and he flew direct to New York.

They had disassembled their weapons and distributed the parts between both sets of suitcases, so no one could find a complete weapon on either of them or even on the same flight. Kazimir had been an arms specialist in the Georgian Civil War and could break down and reassemble firearms from their bare bones. He loved guns and all things that blew up, and he was also an excellent marksman with a knife. It made him a tremendous asset to the Project. The plan was for Mannfort to rent a car at JFK Airport, and Kazi would take the Air Train, so they'd meet up at Jamaica station in Queens.

Kazi had already picked out a hotel on Long Island not far from Lister's office. It was much less glamorous than his usual digs, but it would attract less attention. That part of Long Island appeared to be a sleepy stretch where not much happened; no one was going to suspect them in "suburbia." Americans took their peaceful way of life completely for granted.

First order of business would be to "persuade" the Turkish toad to be more cooperative. Kazi had supplied Mannfort with some in-flight reading about the fool, Rufini, and how he had been acquired, and what buttons they could push to terrify him. Rufini had failed to neutralize the lady doctor, but it seemed he had been quite useful in getting potential clients for Kordec, so Mannfort would hate to waste him if it wasn't necessary. Mannfort scratched at his face, wishing he could get under the mask.

Chapter 51

The next morning, Troy pulled the Jeep into the parking lot behind the office. Tobi felt irascible; seeing patients right now was not where her attention was, and her mind kept straying. She also felt vulnerable leaving the car back here, but she hated going in the office through the front, and at least the Jeep wasn't recognizable as hers. There were already patients waiting on line outside that she would have had to push past and then explain to them why she wasn't opening up the doors yet. It was 7:50 a.m., and she still wanted a few minutes to get her bearings before putting on her professional face. At least Ismar's Mercedes was nowhere in sight.

Troy walked her in to make sure the place was secure and Tobi introduced him to Esther and Mandy and explained he would be hanging out in the break room for the day. Then he went around the building to the bagel place next door to get breakfast. It had been a long time since he'd had a real New York bagel. They'd both agreed she was pretty safe in the morning at the start of the work day.

Her work email pinged and she reluctantly checked it. The frequency of Emergency Department transfers was being evaluated, and apparently, she was one standard deviation above the market mean, but the notice said no action was indicated unless she were two standard deviations above the mean. That would actually be a huge difference. The email recommended discussing cases with colleagues before sending to the ED to see if there were a way to treat them outpatient. Lovely, she thought. Did they think she turfed to the hospital if she was busy in the office?

The only people she sent to the ED who could reasonably be treated outpatient were those whose insurance did not allow her to get outpatient studies because they needed a referral from their primary care doctor. Waiting for that referral could take weeks, and often the patient could not safely wait that long. Sometimes she sent patients due to dehydration, and sure, she could give IV fluids in the office, but it would mean tying up a room for several hours, which would increase wait time, decrease her Press Ganey scores from all her other patients, and she wouldn't be able to get stat blood work on them like the ED could.

Why was B. Healthy emailing her about this, anyway? Oh, she suddenly got it. They were trying to cut the costs for the emergency departments, now that they were part of Hospitals for Health, especially since if they discharged someone who bounced back in a few days, they'd get penalized on their compensation. The hospitals were in a bind too. If they admitted too many people, the insurance companies balked and threatened to deny payment, and if they discharged a patient who later had to come back, they were fined. Their answer was to try to keep people from coming to the emergency department in the first place. America was no place to get sick.

Well, maybe if B. Healthy staffed their sites adequately, Tobi could hydrate some of those patients in the office, but as for those who needed treatment that only the hospital could provide, that's where she was going to send them, period.

Tobi walked into room two. She recognized Peter, who was sitting on the exam table.

"Hey, Dr. Lister. My favorite doctor!"

"Aw, thanks, Peter."

"Do you remember me? The last time I was in, you insisted that I go to the emergency room. I was so resistant, I made your life hell. They took out my appendix, it was about to rupture! It's a good thing I listened to you."

"I remember hearing about that," Tobi said. Look at that, she thought, an *unnecessary* ED transfer. "I'm glad it worked out. You look good. What can I help you with today?"

"Infected finger. I was scratched by a neighborhood cat, and I guess I neglected it. Now it's all full of pus and there's this *thing* growing over my nail, and it hurts."

Tobi looked at his index finger. "You have a paronychial abscess—that's the pus pocket, but you've also got a pyogenic granuloma."

"A pyo-what?"

"It's just extra tissue that was hyper-stimulated and has started growing over the nail. We'll have to remove that."

Peter pulled his hand back. "That sounds painful. Can't you just lance the pus part and give me antibiotics?"

"I'm going to do both of those things, but that won't get rid of this extra tissue. Don't worry, I'll numb your finger first."

Esther came in to assist, and after doing a digital block to numb Peter's finger, Tobi used a finger tourniquet to stop the bleeding, lanced the abscess, and drained it, and cut away the granulation tissue with a scalpel, then cauterized the area with silver nitrate.

"I didn't feel a thing! Thanks, doc."

Tobi got Peter's paperwork together and sent him a script for an antibiotic. Then she documented the history, the review of systems, the exam, the procedure, the billing portion, and the tetanus shot given on the opposite arm to the injury. These days they were required to fill in not just the lot number and expiration date, but also the NDC code on the vaccine. Again, because they could no longer be reimbursed for it otherwise. She tagged the abscess culture to be sent as well.

As usual, the documentation had taken longer than Peter's evaluation and treatment; it seemed that ninety percent of charting was done for the sole purpose of satisfying the insurance company. At least she felt like she'd done something useful for a change, instead of dodging antibiotic requests for colds. Maybe it would be a rewarding day—if she didn't have to send anyone to the hospital and start worrying about that now too. Her nerves were on edge.

Chapter 52

Kazi came down the steps of the elevated train, or "el," as it was referred to, and hopped in Mannfort's rented BMW on Archer Avenue in Jamaica. He gestured at the street as they pulled into traffic.

"Mannya, this city is disgusting. Trash everywhere, and dirt! It's amazing, it's supposed to be such a rich country. But, look, I found connections. The hacker was communicating by email with a couple of places. One looks like the American Medical Association, which could be a big problem for us. The other is an organization called Executors for Our Earth. It's based out of California, US, and there are a lot more emails between them. Owned by some overgrown hippie type. Look at this guy. Isn't he too old to have his hair this long? Bloody Americans." He held up the picture on the website.

Mannfort grabbed at Kazi's phone. "Let me see that face!"

"Easy, Mannya, you're driving! The Americans drive like piss. We can't get stopped for a stupid auto wreck."

"That's him! That's the guy from the dive shop!"

"I thought you killed the guy in the dive shop."

"No, the other guy. The one who came in crying, the one that divemaster knew. Sokowsky's friend, I'd have bet on it then. After we're done here, we have to go to the west coast and find him, find out what he knows, and annihilate him too. The list is getting long,

Kazi, too many people involved. It's becoming a mess. That damn Sokowsky! Didn't have the grace to just die like we thought. What was in the emails?"

"I haven't figure that out yet, he encrypted all of them. All I can tell so far is where they were sent to; I can't read any of them yet."

"Any emails to the sister?" Mannfort asked as he rubbed his nose where the mask had been irritating him. Even though he'd taken the thing off in the first men's room he'd found, it felt like he was still wearing it.

"*Nyet*, I didn't see any. Mannya, maybe she knows nothing. This could be an unnecessary risk we take. Let's just knock off the toad and go home."

"At this point, it is irrelevant. They all have to go. You really think Sokowsky did not talk to her in all these years? At the very least, now she knows *someone* wants her dead, even if it is just a miserable, incompetent fool. She will start asking questions that we cannot afford."

Chapter 53

The next patient was Linda in room three. She was wearing skin-tight blue jeans and a heavy, brown cable sweater. Her boots were made of fake fur and came to her midcalf, and she looked uneasy as she sat on the exam table.

"Hi, I'm Dr. Lister. How can I help you today?"

"Hi, doctor. I found a spider walking on my hand last night. I have a phobia of spiders, they terrify me."

Tobi pulled on some gloves and walked over to her. "No worries, we'll fix you up. Let's see your hand. Did it bite you?"

"No, I screamed and shook it off."

"Oh," Tobi was puzzled. "Do you have any bleeding or itching?"

"No."

"Did it leave any marks?"

"No."

"Do you have any pain?"

"No."

So much for a rewarding day. Tobi struggled to find her compassion. This person was obviously suffering, it just wasn't from a spider bite. "So, what brought you in today?"

"I told you. I saw a spider on my hand, and I'm deathly afraid of spiders."

Tobi took a deep breath. She examined Linda's hand carefully and there was no evidence of anything amiss. She also listened to her heart and lungs and looked in her mouth.

"Well, Linda, it's good news. No problems from the spider. You're going to be fine."

"Are you *sure*, doctor?"

"Yes, everything is fine. The spider didn't bite you and everything looks normal."

"Oh, thank God! What do you think I should do?"

"About the spider? If you see it, kill it. But you may have scared it as much as it scared you, so it may hide from you now. I wouldn't worry about it."

"Okayyy, if you're sure …."

"I'm totally sure. Don't worry."

The day passed in much the same way. It seemed like the neurotics were out today, coincident with the full moon, but Tobi didn't have the patience she ought to. She was having difficulty concentrating, and she guessed it was a blessing she did not have anyone who was truly sick. Troy had brought bagels, lox, and cream cheese for the whole office, which made him quite the hero, and it irritated her. She had not yet decided if she was going to forgive him, or if she wanted him to have any part in her life after this was all over, but there he was, playing up to her staff. They would no doubt soon be gossiping behind her back about the doctor's "friend."

Her phone beeped with Reggie's text.

Hey, kiddo. Just checking in on you. Any spooky noises going 'bump in the night'? Let me know you're okay. Holler if you need anything.

Tobi smiled. Reggie always made her feel like she wasn't alone. She felt guilty not telling him about Ismar's attempted break in, but the thought of starting that conversation was exhausting and she certainly didn't have time to answer all his questions while seeing patients. She'd apologize and fill him in later. Besides, she'd have to explain Troy, and *that* would be an even longer conversation she wasn't ready for. She hadn't explained it to herself yet.

Nikolai was the next patient. Esther brought him into a room and triaged him and then gave Tobi a summary of his problem.

"So, he was at the dentist this morning for a procedure," Esther reported, "and they numbed him up. Now his ear feels funny, and he noticed blood coming out of it."

"Hi, Nikolai, my name is Dr. Lister. How can I help you today?"

"Hello. Yes, I had a tooth filled this morning, and now my ear is bleeding." Nikolai had a Russian accent but seemed very comfortable speaking English. "He gave me two shots in my mouth, isn't that too much?"

"Not necessarily," Tobi shrugged, "sometimes it takes more than one to make the area numb. Was it just a filling, or was it an extraction or root canal?"

"No, just a filling."

"And now your ear hurts?"

"No, I actually can't feel my ear well at all, it feels strange, but I touched it, and there was blood. He had to have done something to it."

"The strange feeling is probably from the novocain." Tobi couldn't imagine how a dental procedure could produce tympanic rupture. She asked him all the standard questions. Was there fever? Sore throat? Sinus congestion? Had he been swimming or flying recently? He answered no to all.

"Did you stick anything in your ear?" she asked. Also, a standard question, usually aimed at eliciting a history of an overly vigorous use of cotton swabs.

"Well, yes, I stuck my key in it."

"Your key? Why did you put your key in your ear?" Tobi had seen all kinds of things land in ear canals, but keys were a first for her.

"I had an itch," Nikolai said, as if people did that every day.

"Oh," Tobi said. "Did you use the key *before* you noticed the blood?"

"Uh, yes," Nikolai answered, but he still didn't seem to understand where the questions were going.

Tobi took the otoscope and looked in his right ear. Sure enough, there was fresh blood on the floor of the ear canal, just inside his ear. The bleeding had stopped, but the ear canal was pretty scraped up.

She stepped back. "Nikolai, you cut the inside of your ear with your key. It's lucky you didn't go all the way in, you might have damaged your ear drum. Umm, it's really not a good idea to stick things—especially sharp things—into your ears."

Nikolai stared at her. "It wasn't from the dentist?"

"No, not at all. Except that you probably didn't feel yourself doing it because of the anesthesia the dentist used. But no … you did this to yourself." Nikolai's face was impassive. "You should let the shower water hit the side of your face to rinse your ear, and I'm going to give you an antibiotic cream to use, called mupirocin. Just put a little bit barely inside the ear canal a few times a day for two to three days, so it doesn't infect." She was about to describe the use of the cotton swab for this, then checked herself. "I only want you to apply it with your little finger. Do not use anything else but your finger, okay? And just a tiny bit. Oh, and wash your hands first."

Give this guy a cotton swab, Tobi thought, and he'll be back with a perforated eardrum tomorrow for sure. Anyone who had ever worked urgent care or emergency medicine believed in the moon's influence, and today was a flawless testimony.

Chapter 54

Mannfort picked through the contents of his emptied suitcase on his bed and went through the door to Kazi's adjoining room. Mannfort had wanted to make it look like they did not know each other, but there was no other way to get adjoining rooms and neither of them was going to carry weapons parts through the hallway. Kazi had already started reassembling his equipment.

Between them, they had brought two semiautomatic rifles, two Makarov pistols, and the ingredients to make a variety of explosives with just a few local purchases. Somehow, they'd managed to avoid the dogs sniffing around at customs. Mannfort had wanted to mail ammunition ahead of time, but Kazi told him it was not needed. There was a sporting goods store down the road from the hotel, and it was easy to buy bullets in America. Kazi had been right; a quick stop had gotten all the ammo they would need.

"What's that?" Mannfort asked, pointing at a knife lying on the bed. "How'd you get that through security? Kazi, you could have jeopardized this mission."

"It's Grivory, I had it pinned to my leg under an air ankle brace. I just bought it."

"Never heard of it."

"It's a synthetic, Mannya, you need to stay up to date with progress. It's a polyphthalamide. Strong, weather-resistant, holds an edge nice, and it's not metal, so gets past security, especially if you bury under a plastic brace. I don't go anywhere unarmed. I just haven't had time to practice with it yet; it's lighter than my usual blade."

"Well, don't miss if you throw it," Mannfort said.

Chapter 55

The Lenman's were in the next room. Mrs. Lenman was there for a bad cold this time.

"Happy New Year, Dr. Lister. Look, my hand is all healed up! I was so happy to see your name on the board."

"That's terrific. How was your Thanksgiving?"

"It was wonderful. And Harry finished the soup for me, so we were able to bring it along."

"It's the first thing I've cooked in years," Mr. Lenman said.

Tobi chuckled. "Well, then it was a good growth experience, but I'm sure you would have had a great time even without it. I can't imagine there was a shortage of food."

"Oh, no, God forbid! But we did get some news of our oldest grandson. I don't know if I've ever told you, he has a drinking problem—"

"*Had* a drinking problem, Mildred, the boy has really turned himself around."

"Yes, Harry, you're right. He's been going to those 'As' and it seems to be working. He's coming up on one year completely sober. We're so proud of him."

"That's fantastic!" Tobi said. "That takes a lot of self-discipline and major life changes."

"Yes, yes, and that's not even the best part. You see, he did a lot of damage to his liver, and he's been very sick. How long was he drinking, Harry?"

"Over twenty years, Mildred, he started in his teens. None of us even knew!"

"Yes, twenty years. So, he has a liver that doesn't work so good. But a nice man came to him and told him that now that he's been sober almost a year, he's going to try to get him on the liver transplant list. They wouldn't even consider it before, but now that he's been so successful and hasn't had a drink—"

"So, we've decided to mortgage our house to help him pay for this program," Mr. Lenman said. "They will help get him to the top of the transplant list, and then they cover the surgery and all the medication and rehabilitation afterward, and homecare too. His Medicaid will never cover all that."

Tobi's head jerked up. "What's the name of the program?"

"I don't remember, but the man was so nice," Mrs. Lenman said. "Of course, our grandson doesn't have the money for it, he hasn't even been able to work the last few years, poor dear. But that's where we come in. Right, Harry?"

"Yes, Mildred, it's the least we can do for him." He turned to Tobi. "So, we can finance it or pay it all up front. Either $15,000 a month for three years, or we can give them a lump sum of $400,000 and it covers him forever. That's a huge discount!"

"Do you know, Dr. Lister," Mrs. Lenman said, "he's the one who's always been the nicest to us, no matter what he was going through. He always remembered his grandmama and grandpapa."

Tobi wanted to scream. "What is this company called? Have you checked them out?"

"Oh, yes, we will," said Mr. Lenman.

"I think it's called Kodiak."

"No, Mildred, that's a bear. It's got something with a cat in its name."

Tobi didn't think anything could put her into shock by this point, but she struggled to breathe. Not the Lenmans! She stood up and walked over to them and took each of their hands.

"You mustn't do this, not with these people. It's 'Kordec,' right? Is that the name? It's a—a scam. And worse. They'll take your money, and your grandson—he won't be safe. Please, do not do this."

Mrs. Lenman looked near tears. "We thought you'd be so happy for us."

"I'm ecstatic about your grandson's sobriety! But this company ... I've heard terrible things about them. They're not good at all. They'll take your hard-earned money and you won't be happy, please trust me on this! Have you had a lawyer look at their contract?"

"Both our son and daughter-in-law are lawyers. They poo-pooed it, but they don't like us much. That's why we have to bring soup for the holiday."

"Then you must show it to someone else." Tobi felt frantic and for a moment considered hiring a separate lawyer for them herself. She suddenly realized that by talking to the Lenman's this way, she was nailing the target to her back, but there was no way she was going to let them go through with this. "Please, promise me you won't mortgage your house, at least not without a lawyer."

"The nice man has a lawyer for us, just to make sure everything is fair," Mr. Lenman nodded.

"No, you must get your *own* lawyer!" Tobi realized she was shouting and the Lenmans looked distraught.

"Please, trust me," Tobi said to them. "These people are not good people, they will just take your money, and your grandson ... he could end up getting hurt. You know I only want the best for you."

The Lenmans looked bewildered as they shuffled out of the office, and Mrs. Lenman dabbed at her eyes with a tissue.

Tobi wished the office would slow down for a few minutes so she could talk to Troy. This was worse than they had thought. The Lenmans' grandson wasn't even on a donor list yet. But there didn't seem to be a moment when there was no one waiting to be seen; it was a steady stream all day, and she found herself going through the motions while her mind raced a million miles a minute.

Troy had parked himself in the breakroom with his laptop and was doing foundation work, answering emails and talking to donors and politicians. His current project was to protect hibernating bears. Not a climate issue, but he was completely incensed, and if Tobi had had the luxury to look beyond her own predicament right then, she would have joined him in that sentiment. It was bad enough the government wanted to legalize killing the endangered species, but they were doing it while the bears were sleeping in their caves, and killing the cubs too! Could you get any more cowardly than that?

Chapter 56

Ismar Rufini drove his Mercedes down the long, curving eighty-foot driveway toward his garage. The mansions in Centre Island were all recessed for privacy, and he enjoyed the thick array of evergreens that accented a stone-lined path, which circled the manor and went around the back. The sun set very early in January, and the house was in shadows, except for the timer light. His wife was supposed to be home, cooking his dinner. If she were out with her friends again … these American women! They didn't know their place.

His knee was inflamed and stiff and he wasn't wearing a brace because he couldn't drive with it on, so he limped inside with his cane and shook the snow off his shoes as best he could in the long foyer. The kitchen was completely dark down the hall. He kept a warm, fluffy pair of slippers by the door and donned them slowly as he called out her name.

"Jennie?"

No answer. He hobbled through the house, puzzled and frustrated. He was hungry and in pain, and there were no enticing aromas coming from the kitchen. He really just wanted to put his leg up and have her wait on him. A nice glass of wine and some hummus and pita while waiting for dinner would have been nice. He shuffled past the living room, dining room, and sitting room, where the fireplace was cold and drafty. No fire, either! She was probably out shopping with his money. The outside light was on in the backyard. That was strange. It hadn't been warm enough for Jennie to be outdoors in months now. He walked over to the glass doors and peered out from behind the curtain and caught his breath.

There was an oddly shaped but somehow familiar, macabre silhouette lying across the steps leading down into the snow-covered, manicured backyard and the inground pool, which was now closed up for the winter. He looked more carefully, and saw blonde strands covered with dirty snow, or something … he opened the door and hobbled out.

The cold bit into him immediately without his coat, and a gust of wind pushed him back until he nearly fell over. His fluffy slippers were no match for the ice underfoot. He inched tentatively forward with the cane and felt himself wretch. He turned to the side and lost his lunch in the flower bed.

Jennie was lying across the path, her head still and lying on the stone, blonde hair tossed aside and covered with blood. Her body looked crumpled and broken, her neck twisted to the left and her legs extending in directions her joints shouldn't be capable of attaining. Her eyes were wide open.

Rufini gasped and grabbed his chest in pain. He told himself he was too young to have a heart attack—he was only thirty-eight years old. He looked around several times before he tried to creep quietly down the steps, but he slipped on the icy stoop when he couldn't bend his knee and landed on his butt. Cautiously, he reached over to check for her carotid pulse, but he was already sure he would not find one.

Chapter 57

By the time she was done for the night, Tobi was completely exhausted, and still imagining Ismar, or some other faceless, sinister foe jumping out at her. Troy suggested they go out to eat, but she was too tired, so he ordered from the Japanese restaurant. She told him about the Lenmans' situation as they drove to pick up the food.

"I understand why you did that," said Troy, "but it wasn't smart. You've just made it personal for them to get you out of the way. Until now, it's been 'strictly business.'"

"How could I not tell them? The whole thing is ridiculous. The Lenmans are in their eighties, how can they pay off a second mortgage? Their grandson is not getting on any transplant list with less than one year sober, and if he *does* get on the list, he's a dead man when his name comes up. So now they're creating anxiety over potential future costs to get patients to invest instead of just going after imminent procedures. You would have told them!"

Troy did not deny it.

"Makes sense. This way, they can get money out of their clients for longer," he said.

"We have to *do* something!"

"We have to expose them without putting you at further risk," Troy said. "Who can you absolutely trust?"

"Hopefully, Daniel Comet. But, do you really think B. Healthy would get involved in something like this?"

"Unlikely. Sounds like they're a hundred percent capitalists, so if there were money to be made … but if they got caught, it would ruin them, and they'd lose everything. Too many risks. I'd say they're probably not aware. Guys like these are heartless money mongers, but their business isn't generally murder, not actively, anyway. People may die from negligence, but they don't count that the same way."

Troy parked the car at the restaurant and looked at her meaningfully. "We go in together. From now on, you're not going anywhere without me until this is all over."

Tobi did not argue, but preceded him dutifully into the restaurant, so no one could sneak up behind them. Troy's hand rested on her shoulder, but she still glanced behind them constantly. Troy stuck to her like glue, which was both comforting and annoying, and contributed to her fatigue as she fought the impulse to succumb to feelings she hadn't had in almost two decades.

He insisted on buying and she let him, and they headed home. She was acutely aware of how different her house felt now. No longer the safe oasis among the trees, she found herself peering behind every bush and every parked car, and once they were inside, she wanted to check all her rooms, closets, and windows before relaxing. Pantelaymin attached herself to Troy's legs and purred loudly until he shared some of Tobi's white tuna with her. Traitor, she thought.

Ellie called.

"Tobi! Did you hear? Ismar's wife is dead!"

Tobi nearly choked mid-swallow. "What? What do you mean? How do you know?"

Tobi started shaking and Troy sat up, on full alert. She put the phone on speaker but placed a finger to her lips, eyes glued to the screen.

"You know my husband is Director of EMS Services, and they responded to a call at his house. Ismar found her—she's dead!"

"How did she die?" Tobi asked, afraid to hear the answer.

"Right now it looks like she might have slipped on some ice in the back of their house and hit her head on their stone steps. Must have been a super hard fall or maybe she's been taking aspirin, I don't know, she was dead on arrival. Could be a crazy random accident, but why would she even go out in this sub-zero weather? And she wasn't even wearing a coat, so I think they're looking at Rufini as a potential murder suspect! I don't think he'd kill his wife and then call the police, do you?"

Tobi's throat was constricted and she couldn't speak. "I … I don't know, Ellie. I gotta call you back." She hung up the phone and brought her knees to her chest and then wrapped her arms around them. She started rocking back and forth.

Troy came over and enfolded her in his arms. "It's alright, you're going to be alright. I won't let anything happen to you; I swear it."

Tobi felt ashamed. She was supposed to have implacable strength, it was how she had survived all her life. But right now, she was falling apart. Some disconnected part of her brain was saying that Ismar had quite enough to deal with right now, he wasn't coming for her, but her blood felt like ice in her veins.

"Rufini won't come here now, right?" she asked Troy. "He's got to be too busy with the police and his wife, and everything … why would he kill her anyway?"

"He probably didn't." Troy clipped his words.

"Why would *they* kill his wife?" she asked.

A moment went by and Troy said nothing.

"Oh. Because he didn't kill me," she murmured.

Troy looked at his watch. "It's nine-thirty, that means it's ten-thirty in the morning in Port Douglas." He pulled out his phone, tapped the screen several times, and put the speaker on once he was connected.

"Good morning, inspector. It's Troy DeJacob. Do you have a moment?"

"Yes, Mr. DeJacob. How can I help you?"

"I found my friend, and she *is* in danger. There was an attempt on her life, but it's been difficult corroborating the facts with the police."

"I am so sorry! Is she okay? How can I help?"

"We are going to have to go to the FBI. Is there any way you can help us validate what has been happening, both in Port Douglas and with this insurance company? We seem to be running up against brick walls. Even the medical institution my friend works for seems to have been, let's say, 'influenced.'"

"I'm not sure how much help it would be," Bent said, "but I can try. There's an FBI field office in Canberra; I will give them a call. I'll need your address in New York and your friend's name, as well as the name of the organization she works for. I'll tell the FBI everything we have so far. Unfortunately, we've made no further headway on the murders of Marcus and Freddie, but it's looking like your Robain's—Reuben's—death was a true accident."

"You have my deepest gratitude."

"No worries. I'll call you back when I know something."

Troy gave him Tobi's name and address and spelled out B. Healthy, LLC.

He hung up and Tobi looked at him. His eyes were soft but intense, more blueish brown today than green, and a few strands of grayish hair kept falling onto his face. The left side of his forehead was still purple and swollen, but he didn't seem to notice it.

"You need to call your former medical director," he said.

Tobi glanced at her watch. It was late, but not horribly so. She looked at Troy's face and then picked up her phone again. It seemed like it rang forever, but Daniel picked up just before it went to voicemail.

"Hey, there, how are you? It's been a while."

"Hi, Daniel," Tobi said, trying to keep her voice even. "Did you hear about Ismar Rufini's wife?"

His voice became suddenly serious. "Yes, I did. What a fluke accident. Horrible."

"Daniel—" Tobi froze. What if he didn't believe her either?

"What is it, Tobi?"

"I don't think it was an accident."

There was silence for a long minute. "I'm listening," he said.

Troy nodded at her and she continued.

"Daniel, I think she was murdered." She swallowed hard. "Rufini followed me home two nights ago. If it weren't for a friend of mine who stopped him from messing with my car, and then from breaking into my house ...."

The line was still quiet. "Are you still there?"

"Yes, I'm here."

"Steve doesn't believe me ... he's been acting strange, and the police don't believe it was Rufini because his wife vouched for him, but now she's dead, and I'm really frightened."

"Do you think Rufini killed his wife?"

"No, I think whoever Rufini is involved with killed his wife. And I think Rufini has been stealing patient information from B. Healthy. I need your help."

"You know I'm here for you, Tobi, but why me? What can I do?"

"Hospitals for Health can look at our patient records," Tobi said. "You probably think I'm crazy, but I swear I'm not making this up."

"Tobi, I take what you say seriously, you know that. Why don't you start from the beginning?"

"Okay, so a month or so ago, Rufini swapped my tablet in the office, and Ellie told me he was doing the same thing on the south shore with Monica."

Tobi told Daniel everything, including the details of Amelia's father, Antonio's, car accident and the Lenmans' intention to mortgage their house.

"They're all using an insurance company that covers only high risk patients, called Kordec—"

"Yes, we've been looking at them."

"You have?" Tobi felt like a hundred pounds had been lifted off her back.

"Yes, their stats are questionable," Daniel said in his usual unruffled voice. "Their premiums are large, but their scheduled payouts are very small. We try to accept it anyway since those patients have to pay such high premiums and we don't want to leave them high and dry. We're still owned by physicians, you know, and we try to give back to the community. I think we're one of the last hold-outs. So far, we haven't had to put in a claim for anything really big. Which is strange, given the types of conditions they insure."

"Why do you think that is, Daniel? Do they all die first?"

Silence.

"I'm not really supposed to discuss this, but yes, they seem to. But this population is by definition at high-risk for mortality."

"But what if that's not it? What if it's by design? Are they dying from their disease or from something else?" Tobi tried to keep her voice as level and tempered as Daniel's. She envied how unflappable he was, always steady as a rock. A rock with a heart.

"Where are you going with this, and how did you become involved?"

"Because … it looks like my brother wrote their original software."

"I thought your brother died a long time ago."

"So did I. Apparently, he just went into hiding, from these people. He actually died a few weeks ago, but he'd been hacking into this Kordec company, and they figured it out, and now they're after me. It looks like Rufini works for them! And now *he's* been trying to get rid of me."

Tobi felt like she sounded hysterical, so she shut up abruptly, but then, she couldn't stand the silence. Troy put a steadying hand on her arm. His blue-hazel eyes held her like an anchor in a violent ocean.

Daniel cleared his throat. "I believe you, mostly because I can't imagine you making this up, and no one has been talking openly about Kordec yet. But do you have any hard evidence I can bring to Hospitals for Health?"

"There are two dead bodies besides my brother's in Port Douglas, Australia. Then there's Antonio's car accident and Rufini's wife in Centre Island. The Australian police are hopefully getting in touch with the FBI tonight. Can H for H track the charts Rufini has been messing with? I don't know who else at B. Healthy is wrapped up in this, but it feels like Steve Chagall just went over to the other side."

"Steve has been rather distracted this past week," Daniel said. "We had a meeting regarding protocols that we'd like to see B. Healthy implement if we are going to share a name, and he was not focused at all. Okay, Tobi, I'll make some calls tomorrow and will check out these Kordec patients. Meanwhile, what are you doing to stay safe?"

"Oh," she smiled for the first time. "I seem to have picked up a personal bodyguard."

"Male or female? Is this person qualified in the muscle category?"

"Daniel, how sexist of you! There are plenty of well-muscled, well-trained women out there."

318	Debra E. Blaine, MD

"Okay, that's fine, as long as this one is strong and fast. Do you keep a gun in your house?"

"No. I thought about it once, but since the only reason to have a gun is if you plan to shoot it one day, I decided against it."

"Alright, well keep your eyes open. You and your bodyguard."

Tobi got off the phone and slumped in the kitchen chair. Troy put an arm around her and gently nudged her up and over to the living room sofa.

"You need some rest. You're a mess," he said softly.

She didn't even argue. She had no clever words to come back at him and she was so tired. She sat down next to him, put her feet on the coffee table, and rested her head on his shoulder, feeling his arm behind her back as he enfolded her in warmth. She wanted to weep for all the years she and Ben lost with him and Reuben. And all the years Reuben lived thinking she was angry at him.

She pushed a strand of hair away from her face. "I wish Reuben and I could have understood each other better. I wish he hadn't been so angry with me."

Troy stroked her hair and his thumb touched a single tear on her face and brushed it away. "He wasn't angry. He named his dive shop 'Tobi's,'" he said, as if that explained it all.

"It was all so *stupid*! All those arguments over *money*!"

"He felt the same way, you know. He was just trying to get your mother off his back, so he gave her whatever she wanted, but once he'd had some distance, he realized you couldn't contribute to your mother the same way, not while raising Benny all alone. And he was tormented about not telling you he was alive, but he was genuinely afraid. At one point, I told him I didn't care about my promise, that I was going home to tell you the truth. But that night we read about the surgeon in London who'd been killed. Reuben had been following him from an internet café in Cairns, and he thought the doctor was trying to expose the scam. When the doctor was murdered, it scared us both. They never found the killer, but the inspector in Port Douglas told me they were pretty sure it was this Tzenkov guy, they just couldn't convict him."

Troy looked at her sideways, and Tobi knew he was checking to see if she were still awake. She let her eyes close completely. Too tired to move, too tired to fight. The soft leather Natuzzi sofa was famous for putting her to sleep. Pantelaymin jumped up and settled into the crease between their bodies and starting bathing herself. Troy stroked the cat with his free hand and Tobi drifted off to the vibration of her purring.

Tobi woke up stiff and sore. Troy was alert in a heartbeat. She sat up and stretched. "I need to go to bed," she said.

They walked upstairs together, and she lay down on the king-size bed and he lay down on it as well.

Before she could say a word, he touched her lips with his finger. "Shush. I promise to behave. It's a big bed."

Tobi was too tired to argue and fell asleep instantly.

Chapter 58

Tobi woke up in the morning to the sound of the shower down the hall. For a minute she felt like she was still in a dream, and she found herself thinking about the Shabbat morning prayer: *Thank You, God, for restoring my soul to me; how great is Your trust.*

There had been something so normal about sleeping next to Troy, as if she had never been away from him. She felt more relaxed than she had in ages, not just since Rufini had started poking around in her life. She closed her eyes and wished the moment could continue forever.

Troy poked his head into the bedroom. "Up?"

"Yeah."

"How'd you sleep?"

"Not bad, actually," she lied. She'd slept great.

Troy's hair was wet and pushed back behind his ears, but he hadn't combed it through yet. There was something very seductive about the way it was tousled. He had a deep purple towel wrapped around his waist and his chest was still wet, dripping on the carpet. He had gained a couple of pounds from what she remembered, but his muscles still rippled as he moved his arm to lean on the door frame, and the gray hairs on his chest were wirier than the blonde ones had been. He noticed her looking at him and grinned mischievously.

"You promised you'd behave," she said, but she couldn't keep from smiling herself.

He laughed. "I haven't done anything."

"Yes you have. You're—there. In a towel. You're taking unfair advantage of a girl in dire straits."

"Okay, okay, but it's the first time I've seen that smile in a very long time. It was worth it."

It might be the first time in a long time that anyone has seen it, Tobi thought.

She went into her own shower and tried to flee from her feelings under the hot spray. She told herself she couldn't take him back in her life now; she'd been living alone too long to get used to having someone around *all* the time again. She liked her privacy. Panni was very respectful of her solitude and affectionate in such a non-intrusive way. And she liked that the only mess in the house was her own. She suddenly remembered all of Troy's mail strewn around the kitchen *and* dining room tables. Piles of photos and calendars and announcements that overflowed from his office into their common space. She hadn't had to deal with that in years—even Ben took his stuff with him when he left, so when he was home, she didn't mind the clutter because she knew it was so temporary. She blew out her hair and headed for the stairs, telling herself her decision was made. She was not getting involved with Troy again.

Her phone pinged with Reggie's text.

Hey, are you alright? Haven't heard from you. Coming tonight?

She frowned. How would she ever explain all this to Reggie—or any of her friends? Tonight was Shabbat, and she never missed a service. She was definitely not going to start now, but how would she introduce Troy? It was more complicated than she wanted to go into, and she didn't yet understand what he meant to her after all this time. She thought about asking him to stay home, but she knew he'd never go for it. The problem with knowing everyone in her community was everyone in the community knowing her. And wanting details!

It looked bright and clear outside and Tobi suddenly needed to get out of the house. She answered Reggie that she was fine and would see him tonight, and considered telling him she'd be bringing a friend, but decided against it.

"I need to get out of the house. Let's go for a walk somewhere pretty," she told Troy. "How about Caumsett, we can hike the trail."

Troy frowned and his left brow puckered. "I'm not sure being in a wooded area is a good idea right now. I'd rather we were out in the open where we can see who's around us. How about the boardwalk at Jones Beach?"

Troy insisted on making a stop at Citibank and went to his safety deposit box, where he asked for the private room to access his things. Tobi watched him rummaging around and gasped when he pulled out a revolver, loaded it with bullets, checked the safety, and stuffed it in his pocket.

"I didn't know you owned a gun."

"Well, now you know. And I have a license to carry, so don't worry. I just hope it works after all these years; it hasn't been cleaned in ages."

"You left a gun here when you left?" Tobi was incredulous. "Why?"

Troy shook his head. "Not really sure. I had the New York carry license, which was a time-consuming application, so I just kept it current. I didn't know when I might need to come back here ... and I think I always *hoped* I would come back here ... and find you ... and I guess Reuben's paranoia got to me. Seems he wasn't wrong. Is it still called paranoia if they really *are* out to get you?"

Now Tobi was shaking her head, trying to absorb what he'd just told her. "Yes, actually, it is. Psychiatric definition of paranoia is believing someone or something is after you, whether or not it's true."

They headed out to the coast.

It was hard to stay disheartened at the beach. The boardwalk was two miles long, and even in winter, there were a handful of cyclists, hikers, and people just gazing at the horizon, but the crash of the surf was so deafening, it felt like they were all alone in the world. A person could scream their lungs out and not be heard five yards away.

They were both wrapped in boots, scarves, and gloves, and although twenty-one degrees was not quite as bad as expected with the sun shining down on them, the wind had to be at least twenty miles per hour out here. They kept moving and managed to last forty-five minutes before they couldn't feel their toes and fingers.

They were back at the path to the parking lot and stopped for a last look before leaving the ocean to walk up to Troy's rented Jeep. Tobi could barely feel her legs anymore but lingered to watch the waves crash violently and tirelessly against the sand in white frothy patterns. It was hypnotic. The sun blazed lazily through the dense winter sky and proved itself to be an unwavering match for the frosty haze and the eternal surf. Instinctively, Tobi squeezed Troy tightly.

"It's humbling," she said. "We are just two tiny specks of life in this vast universe. The energy of our souls is infinitesimal next to the interminable power of the ocean. We are really quite insignificant to the Earth. When we wipe ourselves out, do you think God will weep?"

"It would not be the first time," Troy said. "Our planet has had multiple extinction events, it's nothing new. If we humans do not change our ways, long before the year 2100, temperatures will have risen enough to destroy our farms and melt the arctic permafrost. That will cause regional famine and release dangerous dormant bacteria into the air along with huge amounts of carbon that will further accelerate the warming process. We are already starting to see diseases migrate from the tropics across the globe … eventually, the temperatures will be incompatible with human physiology and we will kill ourselves off, but we will likely starve even before that. Some other species will evolve and thrive, though, something more suited to the environmental changes we create, and the Earth will just start over again. Our planet will adapt—without us. The Universe will go on—without us. God will go on … perhaps God will even weep. Until we become some prehistoric era for the next sapient life form to speculate about. We humans are the only fools who think we matter to the Cosmos. We are as nothing …."

"Thanks for the pep talk," Tobi said. "So inspirational."

Troy wrapped his arms tightly around her and hugged her close. He put his lips against the side of her head. "Except we are not meaningless to each other, and *that* is what makes life sacred," he whispered.

"Sounds like you've become an atheist," she said.

"Never," he said. "But as I believe God gives us the means to survive, I believe God also gives us the freedom to self-destruct. We have the intellect to understand what is happening, but the human race may be too ensnared in its addiction to power, money, and ostentation to save itself. God promised never again to eradicate life on Earth—but He didn't promise to keep us from doing it to ourselves. Our lives are but a nanosecond in eternity. It doesn't *matter* to the Earth. It only matters to *us*. So, make way for the next superior life form."

"I think it will be cats," Tobi said.

Troy cocked his head at her.

"Felines," Tobi said, as they started walking again. "They are the most adaptive mammals, more so than wolves, bears, and monkeys. They have survived on more continents and outlived most every other genus. That is, if mammals survive at all. Maybe it will be birds, though, since the land masses are changing. The ones that can fish, that is, like sea hawks. Except they'd have to move to the poles."

Troy stopped walking and turned to her, undoubtedly to gauge if she were serious or not. Tobi managed to keep a straight face for about three seconds before she burst out laughing. He swatted at her playfully.

"But, seriously, it was an interesting *NOVA* episode," she said. "Felines are far more adaptable than canines and most other mammals, and they *have* survived on six continents over the centuries. I just made up the stuff about the bears and the monkeys."

"Why not the whales and the dolphins?"

"Because the warmer temperatures are pushing their food supply out of reach. The fish they eat are moving deeper to cooler water, so they are as screwed as we are. Dolphins need to breathe every ten to twelve minutes. Maybe some whales will make it. Sperm whales can go more than an hour without oxygen, but most whales can't. You know that, Mr. DeJacob." She laughed. "Ben knew that when he was five."

Troy's face was three inches from hers and their frozen breath mingled in the space between them, their breathing synchronized. Tobi's heart was suddenly racing. He looked into her eyes and at her lips, but at the last minute, he turned away.

"Your nose is frozen," he said.

"Always the gentleman," Tobi muttered under her breath as she turned toward the road.

They got back to the Jeep, and Troy circled it carefully, signaling her with his hand to stay back. He looked underneath, inside, back and front, and across the parking lot, all the time with his hand under his jacket on his revolver. Finally, he motioned to her it was safe to get in. All her fears had returned in an instant.

Chapter 59

"Mannya, if you're sure the toad is going to come here to make the hit, why are we here too? It's chancy."

"Because he is an imbecile, so we make sure he does not fail us this time. And since he will be the one they see, he can take the heat. He knows his time is running out. He does not want to end up like his wife."

Mannfort and Kazi had parked down the road from Tobi's synagogue and were huddled in the brush at the back of the parking lot.

"Kazi, your aim is still true?"

"You doubt me, Mannya? I practice every week. It's my favorite sport."

"But you are using the plastic knife. The one you have not practiced with."

"Mannya, a gun will be heard and they will know where we are standing. The knife is quiet. Stealthy," Kazi said. "I don't see the toad, do you?"

"No. If he does not show, we do the job ourselves, quietly, with your knife."

Chapter 60

Troy sat next to Tobi in the synagogue, feeling very out of place. He had meant it when he'd said he would never lose faith in God, but he hadn't been inside a formal place of worship in decades, outside of the High Holy Day services of Rosh Hashanah and Yom Kippur, when there were so many people that it was easy to be anonymous. Although many people seemed to recognize him and doors opened for him because of the foundation, he was still really more of an introvert, and preferred to just be one of the crowd.

It seemed the entire congregation came over to them, their curiosity piqued by seeing Tobi show up with a man, but everyone was friendly, including Rabbi Lilly. While Tobi pulled Chloe aside and confirmed that Larry had not signed up for Kordec insurance and never would, Rabbi personally welcomed Troy, asked where he was from, and wished him a Shabbat Shalom, a peaceful sabbath. The rabbi had no idea how hard he was praying for just that.

There was an *oneg* following the service, with challah, fruit, and little cakes and cookies, where he had to answer a thousand questions. Tobi had introduced him as CEO of Executors for Our Earth, knowing it would strike a positive chord with her community and turn the conversation to less personal matters. At least a dozen people came over to meet him, including the cantor, whose singing had been nothing less than divinely inspired, like a conduit from Earth to Heaven. Troy understood why Tobi loved this place so much.

Finally, all the questions had been either answered or dodged and he felt like he had met everyone, and they walked out and into the parking lot. The air was fresh and clean, but Troy felt immediately that something was wrong. The hairs on the back of his neck were raised and his chest felt heavy when he inhaled. He tried to look around casually, but Tobi was having her own premonition. She whipped her head around twice, peering into the darkness, her hand clutching his elbow.

"I feel it too," he said. The lights were on in the lot but spaced several yards apart, and groups of congregants said cheerful farewells as they got into their cars. When Troy stopped in front of the Jeep, he could not bring himself to open the door for Tobi. It was like some invisible force blocked his way.

Tobi looked at him, and he nodded. They both backed away from the car, and Troy knelt down to look underneath it. As soon as he stooped, he heard a whizzing sound fly over his shoulder and Tobi shout out.

"Stay down, Troy! Don't get up!" she yelled.

He turned and looked at her and saw the knife lodged in her left shoulder. She had fallen and was sitting on the ground, her eyes wide.

"Tobi!"

Tobi pulled the knife out of her jacket and held it out in front of her like she didn't understand what it was.

"Are you hurt?" he asked.

"I don't think so, I think it just buried itself in my jacket. It looks like … what *is* this?"

But Troy did not have time to examine it. He sensed movement behind the car, then turned to see someone leveling a pistol at Tobi. Troy pushed Tobi flat and rolled behind the Jeep, then rose to his knees and lunged at the fat man. Troy grabbed the attacker's hand and pointed the gun upward just as it went off. Troy twisted the man's arm behind his back, making him drop the gun, and the fat man wailed in pain. Troy turned him face down on the icy pavement and sat on him, wrenching the arm tighter.

Shouts and screams came from the temple entrance, and Tobi's friend, Reggie, came running over with his wife Lynn and with Chloe right behind them. Reggie assessed the situation in a second, grabbed the fat man's other arm, and twisted it back as well.

"Rabbi! Call 911! And grab some rope or something to tie his hands up with," Reggie called out. "Where is our security guard?"

Jimmy, the off-duty cop who worked Friday nights at the temple, was at the other end of the lot. At the sound of the gunshot, he'd turned and started running toward them.

Troy berated himself for not having enlisted Jimmy's support when they first arrived. He had noticed the officer standing off to the side, greeting congregants as they came in, but looking slightly out of place. He hadn't seen the security logo on his jacket until they were walking into the sanctuary, and he hadn't doubled back to speak with Jimmy because he knew Tobi wanted to keep their situation quiet. What a mistake! Troy pressed the fat man's face hard into the ground, and he whined pathetically.

"Who are you?" Troy demanded. "What's your name?"

Tobi came over, absently rubbing her shoulder, with Reggie's wife, Lynn, and several others. "That's Ismar Rufini. What the hell do you want from me, you bastard?" She kicked him in the ribs, and he yelped. "Why are you after me? Who sent you?"

Ismar seemed paralyzed with fear and grunted incoherently. Rabbi Lilly came over with Leo, one of the temple maintenance workers, who had brought a spindle of twine. Troy yanked Ismar's arms back hard and wrapped the twine tightly in a figure eight around both wrists, getting underneath his gloves and cutting into his skin, and then tied it off with a double constrictor knot. "Let's see you get out of that."

Jimmy was at their side. "I'm so sorry! I thought I saw movement in the bushes at the edge of the parking lot, and I went to check it out," he said. He looked from the bushes to Tobi, still unwilling to completely turn his attention from them. He holstered his gun and took out his cuffs and stooped down to examine the constrictor knot. "You know, it would be a shame to cut that off in favor of ordinary police handcuffs," he chuckled, and he tucked them back in his belt, but he kept looking around and back at the bushes. "It almost looked like that knife was thrown from that direction."

Troy hauled Rufini up into a sitting position. "Who sent you? Tell me who, right now!"

Reggie was at Tobi's side. "Are you alright, kiddo? You're rubbing your shoulder. What happened, what is this all about?"

"Am I?" she asked quietly. "I think so. It aches a little. He threw a … a knife at me. It's weird looking." She held the knife up, like she didn't know what to do with it yet.

"Oh my God! Are you bleeding?"

"I don't know, it's too cold to take my jacket off and find out." Troy was sure she didn't want to know.

Chloe put her arm around Tobi. "Come, sit down." She opened the door of the Jeep so Tobi could sit on the back seat. "Are you alright?" she asked Troy.

A small crowd had gathered around them. Troy felt humbled by how quickly he'd been adopted into this community.

Troy nodded, then he looked at Rufini again. "I'm only going to ask you one more time. Who sent you?" He lifted Rufini's bound hands behind his back until the fat man howled.

"I don't know their names, I swear. They kill my wife. They are going to kill me." Ismar bawled like a baby.

Troy tightened his grip. "It was you who followed Tobi home the other night, it was you who tried to sabotage her car, and it was *you* who hit me in the head with the wire cutter."

"Yes, yes, it was me." Rufini nodded his head rapidly up and down. "They made me do it."

"Who?"

"I don't know their names. They only say they are from 'the Project.' That's all I know. And they give me money. I wanted to give it back, but they say no."

"Tzenkov? Is that who you work for?" Troy hyperextended Rufini's arms again until he screamed.

Tobi was suddenly at his side. "Troy. Stop. He's a nobody. He's not worth it," she whispered.

Troy barely recognized himself, consumed by a murderous rage. He lowered Rufini's arms.

The sirens got closer and a minute later, blue and red strobe lights lit up the parking lot. Officers Tarman and Westin got out of the patrol car.

Tarmin recognized Tobi immediately. "You guys again," he said.

Rabbi Lilly, Reggie, and Lynn walked over to Tobi protectively.

"He threw that knife at Tobi and when that didn't work, he pulled out a gun. Jimmy has the gun," Troy motioned with his head.

Rufini squirmed when he heard "knife" but couldn't speak; Troy had mashed his face back into the ground.

Jimmy handed the revolver to the Suffolk officers. "I'm 'on the job,' ninth precinct, New York City. This is my side gig." The officers shook hands. "There was definitely something moving in the bushes at the south end of the lot. I went to check it out and then I heard the gunshot and the screams. The knife may actually have been thrown from there."

"What is going on here?" Rabbi asked, but she looked at Tobi and Troy. "You guys don't seem particularly surprised by any of this."

"It's a long story, Rabbi, not one for standing out in the cold," Tobi said.

Officer Tarman looked at Troy. "Is this the same guy who hit you at your girlfriend's house last week?"

Troy saw Tobi flinch when the officer identified her as his girlfriend. "Yes, officer, and he will admit it to you himself. Won't you, *Rufini?*"

"Yes, yes, it was me. I did that. I had to do it, they made me do it, but I didn't throw any knife! I was going to shoot her, but I couldn't do it!"

"You couldn't do it because I stopped you!" Troy snapped back.

"Well, I guess you guys will sleep easier tonight," Tarman said.

Troy let go of Rufini and let Officer Westin pick him up and drag him into the patrol car. Rufini kept muttering, "No knife, no knife …."

"I don't know, officer," Troy said, addressing Tarman. "He was taking orders from someone else."

Westin examined the double constrictor knot, grinning. "Geez," he said, "this is more secure than cuffs."

"Get it off me," Rufini yelled, "it hurts, get it off!"

"Sorry chum, we'll need to cut that off at the station." He pushed the fat man into the back of the car and locked the door while Tarman walked over to Troy and Tobi.

"I'll need you two to come down to the station with me. Dr. Lister, are you injured? Is that blood?"

Troy spun around. Her shoulder! "Tobi …" his voice cracked.

Rabbi Lilly took charge. "No one is going anywhere. Tobi, come back inside and let's get your jacket off."

"We'll call an ambulance," Tarman offered.

"No! No ambulance. I don't do hospitals," Tobi said definitively.

Of course, Troy thought, she's not going to be reasonable about this. The guilt was overwhelming. He'd promised to keep her safe and the knife had sailed right past him and into her.

"Did you all witness this?" Tarman asked.

"Lynn and I were just walking to our car when we heard Tobi scream," Reggie said. "I saw Troy run around the side of the car and tackle that guy just as the gun went off."

Tarman had gone over to Tobi to take the knife for evidence. "There's blood on this knife," he said. "We should take you to the hospital." He looked at it more closely. "This is a very unusual knife." He held it out to his partner. "Hey, Westin, have you ever seen anything like this?"

Officer Westin came over to inspect it.

"I've seen these before, usually when someone is trying to hide from a metal detector. If I'm not mistaken, it's Grivory." He walked over to Rufini. "Where'd you get this? Why do you have a Grivory knife?"

"It's not my knife!" Rufini started jabbering in Turkish. He looked like he was having a nervous breakdown.

Tarman was scanning the parking lot. "I think we need to clear everyone out of here and do a search of the grounds. Dr. Lister, I want you to be checked out in the hospital." As he spoke, several other patrol cars arrived on the scene.

"No, no, I'm fine! It's probably just a scratch."

Troy walked over to her. "Let's go inside and look, okay?" She was never going to just walk into an emergency department, of that he was sure.

They walked back into the building, and Troy gently took her coat off. There was blood caked onto her sweater.

"Damn, I liked this sweater," she said. Chloe, Lynn, and Rabbi Lilly took her into the ladies room to get a better look, and Troy was left to wait with Reggie and Leo. Rabbi Lilly had kindly but firmly recommended that the rest of the congregants go home. Leo was very sweet and asked if they needed anything before continuing to clean up after the oneg.

"Oh my God, it's so lucky you were here tonight, she might have been killed!" Reggie said. "You never did say how you two know each other. I don't remember Tobi ever mentioning you."

Troy laughed. "No, I don't suppose she would have. I didn't leave under the best of circumstances. None of it was her fault; all of it was, well, it wasn't entirely mine—at least I tell myself that. It was circumstance ...." He knew he was rambling.

Reggie said nothing, and Troy felt pressured to continue. This guy was a friend of Tobi's, would she be okay with Troy talking to him? Right now, Troy really wanted someone to talk to.

"Tobi had a brother—"

"I know, he died years ago, like my sister. We kind of adopted each other. Both of us lost our parents and our only siblings."

Troy looked closer at Reggie. He was about their age with a full head of short gray hair, thick mustache, and kind eyes. Tobi was lucky to have him for a "bro."

"Yes, well, her brother—"

"It's not deep, but it needs to be sutured," Tobi said as she came back into the lobby with Chloe, Rabbi, and Lynn. "I'm not going to the hospital. I just texted Ellie, and she'll meet me at the office and throw a couple of stitches in it, then we can go to the precinct. Meanwhile, I need to call out for tomorrow."

"Do you want us to come with you?" Rabbi Lilly asked.

"Thank you, but no. I'll be okay with Troy. You have a bar mitzvah tomorrow morning; you should go home."

Chapter 61

"**D**amn!" Kazi spit on the ground.

"Quiet, you punk, they will hear us," Mannfort whispered. The security guard was approaching, and Mannfort grabbed Kazi's arm and motioned with his head toward the street. "Come on, let's get out of here." They softly retraced their steps out of the brush and headed for the side road where they had parked the car.

"But I never miss, Mannya," Kazi said as they exited the trees onto the side street. "He had to bend down just at that second. I would have had him and the toad could have shot the doctor! Completely unexpected. The knife is tapered differently and is lighter. It doesn't fly the same."

Mannfort shook his head. "Such good fortune to find the hippie here tonight; at least we don't have to travel across the country to California. But if he is here with her, that sister knows whatever he knows. You see? I was right, she has to go. Let them all think the lady doctor was the target, and hopefully the toad takes the heat."

"What if the toad talks?"

"That is a problem," Mannfort said. "We should have neutralized him before; he is a hindrance now. Maybe we can pluck him off on his way to the police station. Follow the patrol car, but Kazi, don't make it obvious. Blend in with the traffic.

Chapter 62

obi sent a text to Steve Chagall as Troy drove to the office. She was supposed to notify the regional lead if she had to call out, but Rufini wasn't going to be much help.

Thanks for your assistance. I was just assaulted by Rufini, who is now in custody, and I'm heading over to the clinic for Ellie to repair a knife wound before going to the precinct. Please get coverage for me tomorrow.

She read it out loud to Troy before she hit send. "I guess that's not very nice, but I'm so pissed at him. I thought he was my friend."

"It's fine," Troy said. "I don't think you need to mince words at this point."

Troy's phone rang through the Jeep's Bluetooth device, and they both jumped.

"Hello, my name is Agent Logan from the FBI. Is this Troy DeJacob?"

"Yes it is." Troy reached over and took Tobi's hand.

"Hello, Mr. DeJacob. We are on Long Island and have been directed to look into some activity that you were involved with in Australia. Where can we meet you to talk?"

Troy glanced at Tobi. "We will be at the Second Precinct in about a half hour. We are stopping off first to get my friend's shoulder stitched up, she was just knifed and nearly shot."

"I'm sorry we didn't get here sooner. Take care of your friend and we will be waiting for you at the precinct."

As they hung up, Tobi's phone rang. "Hey, it's Steve. Are you okay? My God, I'm so sorry. What happened?"

She told him the barest details in an icy voice. "Please get coverage for me tomorrow."

"Of course. Tobi, umm, was there anyone else there?"

Tobi and Troy glanced at each other again. "My congregation, it happened in the parking lot."

"No, I mean, was it just Rufini?"

"That's all we saw. Do you know something we should know?" Tobi asked.

There was silence for a minute.

"I have to go," Steve said. "Feel better, Tobi, and be careful." The line went dead.

***

Tobi had never been in a police precinct before. There was a faint smell of tobacco and the tile walls were a nauseating green. They were brought back into an interview room with Officer Tarman, a man in a black suit and blue shirt and tie, and a woman in a business-casual navy pantsuit and light yellow blouse. The man and woman both had guns just visible under their jackets, and they flashed their FBI credentials. It felt to her like a *Criminal Minds* episode, or at the very least, *The Twilight Zone*. Rufini was nowhere in sight.

"Come in. I'm Agent Logan, and this is Agent Jacquart," he nodded to the woman. "Have a seat. We've been talking to Inspector

Bent in Port Douglas, and there's some question of whether these attempts on your life and the two victims in Port Douglas are connected to a larger ring of violence that we are looking at."

"And they killed a patient of mine up here," Tobi broke in. "And another patient is in serious jeopardy!"

The agents exchanged looks. "We need to know everything you know," Logan said.

Troy interrupted. "First, you need to promise to protect her."

"Of course. We will keep you under constant surveillance. Dr. Lister, what can you tell me about what you have noticed at work?" Logan asked.

Her lips were parched and she swallowed hard. Tarman brought her a bottle of water.

Tobi told them everything she knew, which she realized wasn't actually very much. Most of it was hearsay from Ellie who heard from Monica, and Troy filled in what he knew from Reuben. But she did explain about her heartbroken patient who had lost her father right before the transplant, and about the Lenman's having been approached to mortgage their house for coverage of a liver transplant that was not likely to ever happen. She suggested they talk to her friend, Chloe, since her husband, Larry, had been approached by Kordec to buy a policy, but fortunately, he had turned them down. Kordec would have likely left a contact number in case he changed his mind. Tobi toyed with sharing her conversation with Daniel Comet.

"You're hesitating, Doctor, what is it?" Jacquart asked.

"Well, I did speak to someone yesterday, but I wasn't supposed to be sharing it yet. They're still evaluating."

"Doctor, we are the FBI," Agent Jacquart said gently. "It's not like sharing with your girlfriend, and if you withhold information—"

"No, of course not," Tobi said. "I'm sorry. I was told that Hospitals for Health has some questions about this Kordec insurance too. Seems many of their patients die before getting surgery. I think they just started looking at it. It's not like H for H hasn't been getting paid, so they didn't notice it right away. It's that they never need to put claims in to begin with."

"Yes, we know, we are looking at them too," Jacquart said. "The AMA had been receiving email warnings that were just recently turned over to us. We're just now evaluating them. Who is your contact at Hospitals for Health?"

"Dr. Daniel Comet, vice president."

Officer Westin came in. "Rufini's talking big time, but he hasn't got much to say. He keeps denying throwing the knife, and there are no prints on it. Of course, he was wearing gloves, but it's an odd knife. And it would be strange to bring a knife *and* a gun and then to use the knife first, and from a distance. Someone else had to have been at the synagogue tonight. We looked through the perimeter of the parking lot and found two sets of footprints in the snow at the south end, but no other evidence of who it could have been." He looked carefully at the knife. "I wonder if we can trace where this was purchased … Rufini is a pitiful reject, though. Mostly he just whimpers a lot, and I'm not sure he knows enough to be much help. He's a patsy."

"Now Randy, you'd whimper too, if you just lost your wife and your hands were nearly severed at the wrists," Tarman winked at Troy.

"Yeah, he said he needs medical attention for those wrists and wants to sue. Ha!" Westin laughed. "That wasn't even on us. Then he said he wants immunity. I told him that's not going to fly."

Logan spoke up. "No immunity. We can offer him protection, that's all, and to try to keep him out of the same prison as his employers. We'd like to examine the knife. Did you get anything at all?"

"Just the sources his phone was contacted from, we got those off his cell. So far, they're a dead end, " Westin said. "Mostly disposable phones, no email addresses."

"We can probably help there," Agent Jacquart said. "We may be able to trace where the phones were bought, and at least see if it was from within this country. If not, Interpol wants to be involved as well; it might turn out this is an operation they've been chasing for the last decade. We can also trace his bank deposits."

"You should speak to Steven Chagall too," Tobi said suddenly. She felt a little like a heel, but Steve had turned on her, so chances were, he either deserved police scrutiny or he was threatened himself. He might know something, and maybe he could get protection too.

Logan turned to Tobi and Troy. "Alright. I want you both to go home and stay there. We have a car ready to follow you, and there will be one outside your house 24/7. We are also going to offer some assistance to your gatehouse. Dr. Lister, is your shoulder alright? Do you need any further medical attention?"

"No, I'm okay."

"Like 'house arrest'?" Troy asked.

"No," Agent Jacquart said, "of course not. Just give us a few days. There are sure to be repercussions from whomever is ultimately responsible. They obviously didn't want you alive, and knowing their pawn is in custody will unnerve them even further. It's just the easiest way to keep you safe right now."

"Does Troy have to stay home too, then?" Tobi asked.

Jacquart looked at Troy. "You may be a target yourself at this point. If you need to go out, let the officers know. Someone should go with you."

Officer Westin took Troy's keys. "I'll bring your car around. We don't want either of you out of our sight," he said.

Tobi's shoulder ached as Troy helped her on with her jacket. "I guess I need a new coat, this one's kind of a mess." The blood was dried and there was a two inch hole in the shoulder.

As they walked through the puke-green hallway, the building shook with an earsplitting boom. Tobi and Troy were forced to their knees, and suddenly, people were running everywhere. Troy pulled her back against the far wall, out of the way. "What the hell was that?"

It only took ten minutes for the police to secure the building, but it felt like forever. Neither Tobi nor Troy wanted to interfere. They exchanged worried glances, both of them fearing the explosion had something to do with them. When Officer Tarman came back over to them, he was visibly shaken and he guided them back into the interview room.

"What happened?" Troy asked him.

"That was your Jeep. I think it would be best if you stayed somewhere else for the next few days."

"No!" Tobi said. "They obviously know we're here and can follow us anywhere, right? I'm not leaving Pantelaymin alone. Can't you protect us there?"

"Who—?"

Troy half smiled. "Her cat."

"Doctor—"

"No. I won't sacrifice her, so I'd have to go back there to get her, and then you would have to secure my house first, anyway."

Troy looked at Tarman and nodded. "She's right. I hope your partner wasn't in the Jeep when it ...."

"No, he had left the engine running and was coming back in to get you guys. So, the device must have been on some sort of a timer linked to the ignition. If someone had been watching to detonate, he would have known you weren't in it yet, so he would've waited. We're searching the area but have not found anyone yet."

It was hours before they got home. They waited at the precinct for the police and the FBI to search the grounds, her house, question the guard at the gatehouse, and check Tobi's car in the driveway. Finally, the bomb squad declared the area safe and they were driven home, with a patrol car to remain stationed outside at all times.

Chapter 63

"What do you mean we missed, Kazi? How does that happen?" Mannfort shouted.

"I'm sorry, Mannya, I didn't want to be anywhere around when we blew the truck. We were lucky they parked it in the back of the station, where I could rig it up in the dark without us being seen, but we couldn't stick around! I figured they'd just get in the Jeep and drive away, make fools of the FBI and the American police. I just wanted us to be long gone, so I added the time delay to the ignition trigger. It's very simple, just a couple of wires. Now, every cop in the county is searching for us." He hung his head.

"Did anyone die?"

"I don't think so, Mannya. I'm sorry."

"No, it is good. The American police are quite vengeful when they lose one of their own. It gets personal for them. What are you looking at?"

Kazimir was frowning. "I must have missed this text. It's from the Utah senator. He says we need him and that we should talk. He thinks he can help us. And I just checked, no money was paid to the account." He looked up at Mannfort. "He has never given us problems before."

"He is one of our oldest customers, *nyet*? How much does he pay?" Mannfort asked.

"Ten grand, every four months. He's not one of our richer clients."

"Well, text him back. Ask him what we could possibly need him for and why he thinks talking should delay his payment. He knows the rules, pay first, talk maybe later. What do we have on him?"

Kazi pulled up his file on his phone. "Standard sleaze. Multiple affairs over last fifteen years. Gave his wife syphilis. He's been treated for chlamydia and gonorrhea five or six times. Nothing recent, but he still likes the ladies. Has two women on the side right now."

"How do you know that, Kazi? I thought we only see his medical records?"

"Mannya, you need to develop your imagination. Once we own him, we get his information. We track his cell phone and see who he calls, what he buys, and where it is delivered. We are an insurance policy, we insure ourselves well. Once you are a client of the Project, always you are a client of the Project. How do you think you get your big quarterly payouts?"

"Okay," Mannfort said. "We will deal with him later. First, we have to deal with the lady doctor, the hippie, and the toad. We must get rid of them quick and get out of here. It is getting too complicated."

Chapter 64

Tobi slept most of the next day and woke with her shoulder burning and stiff. *Great, I can add this to the rest of my arthritic wonders,* she thought. But that wasn't really fair. It was a miracle that she had even survived last night; complaining about a bruised shoulder was unreasonable.

She went downstairs and found Agent Jacquart having afternoon coffee with Troy in the kitchen. They both got up when she walked in the room.

Troy walked over to her side and led her to a chair. "I'll make you some tea."

"What did I miss?"

"We've been following the money, it always talks," Jacquart said. "There was a large payment made to the B. Healthy medical director, Steven Chagall."

"I knew it!" Tobi said. "He got all squirrelly on me, like, a week ago."

"That's about when the payment was made. He was very cooperative, even relieved that we were involved. Seems he was threatened *and* paid to keep quiet. He did ask about you."

"Sure he did," Tobi growled.

"His son was in a terrible car accident," Jacquart said.

"Really? His son is, like, fifteen."

"Yes, well, his son was on a bicycle, and was run down by an SUV."

"Oh." Tobi's stomach did a flip-flop.

"We also traced the bank deposits Ismar Rufini has been receiving. They were rerouted several times, but they originated in the Ukraine. That same source has been making much larger deposits to a Swiss bank, and the name Tzenkov has come up several times, along with Boris Gozinski, which we think is the same person. Gozinski left a half print in the hotel in Port Douglas and rented the Maserati that found its way to the bottom of Finch Bay. And with the help of Interpol, Mannfort Tzenkov lit up on facial recognition flying out of Cairns last month after the two murders.

"We haven't yet traced the knife, apparently it's something that can be purchased online. The payment made to Dr. Chagall came from an account that was also used to purchase two airline tickets to JFK this week. One went through Paris and one came direct from Kiev. Interpol has not been able to pull facial recognition yet."

"They're here, in New York?" Tobi asked, her skin turning pale.

"Don't worry, we're watching you and this development like hawks. No one will get through who doesn't belong."

"My neighbors must hate me. Have I put everyone here in danger?"

"We won't let anything happen to them." The agent spoke softly, and Tobi felt like she actually cared. "Your brother was very lucky, you know. It sounds like he figured it all out. Almost no one survived acquiring that knowledge ten or twenty years ago."

Tobi bit her tongue and kept silent. She hadn't been lucky; Reuben had been dead to her. But for Reuben ... he'd had nineteen years to live his life, dive the reef, take beautiful pictures, and make friends. That had been an incredible gift.

"Why did Interpol stop looking for Tzenkov?" Tobi asked.

"They didn't close the case, but the trail dried up, and they started following bigger fish," Jacquart said. "Tzenkov's success was facilitated by starting on the ground floor of new technology and looking like he was part of the furniture. A lot of effort is now going into ferreting out potential infiltration of quantum computers for the same reasons. That would be disastrous."

"I thought that was all still speculative," Troy said. "Are quantum computer drives up and running, then?"

"Not quite, but it's fertile ground for high-tech start-up thieves."

Jacquart left, and Troy started dinner. He had bought fresh salmon and made his own mango salsa to put over it, and he added fresh zucchini and brown rice. There was a bottle of pinot grigio on the table.

"Where did the fresh fish come from, and the wine?" Tobi asked.

"I went out for a bit with Agent Logan. Agent Jacquart stayed here with you."

Tobi picked up her fork and then put it down again without taking a bite. She looked at Troy. "Did ... did you and Reuben email much? Did you see him a lot? Was he with anyone, was he happy?"

Troy put his utensils aside too, and put his hands gently on her shoulders. "He never stopped talking about you, and he felt terrible that this secret broke us up. And no, he never linked up with anyone that I knew of. I think his closest friend was Marco, and I know he never told Marco any of this. Reuben just taught diving, rented and sold equipment, and took phenomenal pictures. I had everything shipped back here. Right now, the FBI is tearing apart his computer, but it all belongs to you, as soon as this is over."

"Why didn't he try to *do* something about it? That doesn't sound like Reuben, to just run away and hide. Maybe for six months or a year, but then—how could he live with himself, knowing all this and doing nothing?"

"It tore him up, and it got worse as the years went by. But he was sure if they knew he was alive, they would assume he'd been talking to you about everything and would either silence you or use you as ransom to get to him—or both. It was a blessing that he was presumed dead, it was the safest scenario for you and Ben. So, he started sending emails to the AMA, but he felt like that was also dangerous, and he wouldn't let me get involved in it, either. No one answered him, but he said he felt the Russians watching him. I think he used a different email account than the one we used, maybe several."

"I'd like to see your emails. I mean, if it's okay with you. Just a little piece of my brother ...."

Troy put his arms around her and buried his face in her hair. "Of course," he whispered. "I certainly owe you that."

She felt herself start to melt into him, and she was too tired to fight it. A little voice in her head kept whispering to wait until this was all over, not to get hooked again simply because of circumstances. Another part of her argued that she might not even survive the next couple of weeks, so what difference did it make anyway? Life was so short, why was she fighting these feelings?

Chapter 65

Blaise Kavandor was fairly pleased with the way the discussion was going. It was their second meeting of the roundtable and Wiseman was all over the Kordec question, pulling up complaints from medical societies Kavandor didn't even know they'd heard from, and even some from overseas. Of course, Wiseman had said, he was not able to discuss the most current developments at the present time, but there was criminal activity going on right now. You're fried, Kavandor thought gleefully. His get out of jail free card had finally come through.

They took a vote and unanimously decided to ban Kordec Insurance from operating in the United States. Kavandor felt an immense relief. The tension leaving his back and shoulders left a buzzing in his head, like he was lightheaded. It took a minute to register, but gradually he realized the buzzing was actually in his jacket. He reached into his pocket and took out his phone, setting it surreptitiously on his thigh to read the text message. Shit, he thought. Well, too little too late, my enemies. Burn, baby, burn. He stuffed his phone back in his jacket pocket, text unanswered.

As the meeting went on, however, he started to have second thoughts. The room felt excessively warm, and he was breathing too fast, fogging up his glasses. He removed them to clean the lenses, while he looked furtively around the room, but thankfully, no one seemed to notice his discomfort. Collecting enough evidence to get Kordec convicted of a crime could take months, and meanwhile, the Russians would be asking him to intervene and get them reinstated to issue insurance policies ... wouldn't they?

Kavandor had to answer the text. They must know by now that he hadn't paid. They didn't have any way of finding out that he was actually chairing this subcommittee, did they? Could he just say it was out of his control, that he thought he might have been able to change the agenda but someone else took charge of it? Maybe he could turn the whole situation into brownie points for trying to warn them. But if the Russians thought they were going down, they'd do everything they could to take him down with them, that was a certainty. Why did he have to be so damn cocky in his text message!

Chapter 66

Agent Jacquart got off the phone and turned to Logan. "That disposable cell that was contacting Rufini is still active. It's texting with someone in DC. They're verifying the trace on it, but it looks like it belongs to the Utah senator, Blaise Kavandor."

"You think our own government is mixed up with the Russians? Why in the world would any of our own people play ball with them to the detriment of fellow Americans?" Logan seemed to lack imagination at times.

"Usually only one of two reasons," Jacquart answered. "Greed or to save their own skin. Maybe both. We're sending a few agents over now to pick him up for questioning."

"Okay, good. I just heard from Headquarters at Quantico," Logan said. "They've downloaded Reuben Sokowsky's laptop remotely. You would not believe how much incriminating evidence there is on that thing. And now that we have the original RKS program that was used to ravage the data, it's easy to find its electronic footprint on thousands of charts in dozens of different EMR programs all over the country. Why in the world didn't he offer that up sooner? All those people we could have saved …."

"All those people we *might* have saved, if it didn't fall into the wrong hands and Sokowsky hadn't been murdered himself," Jacquart said. "One of the names on that list is the former deputy director of the FBI, and Sokowsky would have seen that too. We knew the deputy retired early because of Parkinson's, but we wondered about some of his decisions for several years prior to that. Now it looks like he knew he had dementia years before he resigned. That in itself is enough to make a person hesitate." She shook her head sadly. "I always liked him. I have to believe he let this go unchallenged because his mind was just too far gone to think it through properly. I want to believe that, anyway."

Chapter 67

Tobi's doorbell rang and Agent Jacquart went to answer it. "She's already been cleared," the agent said over her shoulder, and opened the door to reveal Molly Baker standing on the threshold. Tobi froze.

"Dr. Lister, may I come in?" Molly asked. She stepped forward tentatively. "I want you to know that all of us at B. Healthy are absolutely appalled that you have had to go through this. We want to make it up to you and we will do everything we can to assist in the investigation of Dr. Rufini. This is *definitely* not the way we operate."

Tobi did not want Molly Baker in her house, but she couldn't think of a reason to refuse, especially not with the FBI agents present. She also knew Molly was motivated by dollar signs. This was not a good kind of publicity for a medical organization, especially one that claimed people were their priority. On the heels of Tim Meloncamp, their stock must be crashing.

"Don't worry, Molly. I don't believe B. Healthy played an active role in this, except, of course, for supporting an incompetent lead physician like Dr. Rufini. I know he came cheap, but you do get what you pay for. He had, what? One year of clinical experience after residency before you made him lead?"

"Yes, you are right. He was a big mistake. We will be much more careful in the future." Molly fidgeted a moment, looking for a conversation starter. Tobi didn't think she had ever seen her at a loss for words before. She wondered how the straws were drawn, probably no one in corporate had wanted to be the one to make this in-person gesture.

"Those men guarding your house are very nice," Molly said. "I love their Russian accents."

Agent Jacquart's head snapped up. "Russian—no! Those are Agents Steele and Simpson! All of you, get down right now, and get away from the windows!" Jacquart's gun was in her hand in an instant and Tobi's heart was pounding. Logan had his gun out too, and was backed against the front door in the next second, peering out carefully.

"Keep the doors closed and locked and stay away from the windows," Logan said. He and Jacquart slunk outside quietly, moving along the brush line through the snow toward the car parked at the curb. Jacquart turned her head sharply to the side and spoke succinctly into her ear comm, calling for backup.

With three sets of patio doors, a good part of Tobi's downstairs was made up of windows. Troy grabbed her, and after checking inside first, tried to push her into the hall closet, but she vehemently shook her head. "There's no way I'm was getting trapped in there," she whispered.

He nodded, took his own revolver out and started to lead Tobi silently up the stairs. The large patio doors offered an easier escape, but they also offered easier visibility and entrance for the Russians, especially if they used a bullet. Molly was frozen and would not move. She looked like she might start screaming in fear, but Troy put his finger to his lips and when she would not follow them upstairs, he motioned for her to get down behind the couch.

Once upstairs, Troy took Tobi into her study where his suitcase lay on the floor. The windows led out onto the roof where it was only one story high, so it could be used as an escape route if needed, and the door locked, so both exits could be guarded. They heard shots fired outside and a car window shattered. Tobi was insanely frustrated, not knowing what was happening, but she was too afraid to go to the window. She felt far too vulnerable without a weapon of some kind, and remembered her old hiking knife at the bottom of her filing cabinet drawer.

Quietly, while on her knees, she reached into the drawer, feeling around slowly. She hadn't taken it out in years, but her fingers finally closed over its Velcro casing, and she gently pulled it out and took the cover off. It was heavier than she remembered, and she unfolded the blade. Stainless steel, several millimeters thick at the base, and finely tapered at the tip. It was serrated on one side and came to an exquisitely sharp point. The blade itself was only three inches long, a half inch shorter than the hard plastic handle it tucked into, but it was sturdy and when she'd bought it, it had impressed her as a formidable weapon against snakes or other dangerous critters. It was intended for cutting away bramble and roots or anything else a hiker in the wilderness might need to remove or defend against, or just to cut their dinner.

There was a rustling on the other side of the door, and Tobi willed PanniKat to go hide under a bed. Should she let her in? As they both turned toward the door, the window shattered and glass went flying, and Tobi spun around to see a dark haired, middle-aged man with a gun leveled at Troy. Troy was down on the floor and blood flowed from his right thigh. He raised his revolver, looking for his mark, but the man had disappeared behind the window. A second later, there was a shot fired from below the window to somewhere outside, and Tobi heard police sirens getting closer.

Tobi inched over to Troy as his hand went slack and his pistol fell to the carpet. She put a hand on his groin, while looking for a pulse at his wrist. The bullet wound was just below his main femoral artery. She reached into the closet and grabbed a dress with long, thin sleeves. "I never wear dresses, anyway," she said, as she hacked off a sleeve with the knife and tied it tightly over the wound, a couple of centimeters from his groin. He looked pale, and Tobi realized she was utterly terrified of losing him. "Stay with me, Troy, hang on," she said softly, but he did not respond. Somewhere a child screamed and a couple of dogs barked. The room tilted and the world became surreal.

***

Jacquart crouched behind the door of the car. Both police officers were dead in the front seat, a bullet neatly to each one's temple. Logan had gone around back. She heard the shot from the roof and saw a man crouching below the window. As she aimed carefully, a child screamed. Several dogs barked and Jacquart motioned to the neighbors to get back. She flashed her badge and showed her gun, pointing it up to the sky. The spectators moved away but in that second, her back was to the gunman on the roof. She felt a whiz past her left ear and ducked instinctively.

There was another shot that came from the back of the house. Logan or another intruder? She looked up at the roof again but there was no one on it now. The window was blown open, so she had to believe the assassin had moved into the house. Either that or he had jumped down when she wasn't looking, but he would have had to have been quick.

***

Tobi thought she had been swift tying off the makeshift tourniquet, but as she turned around, there was a man in the room, leveling a gun at her. She looked at Troy's revolver, inches away, but the man snarled at her.

"Move and I shoot. You first, him second."

The accent was thick, but she understood perfectly.

"Kick it over here," the man said.

Tobi looked at Troy. He was barely conscious. The blood flow had slowed down, but he was pale. Her finger strayed back to his radial artery to check his pulse, which was rapid and thready. Then she let go of Troy and leaned back on her hands so she could use her toe to push the gun away. As she did, she felt the knife behind her. She was practically sitting on it.

"You are my ticket out of here," the Russian said. "Get up and come to the window, so I can show them your face."

Tobi's head was suddenly never clearer. He was four feet in front of her. She calculated that from her position on the floor, she would not have the time or opportunity to stand up to get the knife to his chest, and a stab wound in the abdomen might not prevent him from shooting her anyway. But there were other options.

In an instant, a plethora of movie scenes ran through her head. The victim stabs once and runs, but the perp doesn't die, just runs after her even madder than before. She wasn't going to make that mistake. She had to make it count.

She pretended to steady herself with her hand behind her, swaying a little to make it look like she was overwhelmed. She gripped the knife solidly, and as she slowly rose to her feet, she knelt forward. Swiftly, she brought the knife up and jammed the point into his scrotum. He howled like a beast, and doubled over, his head coming down within a few inches of her own, but astonishingly, he did not drop the gun. He was wearing thick blue jeans, and she realized that no matter her conviction, she had hesitated. He started to straighten up, his face like an enraged demon's.

Everything seemed to be in slow motion. Tobi saw his right hand, still holding the gun, coming up in front of his chest and abdomen as he struggled to straighten up. His left hand was over his groin, and the gun was now a foot from her face. With her left forearm, she knocked outward at the hand holding the gun, as she brought up her right and buried the knife in his carotid artery. The gun went off as he slumped to the ground, an expression of disbelief and torment on his face.

It took her a moment to realize she was alive. The bullet had blown through the wall, not her face. She looked around her and saw blood everywhere. She wasn't squeamish, but this was different. She gagged from the smell, and then started to shake.

I just killed a man, she thought. I just killed a human being.

She stood there for a moment in shock, but a moan from Troy brought her back to reality. She looked out the window and saw Agent Jacquart standing below her in the street. Tobi tried twice to call to the agent, but no sound would come out of her mouth. She knelt down next to Troy, but she couldn't speak his name. She shook him gently when the door crashed off its hinges and Agent Logan stood in the frame, his pistol scanning the room.

"Help," Tobi squeaked. "Help him." Troy was barely conscious.

"There's an ambulance coming. What can I do?" Logan asked.

"Hold pressure here," Tobi croaked. Her voice started to come back slowly. "I have a proper tourniquet in the other room." She jumped up, quickly rinsed the Russian's blood off her hands so as not to give any possible diseases to Troy, and came back in ten seconds with gauze and a tourniquet. She applied pressure with the gauze and cut away his jeans with a pair of scissors from her desk, reapplying a tourniquet over the gauze for much tighter control of the bleeding.

Two EMTs came upstairs and Tobi shouted out orders. "He needs oxygen and IV fluids, normal saline, open it up all the way—he's lost a lot of volume!"

Logan took her gently and pulled her away. "Let them work."

"I'm going in the ambulance with him."

The paramedic looked at her sternly. "There's not a lot of room back there, ma'am, you'll be in the way."

"I'm a doctor!" Tobi practically screamed.

"You will be in the way," he said firmly. "We are trained for this; we need you to trust us." He was already inserting an IV, while his partner had oxygen running and was attaching leads to Troy's chest to get a rhythm strip and check his heart.

Logan took her arm. "Come on, wash up, and I'll take you to the hospital."

She stepped back, watching as if in a dream. Some disconnected part of herself noted the loss of her throw rug and couch.

Troy was not conscious, but they took him out on the stretcher with his blood pressure stabilized at 80/55, which Tobi considered miraculous. With Agent Logan's prodding, she cleaned up and changed clothes. She found Pantelaymin hiding under her bed.

"Thank God you're okay, baby." She petted the cat quickly before closing her off in the bedroom and going downstairs. Panni had food and water and a litter box in the master bathroom; the last thing she wanted was PanniKat wandering around the house while the police were all over it, and maybe running outside. They found Molly Baker paralyzed in the living room, still crouching behind the sofa.

"I saw him through the patio door, but he ignored me. I—I don't know why. I thought for sure he'd kill me." Molly was shaking, and her face was drained. "I—Is there anything I can do to help?" she stuttered.

Tobi almost dismissed her out of anger but thought again. "You can have B. Healthy pay for all the damage to my house. And Troy's medical bills. You can pay all of Troy's out-of-pocket medical bills."

Molly nodded slowly. Her eyes were dilated, her face was white, and her lips had barely moved when she spoke.

As Logan escorted Tobi outside, they were joined by Agent Jacquart. The ambulance was already screaming its siren as it headed up the block. An older man with blood on his face sat cuffed in a squad car and stared at her.

"Who is that?" Tobi asked.

"Mannfort Tzenkov. We got him," Jacquart said.

Chapter 68

Tobi paced back and forth in the surgical waiting room. The vascular surgeon had just been in to tell her everything was going to be fine. Troy's superficial femoral artery had been nicked, but Tobi's tourniquet had been effective, and the artery had just been repaired. The resident was just throwing in some skin stitches to close up. Troy was going to have to take it really easy for a while, but he was going to make it.

She felt enormous relief, but she still could not sit still. Thankfully, Agent Jacquart had given up trying to talk to her and was sitting on a nearby chair until Tobi's friends got there. Tobi toyed with calling Ben. She was sure he would drop everything and come running out, and there was really nothing for him to do. Mostly, she just wasn't ready to have the conversation about Troy. She was exhausted, and everything had worked out, anyway; she wasn't even injured. She didn't count her shoulder injury, it seemed like nothing by comparison to Troy. She justified her evasion by thinking generally about how little time there was in a medical student's schedule. He was doing a rotation in interventional cardiology this month, and she didn't want him to miss out.

Tobi had scrubbed her face and hands up to above her elbows, completely disgusted by the Russian man's blood on her. Not that blood made her particularly squeamish, but she had killed this man and by washing off his blood, she had tried to wash off the guilt. Kazimir Nyelko. That's what they'd said his name was. Some distracted part of her brain wondered if one was supposed to say Kaddish over an assassin.

Rabbi Lilly came through the door with Chloe, Reggie, and Lynn close behind. "Tobi! We heard! Is Troy okay?"

"Rabbi!" Tears gushed from Tobi's eyes. "Yes, thank God! He just got out of surgery."

Rabbi Lilly came over and hugged her.

"Ugh, I'm covered in blood, don't touch me," Tobi said. Lilly looked at her, puzzled. Tobi had completely forgotten she had changed her clothes, as encouraged by Agent Logan.

Reggie, Lynn, and Chloe also gathered around her, but she shook even more than before.

"Rabbi. I killed him … I killed him with my hiking knife. It was horrible."

"Tobi, it's okay. Hello? He was trying to kill you," Reggie said.

"I know," Tobi squeaked. "But still—"

Not that she wouldn't have done exactly the same thing if she had to do it over, but taking a life weighed on her heavily. For a fleeting second, she wished Judaism had a confession box like Catholicism. Or that it was Yom Kippur tomorrow, so she could repent in some formal way. That was not their custom, though, and she had never felt any need for an intermediary before. She had always taken her afflictions and her joy directly to God. That's how Jews had done things these last two thousand years, since the ancient priestly order had been mostly abolished, and it had always been enough—better than having a go-between. Clergy was always available for counsel and interpretation of Law, but they did not have the power to pardon.

Judaism emphasized the importance of community prayer, requiring a minyan, or ten people for a formal service, but there were always a few minutes for silent prayer. And for tremendously turbulent emotions, Tobi would sit by a tree or a candle or stare at the moon, and clear her mind of everything but her hunger for the sense of God. She would stay like that until she felt the boundaries of her soul dissolve and she could, for a fleeting instant, become one with something monumentally greater than herself. In those moments, there was only a kind of energy that communicated so much more than words could ever impart. And with it, would come a feeling of healing, of meaningful but indescribable emotion, that could tear away the irrelevancies of her life, and made her feel whole.

"I'm supposed to save lives, not take them," Tobi said quietly.

"Well, you did," Chloe said firmly. "You saved yourself and you saved Troy."

Rabbi Lilly came and sat beside her. "Your rabbi says you did well. The Ten Commandments say, 'Thou shalt not murder.' They do not say 'thou shalt not kill.' In fact, the Talmud tells us that 'if someone is coming to kill you, rise up early and kill them first.' Self-defense is absolutely sanctioned in the Torah."

"Dr. Lister? He's awake and in recovery. You can see him now." The resident let the door fall shut again.

Chapter 69

Agents Logan and Jacquart were tying up their paperwork at the police precinct, where they had been given an office to work from.

"Amazing," Logan said. "If we follow the money, there are seventeen congressman and the former FBI director who have succumbed to extortion rather than come forward, and there are *dozens* who invested in Kordec stock for a piece of the pie. The trail so far designates senators from twenty-one different states and has exposed investments from multiple Fortune 500 companies. And that's just in this country. I wonder if these shareholders knew what these guys were doing and just didn't care or if they only looked at the dividends. You'd think they would investigate their funds better."

Jacquart shook her head. "Well, be sure we will be investigating all of *them* now. I feel like there used to be some things that were sacred, like, just making a buck wasn't a good enough reason to do absolutely anything. What ever happened to personal integrity and honor? Does no one value those things anymore?"

"At my church, they say it's almost the Apocalypse. Sodom and Gomorrah are here and now," Logan said.

"I had no idea you were such an evangelist, Logan. I don't go in much for apocalyptic predictions, but from a strictly historical perspective, I agree. Every great civilization has its decline. In so many ways, it looks like we're living the Fall of the American Empire right about now."

***

Kavandor walked out of the subcommittee meeting feeling sure Kordec was going down. The trick was going to be keeping himself out of sight until they were all put away. What were the chances the Russians would know he'd had anything to do with it? They knew about his appointment to the Health and Human Services Committee, but they would not know about this subcommittee unless they specifically looked, and he hoped they would be kept pretty busy with the FBI and have little time to be thinking about him. He was a nobody to them, after all, right?

As he walked into the hallway, two men in dark suits approached him.

"Senator Blaise Kavandor? We're with the FBI. You are under arrest for aiding and abetting murder and conspiracy to fraud. You have the right to remain silent …."

Kavandor's jaw dropped. He'd been so focused on the Russians, he never considered repercussions would come from his own people.

Chapter 70

Tobi stayed with Troy at the hospital until late evening and then left reluctantly. She had left Pantelaymin shell-shocked and alone in a locked room, and there was nothing more she could do for Troy tonight. Lynn and Reggie had offered their house and were meeting her outside to go get PanniKat, so Tobi walked out into the night, just as Daniel Comet called.

"How *are* you?" he asked. "Geez, I heard you got a knife to the shoulder, then nearly killed in your own home. And your 'bodyguard' landed in the OR. Are you okay? Is he okay? The bodyguard is supposed to protect you both, you know."

"We're both okay. He just had his femoral artery repaired, and Ellie sewed me up a couple of days ago." Or was that yesterday? She was so disoriented about the time. "Did you find out anything you can share?"

"It looks like this has been going on all over the globe, Tobi. Obviously, richer populations are targeted, and they have someone in each venue to act as their mole. Their software is completely compatible with most EMRs, so it doesn't show up as foreign to the system. They can rifle through charts and get lists of seriously ill patients who have hope of cures, but who know the cost of those cures could bankrupt them. They also have a separate database for public figures whose private medical information they steal, and then they blackmail those individuals with what they know. With everything digital these days, anyone with excellent computer skills can hack in and use information to create all kinds of havoc for profit."

"How did Steve get mixed up in all this? I always thought of him as a good guy," Tobi asked.

"Steve had started asking questions because we had alerts put on to monitor any charts that were opened by anyone other than the treating provider or the billing department, and they were going off like crazy. It was an extra HIPAA security feature and when Steve challenged the accessions, he drew Kordec's attention. So, the Russians approached him and offered him money to look the other way. He turned them down until his son was run off the road while bicycling home. Steve got scared."

"I heard about that. Is his son alright?"

"Broken wrist and needed plastics for a facial laceration, and a lot of bruises, both physical and psychological. They threatened that next time he'd be dead."

"No wonder he was such an ass. I guess I can't blame him."

"He told me he tried to warn you by telling you his hands were tied, but he knew you felt betrayed."

"So, what happens now?" Tobi asked.

"So, besides the FBI, we're doing an in-house investigation, as are multiple other hospital entities across the country. The AMA has been pushing for it. And Hospitals for Health has decided to keep the majority of its shares when it merges with B. Healthy. It was going to be a fifty-fifty split, and B. Healthy was trying to convince us to take an even smaller percent interest, which would cost us less in operations' overhead. Most systems are like that now, you know. The lion's share of the business capital comes from entrepreneurs, so doctors maintain very little control. But this experience has scared us. Statistically, this whole scheme could have easily been overlooked, since these people were in such a high morbidity category, but on the human side, our physicians started asking questions about the deaths of their patients a couple of years ago. The scrutiny into that has definitely not been 'cost effective,' and B. healthy didn't see the point. They weren't losing any money on it, and an inquiry might have alienated those patients insured by Kordec, which in turn might have inclined those patients to stop using us, even for unrelated everyday office visits. Plus, it was a time investment to look closely into deaths that were not directly connected to the medical care. B. Healthy thought it was a waste of resources and wanted to terminate the investigation."

"Do you think B. Healthy was involved?" Tobi asked.

"No, I just think they didn't care. Venture capitalists have a different agenda, and it's not people, no matter how much lip service they pay to it. Makes it easier for sinister operations to use them as fronts to exploit individuals."

Tobi wondered if the company would have cared if they had known.

"When does your bodyguard get released? Has he lost his job?"

"Who told you it was a 'he'?" Tobi laughed.

"Agent Logan. I asked if they were protecting you, and he said they were and that you were not alone. Apparently, your friend took down Rufini before he was shot, no small feat given how much that man weighs."

"Said bodyguard also took also took a wire cutter to the head. I guess it would have been kinder for me to have numbed him up before I put staples in his scalp."

"How many staples?" Daniel asked.

"Just two."

"Meh, hardly worth the lidocaine." Tobi could practically see Daniel's mischievous grin.

"He sounds like a keeper, Tobi. But if you need someone to check him out for you, I'll be your acting family in residence. When this is all over, the four of us can go out for dinner. My wife is a keen judge of character."

"Hmm. I'll keep that in mind, if I decide to let him hang around. By the way, what's happening to Ismar?"

"Well, he'll be losing his license to practice medicine forever, and he's going away for a very long time, possibly for life. Nothing to worry about from him. The more cooperative he is, the better it will go for him. First, we have to come to an agreement with the Turkish government; they're asking for extradition. Apparently, he's wanted for crimes there too. They'll probably execute him, so either way, he's not getting out of this. What about you? What are your plans now?"

"Funny, I've been thinking about that," Tobi said. "I just can't seem to picture myself going back to work in a corporate structure. I get about ten headhunter calls and emails a week, I might start answering them. And maybe it's even time to get out of clinical medicine for good."

"That would be a loss, you're a great physician. But I get it. Let me know if you need any stellar references. I might have some connections along the way too."

"Thanks, Daniel. For everything."

Chapter 71

The next day, Tobi walked into the hospital room as Agent Logan was walking out. Troy was dressed and sitting in one of the chairs. "I can't wait to get out of here already."

"What was he doing here?" Tobi nodded at the door.

"I asked him to bring me something from the house. Have you been back there?"

"Only to get Pantelaymin and some of her toys. We're staying at Reggie's and Lynn's, and they invited you to stay too. They've been very good about having a cat around, and Panni likes them. I don't know if I deserve such amazing friends. The whole upstairs is being redone, courtesy of B. Healthy. What a mess. Did they say when you would be discharged?"

"Possibly tomorrow."

Tobi looked at him. The bruise on his forehead was starting to fade, and the staples were almost ready to come out. Had it really been less than a week since he'd shown up bloody at her door? His face was still pale, but he was sitting up easily enough. "Your hematocrit dropped to twenty-four, you know. You need to take it easy."

"I have no idea what that means," he said.

"It means you lost a lot of blood, and very quickly. You really worried me." As she said the words, she realized how accurate they were. Now that he was with her again, what would she do without him?

"So, you've been peeking in my chart? Hmm, did I give you permission for that?" His smile was all mischief.

Tobi was just on the verge of taking him in her arms when her phone went off, with Ben's ring tone.

"Mom! What's going on out there? Are you okay? Your name is all over the news that someone tried to kill you! Why don't you tell me these things?"

"Ben. Hi. I … I didn't want you to worry, and—"

"Worry? Of course I worry! You should have told me! I shouldn't have to hear my classmates say 'Isn't that your mother' and find out that way."

Tobi flinched. "You're right, I'm sorry. But Ben, I was a target because of Uncle Reuben. The last thing I wanted was for you to become a target too. I'd have died first."

"What are talking about? Uncle Reuben?"

Tobi took a breath and realized this was the first time she had been glad that Ben didn't call very often. "Do you remember I told you Troy was messaging me and said it was about Reuben?"

"Mom! If he got you into this trouble and risked your life—"

"Stop, Ben! He *saved* my life. A couple of times, actually. And he's lying here in the hospital right now, because he came back for that exact purpose."

By the time Tobi was finished telling Ben the whole story, she was exhausted all over again, as if she had relived it. Agent Jacquart had said it would get easier with time, but so far, that was proving to be a myth.

"He really saved your life?" Ben asked. "I don't even know what to say. I'm just glad you're alive. I love you. Mom, you could have died! I'm coming home tonight."

"It's not necessary, you should be on your hospital rotation; I don't want you to miss. It's all over, and I'm fine. Not even a scratch—well, maybe a little scratch. God was clearly watching over me. I'd love to see you if you have time, but the house is not even inhabitable at the moment …."

"I think they'd let me take off a couple of days, under the circumstances, and I don't have to stay over, unless you need me to, and if you do, I'll stay in a hotel. I'll be there this weekend—if you're *sure* you're okay. Mom, you've been miserable at that place for years. You need to quit. Work somewhere else, or just retire."

"I can't retire, Ben. I have bills to pay."

"I know, and my tuition is one of them. Stop it. I'll take loans. Your sanity is way more important."

"I have been thinking I need to make some major changes in my life—"

"Good. Why don't you look into that group NY Medical that's been opening up all over the place? They're good people; they even opened several free clinics in the city just to give back to the community. They're owned by a hedge fund, too, but they're run by physicians, and they seem to have a heart. Everyone who works there loves it. This whole thing is crazy."

"I've heard of them, I'll check them out, and I'll start looking around in general. I just got into this rut of staying in one place, partly because they paid well, and the commute was so easy, only fifteen minutes. I don't know, I guess it was also just inertia."

"Let's talk about it this weekend, then. Promise you'll call me if anything changes before that! I can be there in forty-five minutes. I love you."

"I will. I love you too."

Troy was looking at her with a bemused smile. The speaker function had been off, but Ben's voice had been audible without it. "He's very protective of his mom. That's good."

"It was just the two of us for so long ... now he has Rachel, and I'm glad. He went through a lot between his father and me, and I'm very proud of him."

Tobi moved closer to Troy and sat down on the adjacent chair, wondering how a meeting between Ben and Troy would go. She took his hand. "You really did scare me, you know."

She wanted to hug him, but didn't quite trust herself; if she touched him now, she might never let go. Nineteen years of anger had faded to nothing, but she was still afraid to open her heart again. News flash, it was opening without her permission. That's what hearts do; they don't listen to reason. She was suddenly afraid her whole life was about to change forever. Well, her life wasn't exactly so terrific in its present state, was it? So, maybe that was a good thing.

Troy continued to look at her. He licked his lips nervously, and Tobi saw the sweat on his brow. It wasn't that warm in the room, and it reminded her how weak he must still be, even with the transfusions he'd received.

"What?" she asked.

"I have something of yours," he said. He took his hand back and pulled something out of his pocket. He tried twice to speak and had to stop. "I wish I could do this properly, but I feel like I need to do it right now. Then he opened his hand and Tobi saw the little square box.

"No, no, no, Troy! We've been reacquainted for less than a week."

"No, it's not what you think. Well, it is what you think, but not in that way. I'm having a hard time with this."

He fumbled with the box and opened it. Inside was a round diamond in a platinum split shank setting.

"I had just bought this when Reuben told me his predicament. I never got to give it to you, but it's been sitting in my safety deposit box at Citibank ever since. I hope it still fits."

"Troy, I just barely managed to forgive you. And, yes, to admit to myself that I still love you. But please don't ask me to make a commitment like that. And—what would you have done if you'd already given me the ring when Reuben came to you? Would you have broken our engagement?"

"I have no idea what I would have done. But I hadn't yet, and I made the decision that seemed the most ethical one at the time. I sacrificed my feelings—"

"Our feelings! Mine and Ben's too."

"Our feelings, especially yours and Ben's, because you had no say in it. When I look back, I don't know if it was the right thing to do." His voice cracked. "I did the best I could. I hope one day you and Ben will forgive me."

Tobi's heart felt like a pretzel, and her eyes were watering.

"Tobi, this is no longer the engagement promise it would have been. And it is not really an apology, either, because no material thing can make up for what you—and I—went through when I left. Please just take it with no strings attached."

"I don't know, Troy. I don't think I would ever get married again. I mean, what's the point? It's just paper. Ben is all grown …."

He leaned forward and put his finger over her lips. "Tobi, all this means is that I love you. That has never changed, and it never will. It's so long overdue, but, please, take it. It belongs to you. It has always belonged to you."

Tobi realized she had tears in her eyes. She leaned over and stroked his face gently, very aware of the fragile major artery in his right groin. "We have to keep your blood pressure down right now, you know." Awkward moments produce the stupidest comments.

Troy smiled and gently pulled her face to his and their lips locked. Like a rubber band that had suddenly snapped, all her resistance vanished, and nineteen years melted away. Their hearts collided and became one all over again, and, as if they had never been apart, bonded more fiercely than ever.

ACKNOWLEDGMENTS

My greatest thanks goes now and always to my son, Daniel Leisman, for his love and his unwavering belief in me in whatever venture I embark upon. You have always inspired me to strive to be the best I am able and you have given me my raison d'être since the day you were born.

Probably the most influential person in the creation of this book is Rich Krevolin. A screenwriter, consultant, playwright, and professor, I joked that I earned my masters from him, just minus the certificate. Thank you, Rich, for your patience and your tutelage, for teaching me how to build suspense, keep pace, and for generally holding my hand through the many revisions of this novel, beginning with helping me decide if it would be a novel or a nonfiction exposé. The thriller motif is all because of you.

To Ellen Gelerman, it has been such a joy to share this journey with you. We have tackled child rearing from ages two to twenty-seven together, and all the delights and disasters that accompanied those times. But this past year, we finished writing and had our first novels accepted for publication together, and we did it sharing our frustrations, anxieties, and elation. I can't imagine what life would be like without your friendship, love, and support over this last quarter of a century. Here's to twenty-five more.

Huge thanks to my beta readers for their time, encouragement, and suggestions. Maxine Cohen, Joyce Tisman, Maggie Farkas, Brad Elbein, Rebecca Stanley, and Jiya Kowarsky.

Thank you to Rabbi Susie Henneson Moskowitz for Judaic consultation and day-to-day love, wisdom, and support. You are always an inspiration, and to me, you are the quintessential rabbi.

An enormous thank you to the accomplished professionals who took the time to read and review this book for me. Dr. Kenneth Kamler, Rabbi Michael Cahana, and Ed Hershey. A doctor, a rabbi, and a journalist walk into a bar to discuss a book ….

Thank you Rabbi Todd Chizner, for validating my leap of faith into this unfamiliar world and reminding me that faith is more than prayers or the belief in God, but it is the willingness to step off the precipice and trust God to guide me into an unknown future.

To Dr. Steve Goldberg, I am grateful for your friendship, your encouragement, and your support, not just this past year, but for the last decade or so that it has been my pleasure to know and work with you.

This would not be complete without acknowledging the amazing people at Warren Publishing. In particular, Mindy Kuhn and Amy Ashby, for their support, enthusiasm, knowledge, and talent. You both have made this process such a pleasure and are sterling guides as I venture into this foreign field. It is like learning a new profession, and you have been patient with my frustrations and held my hand along the way. I could not have asked for better. Thanks also to Monika Dziamka for her insightful developmental edits. And of course, to author Jennifer Hurvitz Weintraub, who I met on a fluke and she proceeded to adopt me into her life, into the Warren Publishing family, and who has promised to introduce me to the world of podcasting. You always go above and beyond!

Finally, thank you to all my family, friends, fellow congregants, neighbors, and coworkers who have continuously asked "is it out yet" and have given me courage to take this step. Back when the manuscript was only about sixty pages, I wondered if anyone outside of medicine could possibly be interested in physician-patient encounters. Thank you to Fern Bernstein, who repeatedly assured me they would, and insisted that lay people like herself were, in fact, extremely curious to know what happens on *The Other End of the Stethoscope*.

ABOUT THE AUTHOR

Debra E. Blaine was born in New York City and grew up on Long Island, NY. With a passion for the humanities, she received her BA in Philosophy and Hebrew at the University of Texas at Austin, before going on for graduate studies in Comparative Religion at Temple University. She ultimately changed paths, and attended Baylor College of Medicine to earn her MD in 1987. She returned to Long Island for post graduate training and has practiced Family and Urgent Care medicine on Long Island and Queens for nearly thirty years.

The changing face of medicine, which reflects the changing attitudes of Western society, has compelled her to return to her earliest dreams: to engage with and attempt to influence our world through writing and the exchange of ideas. A world increasingly scourged by greed in so many corners, and so far adrift from the practices of integrity, gratitude, and kindness that should be our primary values.

Dr. Blaine has a grown son who is her greatest source of pride. She is on the Board of Trustees of her synagogue, and she loves animals, nature, and being outdoors. She lives with her cat in Suffolk County, Long Island.